MW01000615

FRESH COURAGE TAKE

FRESH COURAGE TAKE

COME TO ZION
VOLUME 3

DEAN HUGHES

DESERET
BOOK

SALT LAKE CITY, UTAH

For my grandson
Samuel "Sam" Hughes Russell

Library of Congress Cataloging-in-Publication Data

Hughes, Dean, 1943–   author.
  Fresh courage take / Dean Hughes.
    pages cm—(Come to Zion ; volume 3)
  Sequel to: Through cloud and sunshine.
  Summary: In this concluding volume to the Come to Zion series Will and Liz, 19th century Mormon pioneers, leave Nauvoo, Illinois and cross the plains to reach the Salt Lake Valley. Meanwhile Jeff and Abby, living in the 21st century Midwest, face decisions about moving from Nauvoo to go to graduate school.
  ISBN 978-1-60907-873-7 (hardbound : alk. paper)
1. Mormon converts—Fiction. 2. Mormon pioneers—Fiction. 3. Religious fiction. I. Title. II. Series: Hughes, Dean, 1943– Come to Zion ; volume 3.
  PS3558.U36F74   2014
  813'.54—dc23   2014000226

Printed in the United States of America
Edwards Brothers Malloy, Ann Arbor, MI

10 9 8 7 6 5 4 3 2 1

PREFACE

If you have read the first two books of the *Come to Zion* series and you are now struggling to remember what happened in those two books, let me offer you a brief plot summary. (*Spoiler alert:* If you haven't read the books, don't read this outline version. It's a bare-bones summary and makes the books sound quite boring.) In Volume 1, *The Winds and the Waves,* Will Lewis and Liz Duncan meet in England. They are both taught by Elder Wilford Woodruff and become converted to The Church of Jesus Christ of Latter-day Saints. Will leaves his home and farm to seek work in the factories of Manchester with the hope that he can raise his economic status closer to the level of Liz's family. He meets disappointment in that pursuit, but a situation does open for him to work as a steward to a wealthy landowner. This raises him in the caste system, but when he and Liz marry, they give up everything to immigrate to Nauvoo, Illinois. The difficult sea voyage forces Will to put his faith into action and deepens his trust in the Lord.

In the second volume, *Through Cloud and Sunshine,* Will and Liz suffer through the loss of their first child, but when they take in a motherless newborn, some of their pain is overcome. Will works hard to establish a road-building business. When he defends himself against a pair of brothers who hate Mormons, his family is forced to live with the fear of revenge. Everything Will achieves is slipping away as the old citizens of Hancock County turn increasingly against the Latter-day Saint population. When Joseph and Hyrum Smith are murdered, Will and Liz still hope to make a life in Nauvoo, but they are aware that they may have to leave their beloved city.

In a contemporary plot that runs through the two volumes, Jeff Lewis, a descendent of Will Lewis, moves with his new wife, Abby, to modern Nauvoo. Jeff becomes interested in learning about William and Elizabeth Lewis, his third great-grandparents. When Abby gives birth to a son with a heart defect, their faith is tested. After Jeff is able to find a deeper trust in God and in his own inspiration the child is blessed to survive. The Lewises are still pressed to figure out what they want to do with their lives, but they grow through their callings in the ward, and they develop a satisfying friendship with another couple their own age, Malcolm and Kayla McCord. Jeff and Abby decide that they want to stay in Nauvoo, where they feel connected to the people they love but also to the Saints who lived there in the nineteenth century.

This is the final volume of the *Come to Zion* series. I hope you feel satisfied when you finish it, but I already know that at least a few people are going to say to me: "How can you stop *there?*" The problem I face is that historical fiction is always an extraction, an episode lifted from the flow of time. Wherever I stop, it may seem as though the story is not finished. In a manner of speaking, it can't be. After all, history—time—keeps going. But the arc of a story is found in the development and resolution of character conflicts. True, our conflicts also continue in life, but a storyteller has to find a beginning, middle, and end. I hope this ending feels like resolution, but at the same time, I didn't want to wrap up everything in a way that life never does.

My own ancestor, Robert Harris Jr., who was involved in these historical events, actually made his way to the Salt Lake Valley and found that his family had not yet arrived. He crossed the plains back to Winter Quarters and later brought his wife and children west. He covered nearly six thousand miles, mostly on foot. I thought of having Will make a similar trek, but it's hard to keep a character walking that long and not start repeating oneself as a writer. So I didn't tell Robert Harris's story, but you'll notice that he shows up as a butcher in Company E of the Mormon Battalion, which is what he actually was.

You may find yourself a little surprised by my characterization of Brigham Young. We now call him the "great colonizer," but the fact is, the trek across Iowa was quite a mess. Part of that happened because "Brother Brigham," as people often called him, was still learning, but even more, the weather created almost impossible conditions. Added to that, Brigham had wanted only an advance party to forge the trail, but many of the Saints didn't listen to him. They crossed the river and joined the company, often without adequate provisions, and Brigham refused to leave them behind.

You may also be surprised at Brigham's harshness. He could actually be tender and sensitive, especially to individuals, but he didn't pull punches when he called the Saints to repentance. How do we know that? He rarely gave a sermon or held a meeting without a clerk there to take notes. We have the text of many of his talks. I don't have the full text of his talks when he was recruiting the Mormon Battalion, but enough was recorded during that time that I can say with certainty that I did not exaggerate his "arm-twisting" techniques. He needed to create an army, and he was not afraid to dish out all the guilt he could to shame the men into signing up.

Not everyone liked that, as I portray it in the novel, but Brigham believed the Lord had opened up an opportunity, and he wanted the men of the Church to stand up and be counted.

Perhaps the most difficult issue to understand is Brigham making promises to the wives of the Battalion members and then, in many cases, failing to keep his commitments. While it may be true that Brigham got carried away with his own rhetoric in convincing wives to support their husbands in joining the Battalion, I think there is no doubt that he thought he would and could fulfill the commitments he made. When he made those promises, he had no idea how much illness would strike the Winter Quarters area, or how dreadfully short on supplies the people would be. He had expected much more cash to flow back to him from the soldiers' pay. He assigned bishops to look after the families left behind, but the problems were greater than he could have imagined, and many of those he called were as destitute and sick as the ones they were caring for. Like all of us, Brigham was doing his best, and also like all of us, he was a real person with his share of flaws. As it turned out, however, he did in fact become one of the great colonizers in all of history. Someone needed to be strong to get the Saints to the West and to lead them as they settled hundreds of communities and built "the kingdom." It's a mistake now to look back and wish him a little "nicer." He was the kind of leader the Saints needed at the time.

Levi Hancock is also a real person and not a fictional character. I'm sure he comes across as self-righteous and rather extreme in his religious zeal, but many reports about his personality appear in the journals of the men who marched with him. If you're related to him, you may not like my characterization, but remember that the early Saints, at least stylistically, were quite different from modern Mormons. I think our jaws would drop if we could listen to some of the intense sermons delivered in those days. Some of what

Brigham and Levi said may make us uncomfortable now, but many other preachers in the early Church would sound just as extreme to us today.

The fact is, when we try to understand our own history, we are looking through a translucent veil. It's almost impossible to adjust our minds completely to the perceptions and manners of a time now almost two centuries back. But human beings, in a more basic sense, don't change. They are always driven by the same needs and desires. What I've tried to do is to create the emotions, fears, pain, hopes, and faith of a people who are connected to us directly and who are the precursors of who we are. Truly, there's no accomplishing anything quite so ambitious as I set out to do, but I hope this series has brought readers a little closer to understanding who those early Saints were, and who we are because of them.

CHAPTER 1

Will Lewis was working at the temple quarry. He and some other men had just muscled a large, rough-cut stone onto the back of a wagon, and they had stepped back to catch their breaths. "That'n was a mite heavy," Jesse Matthews said. He tried to laugh, but he was gasping from the effort.

"Aye," was all Will said. He was bending forward, with his hands on his knees. He felt the strain of this heavy work more these days than he once had. The temple at Nauvoo was progressing faster now, and the workers, both at the quarry and at the building site, had been putting in hard days.

Will straightened suddenly and listened. Down the river he heard the dull chugging of a steam engine and, gradually, the slosh of a paddle wheel. A riverboat was heading for the dock at the north landing, beyond the quarry. Will turned to Jesse and said, "If you'll bring up the oxen and get 'em yoked, I'll walk to the dock and see what I can find out."

Jesse nodded. Will knew that he understood. The two of them had been making plans for a new enterprise, but they needed information. They hoped a riverboat captain could tell them what they needed to know. So Will set out, walking fast. He was warm in his mackinaw coat, but the wind off the river was cutting deep today, and as he approached the landing, he felt it even more. It was December 1844, and three days earlier the first heavy snow of the season had fallen. Cold had followed. Work at the quarry would have to slow now, but enough stone was already cut to keep Will and Jesse busy hauling the sandstone to the temple for a few more days.

Will watched the crew of the riverboat tie up at the dock. He waited as a few passengers got off. The boat wouldn't be stopping long, so Will had to make the best of his time. It had been a warm fall, with little rain, and the river was low. The captain had certainly had to navigate with care through the Des Moines rapids. Above Nauvoo the boat could make good time again, but if this kind of cold continued long, ice would soon close the river, and surely the captain would want to reach his destination upriver and then head south before he got locked in somewhere.

Will hurried on board and was met by a big-shouldered man in a blanket coat and a coonskin hat. "You goin' nort wid us?" he asked. Will heard the accent, but he couldn't have said where the man was from.

"No. I only wish to ask a question or two of your captain if I could be allowed to do that."

"What for you ask question?"

"Could I speak to him? I'll explain it to him."

"I ask him, if you want, but he not like. He not like no questions."

But at that point a man leaning over the rail of the Texas deck barked, "I don't like *your* questions, Swen. You ask *stupid* questions, that's why. But I'm happy to talk to this gentleman. What is it I can do for you, sir?"

"Should I come up there, or—"

"Shor. Come on up."

So Will stepped to the ladder and climbed to the promenade deck; then he climbed a second ladder to where the captain was standing outside the pilot's cabin. Will shook hands with the captain, who was a rather delicate-looking man compared to the men on his crew. He was creased and weathered, but he was probably not as old as he looked. He had too much life in his voice to be much more than forty.

"My name's Will Lewis. I live here in Nauvoo."

"Captain Richman."

"I won't take much of your time. I just need your opinion about a business I hope to put into operation, maybe right away."

"What sort of business?"

"I own six teams of oxen, and I—"

"I know already what yer askin'. What about wagons? Do you have enough heavy wagons?"

"I only have one right now, but I could—"

"You git more wagons and I'll give you work next year when the water gets low again. Most of the captains who ply these waters will do the same. In low water, we can't make't through them rapids, and we can't pull lighters along all the time. If a man is downriver, below the rapids—with teams and wagons ready to haul—we'll hire him on the spot. This time through we had to hire wagons in Keokuk, on the Iowa side, but I would rather offload in Warsaw and stay on this side of the river."

"What about winter, when the river freezes? Could I get any business hauling supplies up to Rock Island and Galena?"

Captain Richman folded his arms across his chest and seemed to think. "Now, that's something that hasn't been done so much, but it does git me thinkin'. Some years the river freezes early, and them towns upriver get caught without no supplies. If a boat could git as far as Quincy, and good wagons was there to haul them goods to Galena, both men could make some money—the captain 'n the hauler. Everythin' would sell fer double, at least, up in them parts."

"That's what I was thinking."

"While yer thinkin', think about gittin' caught with your wagons in a blizzard. Or bad mud, later in the season. That's why no one's been doing it, I'd wager."

"The roads get good and hard in the cold, but some years there's not much snow early on."

"That's exactly right. Some years. And then a day later, it's snowin' sideways and you cain't see yer hand in front of yer face. A man can freeze in that kinda storm."

A gust of wind seemed to emphasize the idea. Will hunched his shoulders and pulled his neck inside his coat. When he and Jesse had started talking about an overland hauling business, the weather had been clear and mild. Captain Richman was giving Will some things to consider.

"But the payoff would be more than worth it if you could make it through," the captain added.

"Is there anything I could haul back?"

"Not ore from the mines up there. Lead ore is too heavy fer wagons. The miners keep workin' but they don't ship ore out until the weather breaks in the spring. There might be some business haulin' furs and hides, though. Hides wouldn't stink so much when they was frozen."

"Aye. That's something else to consider."

For weeks now Will and Jesse had been talking about making two or three trips to Galena each winter, with maybe six wagons full of goods. They thought they might make more money from doing that than they made from farming all summer. Will certainly had come to understand that there were more important things in life than owning a fancy home, and he was well aware that the Saints might decide to leave Nauvoo, but he wanted to stay near the temple—which should be completed in the coming year—and he wanted to make a good living for his family. He wanted to serve missions, too, but when he was gone, he hoped the day would come when he didn't have to leave Liz and his boys behind in a two-room cabin.

"You thinkin' of haulin' out of Warsaw?"

The voice had come from behind Will. He turned to see a stout man with soot on his cap and face. The man must have been a stoker—the member of the crew who kept the boiler burning hot. A stoker lived with the heat and smoke of that fire, and, from what Will had heard, he was not paid very well for all his hard labor. This man looked bedraggled, with a worn-out coat, singed at the sleeves, and soot so deep in the wrinkles around his eyes that it seemed part of the texture of his skin.

"In summer, I suppose we *would* haul out of Warsaw. Most haulers work out of Keokuk, on the west side of the river—with the channel closer to that side. But plenty of boats heading upstream stop in at Warsaw and then here in Nauvoo, so it seemed likely there was work to be had on this side."

"This is not your business, Murphy," the captain said. "He came to talk to me, and I told him already, there *is* work. So get that fire stoked up. We'll be pushing off as soon as—"

"You'll end up killt in Warsaw—a knife in your ribs."

"Who's going to stab me? You?"

"I wouldn't mind."

Will knew immediately that the man was from Hancock County. He might well have been in Carthage and been part of the mob, but Will could never quite give up on the idea that reason might get through to a man like that. "Sir, I have no idea why you would want to kill me. I farm a little piece of land east of town. I'm just a working man like you, trying to feed my family. What is it you don't like about me?"

"We know what you Mormons is. Liars, for one thing. You ain't nuthin' like you say."

"Murphy, that's enough," the captain said. "Get that fire goin'."

The man nodded, but as the captain turned back toward Will, Murphy opened his coat and pulled a knife from a scabbard on his belt. It was dull and rusty, but it had a long, heavy blade that would certainly pass through a man's ribs. Murphy held the knife in front of him, the blade pointed at Will. He glanced down at it and smiled, as if to say, *I've got this ready for you, whenever I get my chance.* As the captain turned to look in his direction, Murphy dropped the knife to his side and turned away.

"I tol' ya ta git goin', Murphy," Captain Richman said. But then he said to Will, "You need to think about men like him, Lewis. I don't know all that's happened here, but I hear the talk ever' time we come through these parts. There's plenty like Murphy who has nothin' good to say about Mormons."

"Do you think I'm a man who deserves to be killed?"

"No, sir. Not at all. I'd like to do business with you. You git the wagons and I'll hire you ever' time the water is low."

"How would I know when you were arriving in Warsaw?"

"In season, we come through once a week, regular. But if you saw the flow of water was down, you could be ready for ever' boat that puts in down there—and that's no small number."

"But it would be dangerous for us to wait in Warsaw."

"That's so. But I can't help you with that part."

Will thanked the captain and climbed off the boat. As he walked back to the quarry, he kept thinking of the payoff he and Jesse could receive from just one trip to Galena. Maybe they could pick up a load in Quincy and avoid Warsaw. But another image also kept appearing in his mind. He saw that big knife Murphy had pointed at him.

• • •

Liz Lewis was on her way to Hanna Ells's dress shop. She had walked off the hill and down to Main Street. As she approached the Mansion House, she wondered about Emma Smith, whom she rarely saw these days. Since Joseph and Hyrum had been murdered the previous summer, their wives were doing their best to go forward with life. Emma had given birth to a son, David Hyrum, in November, so she had been confined at home a good deal lately, but even before Joseph's death, the Female Relief Society had discontinued meeting. All the dissent and bad feelings the spring before had interfered with "normal life" in Nauvoo. Still, Eliza Snow and Sarah Kimball made certain that charity work went on as before, and the bishops continued to call on the Necessity Committees to assess needs and care for the poor.

Liz had continued to teach a few pupils in her house, but the small payments she received didn't really compensate for all her preparation and teaching hours. More important, Jacob was two years old now and very busy. Daniel was crawling about—would soon be walking—and Liz was finding it more and more difficult to watch both boys while pupils were in her home.

But Liz and Sarah Kimball had been putting their heads together. They had listened to Brother Brigham's call for more home businesses, and Sarah had pointed out to Liz that many women in town were good seamstresses. "It's fine to sew work shirts for the men," Sarah had said, "but why couldn't we fashion stylish dresses and wholesale them downriver in Quincy and St. Louis?"

This conversation had taken place at the post office, which had been moved to the print shop after Sidney Rigdon had left town. At the time, Liz had told Sarah, "I'm afraid I haven't improved in my sewing *that* much. I wouldn't dare take on fancy dresses."

"Nor I. But what if we worked with Hanna Ells? She could design the dresses, even cut them out, and she could teach us the little tricks of sewing them correctly."

"I don't know, Sarah. I do want to give up my school, but I doubt I could sew enough dresses to earn anything at all."

"I suspect you're right," Sarah had said.

On the following Friday, December 6, they had seen each other at the temple, where a ceremony was being held to set the last sunstone capital at the top of one of the pilasters. Will was excited that all those stones he had hauled during the fall were turning into something so magnificent. But the day was dreary. A light rain fell throughout the raising of the stone, which was delayed by problems with the tackle used to hoist it. During the delay Liz and Sarah continually admonished their boys not to run about and get themselves covered in mud. The women held their parasols and chatted while Will talked business with Hiram Kimball. As it turned out, Sarah had continued to think about her idea for a dressmaking business. "What if we joined with other women," she asked, "and we each learned the art of sewing a certain style of dress—or even one part of a dress? Each of us would become much faster as we practiced."

"That might be our answer," Liz had said, "but I need a larger room and a bigger table to set out the pattern pieces—and to keep everything away from the little boys."

"Ask Will to build another room on your house. You'll need that anyway if your family continues to grow."

"But can we stay here, Sarah? Don't you think the mobs will come after *us* next?"

After the murder of the Prophet, a quiet summer had followed, but it hadn't taken long for Thomas Sharp to begin haranguing the

Saints again. A number of candidates who had Mormon support had won offices in the August elections, and Sharp saw this as a continued attempt by Nauvoo citizens to dominate the county. In September, anti-Mormons called for a "wolf hunt," and they began to attack outlying farms, burning buildings, destroying crops, even beating Mormon farmers. In October, Governor Ford had sent a small militia to stop the attacks, but it was too soon to say whether the trouble was over.

"Hiram says there are plenty of men with cooler heads who don't agree with what was done to Joseph and Hyrum," Sarah said. "He still thinks we can live with people around here, and after a time, they'll decide there's no advantage in driving us away."

"It's what Will says, too."

"Hiram likes the idea of our making dresses—if we can produce them efficiently. He says he has enough contacts downriver to wholesale anything we can produce."

"But you don't need the money, Sarah."

"Don't say that. With so many stores in town now, Hiram doesn't do as well as he once did."

"Well, then, we both need to earn a little more if we can. Let's see what Sister Ells thinks of our idea."

So today the two were meeting at the little dress and millinery shop across Main Street from the Mansion House. Sarah explained their idea to Sister Ells, who remained silent for a time but then said, "I don't know, Sarah. I have a reputation to keep. I sew my own dresses, and I work carefully. I put in many hours, but I can charge what I think is right, and those who want the finest quality are willing to pay my price."

Sarah had a way of standing a little taller, talking a little more forcefully when she felt strongly about a matter, and Liz saw some of that in her now. "Sister Ells, I wasn't proposing that we do shoddy work. With your help, we could all improve, and we could produce many more dresses than you can now. I know there are not so many who can buy fine dresses here, but in St. Louis there's a greater call for nice things. My husband travels down there often, and he has no doubt we could find sale for our work."

"I suppose, if it's out of town, the stitching may not need to be quite so precise."

"I'm not saying that. I—"

"I know what you're saying. But I can't teach you in a week or two what I've learned in a lifetime."

Sarah seemed to shrink just a little. "Well . . . no. Of course not. But a lifetime of sewing must not be easy on your eyes and your fingers, either. If you did the cutting and we did the stitching, maybe you would be relieved from some of that."

"Yes. I was thinking just that. It's worth considering. Could Brother Kimball sell me material for a better price than he has in the past?"

All three women smiled, and Sarah said, "I suspect he thinks not. I also suspect that after we have a little talk, he will indeed give you a better price."

So Hanna Ells agreed to think a bit more about the proposal, and Liz went home to introduce the idea to Will. Of course, he said what she knew he would. "Liz, I do want you to give up the school, but I don't think you have to turn our house into a dress shop. The boys will be swallowing pins and wearing you out with all their pulling at your skirt."

Liz walked to him, put her arms around him, and said, "I can always trust you to come up with the very best advice. Men are smarter than we women are, that's all there is to it."

"And what should I take that to mean?"

"I mean that you just suggested that we build another room on the side of our house."

"Oh, is that what I said?" Will grinned.

"Yes. I need a place where I can keep my sewing things away from the boys—as you just pointed out. I had known that all along, but it was you who thought of adding another room."

"Strange, but I seem to have 'thought of it' without realizing that I had."

"That *is* strange," Liz said. "The words are hardly out of your mouth, and already you're forgetting."

"What about two rooms?"

She stepped back. "What?"

"I've been thinking that we need more rooms. It might be easier to add two at the same time. It wouldn't be a brick home, but it would give us more living space for a family. Besides, I believe I can safely assume that no matter how often I say that you don't need to help make a living for us, you have no intention of listening to me."

"I do listen to you, but I—"

"I know what you always say. But I plan to go into the overland hauling business just as soon as I can build some heavy wagons, and the day will come when Jesse and I will be known as some of the most prosperous men in the county."

Liz knew all about this idea, but she never heard about it without wondering whether Will would get himself killed trying to drive wagons through the area where so many men—especially George Samples—could ambush him. Still, she knew it was not the right time to argue about that. "One room would be wonderful," she said, "but two would be so much better. Mary Ann is still writing to me that she wants to join us here next year. She might have to live with us for a time. Or even if she doesn't, when more babies come, we'll need more rooms."

"Well, then, let's do what we can to keep more babies coming." He pulled her back to him.

"Will! The boys are watching you."

But he kissed her all the same, and then he said, "Those boys know I love you. No harm in that." Liz liked that. And she liked the kiss, too. But for the moment she was most excited about doubling the size of her house. "When could you start—"

"I can fell the trees this winter and get the logs hewn. As soon as spring breaks, I can start building—before planting starts to take all my time. I have wagons to build, too, so there's plenty to keep me busy this winter."

Liz was still a little worried about her sewing skills, and about what Sister Ells might expect of her, but she was pleased that she and Will were talking about the future. During those first months after the martyrdom, everything had seemed dark in Nauvoo. Maybe some light was beginning to shine again.

• • •

Christmas was quiet in Nauvoo, as usual. Will was working at the quarry on days when the weather allowed, but even on the worst days, when he stayed home, he was outside much of the day building wagon boxes. He also began to fell and hew logs for the house, and he cut shorter logs to build a smokehouse behind the cowshed.

A new Seventies Hall was dedicated late in December, a fine brick building where missionaries would be trained and would practice preaching the gospel. Will had gone to look at the building a few times in recent months, and he was impressed by the quality of the workmanship, all the white pine pews with carved details in the woodwork. But Will's interest was greatly heightened when he was asked to meet with President Young one day early in January and was called to serve as a seventy himself.

"You understand that this is a missionary call," Brother Brigham said to Will. They were sitting across a big oak table from one another, and as President Young spoke, he leaned forward and looked straight into Will's eyes. His reddish hair, which flared out over his ears, fell forward a little. Brother Brigham was a big-chested man who had worked in the building trade—carpenter, glazier, painter—before giving so much of his time to the Church. He wasn't quite so jovial and conversational as Joseph Smith had been, but he was straightforward in his talk, and practical. He concerned himself with the details of creating Zion—building the kingdom of God both in the real world and as a spiritual kingdom.

"Aye, President Young. I know that. But are you asking me to leave now?"

"No. Not yet. But it won't be long. We need to change many hearts hereabouts—and across the world. Tom Sharp is doing everything he can to spread the worst kind of lies about us. We can't sit by and allow him to tell the world what we are. We need to go forth and set the record straight."

Will was nodding. "I've had some thoughts about that, President," he said. "The folks in this county see us only as competitors. I've wondered, maybe we can partner with them more often so they receive some benefit from our presence here."

"What kind of partnerships do you have in mind?" Brother Brigham leaned back again. Will thought he sounded—and looked—a little skeptical.

"On the other side of the river, overland haulers lighten the loads of the riverboats and transport goods around the rapids. There's work to be done on this side, too. I've talked to a riverboat captain who said he could give me plenty of work. I could even transport goods to Galena in winter, when the boats can't get through."

"I've thought of this myself," Brigham said. "But I don't know that our people can drive wagons into Warsaw and expect to come back unscathed."

"That might change if we form a partnership with Warsaw men.

If someone there was making a living by working with us, he might put out the word that I—and the men who worked for me—needed to be given free passage in and out."

"Why don't they just take that business themselves and keep us out?"

"They could. But I'm the only man I know around here who owns six teams of oxen, and I'm willing to build the heavy wagons I need. I'm working on that now. A man in Warsaw would know he could partner with me without much capital investment, since I've gotten things started."

Brigham considered for quite some time before he said, "On the one hand, you're surely right. If others in the county can benefit from businesses we start, they may think we aren't so bad to have around. But the hard truth is, that will never happen. They're already too set against us. As I see it, if we stay here, we must separate ourselves from the gentiles. The devil's in them, and there's no way to change that."

"But shouldn't we try? I have to believe that most men don't like to kill and thieve and take advantage of others. If we go to them in a humble way and just say, 'Let's partner up, and we'll both come out ahead,' I think some will like that."

Brother Brigham was shaking his head. "Some might take your offer and like it, but too many more would be jealous of the ones who were making something of themselves. These are rough characters out here on the edge of the country. Most of them wouldn't listen to God if He dropped down out of heaven and gave 'em a knock on the head. My advice is to stay away from them. You have a wife and two sons to take care of. Nothing will be served if you get yourself killt."

"That's what Liz tells me, too." But Will wasn't quite ready to give up his plans. Thoughts of starting a new business had provided his brightest hope these last few months, and he hated to let the idea go.

"From what we're hearing, Brother Lewis, Nauvoo is likely to lose its charter in this session of the legislature. The state senate already voted against us, and the house will probably do the same. There are still those who want nothing more than to get us out of here. It may be, your greatest work will be in helping the Saints migrate west. Joseph told me many times that we would end up in the Rocky Mountains someday. I doubt we'll ever build up the kind of society we want to have until we separate ourselves from Babylon and learn to do for ourselves."

"I'd rather be with those who stay here where we have a temple. Others will want to stay, and I could be the one to give them work."

"You're to be commended for that, Will. But stay with the Saints. Don't go after the money you think the gentiles will offer you. We're talking about building a wing dam in the river. It would power mills and factories. If we aren't forced out, some will stay here and build Zion while others go forth and build up new stakes. But we'll let the anti-Christs build their own hell and then live in it."

Will nodded—and smiled—and he even gave in a little more to what might turn out to be the inevitable.

Brother Brigham stood up. "Bring your family to the Seventies Hall Sunday afternoon. There's a meeting at three o'clock. We'll ordain you—and a good many more. We have to make this city operate effectively, but we can never stop spreading the truth, either. So if we call you to serve a mission, be ready to put all else aside."

"I will, Brother Brigham. I always will."

• • •

On the following Sunday, Brigham Young placed those big carpenter's hands on Will's head and ordained him. He blessed him that he might teach the gospel, but he also said, "I bless you with wisdom and strength to help build a city of God, whether it be in this center place of Zion or in a wilderness far away."

CHAPTER 2

Abby Lewis put baby William down—for the night, she hoped—and she sat down in a recliner to watch the news on TV. It was only when she heard Jeff's whisper, close to her ear, that she realized she had fallen asleep. She felt her body jerk in response.

"Oh, sorry," Jeff said.

She opened her eyes to see Jeff smiling at her. "What time is it?" she asked, but her voice surprised her—the roughness, as though she had been asleep quite a while.

"It's eleven thirty—or, I guess, a little later than that. Malcolm and I worked longer than we expected to, but—"

"You always work longer than you expect to." But she sounded cranky, and she didn't want to take that tone. Jeff was burning the candle at both ends, trying to finish up the work on their own home, serving in the elders quorum presidency, and still getting up early every morning to drive from Nauvoo to Fort Madison, Iowa, to work. She didn't like how many hours she had to be alone, but she also didn't want to make Jeff feel guilty. So she added, "I tried to stay awake, but I just . . . didn't make it."

"It's my fault," Jeff said. "We hardly ever seem to . . . you know . . . get together these days. But I told Malcolm already, I'm staying home tomorrow night."

"Okay."

She let her eyes fall shut and was already starting to drift when Jeff slipped his hands under her legs and was about to pick her up, like a little girl. "No. Don't do that," she said. "I'll get up."

But Abby did let him help her to her feet, and then she trudged down the hall to the bedroom. By the time she had changed into her pajamas and gone into the bathroom to brush her teeth, she was actually quite awake.

It was June in Nauvoo, and in the last week or so the weather had turned hot. It was good to have central air conditioning this year, after what Abby and Jeff had gone through the summer before, but the air outside was so humid that the windows had steamed up, and even with the air conditioner running night and day, everything in the house felt damp. At least William was sleeping through the night most of the time, and he was as healthy as any baby—even though his life had started with open-heart surgery. He was growing so fast that Abby had had to buy all new clothes twice.

"Jeff, did Brother Poulsen get hold of you? He called, and I told him he could reach you on your cell."

Jeff had sat down on the bed to pull off his shoes, but he looked up at her now. She saw something in his face—some concern that she didn't want to see. "Yeah. He called." He stood up and took hold of her shoulders. "I'm sorry, but I don't think we're going to be able to buy the Poulsens' house."

"But weren't we just going to rent, with the option to buy?"

"Yeah. But he can't get a loan for the house he wanted to buy. He scraped enough together for a down payment, but now the bank is saying that he has to get his old house sold, not just rented. If we moved in and then decided we wanted to leave after a while, he could end up with two mortgages to pay, and they don't think he can handle it."

Abby felt the disappointment. She had picked out carpets and drapes for the house they were living in, and tile for the kitchen, but she really didn't want to be in the house when all that finally got installed. More than anything, she didn't want to live with the moldy tile around the bathtub; Jeff had promised he would wait until they moved and then would come back and tear out everything and rebuild the bathroom. With that being their only bathroom, she didn't know how they could stay in the place while he remodeled. "Couldn't we sign a long a long-term lease?" she asked.

"Well, maybe. We talked about that. He said that if we would sign a two-year or maybe even a three-year lease, he could take that to the bank and see what the loan officer might say. But I don't know. Would you want to do that?"

"We're staying, aren't we?"

"I guess so. I just thought I ought to talk to you about it first. But I don't mind signing if you're okay with it."

That wasn't what Abby heard. Jeff was trying to sound easy and natural, as though he weren't struggling to make that kind of commitment, but Abby knew better. She walked to the bed and sat down, and then she took hold of his arm and pulled him down. He crouched in front of her, on his knees. "When you think of staying with the same job for three more years," she said, "how do you feel?"

Jeff wouldn't look at her. "Well," he said, "I don't think that's the right question. It's like asking whether you can keep any routine— *your* routine, for instance—going on forever. It's not very exciting to think about. But if you take it one day at a time, just keep doing your best, it turns out—you know—that time goes by and it's not so bad after all."

"Is that a way to live?"

"That's how everyone lives. We do what we have to do. I love Nauvoo. I love working in the elders quorum presidency with Malcolm. I like the people I work with. So why should we pick up and leave? I don't mind signing a three-year lease."

Abby bent forward and kissed him on the forehead. And then she held his face next to hers. "I love you, Jeff. I appreciate what you're willing to do for us. But I remember what you were like when I first met you. You were so excited about life and all the things you wanted to do. You can't—"

"Abby, I was a college kid. Everyone at that age thinks he's going to cure cancer or something—you know, leap over tall buildings in a single bound."

She leaned back enough to look into his eyes. "So just two years later, you're ready to give up all your hopes?"

"Everything changes, Ab. When I decided to go into computers, I told myself that I could come up with some sort of breakthrough software that would change the world, or maybe work with a company in Silicon Valley, and . . . I don't know . . . be really inventive and creative. But you have to remember, that was my way of accepting that if I couldn't be a history professor and live the 'life of the mind,' then I'd make the best of being a computer geek. The truth is, I'm not an engineer at heart. I don't know that I could ever invent anything all that great. So why not help a team that builds blades for wind turbines? That's a good thing to do—as good as most things people do in their careers."

Abby had that old feeling again: no matter how hard Jeff tried to tell himself that he could live with the work he was doing, she knew he was giving everything up for her. "I don't want to sign a three-year lease," she said. "Not even two. Buying the house would have been different. We could have fixed it up and maybe made some money if we sold it. But a long-term lease doesn't get us anything."

"Well . . . the truth is, it probably wouldn't help at the bank anyway. Brother Poulsen already told me that. Leases can be broken, so it really doesn't change anything. But we might want to try it and—"

"No. Honey, we can't. We've got to figure out some other answer. Did you sign up for that history class in Macomb?"

"Yeah. And that's the thing. If Malcolm and I can get our houses finished, I can take classes when I have time, and maybe I could do some writing on my own. You know, be a sort of part-time historian but not a professor. My dad worked at a job that he felt no passion for, but he still had his music. I can do something like that."

"Well . . . let's see what we can work out. I'd still like to see you go back to grad school."

She watched Jeff, saw that he was thinking things he didn't want to say. But finally he nodded.

"Go brush your teeth," Abby said, "and then come to bed. I'm awake now."

That did make Jeff smile.

• • •

All the next day, at work, Jeff thought about the conversation he and Abby had had the night before. It was always easy, in theory, to tell her that he was in for the long haul, but his days seemed to last forever. Almost all his work was maintenance and troubleshooting. Computers, no matter how long he worked on them, were frustrating to him. Somewhere between all those ones and zeroes, they found space for belligerence. It was true that challenges actually made his day better. They made time pass more quickly. What he never felt at the end of a day was much in the way of satisfaction. He did like to solve problems for the people he worked with, but he rarely felt as though he had learned anything or become something more than he had been when he pulled himself out of bed that morning.

But that was probably too much to ask and he knew it, so on the way home from work that day he resolved—once again—to stop feeling sorry for himself. What more did he need than a good family, good friends, and a clear sense that he understood what mortality expected of him?

He was also relieved when he arrived home that Abby didn't come back to the subject. "I know you told me that you wanted to be home tonight," she said, "but Kayla and I want to see Vocal Point while they're here, and tonight might be the only night we can go. We were thinking we could go down in time to see 'Sunset by the Mississippi,' too. Sister Caldwell keeps telling me I have to come and see her one more time before she and Elder Caldwell go home from their mission."

Vocal Point was a men's a cappella group from BYU. Abby had heard about them and bought one of their CDs. Since then she and Jeff had become fans. "Yeah, let's do that," Jeff said. "Will we just take all the kids with us?"

"Afraid so. Kayla's little girls should be okay. If William fusses, I'll walk back on the grass, far enough away not to bother anyone."

"You'll have to spray yourself well. With this heat the chiggers are coming on strong."

However much Jeff wanted to see Vocal Point, he had really been looking forward to having some time to read. He wanted to start getting ready for the class he would be taking that fall. He knew it would be hard to keep up all semester if he was still as busy as he was now. He shook that feeling off, though, and said, "Why don't we run down to the DQ in Hamilton? Then you won't have to cook."

"Kayla and I are ahead of you on that, too. We can't all get in one car, but we're meeting them there in—" she looked at her watch—"half an hour."

So Jeff changed his clothes, and he took a few minutes to play with William, who loved to have his daddy home. Then they drove down along the river. Jeff thought of all the worrisome drives he had made to Quincy the winter before, and he reminded himself how blessed he was to have little William in his car seat, babbling, even fussing a little, when less than six months back they had wondered whether the little guy would be alive. They met the McCords at the Dairy Queen and ate, and then they all drove back to the historic section of Nauvoo. They got there rather early and were able to get good seats, and the little girls were quite patient to sit and wait. Sophie was almost four now, and Amelia had just had her first birthday. She was sitting on her daddy's lap, more content than William ever seemed to be.

The babies were not quite so enthralled with watching the missionaries perform on stage, and Abby and Kayla each had to make a trip to their cars to feed them, but Jeff was surprised at how much he enjoyed seeing the show again. He knew quite a few of the senior missionaries now, and seeing the sisters up there in their long dresses and aprons, and the men in their vests and straw hats—with sweat running down their faces—was really quite touching. The show was cheesy, with lots of lame jokes and silly acts, but that was part of the fun of the whole thing.

After the show, Jeff and Abby talked to the Caldwells for a few minutes. They would be leaving soon, and they were excited about getting home to their family—but also nostalgic about leaving Nauvoo. Sister Caldwell told Abby, "I didn't want to git up on that stage when we come here, and now I hate to git off. I'll never ever do such a thing agin in my life. I kinda like struttin' around up there."

Abby laughed. "And you do it well," she said. "But it's your visits that I'll miss. You were a mom to me when I really needed one."

"It's the only thing I know how to do, deary," Sister Caldwell said, "and it came natural with the two of you. I love ya like you're my own kids."

Jeff hated to see the Caldwells leave too, but something else was on his mind at the moment. He had noticed all evening that something was wrong with Malcolm and Kayla. They seemed subdued, and Kayla, who usually prattled on in a steady stream, was surprisingly quiet.

Before the second show, Jeff made an attempt to get William to look at the fireflies—with little response. When Malcolm walked out with Amelia, who was old enough to track the flashes of light, Jeff had a chance to say, "Is everything okay, Malcolm?"

"Well . . . maybe. Maybe not. I'll talk to you about it later."

But that sort of ruined the evening for Jeff. Vocal Point was wonderfully tight with their harmonies. Jeff loved their variety of song choices and the fun they had in introducing their numbers. Still, he kept thinking, "Something's happened to Malcolm and Kayla. I've got to find out what's going on."

So at the end of the show, Jeff asked again, and Malcolm said, "I wasn't going to bring it up tonight, but now that I've said something, I better tell you the whole thing. Why don't you stop at our house on the way home for just a few minutes?"

By the time Jeff and Abby were in their car, Abby was saying, "Something's gone wrong. I think Malcolm's lost his job."

"I know. That's what I'm thinking, too. We're going to stop at their place and talk for a few minutes."

So Jeff drove to the McCords' house, and he and Abby waited while Kayla got their kids down, and then the four adults, with

William asleep in Jeff's arms, sat down at the kitchen table—a table they had shared many times.

"Well," Malcolm said, "I guess I've known this was coming for a long time, but it came out of nowhere today. My boss told me he's losing too much money. He can't keep the place going any longer. He's going to have a big 'going out of business' tire sale starting the first of July, and by the first of August we'll be closed."

"Have you thought what you're going to do?" Jeff asked.

"Not really. I guess we should have done that by now, but we just kept hoping this wouldn't happen. I'd like to go to college, but I don't know how we'd feed the kids in the meantime."

"I told him, I can go to work," Kayla said, "and he could work part-time and go to school. People do that all the time."

"The only thing is, it's not like we're twenty years old and just starting out. We have the girls to think about, and I have no college credits at all. I doubt I could go full-time, and if I didn't, it would take me forever to get a degree."

Kayla looked at Jeff. "I keep telling him, he's only twenty-seven. We *are* just starting out. Now's when he ought to go back to school. It's only going to get harder later on."

Jeff had an idea. It was something he and Malcolm had actually talked about. He let the thoughts run through his head a little longer as Abby expressed her agreement with Kayla. By then, Malcolm was saying, "But it's more complicated than that. It's hard to move at this point. If we sold our house now, we'd lose money, not make any—and the truth is, we probably couldn't find a buyer."

"Don't they have a college down in Keokuk?" Abby asked.

"Yeah, they do," Malcolm said. "Southeastern Iowa has a campus, but it's just a community college. I could do a couple of years there and hope housing prices get better by then. But where's this part-time job that Kayla wants me to find? There's just not much work around here right now."

"Okay, wait a minute," Jeff said. "I've been sitting here thinking about something. Let's look at this whole thing a different way."

Jeff saw all the eyes turn toward him.

"We've kicked this idea around before, Malcolm. You and I—especially you—know how to remodel houses. And that's what a lot of people are doing now. They can't afford to buy a new house, or can't get a loan, so they fix up the one they're living in. I talked to a builder over in Fort Madison a while back, and he told me he wasn't building new houses, but he was doing a lot of remodeling. He said that he was getting so much work—and it was on both sides of the river—that he couldn't handle it all."

"But there's quite a bit we'd have to do to get started," Malcolm said. "Me and you get by with the tools we have, just working on our own places, but to do professional work, I'd need to invest in better equipment—power saws and routers and lots of stuff. And then, I don't know, the business end of the thing scares the heck out of me. If a guy bids something too low, he can work really hard and not make a dime. I don't think I know how to figure out a bid."

"So were you thinking you would do this on your own? I thought we talked about going into business together."

"Would you quit your job?"

"I don't know. I'm just throwing an idea out for us to talk about. I think there's money to be made. Between the two of us, I think we could learn to figure bids and handle the business part of it. I could probably create a website and get our names out there so we wouldn't have any advertising costs."

Jeff was watching Abby, and he could see already that she didn't want to make eye contact with him. He had actually allowed himself to get rather excited about this, but the feeling was passing quickly as he studied her.

"Could we make enough money to feed two families?" Malcolm asked.

Jeff didn't know how to answer that. He could see that his idea was about to die a quick death.

And then Abby said, "What about insurance? If neither one of you had a job, could we afford to pay for our own health insurance?"

That had always been Abby's question, and Jeff didn't have a good answer. During the time he had been out of work, they had had COBRA to fall back on, but if he quit his job, he wouldn't have anything this time.

A long silence followed Abby's question, and Malcolm and Kayla, who had started to light up a little, were looking down at the table again. But it was Abby who surprised Jeff. "Hey, I'm not against this. I'm really not. It might be the answer for all of us. I know Jeff would like it better than what he's doing. Maybe we just have to figure out a transition. What if Jeff keeps his job at first, and does the marketing and helps with the bidding? Malcolm would have all day to work, and Jeff could help at night."

"What about our own houses?" Kayla asked.

"We've got them both to the point where we can stop for a little while and not do any more big projects," Abby said. "I was talking to Brother Robertson on the phone the other day, and he told me to move ahead on the carpets and all the decorating stuff, but not to feel that I have to do everything right away. I was telling him how hard it was going to be to do the bathroom while we're living in the house. He just said, 'If you can live with the bathroom as is, wait until later to fix it.' He said that Jeff has done enough work on the house to earn our free rent for the rest of their mission."

"That's good," Malcolm said. "I can stop where we are on our house—we wouldn't have any choice, really. But if I was working full-time, I could get a lot done on any jobs we took. I have no trouble with being the main one doing the work. I'm just thinking that it might take quite a while to get some cash coming in. My boss told me he couldn't give me much in the way of severance pay. He's going broke as it is."

"I think we'd have to look at it this way," Jeff said. "We'd be partners. If I'm the one with a regular job, and if that's all the money we have for a while, half of it would be yours. Since Abby and I have no house payment, we've been saving a little toward a house, so at first we could help you pay your bills and buy groceries and stuff. Once we do have income from the business, that would add to my work income, and we'd divide from there."

"I think that's probably a perfect way to end a good friendship."

"It will be if we're selfish and greedy and inconsiderate. But we're brothers, Malc. And I think that's the kind of partners we would have to be. Everything would be out in the open. We'd just slice all our resources right down the middle."

"Jeff," Abby said, "if the business did well enough, would you be willing to quit your job?"

"Willing?"

"I know I've made you feel like I'd die of fear if you ever quit, but I think you have to go into this believing that it really *is* a transition, and you would be working toward the day when you could quit. I don't see why you couldn't start building new houses, once the economy is doing better."

Everyone was staring at Abby now.

She laughed and said, "Hey, don't look so shocked."

"Who are you, and what have you done with my Abby?" Jeff asked.

"I want you to be happy," Abby said. "And I want Malc and Kayla to stay here with us."

Tears had filled her eyes. Kayla's too.

"I like this," Malcolm said. "I feel like a ton of bricks has been lifted off my shoulders."

"Well, then," Jeff said, "let's make it work."

CHAPTER 3

Will was serving another mission. On January 24, 1845, the Illinois State House of Representatives had followed the example of the senate and voted to repeal the Nauvoo Charter. Officially, Nauvoo no longer existed, nor did the Nauvoo Legion. Brigham Young had feared this possibility and had called a few dozen seventies and elders to campaign in nearby counties to convince the people of Illinois that Mormons and gentiles could live together in peace. But the charter had been repealed before these brethren could set out to do their work. All the same, Brigham had clapped his hand on Will's shoulder and said, "The enemy can take away our charter, but we're still here, whether any sheet of paper sanctions us or not. We'll operate under priesthood authority, and the Lord will guide us. Bear testimony to the people that we're not such rascals as they think we are."

So Will had set out, and he had decided to do something Brother Brigham hadn't told him to do. He had already made up his mind that he wanted to talk to Thomas Sharp, editor of the local newspaper that had run the most inflammatory anti-Mormon articles over the months. If Sharp's heart could be changed, much of the trouble would soon end. He knew it was probably a fool's errand to see the man, but he had long imagined himself sitting down with Sharp, and in his daydreams he always said the right things, penetrated the man's thick skin, and started a discussion that began to set things right.

Now, however, Will was standing on Main Street in Warsaw, and across the street he could see a sign on the front of a little brick building: *Warsaw Signal.* Reality was sinking in, and Will was doubting himself. He had read the outrageous claims in that newspaper for two years now, and he wondered whether he could walk through the door and even come back out alive. When he had set out that morning from Nauvoo, he had believed his idea was inspired. Now he was thinking he should pull his hat down low and head out of town.

But he walked across the rutted, hard-frozen street, if for no other reason than because he had come this far and didn't want to listen to his fears. He opened the door and stepped inside. The smell of linseed oil from the printer's ink was in the air, and in the back of the room a young man was pulling a large sheet of paper off a press. It was all very much like the print shop in Nauvoo, and something in the familiarity made it seem that these were men like himself.

"What can I do fer yuh?" the young man asked.

"I was hoping to speak to Mr. Thomas Sharp, if I could, please."

"What about?"

"I merely want to meet with him if he's here today and could grant me a few minutes of his time."

"Who are you?"

The young man could not have been much over twenty, but his hair was thinning, and he looked pale, as if he had never worked outside a day in his life. It was his suspicious look, however, that had begun to worry Will. Surely, the boy had heard Will's English accent, and just as surely, he knew that most of the Englishmen in Hancock County were Mormons.

"My name is Will Lewis." Will hesitated, and then decided to be forthright. "I'm from Nauvoo. I hope for better days ahead for our two towns, and I want to express that hope to Mr. Sharp."

Will heard a chair slide on a wood floor somewhere, and then a man appeared in a doorway at the back of the room. Will had seen him before, knew who he was. Thomas Sharp.

"You want to convince me to love the Mormons, is that it?" the man asked, and he smiled. He seemed almost friendly.

"Aye," Will said. "I think it's time we learn to understand one another a little better and make the best of things."

"And how long do you suppose it will take you to change my attitude toward a people I hate with all my heart and soul?" Sharp was still smiling.

"Half an hour might not do it. But we might make a start."

"I'll give you ten minutes—only because I never thought a man would be so bold—and *foolhardy*—as to walk into this town, and into my office, and think to change everything I believe." He motioned for Will to walk back to his office.

So Will took that walk, praying all the way, and sat down. Sharp stepped behind a desk piled with papers and sat down too. He looked just a little wild, his hair long and scattered, his face not recently shaved, and his cravat loose around his collar. Will was surprised all over again to be reminded how young the man was. "What did you say your name was?" Sharp asked.

"Will Lewis."

"What part of England are you from?"

"Herefordshire. In the Malvern Hills. Do you know where that is?"

"Can't say that I do."

"It's not too far from Gloucester."

But that seemed to mean nothing to him either. "And how old are you, if you don't mind my asking?"

"Twenty-six," Will replied.

"That's what I was guessing. We're exactly the same age."

It was strange for Will to think that a man his own age could wield such power and influence in the county. On paper, Sharp's bitter verbal attacks had always seemed to come from a much older man.

"And who sold you this crazy idea that Joe Smith was a prophet of God and Nauvoo was the land of milk and honey?"

"I was taught by Wilford Woodruff, an Apostle. He—"

"I know the man. He's as crazy as Joe Smith was. He sees visions everywhere he looks. Aren't you any smarter than to believe such hogwash? You have some education, I would wager."

"A little. But I was a tenant farmer in England, with little hope to become anything else."

"I've always thought that was the draw for the English and Welsh who come here. Someone told you that you could own your own land, get a fresh start on life. The religion looked like something you could embrace, just to move up a little in the world."

"I'm certain that was part of what made me listen at first. But I came to believe—"

"No, no. I don't want to hear all that." Sharp ran his fingers through his hair and leaned back. "But I like that you admit that the land was an attraction. You don't seem quite so loony as most of the Mormons I've talked to. So tell me what you came to say. I want to hear it." He spread his arms wide, as if to say, *The time is now yours, sir.*

"I believe that everyone in the county can prosper. Instead of competing with one another, why not enter into enterprises together? Many of our people are trained craftsmen. If our two towns, along with Carthage and the other towns hereabouts, would seek out capital support and establish mills and factories, we're located in a perfect place to export our goods down the river and eastward on the Ohio—even across the ocean. I don't think men have to share religious beliefs in order to respect each other and get along as neighbors."

Sharp was laughing by now. "So you want us to start businesses together—now that you're scared for your lives. You didn't arrive in our county with that attitude. The first thing you did was to build up a mighty army, and then you showed us that you could take over our economy, our politics, and everything else, just by your sheer numbers. I never once heard Joe Smith say he wanted to build *factories* with us."

"You have to understand," Will said, "in the beginning, those who came to Nauvoo were still licking their wounds from being driven out of Missouri. They came to find a place to settle, and they wanted to build up their own society. They were still fearful about how they might be received. But that's what I'm advocating: a change from all that. Our people may have voted mostly the same in the past—because they had common concerns—but if our concerns were united with yours, you wouldn't have to worry about voting blocs."

"Oh, thank you, Mr. Lewis. You're opening my eyes. Now that you've lost your insane leaders, and lost your charter—and with it, your army—you want to be friends. You want *our* capital to open up jobs to *your* craftsmen. You want—"

"I didn't say that. I'm saying that we live in this county together. We ought to find ways to work together, not against each other. Most of us believe in Jesus Christ and—"

"Don't start that. Don't tell me that you're *Christians.* Christians don't steal horses and pass counterfeit money, and they—"

"Governor Ford himself looked into all that, and he said it wasn't true. As much as anything, people believe that we do those things because *you* keep claiming it in your newspaper." But Will didn't want to sound angry. He took a breath and said, more quietly, "I believe with all my heart that our people are mostly good, and I believe the same about the people of Warsaw. As long as we live here together—"

But Sharp was suddenly on his feet. "We will *not* live together much longer. We will *never* be compatible. You came here to take over, and you couldn't do it. Now you better come at us full force and conquer us—drive us into the river—because it's either that, or we conquer you. Mr. Lewis, I *vow* to finish what we started with Joe and Hyrum. If you didn't get the message from that, then accept the message from me now. Get out *with* your life or take a ball in your chest—but don't come here and talk to me about being friends."

Will stood up too, but he spoke calmly again. "Mr. Sharp, I own land here, the same as you. If you don't like my being here, I understand that. But how can it be right to kill people, burn their houses, drive them away—only because you disagree with their religion?"

"Yours is not a religion, Mr. Lewis. It's a band of fanatics. It's men claiming to see visions and then ordering around dupes like you who can't see through their madness. It's men with harems, clutching innocent young women to their bony old bodies. Don't tell me that that's a *religion*."

Will wasn't going to listen to any more of this. He had tried his best to offer an olive leaf, but he could see now, Brother Brigham had been right about Sharp. "I'm sorry I bothered you," he said softly. "I only wish you could know our people. Most of them are honest men and women who try to do what's right. You describe us over and over in your newspaper as thieves and counterfeiters, but I've lived here the better part of two years, and I don't see the people you're talking about. Joseph Smith was nothing at all like the man you describe. I looked him in the eye on many occasions, and I knew his heart. He was as good a man as ever lived."

"Listen, Lewis, you can believe all that, but I knew the real Joe

Smith. He insulted me and called my newspaper a filthy rag. I saw no *Christianity* in that man."

Will was on the edge. He wanted to grab Sharp by the neck and slam him against the wall. Instead, he took a moment to control his voice, and then said, "You raise an interesting question, Mr. Sharp. I find myself asking what Jesus would call the hatred and lies you print in your paper—and your editorials that advocate *murder.* 'Filthy rag' might not be too far off."

Sharp came around the desk with his fist doubled up, but Will didn't back off a step. Sharp stopped short and only poked a finger toward Will's face. "I looked that man in the eye too, you know. Just before he breathed his last. He didn't *prophesy* at that point."

"Then you admit that you were there? In your paper, you lied about that. You said that Mormons attacked the jail themselves. Don't you ever get sick of yourself, with all your lying and distortion?"

"Get out of here."

"Thank you. I'm happy to leave." Will stepped toward the door, but then he turned back. He hated to think that he had made things worse, not better. "I would still hope that you would think about what I've said today. We've both expressed our feelings, and maybe that had to happen. But it just seems to me that a war between us will do no one any good."

Sharp was smiling again. He brushed the hair out of his eyes, and, surprisingly, he stepped forward and reached out his hand to Will. "You stick to your text, I'll say that for you, Lewis. And I honestly hope you get out of town alive. You have more courage than good sense."

"You might be right about that," Will said. He shook the man's hand, and then he set his hat back on his head and stepped to the door.

"I'll tell you something you need to know, Lewis. When you

Mormons first came here, I had no hatred for any of you. You brought your trouble upon yourselves. Every bit of it."

"But, Mr. Sharp," Will said, "Joseph Smith told me himself that he invited you to Nauvoo, met with you, tried to make a friend of you."

"Oh, yes, he tried to pull the wool over my eyes. But the first time I criticized him, he denounced me and my newspaper. I found out early just what sort of man he was."

"No. You never knew that." He took one step back toward Sharp. "And yet, you killed him. You'll pay for that even if these corrupt courts never convict you."

"Get out of this county, Lewis. You and all your people. If you don't, you *will* die. Do you hear that? I feel no guilt when I kill a rat, and I'll feel no guilt when I kill you and your wife, or even your babies. You may have been a decent man at one time, but you fell in with people who lost their right to live with other citizens. The only solution for dealing with your kind is to wipe you off the earth."

Will had to make a choice. There were so many things he wanted to say. And more than anything, he wanted to knock the man on his back. But he felt sad, too, that his good intentions had backfired on him. He thought of Joseph, and he thought of Christ, and then he said, "I'm sorry you feel that way. I will continue to pray that with time, you'll change your mind about us."

But as Will walked from the office, he heard Sharp say, "*Nothing* will ever change my mind."

• • •

Liz was alone again. But nothing seemed the same this time. Daniel was walking, and he was a livelier little boy than Jacob had ever been. In fact, he seemed to inspire Jacob to explore the house more than he had before, and the two loved, above all else, to go outside. They usually didn't last long in the snow and cold, but they would not be back inside long before they wanted to go out again. Liz liked to get out herself, even with snow on the ground, and she thought it was good for the boys to become hearty and self-confident about facing the elements. All the same, what Liz needed now were the two other rooms that Will had promised to build in the spring. She was no longer using her house as a school, but she was sewing as many hours as she could free up each day. She still had all the same chores—never-ending, it seemed—but she was gaining some efficiency in dealing with the milk and butter making, and Will had left her a mighty pile of firewood. Both boys seemed to wear out enough to go to bed quite early, and while they were asleep she could sew without interruption.

What pleased Liz most was that the quality of her work had improved in the weeks since she had been sewing dresses. Not only could she fit the cuttings nicely, but she had developed a neat little stitch that looked quite professional.

Today, however, Liz was worried. She was taking a dress to Vilate Kimball, wife of Heber C. Kimball, one of the Apostles. Fortunately, the Kimballs lived just under the bluffs, so Liz could take her boys and walk down quickly, but Vilate had always seemed such a pretty, elegant woman, and Liz felt nervous around her. Sister Ells had taken Sister Kimball's measurements and had cut the fabric for the dress, and Liz felt satisfied with the sewing she had done, but she didn't want to seem uneasy and awkward. Liz always pretended to be confident, no matter what her circumstance, but the truth was, when she met the "great ladies" of Nauvoo, she felt inadequate. Her mother and father had always looked to their "betters" with a certain awe and humility, and Liz knew she had inherited some of that.

She folded the dress carefully and wrapped it in brown paper, then took the boys and hiked down through the woods. The trail had been used a good deal since the last snowstorm, so she had no difficulty getting through the woods, but the boys kept running ahead, slipping on hard patches of snow, and they didn't listen when she pled with them to come back and stay with her. She finally had to carry little Daniel, who simply couldn't keep up with Jacob. Daniel was going to be bigger than Jacob someday, but he was not quite a year old and was still very unstable on his little legs.

By the time they reached Vilate's house, Jacob wanted to be carried too, and he was out of sorts when Liz didn't have an extra arm to lift him. The Kimballs lived in a log house with a brick addition built onto one side. It was a humble house for such honored people in the community, but it was quite a large place.

It was Sarah Noon, a woman Liz had seen with Vilate before, who opened the door. She was English and a few years older than Liz. Liz had assumed at first that Sarah Noon was a widow, but Sarah Kimball had told Liz that she had been married to a ruffian who had beaten her, and she had divorced him. Liz also knew that Sarah Noon helped Vilate a good deal, and the Kimballs apparently provided for her. Liz had stopped to talk to Sarah and Vilate one day when the two were working together in the garden, and the impression Liz had taken away was that they treated one another as friends, not merely as employer and employee.

Of course, Liz knew what some people said—that Sarah Noon was married to Heber, the same as Vilate, but Liz didn't think that was true.

"Come in, Sister Lewis," Sarah said. "Sister Kimball said you was comin'. It's a dress to fit, if I remember right?"

"Yes." She handed the package to Sarah, and then she picked up Jacob and carried both boys inside. She knelt by them. "Jakey, Danny, you must be good boys now. No running about. Mummy won't be long."

"Oh, don't worry, Sister Lewis," Sarah said. "We have four young boys here. I'll take yours to play with some of ours."

It seemed a strange thing to say. Liz remembered having seen the Kimballs with five children, three of them little boys, but who was the fourth, and why had she said, "to play with some of *ours*"?

"Do you live with the Kimballs, Sister Noon?" Liz asked.

"Oh, no. I have two daughters at home, old enough to work a little and look after themselves during the day when I come here to help Sister Kimball. I do bring my little son with me here each day."

Liz nodded and didn't ask anything more. She knew she had already gone too far. But Sarah didn't seem embarrassed by the question. Somewhere, in another room, Liz could hear children laughing and calling out, and she was sure Jacob and Daniel would like to be part of that, so she relaxed a little. The children sounded busy and boisterous, which made Liz feel that she needn't be ashamed of her own mothering skills.

About then Vilate opened the door to a room that was straight back from the front door. She looked serene, considering the noise from the children, and Liz could see proof of what she had guessed from the style of the dress she had been making. Sister Ells had called the dress a "wrapper," a loose-fitting design with a high waist. It was clearly designed for a pregnancy.

"Oh, thank you, dear. Is that the dress I ordered?"

"Yes, ma'am."

"I'm Vilate, not 'ma'am.'"

Liz smiled and stopped herself before she called her "ma'am" again.

"Let me try it on quickly," Vilate said. "I don't see how it could do anythin' but fit." She laughed.

Sister Noon was holding the boys by the hand as she led them from the room. Little Daniel was looking up at her, seeming perplexed. Sarah bent, picked him up, and carried him to the door. He looked back over Sarah's shoulder at Liz, but he didn't cry.

"It's all right," Liz said, and she gave him a little wave. She stepped to a nearby dinner table and pulled open the brown paper. She lifted the dress by the shoulders and shook it out a little, and then she carried it to Vilate. "The fabric is so pretty," Liz said. "Did you choose it yourself?"

"Yes, but don't tell Heber. When he gits the bill, I'm hopin' that he assumes it was all Sister Ells's doing."

The skirt was a medium-weight cotton with little rosebuds in the print, but the bodice was a rich, rose-colored velvet. It was certainly not a housedress, but it was not really a gown, either. It was something she could wear to a party or a play, but also nice to wear at the grove or at other church meetings.

"When he sees you in it, he'll forget all about the cost," Liz said. "I'm sure of that."

"Oh, I doubt that. I'm too old to take his breath away, the way he used to say I did." She laughed, and then she took the dress and returned to her bedroom.

It was true that Vilate was no longer a young woman. She certainly had to be close to forty. But she was slender and quite tall, and her face was unwrinkled, her gray-blue eyes quite brilliant. Liz thought she was beautiful.

Liz was suddenly alone, and she liked having a chance to look around. The house may have been built mostly from logs, but it was roomy inside, and beyond the dinner table was a beautiful glass-front cabinet with a display of blue and white dishes that could only have come from the potteries in England, where Brother Heber had served two missions. Everything looked much finer than the things Liz had in her little house.

In only a few minutes Vilate was back in the main room of the cabin, wearing the new dress. "It fits perfectly," she said, "and there's room to grow." She laughed again and seemed entirely at ease with Liz.

"Good. Just let me look at the fit in the shoulders, and then I'll pin up the skirt for hemming and we'll be finished."

"The shoulders feel perfect. Just pin it up."

So Liz asked her to stand erect, and she knelt and began to fold and pin the fabric in place.

"It was nice of Sarah to look after my boys," Liz said. "I was worried they would make a mess of your house while I was doing this."

"Sarah is a blessing to me, Liz. I don't know what I would do without her. We're sisters now. That's how we think of one another."

"We're all sisters. That's what I love about Nauvoo."

"Yes, that's true. But this is more than that. Maybe you understand what I'm saying."

Liz's question was answered, and Vilate was not ashamed. Liz had felt uncomfortable when she had only suspected, but Vilate's forthrightness—and her obvious love for Sarah—seemed to take away the mystery and strangeness of the situation.

"Life surprises us sometimes," Vilate said. "We think we know exactly where we're going and what to expect, and then the Lord tells us to turn a corner that we didn't know existed. When He speaks to us in a clear voice, though, and tells us even something we think we don't want to hear, there's no mistaking the command. Something that seemed undesirable can become just the opposite."

Liz understood what Vilate was telling her, but this wasn't a conversation she wanted to have. This way of living may be all right for the Kimballs, but it wasn't right for Liz and Will. "I know what you mean, Sister Kimball," Liz said, and she tried to keep her voice light and conversational. "I never expected to be in America, never expected to live in a log house, never thought I would churn butter or chop wood. But the Lord called us here, and I'm so happy we listened to the call."

"I'm glad to hear you say that, Sister Lewis. A good many are still leaving the city, chasing after some of these false prophets. We need you young people to stay strong and stalwart."

"I don't know how strong I am. And I do get scared when Will is gone—as he is again—but still, I feel confident that the Lord is with us."

Liz was putting in the last pin when Vilate said, very gently, "Sister Lewis, I'm certain we have hard days ahead of us. But I feel calm. We have to keep trusting, that's all."

Liz felt Vilate's assurance run through her own spirit. And afterward, as she walked home, she told herself that she wasn't going to fret about quite so many things as she had in recent months. Vilate and Sarah Noon were sisters, and both seemed happy. Sarah had certainly needed someone to support her, so maybe that explained the Lord's instructions to the Kimballs—and to Sarah. But Liz's circumstances were entirely different, and she was glad for that.

So Liz resolved that she needed to keep the faith and not worry so much about the rumors she heard, or even about the future of the Saints. She merely had to accept the Lord's will and keep her eye on the path ahead. No one could take away the peace she felt unless she lost her faith in the Lord.

CHAPTER 4

Will was frustrated. His previous mission had been difficult, serving in the South, but convincing the people of Illinois that Mormons were decent people was proving impossible. He had expected to find plenty of allies in Quincy, where the Saints had been so well received when they had first fled from Missouri. He did find some folks there who regretted the plight of the Mormons, but one of the newspapers had begun to editorialize in favor of those demanding that they leave the state. The editor argued that Mormons could never be integrated into the society of "normal" people.

Will walked from town to town. He usually met with newspaper editors and town officials, and the farther from Nauvoo he walked, the more friendliness he found. But almost no one was willing to put him up at night, and it was too cold to sleep in haystacks, so he spent far too much of his hard-earned money on taverns where he could pay for his keep. By the early part of March he had worked around to the southern part of Illinois, and now he was making his way home. He hoped that a few editors would be less likely to print only one side of the story after talking to him, but he didn't think he had converted anyone to his point of view.

One editor told him, "If the Mormons were all like you, I suspect no one around here would have trouble with your people. You seem a fine fellow."

"How many of us have you met, sir?" Will had asked.

"Well . . . only you, I suppose. But I've heard about the others."

"Why don't you come to Nauvoo and see just how many are exactly like me? It's rumors and accusations that form most opinions about us."

"I suppose there might be something to that," the man had said, but he hadn't promised to come to Nauvoo to see for himself.

Will made his way to Quincy again, and then walked north. He stopped in the Morley settlement and stayed with Solomon Hancock and his family for a night, and then he trudged on toward Nauvoo. He was eager to get home, but he was not pleased with what he would have to report to President Young.

Will had decided to avoid Warsaw. He stayed east of the town and headed for Golden's Point, away from the river, but as he neared Green Plains, he knew he would be better off to avoid some of the rabid Mormon haters there. Levi Williams, a minister in Green Plains, had been one of the leaders of the mob that had killed Joseph and Hyrum. So Will cut through a wooded area and then walked across some fallow fields. What he recognized, however, was that he would now be coming very close to George Samples's farm, and that was another place to avoid.

And yet, when Will spotted George's farm, set back close to a grove of trees, he suddenly wanted to talk to the man. He knew he held a grudge against George and Blake. After all, these were the men who had lain in ambush to kill him. But when Will studied Christ's teachings, as he had done a great deal during his mission, he desired to be a better man. He had to wonder whether there was something he could do to end the trouble between him and the Samples brothers.

The more he thought about the matter, the more he believed that he had been led toward George's home. He decided that having failed to change Thomas Sharp's mind—and so many others—if he could at least make things right with the Samples brothers, maybe he could think of his mission as a success.

So Will walked to the front door of the farmhouse—a log cabin, badly chinked, with a sod roof that drooped so badly it appeared ready to fall in. When Will knocked at the plank door, he knew he was putting his life on the line, but he waited all the same. Suddenly, a black dog—some sort of mongrel sheep dog—charged around the corner of the house. It stopped short of attacking, but it bared its teeth and barked furiously.

Will stood his ground until George opened the door. The man looked confused at first. He even stepped back, as though he expected Will to be wielding a weapon.

"Could I speak with you, George?" Will asked.

George couldn't find his voice. He looked more disheveled and dirty than ever, as though he had never changed his clothes or combed his long hair since the day Will had left him on the Carthage Road. His only response was to shout at the dog, "Stop that!" The dog shuffled backward and hunched down as though it knew better than to ignore George's command.

"George, I still want peace between us. I was just wondering if there's anything I could do for you and your brother. I know these have been hard times for you."

"Get out of here," George finally managed to say.

"I was just wondering how Blake is doing now. Is he able to get up and around, or is he—"

"You might as well've killt him, Lewis. He sits all day, just starin'. He don' know whar he is."

"But, George, you were going to kill me. I was just fighting back."

George stared at Will. Finally he did say, "We shoulda killt you when we had a chance. It's what you had comin', an' still do." He moved his hand down to his belt and felt along it until he grasped the handle of a knife, still in its scabbard.

"All right. You have your opinion about that, and I have a different one. But all that's in the past. What I was wondering was whether you have enough food to last you through the rest of the season—until you get another harvest in. I still feel bad about the way things turned out, and I'd like to help out, if I can."

George pulled the knife from its scabbard. "Leave now or I'll cut you open from yer belly to yer throat."

"All right. I'll go. But there's no reason we can't end this feud between us. I'm not asking you to be friends; I just think it's time we—"

"You got somethin' wrong with you, Lewis? You never understan' nothin'. When spring breaks, the war is on. The people aroun' here is gittin' together. We'll kill yuh this time. Ever' one of yuh, if that's what it takes." George raised the knife higher, held it even with his shoulder. He could strike with it any time he wanted, but Will wasn't worried. He knew he could dodge it quickly enough. In the back of his mind was still the trust that the Lord had sent him here, that this was the culmination of his mission.

"I don't know how your crops turned out this last year. Did you harvest enough to get you through until spring?"

"I don't need nuthin' from you, Lewis. Jist git away from here."

"All I'm asking is if you could use some corn, or maybe a cut of bacon."

George made his lunge. Will sidestepped and then slammed the man's forearm with such force that the knife went flying. And just as quickly, Will jumped down in the dirt, grabbed the knife, and came up holding it raised and ready.

"I'm not going to use this, George. You're in no danger from me. But don't try to kill me again. I'm a stronger man than you are, and I'm faster. You should have learned that by now."

George was easing his way back.

"Step into the house," Will said. "I want to talk to your brother. Maybe you don't want my corn, but I want to hear from Blake that he's not going hungry."

Will stepped forward before George could shut the door in his face. As the man gave more ground, Will moved ahead. There was a low fire burning in the fireplace, but that was the only light. Will glanced around and saw that the cabin was squalid, with little furniture and the stench of human waste in the air. Then he saw Blake sitting on a broken bed in a dark corner. The man didn't react to Will's presence. His face was mostly dark, covered by his black beard and by shadows, but his eyes were reflecting the firelight, and Will could see that they didn't move at all.

"I regret that I did that to him," Will said.

"You're the craziest man I ever knowed," George said. "You don't know what you done to us." But this was more subdued than hostile. Will was the one with the knife now.

"George, listen to me. From the beginning you've hated me, but never for any reason that I can understand. The fact is, I don't like you, either. But I'm not talking about us being friends. I just want to be sure you're not starving."

"I don't want yer handouts."

Will was losing his patience. "All right. Fine," he said, too sharply. He saw Blake flinch at the sound, and he lowered his voice.

"I was down this way, and I wondered how you were holding out. That's all."

"Here's the only thin' I have ta say ta yuh. I vow I'll kill yuh yet and float yer carcass down the river. Yours, and yer wife's, and yer little boys'. And ever' other Mormon, from ol' Brigham on down. Now use that knife if yer goin' to. Otherwise, git out of my house."

Will turned the knife around, held the blade lightly in his fingers, and then handed it back to George. "You use the knife if you want to. I have no desire to harm you."

George took the knife and stood silent for a time, staring. Will nodded, and then he turned deliberately around. He stood for a moment, so his back was an easy target, and then he walked slowly to the door. He knew George wouldn't stab him. He also knew that he hadn't accomplished anything that he had hoped to do—not here, and not on his entire mission. When he reached the front step, Will turned back. "George, one of the great regrets of my life is that you and I had this trouble. If I can help you and Blake in some way, I hope you know I would like to do that. I wish I were a better man than I am. And the truth is, you're a sorry excuse for a human being yourself, but I still think we could have handled this better than we did."

George was mostly in the shadows, back in the house, but Will could see in the man's face that he had no idea what had just happened to him.

• • •

When Will returned from his mission, Liz could see his disappointment and hear it in his voice. But what worried her more was how little he wanted to talk about his experiences. She had the feeling he was holding back so that she wouldn't know the depth of the hostility he had experienced. It was late March, 1845, and the weather was improving, spring coming on, but Will had hardly spoken of plowing and planting—the things he usually talked about in the spring. She thought she knew why. There was a great deal of talk in Nauvoo about finding a new home where the Saints could live the gospel and not worry what their neighbors thought of them. In every issue of the *Times and Seasons* and *Nauvoo Neighbor* there were articles about "Upper California"—the Rocky Mountains and the land beyond. John Taylor praised the valley of the Great Salt Lake and the Bear River Valley as a region with a good climate, an area remote enough that the Saints could live there in peace.

Liz found herself thinking more and more that leaving Nauvoo was the best answer. She was tired of the panic she felt that George Samples would try to burn down their house—or the fear that a mob would attack the city. She was also tired of hearing what Thomas Sharp wrote in his newspaper, or learning of threats in the outlying settlements. Sometimes Will tried to explain to her why people in the county hated Mormons so avidly, but she looked about herself and saw good people—devoted brothers and sisters—who only wanted to live simple lives, raise their children, and build up a place where love and kindness prevailed.

Liz wanted her little boys to be happy and healthy, not afraid, and she wanted them to love the gospel as much as she did. If all that could happen only somewhere in the wilderness of the West, she thought she could accept that. Still, she feared the cost of that kind of migration, wondered whether she could hold up under the demands. She no longer thought of going back to England. She knew that she never would, and no matter how much she missed her mother and sister, she knew she and Will were happier here than they would have been had they stayed in England and always wondered about Zion. But she longed for peace and hoped that she wouldn't always be afraid.

On March 16, Brigham Young had announced that Nauvoo would be reorganized as a "town," as defined by state laws, only one square mile in size. The name of the town would be the "City of Joseph." His emphasis, at least for many of the Saints, was on remaining in Nauvoo, not leaving. A new police force would operate under the direction of the priesthood, with deacons quorums serving under bishops, patrolling the community and guarding against attacks from outside. Hosea Stout would oversee the force, as he had before. The Nauvoo Legion was officially disbanded, but the volunteer soldiers were still ready to protect the city. Immigration from Britain would be encouraged again, and work on the temple would be pushed forward faster than ever. Bricklayers were to be called to resume work on the Nauvoo House, and a new Music Hall had recently been dedicated, near the temple.

Brigham Young and Heber C. Kimball were also admonishing members to turn Nauvoo into a garden. The Saints should plant every undeveloped lot, every open space, and cultivate the entire Big Field. Members needed to make their own cloth, too, and sew their own clothing, and the shops in the city needed to supply shoes, bonnets, and household implements. The time for depending on imported items needed to end, and the Saints would have to learn to be more independent and self-reliant.

What Will had told Liz, however, was that, without announcing their intention, Brigham Young and the Twelve were planning to send a group of men west to seek out a place of refuge. One possibility was that only a portion of the members would migrate to the West, and the "center place" of Zion would remain in the City of Joseph. But a plan was also to be prepared in case extreme measures had to be taken in order to save the Saints. Will had learned, from talking to William Clayton, that the Council of Fifty was meeting often, and they were still the ones who would direct the secular concerns of the kingdom—and the exodus, if it became necessary.

Above all, Brigham had preached, forcefully, that it was a time for retrenchment. If the Saints wanted to be blessed by the Lord, they had to end their wicked ways. Liz wondered sometimes whether Church members were nearly so wicked as Brigham made them sound, but he wanted dancing to cease—even though he liked to dance himself—and he wanted light-mindedness to be brought under control, Sabbath breaking to stop, and he wanted to hear no Latter-day Saint use the name of the Lord in vain. Liz knew that he was certainly right; she only wished that Brigham would soften his speech a little and admonish the Saints in a milder way—the way Joseph had done.

For Liz, this was a strange time, and she knew that everyone in the city was feeling the same thing. The goal was to finish the temple, build Zion, and go forward in the hope that the Lord would intercede and allow the Saints to keep their city. But the leaders were looking west, and everyone knew it. Liz wondered every day when this delicate peace would end and violence would break out again.

On Sunday, Will and Liz were invited to dinner with the Benbows and some of the other English Saints. Brother Benbow sent a young man who worked for him with a little carriage, and Will and Liz, with their boys, had a nice ride out to the farms east of town. It was a sunny day, still a little chilly, but the first redbuds were opening in the woods, and the birds were joyous about the sunshine. Liz liked that "her three boys" were all together again. Will seemed more lifted in spirits than he had been since coming home.

The English Saints enjoyed the time together, and Liz felt comfortable with them. Many were people she had known in the Malvern Hills. She liked the cadence of their speech, the familiar style of joking and laughing, and she liked that now, with the better part of a year having passed since Joseph and Hyrum had been taken from them, they no longer spoke so much of that tragic time. There was surely a good deal to worry about, but without saying the words out loud, Liz heard in the voices of her friends some growing optimism. Most had settled in, satisfied with their land and their houses, however simple, and she heard talk of the future. Some speculated that they might remain in Zion, and others seemed to think that settling in the West would be better. But at least the darkness of the previous June—when gloom had been hanging in the valley like fog—had mostly cleared.

After the dinner, Will and Liz walked to Jesse and Ellen's house, just to share a little time together before the Lewises took the ride back to town.

"You would na' go wrong ta move out here ta yer farm," Ellen told the Lewises. "You would like the livin' here—with ones that know the mother tongue."

Liz laughed, but she said, "I *would* like it. Will still wants to build a nice house in town, and only farm here, but a fancy house is not important to me. I like the prairie, and I would see Will more if he didn't have to work so far away from home."

The Matthews children liked to entertain the little Lewis boys. They were excited now to take them out to the cowshed to see a new litter of kittens. Liz was happy for the chance to sit at the kitchen table with Ellen and Jesse and not have to worry about the boys for a few minutes. She was pleased to see that Jesse and Ellen's little house was better furnished than it had been at first. The partnership Will and Jesse had agreed upon really had made a difference in all their lives.

"We may decide, in time, to live here by you," Will said. "But for the present, with everything about the future still in question, I wouldn't want to start another house, even a better one in town."

"I know that some o' the people 'round here—Tom Sharp and them like 'im—still call for war," Jesse said, "but I wonder if most folks in the county want nothin' more than ta git their crops in the groun'. It might be, they don' care so much 'bout drivin' us out as they claim. If we keep on, and do na' bother 'em, maybe they will na' bother us neither."

Liz watched Will. He knew plenty and wasn't saying much. But he did say, "I hope you're right. I was talking mostly to newspaper editors and town leaders on my mission, and they're certainly full of loud talk. It might be, the people themselves don't really care so much."

"But it's the newspapers what riles others up," Ellen said. "They keep the hate goin' when maybe the farmers would let it go."

"That's true," Will said. "Those men can fan the flames. And men like Levi Williams make it seem that life can ne'er go on so long as we're still here."

"What will they do, then?" Jesse asked. "Will they come after us this year?"

Will took his time, even glanced at Liz, before he said, "I don't doubt the talk will keep up. But they know we have the numbers on our side, even with most of our weapons gone."

"What about those Samples boys?" Jesse asked. "Will they be puttin' a mob together?"

Will was sitting where the light from the window was across his face; Liz saw something in his eyes that she had noticed often since he had come home—a worry that he didn't want to talk about. "I stopped in to see those boys," he finally said. "Blake is in bad shape, and George will never forgive me for the damage I did to his brother. He's the sort of man who won't come after me alone, but he might do what you say—round up some others. If I were to wager, though, I'd say he won't do that. I don't think he's brave enough to take me on here in Nauvoo."

Liz couldn't believe what she had heard. "Will, what do you mean? You actually went to his house?"

"I did."

"But why?"

"I was just worried that they might be going hungry. I offered to give them some food. It was just a little peace offering—to see if I couldn't end the troubles between us."

"What did he say?" Jesse asked.

Will smiled. "All in all, I'd have to say that he wasn't interested in feeding at my hand. He pulled a knife on me and ordered me out of his place."

"Will, what were you thinking?" Liz asked. "He could have killed you."

"I know. But I wanted to make the offer. It just seemed right to do it."

Liz sometimes wondered whether she would ever understand the way Will's mind worked. Those men had tried to kill him, and yet he acted as though he owed *them* something.

But Will was quick to change the subject. "I stopped by to see Oliver Hyatt, too. I asked him if he wanted to partner with us, if we start our hauling business this summer."

"Does he want to do it?"

"He said he wanted to think about it. He's wary about what people might do to him. Still, he said he may do it. And if he doesn't, we have time to find someone else. Low water won't be coming 'til late in the summer, and we still have to get some wagons built."

"And what if we leave Nauvoo before long, Will? Won't that be a waste of money?"

"We'll need wagons to go west, if that's what we end up doing.

Cargo wagons are heavy, but it might not be bad to have something like that out on the prairies. And if we had more wagons than we needed for ourselves, I think we could sell them."

"Knowing you," Liz said, "you wouldn't sell them. You would give them to the poor."

Everyone laughed, and Will smiled. "That might not be such a bad thing either."

"Liz is right," Jesse said. "For a man that hopes ta git rich in business, you don't really know how to hold on ta yer money. You think more on us, and on the Johns family, than you do on yerself."

"That's not so. It's worked out well for all of us."

"Aye," Jesse said. "It saved us, sure."

"Let's see what those little ones are doing," Will said.

Liz put her hand on Ellen's forearm. "That's what he says, that he wants to look after the children, but he feels cooped up if he stays inside more than a quarter of an hour. He likes the smell of a cow-shed better than pork frying in a kitchen."

"There might be a wee bit of truth to that, Lizzie," Will said. "But mostly I want to see what Jesse has done with his shed and his corral. He's been making some improvements this last winter. He's told me all about it."

So Will and Jesse walked outside, and Liz looked at Ellen. "Those two are a pair, are they not? They'll always be farmers at heart, even if they talk so much about business."

"They both have good hearts, Liz," Ellen said, "but they prod each other on in ways they prob'ly should na' go. I do na' like this talk of making partners in Warsaw, and hauling goods up and down the river."

"I'll tell you what they are. They're innocents in a wicked world. They think these things up together, see it all in their heads, but they don't see the dangers. How could Will knock on the door of those Samples brothers?"

"He's lucky to be alive—that's all I can say."

Liz thought of Will, always trying to do the right thing, always thinking the best of people, even offering help to a man who had tried to kill him. "But we're blessed to have them," she said. "They're good to us, and good to the children, and they kneel down with us and call on God to look over us. I think maybe we'll hold on to them, in spite of all their faults."

Ellen was smiling and nodding, too. "We'll need such men if we're goin' ta cross this whole land and start all over one more time."

"Can we do it, Ellen?"

"I tell mysel', sometimes, 'No, I ca na' go so far.' But we may not choose for oursel's in the end."

"I know." Liz thought of the ocean and all it had cost Ellen. "We've done things we thought we couldn't. We'll do what we have to, if it comes to that."

"But we can na' give up our hope. Maybe the Lord will protect us. Maybe we'll stay where we be."

It was what Liz hoped, too, but in spite of all Will's talk of business and farms and houses, she had seen that his mission had changed him. She had the feeling that what he wasn't telling her was that trouble, more than anything, was what lay ahead.

CHAPTER 5

It was Halloween, and Mulholland Street was decorated with carved pumpkins: on the sidewalks, in storefront doorways, and propped up on plastic stands or on hay bales. The Lewises and the McCords had taken their kids—with William in a stroller—and walked up and down the three or four blocks of town just as the sun was going down and all the jack-o'-lanterns were beginning to glow.

Nauvoo had filled with visitors from all around the area, and finding a parking place was not easy. Along with the display of jack-o'-lanterns, there were street vendors selling food, local folks wearing costumes, and a small-town carnival atmosphere.

William was getting restless in his stroller, so when Abby saw a parade approaching, she got him out and held him so he could see. He was nine months old now and taking great interest in the world. At home he was pulling himself up to the furniture, and Abby was sure he was going to take off walking before long.

The parade consisted primarily of townspeople, especially kids, dressed up in costumes, but some of the senior missionaries showed up on a horse-drawn wagon. They were playing kazoos and toy flutes. Abby loved that the missionaries were part of all this.

The parade lasted only fifteen or twenty minutes, and then Jeff took William and they all walked down the street again. Malcolm was walking ahead of Abby when she heard him say, "Mayor Ken, it's better than ever this year." Malcolm reached out and shook hands with a young man in a T-shirt and shorts. Abby, wrapped up in a warm coat, couldn't imagine that this man—apparently the mayor—wasn't cold, but he showed no sign of being uncomfortable.

"Hey, it's great, isn't it?" the mayor said. "But don't give me the credit. I only helped put the pumpkins out. People have been working on this all week." He was grinning, and Abby could see he was thrilled with the way the evening had turned out.

"Have you met the Lewises?" Malcolm asked. "Jeff and Abby, this is Mayor Ken Carter."

"I've seen you before," Mayor Carter said. "Didn't you help us carve pumpkins last year?"

"Yeah, I did," Jeff said. "And I remember seeing you. But I didn't know you were the mayor."

"I guess you don't think I dress like one." He laughed.

"You look *perfect*," Jeff said. "I think neckties are greatly overrated."

"Hey, I don't even own one," Carter said. He did seem awfully young to be a mayor, but Jeff liked him instantly. "Was it Jeff and Abby? Did I get that right?"

"Yes." Jeff shook hands with him. "And this is William."

"Oh, all right. Now I remember. He's the one who had the heart surgery last winter."

"That's right," Abby said. "I'm amazed you know that."

"That's all anyone talked about there for a while. But he looks great now. Good as new."

"He is. He's just a normal kid," Jeff said.

"So have you moved here to stay?"

"I think so," Abby said. "Jeff works in Fort Madison. We've been fixing up a house for some people, but we're looking for one we can buy."

"That's great. We need young families. Too many kids grow up here and then move away."

He chatted a few more minutes, and then he walked on down the street. Abby could hear his big laugh as he greeted others. She loved that the mayor was such a regular guy, but what she liked even more was that he cared whether she and Jeff stayed. It was nice to live in a town where people could know one another, where even one family's coming or going made a difference.

Jeff and Malcolm bought everyone hot dogs for dinner, and then they all headed to the McCords' house, where Jeff and Abby had parked.

"Come in for a minute, Abby," Malcolm said when they got there. "Jeff and I have something we want to talk to you and Kayla about."

Abby was pretty sure what Malcolm had in mind. It was what all of them had been talking about the last couple of weeks. Jeff and Malcolm were way too busy with their business, and they weren't sure how they were going to be able to manage everything. It sounded as though Malcolm wanted them to help solve the problem, but she wasn't sure there were any good answers.

They all went inside. Kayla's girls wanted to play with William, so Abby took him to their room, which obviously pleased him. When she came back to the living room, she sat down next to Jeff on the couch.

"So have you guys decided what you want to do—without consulting us?" Kayla asked.

"No. Just the opposite. We have some thoughts—and now it's time for all of us to talk," Malcolm responded.

Kayla sat down on the arm of an old overstuffed chair that Malcolm was sitting in, and she put her arm around his shoulder. Kayla always talked of losing weight, but lately she had actually made some progress. Abby thought she looked great. She wasn't a beautiful woman, but there was a mildness about her—her eyes soft and pretty—and a sense that she accepted herself, didn't need to be the center of attention.

"You know what a mess things have been lately, with me and Jeff gone so many hours every day," Malcolm said. "Well, we had a long talk today, and we figured out one way we might be able to make things work better. But we need to find out what you two think."

Abby told herself to listen, not to say too much. She had sometimes come on too strong in these situations.

Malcolm looked at Jeff at that point, as though he wanted Jeff to do the talking. "Well," Jeff said. He took hold of Abby's hand. "The good news—as you know—is that our business is doing better than we ever expected."

"It's doing *too* good," Kayla said.

Jeff slid forward on the couch, glanced over at Abby, and then looked at Kayla. "Yeah, in a way that's right. We can't keep up with everything while I'm still putting in forty hours a week across the river."

"But if you quit your job," Kayla said, "we don't have enough money coming in yet. I mean, not enough for both families to live on."

"We don't yet. But that's because we haven't finished some of the jobs we started. In the next few weeks we're going to see some good cash flow, and after that, we feel like our income should be steady."

"How soon would you quit?" Kayla asked.

Jeff looked at Abby again—as though he knew that was her question, too. "We haven't decided anything, Kayla. I know I couldn't quit until we build up some savings. But the thing is, if I were working full-time with Malc, our business income would take a hefty jump—just because we could get more jobs done."

Abby had known all along that the goal was for Jeff to quit his job and for the two to develop their business, but she had thought it might take a year or so before the talk actually turned to doing that. It had been easy to talk last summer about making the break, but she wondered now whether Jeff and Malcolm had considered all the implications. "Jeff," she said, "sometimes you still talk about wanting to be a professor. Isn't this about as far away from that life as anything you could think of? Are you sure you would like remodeling for a living if you were doing it full-time?"

"I've really thought a lot about that, Ab. I think I might get tired of working sixteen hours a day, the way we've been doing. But gradually we'll be able to hire men to work for us, and we won't have to do all the work ourselves. If the economy changes, we could go into building new houses, even developing housing projects. It just feels so much more exciting to me than maintaining computers."

It all sounded rather shaky to Abby. She knew that Jeff wasn't putting enough time into the class he was taking in Macomb, and Malcolm had started some classes in Keokuk and then hadn't found time to study and had had to withdraw. But she didn't want to be negative. "All right, here's what I propose," she said. "I'll start looking for a full-time job, one with benefits. That way we would have one steady paycheck, and we'd have insurance. If things got slow for you guys, we would still know that both families could eat and pay bills."

"But what about William?"

"I would take him," Kayla said. "I doubt I could get a decent job, but Abby could make the money and I'd look after the kids."

"We wanted to avoid that," Malcolm said. "We wanted to make this happen ourselves, so neither one of you had to work while the kids are little."

"But Kayla and I could help make it work for a while," Abby said. "Kayla loves William as much as I do—and so do your girls. I wouldn't worry all day, the way I would if our cash flow was a constant problem."

Abby watched the two men, who were both avoiding her eyes. She knew Malcolm was wearing down. He had lost weight that fall, and the guy had never had any flesh on his bones to begin with. But even more, she had noticed the weariness in his eyes lately. It was the same look she had seen in Jeff's eyes for a long time. Abby knew what she had to add. "I don't want to wait very long before we have another baby," she said, "and I don't want to be working when we have two at home. But if I worked for a while, that would at least give you guys time to find out if your business is going to develop the way you think it will."

Abby saw Jeff nod, and that surprised her. Malcolm had seen it too, and he also gave a little nod.

"I think it's the best answer," Kayla said.

"The one thing I don't know," Abby said, "is whether I can find a job that pays enough."

"That's important," Jeff said. "I don't want you working for minimum wage somewhere."

"Well, I'll look, and let's see what happens in the next few months."

"I think we all need to pray about this," Kayla said. "Let's not make any decisions until we all feel sure about it."

"That sounds right," Jeff said, and he took hold of Abby's hand again. "Abby, thanks," he whispered.

The truth was, Abby was frightened. She wasn't sure this was the right answer at all. But she was still glad that she had committed herself to do her part.

• • •

Abby's parents wanted Jeff and Abby—and especially William—to spend Christmas in New Jersey with them. They even wanted to pay for the airline tickets. Jeff held out for a while, then finally said he would go, but he wanted to pay for the flight himself. In the end, however, he surrendered unconditionally and accepted the terms of the offer. His one little victory was to insist that he could only stay for three days. He really did feel that he couldn't miss many days of work, and he especially couldn't leave Malcolm to finish up a project they were working on. Of course, that was clearly all right with the Ramseys, since Abby said she would stay a little longer. But Jeff and Abby both had to be home before New Year's, when Jeff's family planned to visit Nauvoo.

There had been one other part of the bargain. Jeff and Abby agreed with one another that they would say nothing of Jeff's intention to quit his job. The fact was, since making the decision to look for work, Abby had found nothing in the way of a job that offered benefits, so the whole plan was still up in the air. All four were saying that they felt good about the plan, but if Abby couldn't find a decent job, Jeff couldn't quit his.

For now, things were still on hold, and Jeff and Malcolm were still pushing very hard, so it was actually quite nice to have a few hours on an airplane, even with William getting a little restless at the end, and it was even better to have a few days of downtime. Things also started well in New Jersey. Jeff had a feeling that Abby and her mother had had a heart-to-heart discussion about their visit, and Mrs. Ramsey must have been on warning not to get aggressive again. Or maybe it was just that she was so excited about having William with her that she paid little attention to Jeff. Abby's father had always been congenial; he liked to kick ideas around with a young man he obviously considered bright and well-informed. Jeff felt his father-in-law's respect, and that made conversations with him enjoyable.

Abby's sister and her husband were coming over on Christmas Day, but on Christmas Eve, only Jeff and Abby and William were there with Abby's parents. After William went to sleep, the four sat in the living room with a fire—or at least a gas log—in the fireplace, and Jeff and Abby sat comfortably in the elegantly appointed room, at first "catching up" on some of Abby's friends and relatives, and then chatting casually about this and that. But eventually, Abby's father asked, "So how's your job going, Jeff? Abby tells me that you're hoping to rise in the company, in time, maybe get into something more than IT work."

Jeff knew that Mr. Ramsey meant well. He wasn't saying anything Jeff hadn't said, but his tone had made "IT work" sound a little too much like "common labor."

"It's hard to know what might happen," Jeff said. "There's not much room to advance there at the plant in Fort Madison, but the corporation is huge, so other opportunities could certainly open up." Jeff wanted to say that much and nothing more, so he asked, "What about your work, John? Do you still enjoy what you're doing?"

"Mostly. It's the same company for all these years, but different challenges come up every day. I'm never bored." Mr. Ramsey was a handsome man, rather short and compact, with enough gray hair to look mature. What bothered Jeff was that although he liked to talk about current events, or about all sorts of ideas, he seemed guarded about expressing anything personal.

Jeff wanted to say, "Oh, that's nice. Personally, I'm bored every day," but he didn't. He merely nodded.

It was Abby's mom who said, "Jeff, are you checking to see what jobs the corporation has open in different regions of the country? I wonder if you could ever find something here on the East Coast, closer to us."

She had said this very nicely, but Jeff knew her attitude: Get out of the desolate Midwest and find a civilized place to live.

Abby said, "We love Nauvoo, Mom. We're getting to know lots of people around town, and everyone's really friendly. When you walk down the street, people wave and say hello even if they don't have any idea who you are."

"That is nice, I suppose," Mr. Ramsey said. "Teaneck is not a terribly big place, really, but you don't often see that kind of outward friendliness around here."

Jeff was nodding, saying nothing, trying hard to think of some way to change the subject.

"What I hear," Mrs. Ramsey said, "is that people in little towns are friendly on the surface, but they're also quick to talk behind your back. Everyone knows everyone, and that means they know all the gossip they can spread about you."

"We don't find that, Mom. Not so far. But then, there's not much to say about us. What everyone knows is that William is a little miracle baby. People always ask about him. It's like the whole town wants to share him."

"Well, you know, that's exactly what I'm talking about. It's not really their business whether he had heart surgery or not. Is that going to be his label all while he's growing up? Other kids might—"

"No, Mom, it's not like they—"

"It's nice they're concerned, Olivia," Mr. Ramsey said. "They'll forget about the surgery after a time." This had been one of Mr. Ramsey's peacekeeping contributions. He had clearly wanted to stop his wife before she pushed the matter too far.

So that was that, and Abby asked about a cousin, and Jeff took a breath of relief.

The cousin was doing *very well*. He had graduated Princeton and gone into investment banking. He was surviving the economic downturn *beautifully*. He and his wife—who had chosen not to have children for now—had just returned from two weeks in Mallorca, Spain, and Portugal. "He's got more money than he knows what to do with, so he's making the most of it," Mrs. Ramsey said.

"I'd rather have William," Abby told her. "And Nauvoo, Illinois."

A little silence followed, and Jeff stared into the flames. Mr. Ramsey finally said, "Your mom told me how all the LDS people look out for you. I can see where that might be a nice sort of lifestyle."

Jeff appreciated that Mr. Ramsey had learned to say "LDS" instead of "Mormon." Somehow, he looked a little too dressy in his red cable-knit sweater and his expensive shoes, but he had a congenial manner, and he clearly wanted Jeff to feel at ease in their home.

But Mrs. Ramsey was rolling her eyes. "It may be *comfortable* to live in a town like that, but you both need to think about the future." She looked at Jeff, hesitated long enough to lighten her tone, and then added, "What *is* your plan, Jeff? Where do you see yourself in, say, ten years?"

"Well, as Abby said, we're happy in Illinois." But Jeff couldn't resist defending himself a little from the implied accusation. "One thing I've thought about is opening a business of my own. I have a friend in Nauvoo who has some of the same interests I do, and one of these days, we just might try our wings a little."

Abby suddenly sat up straight. "Mom," she said, "I think it's time to cut that pie. What do you say?"

"Oh, yes. Pie sounds good," Jeff said.

"What kind of business?" Mrs. Ramsey pressed.

Jeff knew he had to be vague. "Oh, I don't know. We've had some different ideas."

"Like what?"

"Building, maybe. I think you met Malcolm and Kayla while you were with us last winter. Malcolm's really a craftsman, and I've always liked to remodel and that sort of thing—the way I'm doing in the house we're living in."

"So now that you've graduated Stanford, you want to be a carpenter?"

"No. Not really. Just—"

"A *contractor?* You have stars in your eyes if that's what you're thinking. We have friends who got rich during the boom, and they're flat broke now. That's how building is—boom and bust, over and over."

"I know. But when building drops off, remodeling and repair work pick up."

"Jeff, I can't believe I'm hearing this. That's *handyman* work. Is that what you want to do?"

Now Jeff really was caught. He tried twice to answer, stumbled over his words, and was about to try again when Abby said, "Mom, we decided not to tell you because we knew what you would say, but Jeff and Malcolm have started a little business on the side. Malcolm works full-time, and Jeff helps out. But they're doing *very* well."

"That's good," Mr. Ramsey hastened to say. "I admire how hard you're willing to work, Jeff. If you can make a little extra on the side and build up some savings, that will help you get into a house and—"

"Oh, please, John," Mrs. Ramsey said. "Where's the future in that? He needs to concentrate on his job, make an impression, and move up the ladder in the corporation. He can't burn the candle at both ends for the bit of extra money he can make fixing up kitchens, or whatever."

"Mom, don't do this again," Abby said.

"I'm not *doing* anything. I'm just saying, he needs to put his efforts where they'll get him somewhere. That McCord boy talks like he flunked fourth grade. What kind of *business* is he going to build?"

Jeff and Abby both reacted at the same moment. Jeff tried to say how smart Malcolm was, but Abby drowned him out. She stood, pointed at her mother, and said, "Jeff is thinking about quitting his job, Mom. We weren't going to tell you, but we might as well, so you can throw a fit now instead of later. He and Malcolm are building a good business, and we think it will do really well in time. I'm going to go back to work if I have to, and that will help until the business develops the way we think it will. But I know he'll make a go of anything he does. And don't say one more word against Malcolm and Kayla. They're the best friends I've ever had in my life. I . . ."

But she had started to cry.

Mrs. Ramsey was looking as though she had been struck with a blunt instrument, but she didn't say a word.

Mr. Ramsey finally said, "Well, now, let's not get into a big *thing* about this. Abby, I'm sure you're right. Jeff will make a go of anything he does."

· · ·

Two hours later, Jeff and Abby were in the guest bedroom when a little tap came at the door. Abby knew, of course, that it had to be her mother knocking, but she didn't want to talk to the woman. Abby had bolted from the room after her little tantrum, and as much as anything, she was embarrassed that she hadn't conducted a more adult conversation with her parents.

But Jeff opened the door and let Abby's mom in, and then he stepped out.

"I'm sorry," Mrs. Ramsey said to Abby. "I don't want to ruin Christmas."

"I'm sorry too. I know you have a point about Jeff quitting his job. It has worried me, too, and maybe that's why I'm so defensive."

"You know what your dad just told me?"

"No. What?"

"He said that thirty years ago, he wanted to open his own advertising agency—and I do remember that—but I made such a fuss, he didn't dare do it. He said he's liked his career all right, but he's always wondered whether he couldn't have had more fun, and been more creative, if he had been on his own."

"That really surprises me."

"I know. Me too. But I've never wanted to take any chances. I've always done things the safe way, and maybe that's been a mistake. John said that if he had fallen on his face, he could have gone back to work for a big company. But he still wishes he had found out whether he might have developed a successful business of his own."

"And he's never said that to you before?"

"Never. But he got a little cross with me tonight. He told me that Jeff needs to try this, if that's what he wants to do. The two of you will do fine in the long run."

"Do you believe that?"

"It scares me to death."

"I know. I'm the same way."

"But it's sort of like having babies. Apparently, it's your decision, not mine. I'm ever so much wiser than you'll ever be, but I guess I don't get to run your life for you." She finally smiled.

Abby got up and wrapped her arms around her mother. "Thanks, Mom," she said. "We'll be okay. To tell you the truth, I don't think, in ten years, Jeff will be fixing up kitchens. But we'll be doing okay. We just have to figure out what's going to work for us."

CHAPTER 6

Will was nervous. He and Jesse were waiting at Oliver Hyatt's farm. They had expected Oliver and his hired men to arrive by now from Warsaw, where they had gone to offload a riverboat. The boat might have been late this morning, but it had docked at around the same time each Thursday for the last six weeks. Still, it wasn't the delay that worried Will so much as it was the hostility toward Mormons that had reached a new fervor lately. He hoped that Oliver hadn't put himself in danger.

Will and Jesse's hauling business had done very well since the Mississippi had hit its shallow point, but Will could see trouble coming. The old citizens of Hancock County had been organizing, and Thomas Sharp had been stirring the pot with renewed hatred. The fact was, plans to migrate west were being discussed more openly all the time now, and Church newspapers included praise for "the Western measure" in every issue.

In June, Heber Kimball had spoken at the grove and said that he was only too happy to leave Nauvoo, it being such a sickly place. The Saints would keep their promise to the Lord and finish the temple, and Brigham would keep his promise to Church members and allow them to receive the glorious endowment they were waiting for, but then, probably in the spring of 1846, the Saints—or at least some of them—would begin their exodus.

The summer of 1845 had been good for Will and his partners, but now, in September, the anti-Mormons (as they openly called themselves) had realized that killing the Prophet had not accomplished their hope of destroying the Church. They would no longer tolerate the presence of the detested Mormons. "Wolf hunts" were on the rise again. Will was trying to walk a delicate line. He assumed that he would probably leave with the Saints, but he and his friends were bringing in more income than they had ever seen in their lives, and he wanted to earn all he could before he took his family into the wilderness. The river had been low, work almost constant, and at the same time, he and his partners, with the help of hired hands, were cultivating good crops for the fall. Will also continued to work at the quarry, hauling stones to the temple, but he did that only out of a desire to fulfill his promise to Joseph—and now to Brigham—to see the temple completed. He would have been better off financially to spend all his time with his farm and with his new business.

What Will still kept wondering was whether Brother Brigham would want some members to stay in Nauvoo, look after the temple, and keep a presence in the area. Maybe the old citizens wouldn't worry about a much smaller, less Mormon-dominated community. Liz worried about staying behind if most members departed, but she was even more frightened of moving away from civilization—and Will didn't want to put her through that. So he held out some hope that they could stay.

Right now, however, Will had more immediate things on his mind. Oliver still hadn't shown up. Jesse and two hired men from Nauvoo—Hanford Mills and Stanley Baldwin—were sitting under a nearby tree, their hats over their faces, apparently asleep. Will kept watching the road and pacing back and forth. After a time, Jesse got up and walked over. He leaned against the sod fence and said, "Will, I would na' fret. These boats ne'er come in 'xactly on time."

"I know."

"In low water, they catch on sandbars—things o' that kind."

"I know that, Jesse. But the way the talk is now, I do na' know what might be happenin' to Oliver." Will rarely spoke in his Herefordshire dialect these days, but when he was alone with Jesse, he sometimes fell back to it quite naturally.

"It's us they hate. I do na' see 'em doin' him no harm."

But Will's attention had been drawn to dust rising from the road off in the distance. "This might be Oliver," he said.

Both men waited and watched, and finally Jesse said what Will was thinking, "They be movin' too fast up that hill. It's our wagons, I do believe, but they can na' be loaded down."

The two waited, and as Oliver approached, driving the first of four wagons, Will saw the concern in his face.

Will stepped outside the gate and waited next to the road. "What's gone wrong?" he called out to Oliver.

Oliver didn't answer until he was closer. "There's trouble," he finally said. "We were almost finished offloading the boat when a gang of men with guns showed up at the wharf and surrounded us. They told us to empty our wagons and get out, or they would shoot us on the spot."

"Who were they?"

"Men from town. Some I know, some I don't. But they know I'm working for you—or at least for a Mormon—and they say they won't let that pass no more."

"Can't you talk to—"

"No, Will. There's no one I can talk to now. The war is starting.

One man told me he knew where my farm was, and I better not keep your oxen here from now on or they'd burn me out with the Mormons."

"Have they burned some places already?"

"They claimed they burned some yesterday. They bragged about it."

"Where?"

The hired man who had been driving the second wagon, Silas Jones, was standing alongside Oliver now. "They said it was down by Green Plains," he said. "They was laughin' and sayin' how they chased people outside—women and childern and ever'body—an' then they burned up their houses."

"They weren't shootin' people, were they?" Jesse asked.

"They didn't say. They just said about burnin' the houses."

"Did they say the *Morley* settlement?"

"I don't recall that name. One of 'em said somethin' about Lima."

The Morley settlement was strung out along a road, and at one end was the town of Lima. So that was where the troubles were. Lima was south of Green Plains and not all that far from Warsaw; the Mormons there were in a dangerous spot. Will just hoped no one had been hurt.

"These men were riled up more than I've seen before," Oliver said. "They kept telling the folks who gathered around us that they were getting ready to march straight into Nauvoo."

"Let 'em come," Jesse said. "They won't be quite so brave when they try that."

"They'll get more men—from all around these parts. I don't see any way out of this now. I'm sorry to say it, Jesse, but your people will have to leave Illinois. These men will never stop 'til you're all gone."

Will had to admit that that might be the case, but for the moment he was more concerned about getting his teams and wagons away from Oliver's farm. "We'll get these wagons headed north," he said. "Help me yoke up my other teams. We'll double hitch them to a couple of these wagons and get going. If someone comes around to see what you've done, just tell them you're having nothing to do with me from now on."

"I'm sorry, Will, but that's going to have to be true."

"I know. And I won't try to come back to Warsaw. Maybe something can be worked out—a truce of some sort—but for now, we'll stay away."

"Will, don't even talk about making peace. If you try to talk to them, they'll kill you. I've never seen men so crazy. They ain't thinking anymore—and they surely ain't going to do any talking. They want blood."

"I know. I've seen them like that. I was in Carthage."

So all the men helped round up the oxen, yoked them, and hitched them to Will's wagon and to Jesse's. Will led the way, and Jesse and the other two drivers followed. They headed up the road that Will had graded two years earlier. He just hoped they could get out of sight and on toward Nauvoo before someone decided to come after them.

Will could see what was coming now. He would have to give up his business, his house, his farm. He would have to take his family west. Will wondered what sort of life they could have there. He doubted the land was as fertile or the rains as plentiful. More than that, he wondered what all this would do to Liz and the boys. People had died during the ocean crossing—especially children—but how many more would die on the vast plains, crossing most of the continent? Will didn't like to think about any of that.

Will kept watching for riders from Warsaw, or for people on the road, but no one seemed to be pursuing them. He spoke to his oxen as they crossed the bed of a dry stream, and he touched the nearest oxen with his stick just to push them a little as the teams climbed up the other side of the gulley. As the road leveled out again, a movement in a little copse of trees caught his eye, and he turned to look in that direction. At the moment his head turned, he heard a shot ring out, and a musket ball buzzed past his ear. Instantly, he was off the wagon and down on the ground. He had hidden a pistol in a side box on the wagon, under some tools. He reached up and flipped open the box, then pushed the tools to one side and grabbed the gun. By then he heard another musket shot, followed by a thump. He saw Sam, his lead ox, hunch up, let out a sound like a moan, and then collapse to the ground.

Will tried to think whether enough time had passed for a man to reload a musket before the second shot. It didn't seem so. There must be more than one shooter in the trees.

Sam was lowing mournfully. He had pulled Sassy, still yoked to him, off balance, his neck twisted. And then another crack and another thump. Will saw blood spatter from Sassy's neck, and he watched the big white ox drop down next to Sam.

Will had the pistol, a revolver, and he held it ready, but he couldn't see anyone. He couldn't think what to do.

And then Jesse was next to him, crouching. "Where are they?" he asked in a frantic whisper.

"In those trees, but I can na' see 'em."

"Fire at 'em. If they know we have weapons, they will na' be so quick to coom after us."

So Will leaned around the front of the wagon and fired his pistol past the rumps of his two remaining oxen. An instant later, he saw movement, and he realized that Hanford was running toward the trees. Hanford fired his pistol, then dropped onto the ground. "Clear out or we'll have your hides," he shouted.

Will took a quick step and then dove down next to his wounded oxen. He came up an instant later and fired into the trees. "Let's take 'em," he shouted to Hanford, but he was only going along with the ruse. He was not going to make a charge. He heard movement in the trees and the sound of horses shying and stomping. Then he heard the pounding of hooves as the horses began to gallop.

Hanford jumped up and ran into the trees. He fired his pistol one more time. In a moment, he yelled back to Will, "There was three. They're riding away, fast as they can go."

"Cowards," Jesse said. "They be brave so long as they can hide an' shoot innocent animals, but they ride off soon as they face some'un ready to fight."

"They weren't just out to shoot the oxen," Will said. "The first ball passed right by my head. I happened to turn just then or I'd be a dead man." Will got up and looked down at his oxen, both breathing hard, both dying.

Hanford had returned by then, and Stanley had walked forward from his wagon. All four men stood over the animals.

"These two ha' worked hard for us," Jesse said. "It's not right for 'em to suffer this way."

"I'll shoot 'em," Will said. He raised his pistol, held it close to Sassy's head. Seconds passed, and he kept telling his finger to tighten on the trigger, but he couldn't get himself to do it. "I can't be the one to kill 'em," he finally said. He turned away and said, "Hanford, shoot 'em for me."

Will looked out across the prairie as one shot rang out and then another.

There was a long silence after the echoes of the pistol reports died away, and then Jesse asked, "Shall we carry off these animals?"

Will had been considering. "No," he said. "We can't get 'em up on the wagons. We'd have to butcher 'em first. And there's too much danger in that. Let's unchain the dead ones and take the yoke, and then let's get back to Nauvoo as fast as we can. Those three can't be the only men looking for Mormons to attack." He turned back toward Hanford. "Was one of those men a big, broad man with a black beard?

"I don't know. They was ridin' away. I couldn't see if they had beards."

"What about a big chestnut horse?"

"It might have been. Two of the horses was dark, if I'm thinkin' right, but I can't say for shor."

Will nodded. It was like George to set up an ambush, and maybe he knew that Will had been picking up loads at Oliver's farm, but there were also plenty of men who had seen Oliver leave Warsaw. They would have known where to cross paths with Will and his men.

The men unhooked the chains and released the yoke from the oxen's necks, and then Will forced the other two oxen to step back a couple of paces. All the oxen, even the ones yoked to the other wagons, had begun to bellow now. They had surely smelled the blood, and they seemed to know that two of their working mates were gone. Will got back in the wagon and drove it on around the dead animals. Sam and Sassy were two of his strongest oxen, ones he had had from the beginning, and they were dear old friends. Now that the initial danger had passed, Will felt tired, defeated.

• • •

Liz had heard the news from Yelrome—the name people used sometimes for the Morley settlement. On the previous day, September 10, a mob had ridden onto all the farms. They had allowed the Mormons to carry what furniture they could outside, and then they had told them that they could come back to harvest and haul off their grain, but they could never rebuild. Only a few of the Saints were physically harmed, but families—including little children—had had to stand and watch as men set fire to their houses. One man told Liz, "They went about their business, from what I heard, like they were ridding themselves of gophers or snakes."

"Where are those families going to stay?" Liz asked.

"Brother Brigham's told them to come into Nauvoo and live with other families. A wagon train is already on its way to bring everyone in."

"Is this the end?" Liz had asked.

"I suspect it is. We need to go somewhere where we're not hated. And I guess that's only in some place that no one wants."

"Will they start burning our houses here in Nauvoo?"

"I don't know. I used to say they wouldn't. But everything's getting out of hand now."

Liz nodded. She knew what it was all coming to. But the image that came to her mind was a vast prairie like the one east of Nauvoo, and worse, mountains and deserts beyond that. How could they move into such lands and do anything but struggle and starve?

Liz was tidying up in the house while the boys were playing outside the door, which she had left open. It was a nice day, still quite warm, but the air was not so sultry as it had been all summer. She didn't want the boys wandering far off, but she did like to let them run and be boys sometimes. Jacob was almost three now, and he was good to mind his mother, and Daniel, who was a year and a half, always stayed close to Jacob.

When Liz realized the boys were not as close to the door as they had been, she walked out and looked to see where they were. As she did, she spotted them running hard toward the house. They had been out beyond the cowshed, at the edge of the woods. Liz waited, about to warn them not to go wandering off so far, when she saw the fear in Jacob's face. "Mummy, Mummy," he was saying. "A man. A man."

Liz dropped to one knee and grabbed Jacob and then Daniel. She held one boy in each arm and said, "What man? What happened?"

"A man scare us."

"What did he do?"

Jacob pulled back and looked toward the woods as though he expected to see the man still there. "He said, tell you . . ." He took a breath, his eyes still full of terror.

"Tell me what?"

"Burn our house."

"What?"

"He said, go home, tell your mama, we burn your house."

"What man was it? Have you seen him before?"

Jacob shook his head.

"Did he have a black beard, all spread out wide, like this?" She gestured with her hands to show the shape of the beard.

Jacob nodded.

"Are you sure? Was he a big man? *Very* big?"

Jacob nodded again.

"All right. It's all right. He won't hurt us."

"Will he burn our house?"

"No. He just wanted to scare you. But Daddy will take care of us. He won't let the man come here again."

Liz brought the boys back into the house, and then she waited. There was no window on the north side of the house—the side that faced the cowshed and the woods beyond—so she watched from the window in the big room, and then she walked to one of the new rooms that Will had built, the one in which she kept her sewing. She looked out toward the west. She saw no one, heard nothing, but her mouth was dry, and she could hear her heart beating in her ears. She went to the drawer where Will kept the pistol, but it wasn't there. She realized he must have taken it with him. She had never known whether she could even use it, if it came to that, but her fear mounted, knowing she had no way to defend her little boys. She told herself not to cry, not to let the boys see how frightened she was.

More than an hour went by, slowly, and still she heard nothing, saw no one. The boys played inside, but Jacob kept watching her, clearly still worried. So she sat down and tried to seem composed, but she couldn't concentrate enough to stitch or to do any of her housework. She merely waited for time to pass.

Liz was relieved when Will arrived home sooner than she had expected. But for some reason he had brought all four wagons, empty, and he and Jesse and the other men began unyoking the oxen and leading them to their small corral. They had never done that before.

Liz walked outside. "What's happening?" she asked.

She saw Will's hesitant glance as he avoided her eyes the way he always did when there was something he didn't want to say. Finally he told her, "I guess we're out of business. Oliver drove the wagons into town, the same as usual, but men made him unload and get out."

"What do you mean, 'made him'?"

"They didn't hurt anyone," Will said.

But Jesse told the rest. "They had guns, and they tol' Oliver ne'er to unload any boats again, and for 'im ne'er to keep our oxen from now on. Oliver was scared, an' I do na' blame 'im."

"Aye," Will said. He took a direct look at Jesse. "Let's not make it sound worse than it was. We're all fine, and if they had wanted to do something to Oliver, they had their chance. He should be fine."

Jesse said, "But on the way back—"

"Liz, some men shot two of our oxen," Will said. "But it's all right. You won't have to worry about us going down to Warsaw any longer."

"They shot at Will firs', and missed, and then they shot the oxen. We scared 'em off, but Will was lucky they did na' kill him right on the spot."

Liz watched Will duck his head. She felt sick.

But Will stepped to her, took hold of her shoulders. "Don't fret," he said. "I told you, we won't be going back that way."

"But someone was here."

"What?"

"George Samples was in our woods. He talked to the boys, told them to tell me he was going to burn down our house."

She saw Will's jaw tighten. "Where was he? How did he talk to the boys?"

"I let them play outside, and they wandered up by the woods, behind the cowshed."

"When?"

"More than an hour ago."

"How do you know it was George?"

"I asked Jacob if he was a big man with a big black beard, and he said it was."

Will hurried out to the wagon he had parked by the house. Liz looked out the door in time to see him grab his pistol from the seat. "You men, come with me," he said, and the four of them walked toward the woods, Will holding his pistol in front of him.

Liz didn't think George would still be there, but she didn't like Will going off with a pistol in his hand. If George—and maybe some others—were waiting around for dark, hiding in the trees, she didn't know what might happen.

She walked back to the front door of her house, checked on the boys, and then stepped back outside again. Will and the others were gone longer than she liked, but she didn't hear anything. What she saw when they returned, though, was that Will was changed: shaken and pale.

He stood in front of Liz for a time before he said, "He's killed our sow. Cut its throat."

"Oh, Will."

"He could have come after you—you and the boys."

"No. He would na' do that," Jesse said. "This is what he does. He sneaks 'round and works in the shadows. He would na' dare kill your family. He knows you would find 'im, no matter what, and he's scared of you, more'n anyone."

There was a long silence, with only the sound of a little afternoon breeze rustling the trees. "We have to leave, Will," Liz said. "We can't do this anymore."

"And if we leave, George wins."

"It doesn't matter. It's not just George Samples. It's all of them."

Will didn't respond to that, but she saw the truth in his face. And then he said it. "We will leave, Liz. I can't keep you here where you'll always have to be scared."

CHAPTER 7

It was Sunday, October 6, 1845. Will and Liz were standing in the first-floor meeting room in the Nauvoo temple. The roof was now on the building, and the windows were installed. Although not all the rooms inside were completed, on the day before, Brigham Young had offered a prayer to dedicate this first-floor section of the building. Like many of the Saints, Will and Liz had not arrived early enough to make it inside for that meeting, but today they had gotten in for the afternoon session, even though they hadn't managed to find a place to sit.

Will felt the joy of seeing the temple so close to completion, but he hated to think that after all his efforts to help with the construction, the beautiful place would soon be abandoned. Everything had changed now. Brigham Young and the Twelve had made an official promise to the citizens of Hancock County that *all* the Saints would leave Nauvoo, beginning as soon as grass was growing on the prairie in the spring of 1846.

The last month had been violent, with continued attacks and house burnings. In such a passionate, hateful atmosphere, no one was listening to reason. Thomas Sharp was maintaining that the Mormons were burning their own houses and blaming it on mobs in order to gain sympathy. However outrageous the claim, it was apparently widely believed. A committee of Quincy men had attempted to bring order. They decried the burnings by Levi Williams and his "regulators," but as they negotiated peace with all involved, these very men accused the Mormons of all the crimes that Thomas Sharp so often asserted: theft, counterfeiting, militarism, and "spiritual wifery."

Nauvoo, at the same time, was left with little defense. Men who had served in the Nauvoo Legion before it was dissolved could perhaps organize and fight off the mobs, but they lacked sufficient weapons, and even more, they were weary of being hated and had no desire to enter into a war. Hosea Stout still led a police force of sorts, but the only defense against intruders consisted of the young men of the community, who had been organized into "whistling and whittling" brigades. When they spotted a stranger, or anyone who seemed suspicious, they surrounded the man, saying nothing, only whittling with their large knives, a tacit threat. But fending off a major attack on the city would demand more than boys with knives.

All the rancor had raised tensions high, but predictably, when Jacob Backenstos, who had been elected sheriff that summer, tried to gather a posse to defend the Mormon settlements, he was accused of waging war. Fearful for his life after being chased by a mob, he deputized a Mormon, Orrin Porter Rockwell, to assist him. Frank Worrell, who had been in charge of the guard at the Carthage jail—and *hadn't* protected Joseph and Hyrum—rode toward Backenstos and raised his gun. Brother Rockwell responded by shooting him through the chest and killing him. In spite of all the depredations by the old citizens, this shooting was characterized in the local press as the Mormons on a rampage, killing the old citizens of Hancock County.

There was really no choice. Things would only get worse if the Saints tried to stay. Brigham Young had signed an agreement to vacate Nauvoo. This agreement—along with state troops sent by Governor Ford to enforce the peace—had finally brought relative calm. Those who hated Mormons were suspicious of Brigham's promise to leave in the spring, but they backed off from their open attacks.

Parley Pratt was the first speaker in the afternoon session of general conference. He raised a question Will had thought about a great deal lately. Why would the Lord ask so much labor and expense of the Saints in building the temple—and then allow them to be driven out? But Brother Pratt said this was nothing new; the people of God had always been required to make sacrifices. "Our houses," he said, "our farms, this temple, and all we leave will be a monument to those who may visit the place of our industry, diligence, and virtue."

Will liked that. He liked to think that he and Liz had helped build something that stood for who the Saints were. He looked around the meeting room, which was crowded well beyond its expected capacity. He saw little Brother and Sister Johns standing near the wall, stretching to see over—or between—others who were also standing. Will thought of all that the Johns family had been through since arriving, and how hard they had worked to establish themselves. They had made the best of their conditions, had survived almost constant illness, and had kept the faith. And now, here they were, nodding, looking resolute, ready to join "Israel" on its march into the wilderness.

Brother Pratt stood behind the white pulpit, his big shoulders squared, like a boxer ready to fight. His voice was strong, too, but his tone was gentle. In the West, he said, the air and water, soil and timber were free to all, and "we can become vastly more wealthy, have better possessions and improvements, and build a larger and better temple in five years from this time than we now possess."

Will saw many heads nodding, felt the power in the room. Since the Prophet Joseph had been killed, there had been a good deal of bickering, and many had felt doubts about the future, but today Will felt Brother Pratt's testimony, felt the unity of the Saints who were willing to follow the Twelve. They would do what they had to do, and they would do it with hope and confidence.

Before the meeting ended, Brigham Young arose and asked the members to enter into a covenant to "take all the Saints with us to the extent of our ability" and to leave no one behind. He promised them that if they would serve one another in that way, the Lord would "shower down means upon this people, to accomplish it to the very letter."

The members of the congregation, in one accord, raised their hands. And Will felt something changing inside him. This was the next great challenge, to move as a body, to support one another, and he was fired with desire to be one of those who used his own strength to lift up those who were weak or ill or disheartened.

After the fourth and last day of conference, Brigham Young and the Twelve issued a circular to all the Saints. In it were instructions on building wagons, the width of the wheelbase to use, the sale of property in Nauvoo, the purchase of horses and oxen, and all such practical matters. Will liked that Brother Brigham understood such things and seemed very much in charge. He was not only their spiritual leader but one who could solve problems and make practical decisions.

Will was also moved by the commitment to finish the inside of the temple. "Wake up, wake up dear brethren . . ." the circular cried. " . . . we exhort you . . . to prove your faith by your works, preparatory to a rich endowment in the Temple of the Lord, and the obtaining of the promises and deliverances, and glories for yourselves and your children and your dead."

Will and Liz read the circular together, and then Will raised Liz's hand to his lips and kissed it. They looked at one another and nodded. They would escape these people who hated them, and, in the end, they would build something better. But before they left Nauvoo, they would receive the promised temple endowment.

Still, the anti-Mormon forces felt compelled to keep the pressure on the Saints. In November, Edmund Durfee, a Mormon who had lived in the Morley settlement, returned to his farm to harvest his corn—as his attackers had promised him he could do. But he was ambushed and killed.

When Will told Liz the news about Brother Durfee, she was clearly shocked. "Why would they do that?" she asked. "We told them we'd leave. Can't they see how hard we're working to get ready?"

"They think they have to keep our feet to the fire," Will said. "They're afraid we'll go back on our promise."

"I never imagined there could be so much hatred in this world."

Will took Liz in his arms. "I know. But we can't give in to it ourselves. I feel such deep hatred myself sometimes, it scares me, and I hear the Saints wishing destruction on our enemies. I keep thinking, if we give way to the same kind of anger that we're receiving, we're no better than they are."

"But they're the ones who killed our prophet. We didn't start the hatred."

"That's not how they see it."

Liz pulled away. "I don't care how they *see* it, Will. We could have lived here in peace, if they would have let us."

"I know. I think that's right. But we're not without blame."

"But—"

"That's not the important thing anyway, Liz. Christ taught us to love our enemies. Do we believe that or don't we?"

Liz stood looking at Will for a long time. Finally she said, "It's a hard thing to do. I don't know if I'm capable of it."

"I feel the same way. But we have to try."

And that night Will gave some further thought to something he had been considering. He talked his idea over with Liz. She was shocked at first, didn't even want to talk to him about it, but after they were in bed that night, she said, "Are you still awake?"

"Yes."

"I think you're right," she said. "You should take it to them."

"All right, then, I will."

"Are you sure you feel good about it?"

"I do."

When Will had found his sow with its throat slit, he had slaughtered it, split the carcass in half, and then smoked the meat in his smokehouse. Now he got up early, loaded one of those sides of the pork on his wagon, and drove south to the farm where the Samples brothers lived. He stopped far enough away that no one inside the house would hear his wagon, and he hoisted the pork onto his shoulder, walked to the front step, and quietly set the meat down by the front door. And then he returned to Nauvoo. He didn't know whether George would know where the meat had come from—or whether he would take offense—but he told himself, the brothers would eat better that winter. It was something he could do for them.

• • •

Liz was glad for a good harvest, and she was glad that Will was getting wagons ready for their departure. At the same time, there was much to worry about. Spring would not be an easy time to set out for the West, with their stores at the low point of the year. Still, she was not sorry for the loss of some of her pork. She felt better about it than almost anything she had ever done, even though she was worried about their own supplies.

Brigham Young was instructing the Saints often these days, and the Twelve had published a list of needs for a good "fit-out" for the difficult trek. Each family should have a good wagon, two or three yoke of oxen, two cows, two beef cattle, three sheep, a thousand pounds of flour, twenty pounds of sugar, two pounds of tea, five pounds of coffee, one rifle, ammunition, and a tent. The estimated cost for everything was $250. Liz knew that Will was concerned not just about providing all that for his own family, but about making sure that Jesse's and Dan's and Jake's families were also taken care of.

"We're more fortunate than most," Will had told Liz. "We have good wagons for all of us, but we do need to buy more oxen."

Liz had looked up from her sewing and said, "But Will, we have five good teams. No one else has that many."

"Aye. But we ought to have eight. That's what Parley Pratt tells us we need—two teams for each wagon."

Liz had been counting the oxen and thinking only of their own family and the Matthews family, but to Will, his partnership extended to Daniel and Jake. "We don't have to provide for everyone, do we?" Liz asked.

"Maybe not. Jake is pretty well off. He sold his farm in Alabama. He still has some savings from that. I think he can manage for himself and maybe help Dan a little. I just don't know whether he thinks that way. He's not been here as long, and I notice that he still hasn't grasped, entirely, what it means to be part of Zion."

"But, Will, how many people are going to be able to buy two teams of oxen and beef cattle and sheep and all the rest? I know very few who can acquire all that."

"Brigham talks about a pioneer group, well fitted out, making the long trek and planting along the way for those who will come after. I'm sure he knows very well that most people won't be able to provide so much for themselves, but I'd like to be with that first company, and I don't want to leave our friends behind."

"Will, we don't have $250. Nothing like it. How can we—"

"We might have, if we can sell this lot in town along with our farm. Brigham keeps telling us to get what we can for our property, and the Church will try to sell everything it can find buyers for—the Masonic Hall, the Seventies Hall, the armory, everything."

"The temple?"

"I don't know about that. We're finishing it so we can receive our endowments, but some say that it will bring a better price if it's finished inside."

"But we can't do that. We've put *everything* into that building. How can we let someone desecrate it?"

"Leaving it standing empty is a kind of desecration. It would be better if people of faith, of one kind or another, owned it and looked after it."

That was something else that Liz had a difficult time thinking about, but Will was right: she did hate the idea of all their work and money going into a building that would stand empty and finally fall apart from lack of care. "Who would buy this house, Will? Or our farm? Won't people just wait until we leave and grab what we've left behind?"

"Maybe. I don't know. But there are people who'll want a proper deed. I'm sure they'll be looking for the best price they can get, but at least some of the land will sell, and we have the winter and early spring to find buyers. Some people will want to do the right thing."

"And where do you see evidence for that?" she asked.

"I just believe most people know what's right and what's wrong. And they don't like themselves when they do what's wrong."

Liz was smiling at him.

"You think I'm too trusting, don't you?"

"No, I don't," she said. "I think you're so good that you assume everyone else must be like you. And I'm glad that's the way you are."

But Will didn't believe any of that. He fought his own inner fights every day. He resented the loss of his property; he was enraged when he read what Tom Sharp continued to write; and his feelings toward the men who had killed Joseph and Hyrum could probably only be described as hate. He wanted to follow Christ, but he fell short in every way. What he knew, though, was that he believed what Christ had taught, and he didn't ever want to give up on walking in His footsteps, however far behind.

• • •

Nauvoo had turned into a workshop. Every public building had become a wagon factory, and blacksmiths and wheelwrights were working almost around the clock. At the same time, work on the interior of the temple was going forward as never before. There were no more stones to haul from the quarry, but there was finish work and painting, and there was rubble to be cleared and wooden cranes to remove. Will and Jesse worked on all that, and they sometimes went inside, away from the cold, and helped where they could. The men who had installed the circular stairways and were now finishing the woodwork were fine craftsmen. Will and Jesse didn't have the training for that kind of work. Will knew that the grip of his right hand was awkward and he might mar the finer work, so instead he carried lumber and was a little vain about showing that he could heft more boards at once than any man there.

In early December the endowment sessions began. All day, every day, men and women who were worthy were invited to the temple, and those who had been endowed and trained to officiate, both men and women, carried out the ceremony in the attic of the temple. These rooms had not been finished, but Will had seen workers install canvas partitions, and one day he had seen men carrying plants into the building. "It's to make a place like the Garden of Eden," the worker had told Will. But Will didn't know what happened in the endowment ceremony, and he had no idea why a garden would be part of it. What he knew was that he and Liz were eager to receive their blessings. One seventies quorum after another was being called in, but Will's was one of the last to be formed, so his turn hadn't come yet.

Will had other matters to worry about. He had placed an advertisement in local newspapers offering his town lot and farm for prices that were more than fair, but he had not received a single response. He was hearing the same from others. Some had managed to get a few dollars for their property, but mostly, people in the county were doing what Liz had suggested they might do: merely wait for the Saints to leave. Will still thought some might want to possess a clear title, and maybe, as spring came on, interest would mount.

Will had been fortunate enough to save a little money, and he had a few possessions he was able to use for bargaining. He wanted to take some of his tools with him, but he doubted he could weigh down his wagon that much, and certainly he couldn't take his iron-clad plow. He found a man in La Harpe who was willing to trade teams of oxen for the plow, his grader, and some extra rigging. Will had known that he should have gotten three or four teams, young ones, for the value of this equipment, but he had acquired only two teams, neither of them as hale and strong as he would have liked. Still, he had seven teams now, and Jake said he could purchase his own. That meant everyone had a wagon and at least two teams, with an extra team should one wear out.

Will and Liz talked to people every day who were thrilled with their experience in receiving their endowments in the temple. They were clearly not at liberty to tell all they had learned in the temple, but that made the experience all the more individual and holy. Will and Liz talked almost every day about having their chance to go.

Anti-Mormons apparently had too much time to think during the winter. Many of them obviously wanted to press Church leaders to keep their promise to leave. Word of lawsuits and attempts to arrest the Twelve for the destruction of the *Nauvoo Expositor* press circulated almost every day. As the month of January ended, rumors abounded that federal troops had gathered in St. Louis and were prepared to stop the Mormons from going west. Government officials were supposedly afraid that the Saints would ally themselves with the Mexicans or the British and work against the acquisition of western lands for the United States. Will learned that it was Governor Ford himself who had warned Brigham and advised that his people leave before they were stopped.

The plan had been for a party of young, strong men to start first and blaze the trail, but all the threats of arrests made the departure of Church leaders the first priority. Word spread that an advance party of leaders and those who were prepared to leave would begin right away, and others would follow as soon as they could. On February 4, a few wagons crossed the river on flatboats. The river had remained unfrozen all winter but was flowing with large chunks of ice.

Will felt a desire to leave with all those who were crossing, but he also knew he wasn't truly prepared. What worried him most, however, was that he and Liz hadn't received their endowments. President Young didn't leave with the first party, and he and other temple workers were staying in the temple almost around the clock, but hundreds had still been unable to have their opportunity. Will and Liz finally left their boys with Nelly Baugh early one afternoon and walked to the temple. They were able to get inside, out of the cold, and wait in the crowded meeting room on the first floor with hundreds of others. Some had been waiting since early that morning.

Nothing taxed Will's patience more than sitting and waiting, but he told Liz he thought they had better stay; this would probably be their last chance before the leaders all crossed the river. The day dragged on, however, and finally a man stepped into the meeting room and said, "Brother Brigham just walked out the door. He told some of us that he had to get packed up and ready to leave Nauvoo. He wants you to know, there will be a new temple in the new Zion, and your time will come to receive the endowment. But he's in danger if he stays any longer; he must leave."

A painful stillness filled the room. Liz finally whispered, "We can't go without our promises, Will. It's what we've all worked for, all these years."

Will was suddenly on his feet. "Brother, are they still going forward upstairs? Is someone doing more endowments?"

"Yes. For now. But the leaders have to leave. It's the same for all of them. You can stay, I suppose, but I don't know how many more will have a chance."

Again the quiet, and then whispering began, as couples considered what they would do. But no one left. "We'll wait," Will told Liz, and she nodded. Will closed his eyes and prayed, and when he opened them, he saw that Liz had been doing the same thing.

A couple of hours went by, and groups were called out now and then and guided up the winding staircases, but more important, Brigham had returned to the temple. He had told someone, "I can't walk out on all these good brothers and sisters."

When Will and Liz finally made it upstairs, it was past midnight, but they felt fortunate. Hundreds more were still waiting. As it turned out, Brigham stayed two more days and continued to conduct endowment ceremonies almost around the clock.

Will had had no idea what to expect, but inside the temple he was taught much about the meaning of life, both mortal and eternal. He made promises to God, and he was promised great blessings in the eternities. There were moments in the ceremony when he was brought to tears as he envisioned all that he and Liz could be in the next life.

When they came out into the cold Nauvoo night, they held each other, and Liz told Will, "I feel as though I can withstand anything now. We'll manage this. We'll do what we're called on to do. But we mustn't ever forget what we learned tonight."

Will felt the same. Nonetheless, as days passed, and his land still hadn't sold, and departure was still not possible, he realized that the two of them were about to begin a journey more difficult than anything they had ever attempted.

CHAPTER 8

Jeff's parents and all three of his sisters were in Nauvoo. They had flown to St. Louis and rented a car and had arrived late in the day on December 29. Jeff had worried about finding room for them, but they had rented a condo east of town. Jeff's mom had actually wanted to sleep on the floor of their house and be close to her grandbaby the whole time, but Dad said he needed a bed, and Rachel, Julie, and Cassi preferred to have a place with two bathrooms.

The girls fell in love with little William immediately and showered him with constant attention—which he loved. Julie and Cassi had said on the phone that they were hoping for snow, but that enthusiasm abated quickly for the Las Vegas girls when they were confronted by Nauvoo's winter air. Rachel knew about cold, this being her fourth year at BYU, and she was the one most fascinated by the Mormon history sites. Cassi, who hoped to be heading to Provo herself in the fall, also showed some interest, but Julie talked to her incessantly—even during tours—and her conversation never had anything to do with history.

The family had only two days to see all the historical sites they could, so they filled the first one by running to Carthage to see the jail, then seeing as many of the houses and public buildings in Nauvoo as possible. Jeff's mom, Alicia, was especially interested to see Sarah Granger Kimball's house and the upper room in the Red Brick Store. She made sure that her daughters learned about the beginnings of Relief Society, and she made her own pitch about the Prophet saying that the Church never was "perfectly organized" until the Relief Society was created. Jeff was glad to see that Rachel really was moved by the idea of being where all that started, and she seemed especially touched when the tour guide from the Community of Christ pointed out that the first temple endowments had also been performed upstairs in the Red Brick Store.

At the end of the day, Jeff's mom stepped close to Jeff and whispered, "Try to find a little time to talk to Rachel while she's here."

"Okay. Why?"

"Just talk to her. I think she would like to have some time with her big brother."

Rachel had always been fairly serious, and certainly quieter than anyone else in the family, but Jeff had noticed all day that she seemed somber, as though she had something on her mind. So on the following morning, New Year's Eve, he drove out to the condo, chatted with those who were out of bed—which did not include Julie and Cassi—and then said to Rachel, "Hey, do you want to go for a little ride with me before you all head into town again? There's something I want to show you—not too far away from here."

"Okay," she said. But she sounded a little suspicious. Still, she got her winter coat, which was draped over a chair in the living room, and the two walked out to the car. As soon as they got in, however, Rachel said, "I guess Mom told you what happened."

"No. What do you mean?"

"Come on."

"No, really. She didn't tell me that anything had 'happened.'"

"So what's this all about?"

"Grandpa Lewis had a farm out this way. I just wanted to show you where it was."

"Why me?"

"Because you seem interested in that kind of stuff. And besides, I wanted to talk to you. We used to be buddies, and I don't see you much anymore."

She seemed to like that. She patted his shoulder. "Thanks," she said. "So what do you want to talk about?"

"You seemed sort of sad yesterday—and that worries me. I was just wondering how you're doing."

He glanced toward her and saw that tears had filled her eyes. After a few seconds, she said, "I didn't think it showed." Then she added, "But thanks for worrying about me. How come I never meet guys like you at the Y?"

Jeff watched his little sister, thought how pretty she looked. But she was the sort of woman who didn't make a big splash with the way she dressed or with her personality. She could easily blend into a big student ward without many guys noticing how soft and lovely her blue eyes were or how interested in her world she was.

Jeff drove out along a gravel road to the south, and he let Rachel have some time to think. When he came to the spot where the road intersected with another dirt road—the eastern end of Parley Street—he pointed off to the right and said, "That field out there was Joseph Smith's farm, and the one to the left was the parade ground where the Nauvoo Legion came for training."

She nodded but didn't say anything.

"So what's going on?" he said.

"Nothing, Jeff. Really. That's the stupid part."

"Come on. Talk to me." He eased the car forward and turned east on Parley, then drove very slowly.

"It's embarrassing, it's so stupid." She looked out the side window, away from Jeff. "There's this guy in my ward I thought I liked. A guy named Tyler. He's good-looking and . . . well, you know . . . I had a crush on him. He didn't ever ask me out or anything, but we were in the same family home evening group, so I saw him quite a bit. For a while he seemed to pay attention to me, and I got it in my head that something was happening. And that's the whole story. It just didn't go anywhere. I don't think he's dating anyone; he just stopped talking to me as much as he had there for a while."

"Guys don't want to date these days," Jeff said. "I think they're all scared of getting into a relationship before they finish school."

"That's about right. Most of them say they aren't getting married until they're at least thirty. They're always joking about 'not getting tied down.'"

"Well, something will work out for you one of these days."

"Maybe. I don't know. But I always thought I'd go to BYU, find a cool guy, get married, and have a family—you know, the whole Mormon thing. Now I'm a senior, and Dad is after me to graduate, and I just keep thinking that if I leave college without finding someone, my odds will get worse and worse."

"*Are* you going to graduate this year?"

"No. I've changed my major twice. I need to go another year— much to Dad's disappointment. But I don't think another year will matter that much. I don't know how to . . . *attract* guys. I think they're all looking for cute little beauty queens with more *physical assets* than I have." Rachel laughed and so did Jeff.

Jeff had no idea what to tell Rachel about finding a husband. He turned onto another gravel road, watched his odometer, and drove about half a mile. "Okay, it was about right here," he said. "William

Lewis, known as Will, and Elizabeth Lewis, known as Liz, had a farm right about here. From what Grandpa said in his life history, they actually lived in town, right there across from our house, but he farmed out here. I found his property on the plat maps down at the Lands and Records office."

There was actually not much to look at—just a flat piece of land with a stubble of cornstalks across it, and some patches of snow. "Grandpa Lewis was the first man to plow this ground. I just think that's kind of cool to think about."

"It's a neat thing to try to picture. Would he have used horses or oxen or what?"

"Actually, he owned a bunch of oxen, and besides plowing his own land, he plowed other people's fields—you know, for hire. He graded some of the roads in the county, too, but I'm not sure if they were ones that are still around."

"What was he like, Jeff? And what was Elizabeth like?"

"They were just people, like us. They went through hard times. They lost a baby, and it about broke their hearts. They built a log house and started this farm, and then they had to pull up and leave everything. But Grandpa was pretty down to earth. He never claimed to find 'faith in every footstep,' the way we like to say now. He and Grandma did what they had to do, and they got discouraged, but the impression I get is that they didn't spend a lot of time feeling sorry for themselves."

"The way I'm doing, you mean?"

Jeff looked over and smiled. "Well, let's just say, you're a beautiful young woman; you're not yet twenty-two; you have a good brain and a good education; and you don't have to churn butter or walk across the plains."

Rachel smiled too, but she said, "I think I'd rather walk across the plains than wait for some guy to notice that I'm alive."

"I get what you're saying. The great blessing of Will Lewis's life, as far as I'm concerned, was that he never had to mess with computers."

"Do you still hate your job?"

Jeff was taken by surprise. Had he ever told her that he didn't like his job, or had she merely surmised as much from things he sometimes said? He looked at that stubble of corn, and beyond to a line of leafless willow trees in a little gulch. Clouds were hanging in the river valley today; that snow the girls had talked about seemed a possibility. But the gloom only made Jeff think of all the days he had driven up the highway, not far from where he had stopped the car, on his way to Fort Madison.

"Well," Jeff said, "I'll tell you what. I don't particularly like my job, but I don't think I'd like to plow that field with a team of oxen, either. A man has to provide for his family, and that's been true for-ever. It's only in our age that we've started to feel sorry for ourselves if we can't spend our days exactly as we please. I really have made up my mind I'm not going to pity myself anymore. So when I give you that advice, I mean it for myself, too."

"Don't you think Grandpa Lewis ever wished he could do something else?"

"Actually, I know he did. He tried to get a business started here, hauling cargo overland. But I don't think he cried in his pillow at night because he wanted to sit in the woods and write poetry—or whatever. He had only so many options and he went after them. I can do that too."

"Are you really going to start remodeling houses for a living?"

"Yeah. I probably am. What are Mom and Dad saying about that?"

"You know Dad. He can't believe he spent all that money on Stanford only to have you work at something you didn't need a college education to get into. And then Mom is all, 'Is that what you think college is—*job training*?' But I heard her tell one of her friends, 'The boy was meant to be a professor. He'll never be happy as a builder.'"

Jeff nodded. He took another long look at Rachel, and then he said, "Well, Sis, you *are* beautiful, and—"

"Come on, Jeff. That's just not true."

"Hey, have I ever lied to you?"

"Yes. Many times.

"Only when we were kids. But I'm not lying to you now. You don't do much with makeup to show off your beautiful eyes—and your skin doesn't need any help—but any guy worth having will see not only how you look but who you are. And you are, my dear sister, *beautiful.*"

She seemed to accept that, but her eyes filled with tears again. "I wish you were around more often, Jeff. I really miss you."

"I feel the same way. But we'll always see each other. When Grandma and Grandpa Lewis said good-bye to their families back in England, they were pretty sure they would never see them again."

She sat back and looked out across the land again, as though she wanted to get those grandparents into her head.

"I'll tell you what's going to happen to you, Rach."

"What?"

"Something." He waited for a moment, and then he added, "That's what always happens. We grow up picturing our lives, thinking we have a lot of say in the matter—and we do have some—but *something* happens. The test in life is to deal with whatever comes."

"In Young Women, the teachers always made it seem like the outcome was automatic. You fell in love, you got married. But I have two friends who are divorced already, and a guy I knew in high school is dying from cancer."

Jeff put his hand on Rachel's arm. "But that's the point. We come to mortality for *experience,* and if everything went the way we wanted it to go, we wouldn't learn much of anything. It's always been like that. Grandma and Grandpa got kicked out of their home and had to cross the plains. We get knocked off our plan A, and then we cross whatever plains God puts before us. But, like I said, I'm going to try not to feel sorry for myself anymore."

"It's a good plan. And Tyler's actually kind of dumb, if you want to know the truth. If he liked me, I probably wouldn't like him."

They both laughed.

"I wonder what we'll write in our life histories, Rach. And I wonder what our great-grandchildren will think we were all about."

"At least we know that Grandma and Grandpa Lewis were pretty tough."

"That's right. And that's what we have to pass down to the generations that come after us."

· · ·

Snow began to fall later that day—not a lot, but enough to turn the lawn white. Julie and Cassi ran out to touch the stuff. They even made a few snowballs and threw them, but they didn't stay outside very long. They came in looking thrilled and rosy but glad to be back in the warm house.

Dinner on New Year's Day was nice, and Abby was happy to have her rebuilt kitchen to work in. She was also pleased to have nice carpets on her floors—newly installed. The house had been a mess for a time while the carpet layers worked, but the inconvenience was worth it. Jeff really had done a wonderful job on the house, and she knew the Robertsons were going to be pleased with his work—even if the bathroom was still a mess.

It was fun to have a houseful of people, too, and the greatest fun was to watch the whole family focus on William. Jeff's parents had decided to bring their gifts with them and celebrate a second Christmas. William was almost a year old now and toddling about. He didn't quite understand all the gift giving—he liked the wrapping paper as much as the presents—but he was a happy little boy who loved all these aunts who fussed over him, and he loved being bounced by Grandpa and hugged by Grandma. It was a rest for Abby to have everyone looking after him, but it was rather chaotic, too, with all the noise that Abby had never really known in her life. The holidays in her own home had always been rather sedate, with lovely dinners on expensive china and pleasant talk—none of this squealing and teasing and battling like what went on between Julie and Cassi.

So when it was all over on January 2, and the Lewises had said their good-byes and driven away, Abby was sort of relieved—and at the same time surprisingly lonely. Jeff had taken the day off, so that was nice, but she knew he would head out early the next morning, and he had already said he would have to work late with Malcolm the following evening. It was hard for her to face such long days and evenings. She and Jeff still had only one car. He sometimes let her drop him off where he was working in the evening, if it wasn't too far away, and that gave her a chance to run to a grocery store or a drugstore in town, or even to make a trip to Keokuk. But just as often, she was alone with William all evening.

Jeff and Malcolm were starting to see substantial income from their work, but they had had to pump a good deal of the money back into purchasing power equipment and tools. They had also experienced their first runaround in getting paid for a job they had completed. Abby had noticed that a little more realism was setting in with Jeff and Malcolm, and she was glad of that. She didn't want Jeff to give up his job before they had enough income to live on.

On Christmas Day, back in New Jersey, Jeff had promised Abby a wonderful present. He had already given her a beautiful sweater and skirt for her Christmas present, along with fun little gifts for her stocking, but on this day, with the house finally empty, he kept his promise and bundled up William and took him outside—which William loved—with a vow to stay away long enough for Abby to have a nap. She actually didn't sleep very long, but even just the idea of it was wonderful. There had been so many times in the last year that she would have given almost anything just to have a little more sleep. She was doing better now, with William still taking a nap every day, but it touched her that Jeff understood how much she loved to have a little time for herself. What she wondered, however, was whether *he* would ever get enough sleep. The man didn't know how to nap, and he simply never slept a full eight hours.

When Abby's boys returned to the house, William's plump little cheeks were bright red, and his eyes were wide and happy. "Will, tell Mommy, *snow*. Say it, *snow*." Jeff waited, tried a few more times, but William was pointing at the door, obviously wanting to go back outside. "He was saying it out there," Jeff said. "We made snowballs and threw them. I told him *snow*, and he said it."

"He was probably saying *no*. That's a word he uses quite often."

"Well, it did sound like *no*, but he knew what we were talking about, and he loves the stuff. I thought he'd get too cold in a couple of minutes and want to come back in, but he didn't. In fact, he didn't want to come in even now. But hey, how come you're up already?"

"I fell asleep for a few minutes, but that's about it. I'm starting to be more like you, I guess." She took William from Jeff and unzipped his snowsuit.

"No," William said.

"See?" Jeff said. "He said *snow*."

"No. He said *no*. He wants to go back outside."

Jeff laughed. "No way. I'm too cold." He helped pull William's snowsuit over his shoes, and then he tossed William in the air a couple of times, which made him laugh.

A little while later Abby fed William and then put him down for a nap. When she walked back to the living room, she said, "You wore him out. He fell right to sleep."

"He wore me out," Jeff said. "My eyes have been going closed reading this book—and it's one I've been waiting to read."

Jeff's parents had brought him several Mormon history books—some new ones that were Christmas presents, and some others they had had around the house. The one he had started to read was about the Mormon exodus from Nauvoo. Jeff had told Abby about some of the trials the early Saints had had in crossing Iowa when the weather was so bad and so many were sick.

"Why don't *you* take a little nap?" Abby said.

"You come with me."

She laughed. "That's not a nap."

"I won't mind if you keep me awake."

"Let's wait, and we'll put William down early tonight."

Jeff nodded. Abby appreciated that he never pushed when it came to such matters.

"Jeff, your mom and I had a good talk last night. She thinks you ought to go to grad school."

"I know. I talked to her about that too, and I understand where she's coming from. But we need to stick with our plan for now. For one thing, I can't run off and leave Malcolm. But I think we're going to do very well with our business. We've got a good check coming next week when we finish this job we're doing, and we don't have to reinvest any of it. It's the first time we won't have to skimp by. I really think the worst of that is over."

Abby sat down in a lovely emerald-colored upholstered chair she had purchased to replace the old recliner. Jeff was sitting in a matching chair with his reading lamp turned on. "I guess there's no chance we could buy another car," she ventured.

"We can start thinking about that. I know how bad it is to be stuck here without one all day."

"But if we had a car payment, you'd have to stay with your job longer, and then we're back where we started. I thought it was such a great idea to go back to work, but I'm starting to think I'll never find a job that would actually help out all that much."

"Here's what I've been thinking. I've created quite a nice web site for our business, and I've figured out some ways to push people to it. We still get most of our business from word of mouth—our customers just telling other people that we did a good job for them. But the other day I wrote a little article on how to change out old windows—what some of the problems were, and what some of the good products are that people could use. I got a lot of hits from that. Every time I add something to the site, it jumps up on the Google rating. The best thing I can do is keep more stuff going on there all the time."

"Yeah. Like you have plenty of time for that."

"That *is* the problem. But I got thinking, what if you wrote some little articles on decorating ideas? You know, something about color coordination, or choosing fabrics, or—well, I don't know what I'm talking about. But you would know some things to write—just stuff for amateurs who want to fix up their houses. A guy might look up something on how to change out a toilet, but women might be looking for fuzzy toilet seat covers, or whatever. We would keep driving people to the site, and you would be helping, but you wouldn't have to leave home."

"I could try to think of a few things, I guess, but what difference would it make? You have all the work you can handle as it is."

"I'm actually thinking of something a little bigger than just advertising our business. I'm thinking I could create a regular blog on remodeling, and maybe you could do the same with home décor. If we had enough people looking at it, we could start to sell advertising space. It might become a business in and of itself."

"But what about Malcolm and Kayla?"

"They could help us with ideas, but I don't think they would want to do any writing. Still, all the profit we made would go right back into the business. We'd split with them, the same as with all our remodeling projects."

Abby was glad to know that, but she didn't see that they could make much selling ads. "I still wish that somehow I could find a job—with benefits—and get you out of your job, so you and Malcolm could have a night at home once in a while."

"I know. And I'm glad you're willing to do that. But I'm okay for now, and I doubt you'll find anything worth your time."

Abby was pretty sure that was true. Still, she had been praying for an answer. A year ago, she had sometimes wondered whether God was listening to her, but she didn't feel that way now. She really believed that the Lord would guide them. She knew that there would always be things to deal with, and nothing would ever turn out quite as perfectly as she would like, but she trusted that in the long run they would be okay. "I'm not going to be so afraid as I used to be," she told Jeff.

He laughed. But then he said, "You've already changed a lot, Ab. You trust more than you used to."

Abby nodded. She thought that was true.

CHAPTER 9

The weather had been cold in spells, but never cold enough to freeze the Mississippi all the way across. Blocks of ice were flowing, making ferry crossings dangerous, but more of the Saints were making their exodus every day. Will had been called by Charles Rich, a captain of fifty, to lead ten families as a captain of ten. Brother Rich was preparing to make the crossing soon, along with the Apostles, and Will felt that his group should follow, but he didn't want to head into the wilderness without adequate provisions—and he still hadn't been able to sell his property.

One morning a burly man on horseback rode up to Will's house, dismounted, and walked back to where Will was chopping wood. Will put his axe down, and the man said in a deep voice, "My name's Asa Barnes. I unnerstan' yer lookin' to sell this place?"

"Yes, sir, I am," Will said. He reached out his hand. "Will Lewis."

"How much did you want for't?"

"Not what it's worth. I know I can't get that. Make me an offer."

Barnes was wearing a battered felt hat. He leaned his head back now and peered out from under the broad brim, looked around at the house and corral and cowshed. "How much land do you own?" he asked.

"Four acres. About half of it is still in good timber."

"And you have a deed?"

"Yes, sir."

"I cain't offer you much. But I could maybe give you a hundred dollars."

Will had already come to think he would have to sell for less than that, but that wasn't what he said. "I've got a twenty-acre farm east of town. There's no house on it, but it's good land, plowed and ready to plant in the spring. For three hundred dollars I'd let both places go."

Barnes turned and spat a stream of brown saliva on the ground. He wiped his lips, and he smiled. "Them places out there ain't gittin' anywhar near that much," he said.

"Offer me a quarter of what it's really worth, and I'll be satisfied."

"And how much would that be?"

"I'd take two hundred dollars, I guess."

"Well, no. That's more'n I kin go."

Will looked at the ground for a time, and then he looked at Barnes square in the eyes, even leaned toward him. "People tell us that we're so terrible to live around," he said, "that they have a right to drive us out. They've burned down some of our houses, shot some of our people, *demanded* that we leave. And no one, not the governor, not the president of the United States—not a living soul—will lift a hand to protect us. Does that strike you as right? Is that the way things are done in this country?"

"Don't blame me for't. I live way north from here. As far as I care, you could stay right here. But yor all puttin' notices in the newspapers that you want to sell yor land. I'm just takin' a gamble.

I'll buy a few places and see if I kin sell 'em, but I might get stuck with everythin' I buy."

"Take a look at your conscience. Think about a people thrown into the wilderness, with no way to receive a fair price for their land. Then you tell me what you'll pay me, and we'll settle for that."

The man nodded, as if he understood Will's grief, but he said, "A hundred seventy-five, I'll say, and I suspect no one else is gonna pay you half so much."

"What would you pay me with?"

"I raise cattle and sheep, and I know that's something you want to take with you. I could pay in good animals, healthy and strong. You kin look at 'em and we kin settle on what they's worth. We could set out tomorrow morning. It's two days' ride from here. Some others is going, and you could all drive the sheep and cattle back t'gether."

Will didn't like any of this, but he had been asking the Lord for an answer, and this seemed to be the only one open to him. He had oxen, wagons, and almost enough flour, cornmeal, sugar, and tea, but he didn't have beef or mutton, and his friends didn't either. He decided he would make the trip north with Mr. Barnes, and when he returned with the animals, the ice might not be flowing so heavily. If that were true, he and his friends could cross the river. He had also been thinking about Warren and Nelly Baugh. They wanted to be one of the families in Will's ten, and they were worried about supplying themselves, the same as everyone else. It seemed to Will that if he bargained well enough, he might be able to help them out, too.

• • •

Liz was happy when Will returned from his trip north to trade for cattle, and relieved that he felt pleased with the bargain he had struck. But she was startled when he said, "Liz, I think we should leave right away. Tomorrow, or the next day, at latest. I stopped out on the prairie and talked with Jesse. He's of the same mind. We pretty much have what we need, so we might as well go ahead and cross the river."

"But, Will, most people I talk to are waiting for spring to break. What do we gain by leaving now?"

"Our land is sold, Liz, and we promised to leave with Brigham and be part of General Rich's company. They're all going now. Brigham crossed the river yesterday."

"But all that organizing is falling apart now. You told me that yourself." What they both knew was that the companies would not be made up the way they had been planned. Half the people crossing now had not been called to the pioneer company. And many of those who *had* been called were not ready to leave.

"I know all that. But I like to keep my promises." He glanced away for a moment, then looked back at Liz. "Besides, Jesse doesn't want to stay out on the prairie, where attacks will surely come first. And as far as that goes, as more people leave, the danger might be worse here in town."

"All right, then." She nodded, accepting it. "But tomorrow?"

"Let's say the day after."

She took a deep breath, and then she nodded again.

"I need to ride down to Dan's house and tell him," Will said, "and I'll talk to Warren, too. Jesse and Jake will be heading into town in the morning. We'll have to put them all up here for a night."

So he had made up his mind before he had said anything. But that was all right, Liz decided. Once they crossed the river, she thought she might feel free. She was so tired of being scared.

• • •

Two days later, on Wednesday, February 18, 1846, the four families drove their wagons down to the ferry landing. Warren Baugh had decided to wait for warmer weather and growing grass. Nelly would have chosen to go, Will thought, and she shed a few tears to say good-bye, but they promised to see each other someday, out West. Will gave them a few supplies he knew they needed, and they were grateful for that.

When Will's group reached Parley Street, a long line of wagons was waiting. Some people had been there all night. The weather was warm and fair, and the river was much safer than it had been the week before. Many had obviously decided this was a good opportunity to make the crossing. But this meant a long day of waiting, which was hard for Liz and even worse for the little boys. They could play outside, which they liked, but they were confused with what was happening. Daniel, almost two years old, didn't understand much, so he didn't worry. But Liz knew that Jacob had heard too much talk—talk about going far away, pieces of conversations about people being shot—and he had certainly felt the concern of his parents. He kept running back to Liz and clinging to her as though he were afraid the wagon would leave without him.

It was late in the day when they finally crossed the river on a flatboat, pushed across by men with long poles. The mile-long excursion actually seemed to excite the boys, but it scared Liz. The weather had begun to change. A stout wind was blowing, chopping the water, bouncing the wagons, and progress was slow. It was getting dark as they landed on the Iowa side, and the men decided to camp by the river and set out for Sugar Creek in the morning. The boys slept in the wagon between Liz and Will, and everyone stayed warm under their quilts, but by morning snow had begun to fall. That changed everything. The climb up the bluffs was difficult, even with two teams of oxen pulling. The men had to get out and push to help the animals, and that meant the wagons had to make the climb one at a time. Much of the day got away from them before all four wagons were on top of the ridge. By then the wind had turned cold and the temperature had taken a big drop.

Liz had been huddled with her boys in the wagon, wrapped in every quilt they had, while they had waited for Jesse's wagon, the last one, to make it up the hill. Jacob kept saying, "It's cold, Mummy. It's so cold."

Little Daniel was tucked against her body and seemed all right. "Jacob, be a big boy," Liz kept telling him. "We'll build a fire when we stop tonight. You'll get warm."

"I want to go home," he said, and then he tucked his face against her side.

"I know. But we'll have a new house . . . one day. We have to wait just a little."

But Liz wondered how long that would be—and where they would ever have a house again. From now on everything was wilderness to her, and more frightening than she had expected. She was starting to realize that she had only replaced one fear with another.

Liz wasn't happy when Will asked her to "step down for a minute." She couldn't think why he wanted her to do that. But she had told herself that she wouldn't complain about anything. After all, she had prayed that she and her family would be kept safe from the mob, and her prayers had been answered. So Liz handed Jacob to Will, and she kept a quilt around her and Daniel as she struggled to get down out of the wagon. Will helped her, and then he turned her around. "Everyone's walking back," he said. "For one last look."

"Look?" But by then she knew what he meant. She carried Daniel and walked back to the ridge, where she looked out across the valley and the river. There in the distance was the temple, white and glistening. The snow had let up, and the clouds had broken apart enough to send columns of light down on their city, their temple.

"I've never seen the temple from this side of the river," Will said. "I swear it's the finest-looking building in the world."

Tears filled Liz's eyes. The finality of everything struck her hard. "You worked so hard to build it," she told Will. "Everyone did."

He nodded, but she could tell that he couldn't get any words out.

"It's not right, Will. They shouldn't be able to take it from us."

"No, they shouldn't," he said, but nothing more.

All along the ridge, families were standing together, looking out across the dark, broad river. Everything else was white, but the temple shone brighter than the snow. Liz remembered the day she and Will had arrived in Nauvoo, so weak and sick, and with so little in the way of possessions. On that first day they had seen the temple, only just begun, and each day in Nauvoo since, they had watched it, felt the desire and responsibility to help build it, and felt the satisfaction of it growing ever closer to completion.

A week or so back, the temple roof had caught fire, heated too much by a stovepipe. The Saints had created a bucket brigade and saved the building, and then, quickly, had patched the opening. Some said it might have been better to let it burn rather than to allow the anti-Mormons to defile it. But Liz had never thought so. She wanted to believe that somehow the temple would be protected, that it would stand forever just as it looked now.

"We weren't as good as we should have been," Will said. "Maybe that's why we couldn't stay."

"I don't believe that," Liz said. "We did our best. God wouldn't give the victory to those who hate us. He has a new place for us, and it's going to be better."

It was what Liz wanted to believe more than what she truly felt. Her mind was going back to all her memories of Nauvoo. There on those flats by the river she had spent the hardest months of her life, and in a little log house on the hill southeast of the temple, she had given birth to a beautiful daughter, who now lay in a grave east of the city. Liz would never be able to visit that grave again, but she told herself to think of Mary Ann, not the grave, and trust that she would see her baby in another world.

Liz pressed against Will and said, "What we lost is the building itself—and our houses. What we built, we're taking with us."

"We were young when we got here. We've both grown up more than just four years' worth."

"I can't really remember the girl I was."

"You're still the same woman, Liz—just stronger than you ever expected to be."

Will was holding Jacob close, and the boy was crying softly, seeming to feel all the sadness around him. Still, Liz and Will stood for a long time gazing at the place they had called Zion. Liz knew they needed to push on, but she kept thinking, *When I take my last look, it will be the last one ever.*

• • •

Will and Liz and the other families finally walked back to their wagons and continued west to Sugar Creek, just a few miles beyond the bluff. The women drove the oxen, and the men herded the cattle along: milk cows and beef cattle and sheep. They all had live chickens in pens on the backs of their wagons, and they carried bacon and smoked pork and sacks of flour and corn. The heavy wagons were also weighed down with bedding, cooking pots, tents and tent poles, crockery, utensils, and even some pieces of furniture. All that would have been hard enough for the oxen to pull without half a foot of snow on the ground.

What Will could see as they approached Sugar Creek was a scattering of tents and wagons and a few hastily built log shelters. He continued on to where he could see into the valley below, where many more tents were set up on both sides of a little stream that ran from north to south. It was like a little city, the campsites sprinkled over the snow and animals tied up or corralled with makeshift fences. Open fires burned in each little camp. But Will didn't see all that many people. Most of them, he supposed, were huddled inside the tents and wagons and shelters.

Will walked back and conferred with the men from the other wagons. "There are already too many people down in that valley," he told them. "Why don't we find a spot up here on this east ridge, near the trees?"

"Shouldn't we seek out Charles Rich?" Jesse asked.

"I don't even know if he's here. We'll travel with him when we push on, but right now we need to look after our families—get them settled somewhere. It's going to be a hard night."

"We'll face more wind up here," Jake said.

"I was thinking about that," Will said. "I know we might not be here long, but let's get our children protected as best we can. Tomorrow we can cut enough timber to put up a log shelter—three walls to block the wind—and we can use some of our tents for a roof."

"Can we all get inside a little place like that?" Jake asked.

"I see some tall trees in those woods. We could maybe build a place twelve by twelve, or something like that, and then just crowd in together. We could make our fire just outside and maybe trap some of the heat inside those walls." Looking into the eyes of his friends, Will saw how resolute they were trying to be and how worried they actually were. The men hadn't shaved for a few days, and crystals of ice had formed on their eyebrows. Jake, who hadn't experienced much cold weather in his life, was gripping his arms tight around his chest and shivering so hard that Will worried about him.

"We need to build a big fire before we do anythin' else," Brother Johns said. "My childern is almos' froze. And they're hungry, too."

"I know. Let's pull these wagons over against those trees on the north, and we'll form a square. We can keep the animals in the center. Then let's get some wood chopped. Tell your wives and children to stay in the wagons for now."

"We need to hurry," Jake said. "Faith is giving up. She keeps saying she can't face this, and she's got the girls upset and crying."

So the men pulled the wagons together and stopped on a little snow-covered plain near the woods. Jesse and Dan took care of the animals, bringing them inside the hollow of the square, and Will and Jake started gathering wood from under the trees and chopping off dead branches. Will walked to another camp not far away and came back with a stick of burning wood to start the fire. It took him some time to get a good blaze going, but once he did, the children gathered around close. The women had all brought loaves of baked wheat bread with them, enough to last a few days. They heated up cuts of pork and ate it with the bread, and the children all seemed enlivened by that. But the sun was going down, and there was nothing to do but wrap the children in all the quilts they could and let them sleep in the wagons again. Will managed to find a few big rocks under the trees, and he heated those by the fire. These he distributed to each family so they could put them under the quilts, near the children's feet. It would help a little, at least for a while.

Will had Liz lie on a heavy quilt with Daniel and Jacob cuddled close to her, and he wrapped them up. "It's too cold," Jacob whimpered. "I want to stay by the fire."

"Just stay close to Mummy. She'll keep you warm. You'll be snug in no time."

"Where are you going?" Liz asked Will.

"I'll keep the fire going."

"You need to sleep."

"Not really. After a while, if you can't keep the boys warm, bring them to the fire. It's more important that we make it through the night than that I sleep. Tomorrow we'll get a shelter built."

He couldn't see Liz's face, but he heard the fear in her voice when she said, "Will, pray with us before you go to the fire."

So they prayed. Will called upon the Lord to protect his family, and then he walked back to the fire. He placed more limbs on top, then stood as close to the blaze as he could tolerate. Jesse soon joined him.

Will could see in Jesse's face that he was pained by what this was doing to his children. "This is bad," he told Will. "We can't hold out this way very long."

"This kind of cold can't last more than a day or two," Will said. But he didn't know whether that was actually true.

After a time, a man from another camp walked over to Will and Jesse. He introduced himself as Brother Rogers. "How long have you been here?" Will asked.

"This is our sixth night. It wasn't so cold at first. Everything changed today."

"Are people getting by all right?" Jesse asked him.

Brother Rogers stood close to the fire, holding out his hands toward it. He finally looked at Jesse and said, "Everyone's keeping their spirits up pritty good. But the children are gittin' sick. I heard that some died today."

"What can a man do to protect his family?" Jesse asked.

"Not much. But you folks is fitted out good. You should be all right."

"Is someone in charge?" Will asked.

"Brother Brigham got here late Sunday night, and he started git-ting things better organized, but he had to go back to Nauvoo—to git things on track over there. Some of the other brethren are here, and they're trying to direct what's goin' on, but more people keep coming ever' day, and they just camp where they can find a place for now."

"Has Brigham said when we'll push on?"

"No. He don't know yet. No one knows much of anything. Brigham called us together and said we have to wait 'til some of the other Apostles git here. He's goin' to git us set up in companies and everything when he comes back."

"We're supposed to be with Brother Rich. He called me to—"

"That's all changin'. Too many've come who wasn't assigned to any companies. We'll just have to wait and see what Brigham does about that."

"All right, then," Will said. "We'll manage all right."

"It ain't so bad, really. The weather will break one of these days, and we'll move on. It's better than waitin' to get kill't over on the other side of the river."

Will said he agreed, but the next few days were very hard. That first night, in the wagons, was a test of everyone's strength. Before morning, all the women had given up on the cold wagons and had called for help in getting the children to the fire. The parents had sat on logs or stood near the fire and held their little ones, some of them sleeping and some of them crying. And then, as soon as the men could see well enough to work, they started felling trees, trimming them, notching them as best they could.

The day was cold but sunny, and the children were able to move around enough to feel warmer. Daylight made a big difference to them. But the warmer day gave way to a harsh, freezing north wind, and by evening the temperature had fallen even lower than the night before. The men had been able to get three walls built and braced, and they stretched two tents over the top to keep the snow out. Will spread out another tent on the floor, and a layer of quilts, and then everyone huddled together and Will covered them over with more quilts and another canvas tent. He spent most of the night by the fire again, but he did finally squeeze into the bedding and sleep for a couple of hours.

The fierce cold continued, and each day was an ordeal. On the one hand, Will was amazed at the fortitude of the people, many of whom were cheery and optimistic no matter what they faced. Every night Pitt's Brass Band played, and down in the river valley people gathered to dance. But Will was worried about his sons. Both had begun to cough and sniffle, and both looked vacant at times, as though they were trying to think what all this meant, why their parents would bring them out here.

On Monday, all the captains of tens and fifties were called together. Brigham Young, Heber Kimball, and John Taylor had returned the night before from their trip back across the river. The leaders reached a decision that a company would move forward the next morning and begin to identify a route across the Iowa Territory. But the following morning was bitterly cold, and snow began to fall again. The newly formed advance company didn't leave after all.

Will kept hoping that the worst was over, but Wednesday and Thursday were the coldest days yet. Some said that the temperature had fallen to twenty below zero. It was on that Thursday that Brigham Young walked through camp. When he spotted Will, he came over to him. "Brother Lewis," he said, "it looks like you've taken care of yourselves pretty well."

"We're managing," Will said. "I hope this cold lets up before long."

"That's what we're all praying for," Brigham said, "but the Lord seems to know what backsliders we've been. He's letting us humble ourselves before we set off into the wilderness. We'll be better off for it."

"I hear there's cholera in the camp. Are many dying?"

"Yes. There's been a number of deaths. But we don't even have a count as to who is here and who isn't. I told the people not to come until they were ready, but they've come without food or blankets, and then they want to know why God doesn't send a hot wind to melt the snow. Dozens have died—that's all I know—and most of them little children. It makes me cry to see it. It's the fault of those who drove us out in the winter, but it's our own fault, too. We have to establish some order in our camp or we're going to destroy ourselves."

"We have some good men in our little group, Brother Brigham. What can we do to help?"

"I need your food."

Will actually took a step back. Since leaving Nauvoo he had thought of almost nothing except protecting his wife and children, and now the President of the Twelve wanted to take away the one thing he couldn't possibly give up. "How can we—"

"Did you bring as much flour as we recommended?"

"Aye. But—"

"I know. It's not right. But we have people who will starve in the next few days if we don't feed them. I need one of your beef cattle and a sheep or two, and maybe five hundred pounds of flour."

Will nodded. He couldn't get any words out.

"We have more food coming. If I can, I'll replace what you give me. But I can't let people starve, no matter how foolish they've acted."

Will nodded again, but this was almost too much for him.

Jake stepped up next to Will. "Brother Brigham, you can have my animals," he said.

"That will never do, Brother. I appreciate your generosity, but I can't take that much from one family."

Jake was looking at the ground. "We won't need them now," he said. "My wife and I are pulling out. We're heading to St. Louis. Faith and the children can't take this cold—and I can't either. We're not cut out to travel in a wagon all the way to the West."

"It's good to know that now rather than later," Brigham said, and he sounded harsh, as though he had a hard time respecting a man who would give up. But then he added, more gently, "There are plenty of our people living in St. Louis. Stay there a few years if you have to, and then come west when we're better established."

"We've talked about doing that," Jake said. "We'll decide later."

"All right then. But, Brother . . . what was your name?"

"Winthrop. Jake Winthrop."

"Brother Winthrop, don't let this first step away from us become a path on your way to the unholy ways of this generation. If you face the fire with us, you'll be refined. But if you always turn from that which is difficult, you will never become the man you're capable of being. Do you understand that?"

"But my children are suffering too much. I could maybe—"

"I know. I feel the same thing. But that doesn't change anything. When the Lord asks us to do something that seems beyond us, we either rise up and do it, or we slide backwards. Just don't let yourself do that." Brigham shook Jake's hand. "God bless you with strength," he said, and he walked away.

"The man has no patience with weakness," Jake told Will. "And that's what he sees in me."

"I don't, Jake, but I do fear what might happen to you. If you separate yourself from the Saints, you might never return."

Jake looked down at the ground again, and when he finally looked up, he said, "Will, Faith and I love you, and we will always appreciate what you brought to us. But I don't know that we'll stay with the Church."

"But why?"

"This church asks more than we can give, Will."

"It gives back, too, Jake. Get the winter behind you, and rebuild your strength. Come to Zion when you're ready."

"We will if we can. We do believe the Church is true."

"Then stay with us. You can lean on us if you have to, and we'll get you through."

"I don't know. Faith and I talked all night last night when it was so cold, and we decided this was best."

So Will went to Faith and pled with her not to give up, but she wouldn't answer him, and in the morning the Winthrops drove their wagon back toward the river. Will had a feeling he would never see them again. He also saw other wagons leave that day, and he heard of more deaths. It was hard not to feel that the Lord was asking too much right now, no matter what Brother Brigham had said.

That day Charles Rich, who had crossed back to Nauvoo, returned, and he reported that he had walked across the Mississippi, which had finally frozen enough for wagons to cross. That would be a blessing for many who were waiting to make the crossing, but how many would come without adequate provisions? If the ice was a blessing, the cold that had produced it had already taken lives. And it would surely take more.

CHAPTER 10

Will had been working all day building a bridge across the east fork of Locust Creek. Time and again he had walked into the cold water and held posts upright as other men set the beams, and then he had helped to lash on the cross braces and treads. The water was so cold that it had numbed his body. At times he had had to stand in the strong current and brace himself, the water up to his chest. He wondered whether he would ever be warm again—but someone had to do this, and he liked to think he was as tough as any of the men. At least the air was reasonably warm. Such days had been rare lately.

It was April now, and more than a month had gone by since the pioneer companies had set out from Sugar Creek. The plan had been to cross Iowa Territory in about six weeks, but no one had foreseen the difficulties and hardships ahead. The wagon companies were not yet halfway across the territory. In the western part of Iowa there had been crude roads to travel, established more by repetition than by design, but they were mostly washed out now, as were many bridges. When the worst of the cold had let up, Brigham Young had hoped to travel over frozen earth for a time, but the "Camp of Israel," as the emigrants called themselves, had hardly gotten under way before spring rains had set in—hard thunderstorms at times, or steady rain that filled up the creeks and turned them into wild rivers. The roads had turned to mud, slick at first, then gradually deep and sloppy enough to bog down teams and wagons. Progress had slowed to a few miles a day, with everyone walking to save the oxen and mules, and boys herding animals that balked at the mud and searched about in vain for grass to graze.

Will had spent many hours up to his knees in water and mud as he helped one wagon after another push up hills or across boggy stretches of lowland that sucked in animals to their bellies and wagons in over their axles. At night, exhausted, he had fallen into "bed"—quilts laid on whatever ground could be found for pitching a tent. But what worried Will more was that Liz and the boys were struggling, all three of them sick.

It had taken seven days to reach a place called Richardson's Point on Indian Creek, not yet thirty miles from Sugar Creek. Brigham had called for a halt long enough for his people to repair their broken wagons, wash their clothes, rest their bodies, and, in some cases, seek work for a few days. With no grass growing yet, fodder for the animals had been hard to come by. Will had spent two days splitting rails for a farmer, and he and his team of men had brought back a wagonload of corn for the oxen. After a few pleasant days, the camp had been ready to push on again, but the storms returned—rain, even snow, and cold winds.

A number of babies had been born in the camps. Patty Sessions was kept busy moving forward and back in the strung-out wagon train, "putting women to bed," as she called it, but the beds were nothing more than wagon boxes and the conditions were cold and wet and crude.

The weather, the mishaps, the sickness, the weakened state of the animals, even hunger among the Saints—all that had been difficult, but Will was especially frustrated by the confusion. Brother Brigham tried to set rules, tried to keep the companies organized, but the order of travel changed as soon as the companies left their campsites each day. There were hills that took all day to climb as hundreds of wagons lined up and waited. It was challenging for people with lighter wagons or better teams to wait for slower travelers even though Brigham kept telling them to do so, and in open areas the wagons fanned out in anything but a file. Will had been assigned to Charles Rich's company of fifty, but Brother Rich had gone ahead with others to search for the best route. Will kept his three families together, but most days he hardly knew where his company of ten was.

Still, the people were moving steadily forward, and Will was proud at the end of this day when he had helped to finish a sturdy bridge. Hunters from the company had also killed several deer that day. They had brought a cut of the venison to Liz, who had cooked it over the fire outside their tent. Will sat by the fire, wrapped in a quilt. Liz had also cooked cornbread in the ashes of the fire, and Will felt much better as he filled his stomach and warmed his legs. Liz brought his wet clothes to the campfire and staked them up to dry, and she set his boots as close to the fire as she dared. "Are you feeling a little better?" she asked him.

"I'm fine. Never better," he said, and he laughed. He knew people among the company who always buoyed up the others with their optimism and good spirit. He wanted to be one of those people, not one of the whiners, but he also knew that he had been impatient, even harsh, with some of his fellow travelers. "It's you I'm concerned about," he told Liz. "I don't like that wheezing I hear when you breathe."

"But weather like this makes me feel better," she said.

Somewhere, at one of the campfires, someone had begun to sing "The Spirit of God Like a Fire Is Burning." It was a bit of a joke, with everyone huddled by their fires, but soon everyone picked it up, and all through the camp, the familiar tune filled the little valley. It was a good moment, and it reminded Will that he was surrounded by more strength than he sometimes gave people credit for—people making the best of a miserable situation.

But early in the morning, another storm blew in.

It was only a sprinkle at first. During breakfast Will felt a drop or two hit the side of his face. But the heaviness of the rain soon picked up markedly, and people began to head for their tents or wagons. Will and Liz hurried to their own tent, where the boys were still in bed. Once they were inside, the patter of the rain was at least gentle, and Will hoped that he had picked a good enough site, where the rainwater wouldn't run into the tent and soak their bedding.

Jacob had slept late and only now sat up when his mother offered him some cornmeal mush. Will knew he was tired of mush, and he wasn't feeling well enough to be hungry, but he worried how thin the boy was getting. "Eat your food, Jakey," Will said, patting the boy's head and trying not to sound too stern.

Jacob looked at the mush without responding. Instead, he said, "I don't like rain." And then his coughing began again. What was worse was that little Daniel was still sleeping, and he was making that same wheezing sound Will had heard from Liz. Will could only think of pneumonia and what that might mean if either one of them—or all three—had it.

"It's all right, Jacob," Liz was saying. "We're staying here today. We'll be dry. And warm."

"It's not warm. It's cold," Jacob said.

"Get under your quilt with me, then, and I'll keep you warm."

"You always hold Daniel."

"I can hold you both."

Jacob was a sturdy little boy, and strong for his age, but his spirit seemed delicate, and he feared things that Will couldn't remember ever worrying about. But then, he had gone through a lot more. Will didn't know whether his real father would be heading west with the Saints. He only knew he dreaded telling Jacob someday that he and Liz weren't actually his parents. He sometimes hoped that he would never have to do that, that Brother Clarkston would never come around to introduce himself to Jacob.

The rain continued and the day was tedious, but the night turned terrifying as the storm became much worse. Will had to go out in the dark and trench around the tent to keep water running around it, and he had to pound the tent stakes in deeper to hold against the wind. But his family got through until morning, even though enough water had seeped in to dampen the bedding and make the boys cold and miserable. Many tents had blown down in the night, so Will spent the morning helping people move and reset their tents and hang bedding in trees to dry. But not much drying occurred in the cold air. All the same, on the following morning, with frost on the ground, Will's company crossed the bridge and headed on to the main branch of Locust Creek.

Toward noon, Will called for the wagons to stop. He needed to look about for a good camping spot, and the animals needed rest. What worried him now was that the only browse that could be found consisted of small branches and bark from cottonwood trees along the creek. All of the corn was gone, and there was still very little grass.

Will was talking things over with some of his men when he saw a carriage approach from the east. He knew this had to be Brother Brigham catching up with them. The men waited as Brigham jumped down from his buggy and strode toward them. He was even smiling a little as he shook hands with Will and the others. "That was a good bridge you men built," he said. "Thank you."

"Glad we could do it," Will said.

"We need some more fair days like that one so we can start making better time. But for now, we need to let others catch up to us. Two companies are still back at the Hickory Grove camp. It could be two or three days before we can gather up together again."

"There's plenty for us to do. I've got a wagon tongue that's broken, and—"

"No. I have something else for you to do, Brother Will. We can't go on ahead until we procure fodder for the animals."

"Aye, it's true."

"I want you to take two wagons and three men, and I want you to find someone who will sell us some grain or hay. Head south into Missouri. We've run out of settlements out this way, and there's no one to bargain with north of us."

"Do you have any idea where I could find fodder?"

"No, I don't. Pray about it, and let the Spirit tell you where to go. I have a little cash, and that's something most men like to get their hands on, even if it's coming from the Mormons they hate so much."

"All right, then."

"We have two wagons freed up for you. You'll have to go back a couple of miles to reach them. Choose your men and get going just as soon as you can. Make good time, find grain, and then return here. We won't leave until you make it back."

But Will could only think about his family. "Brother Brigham, my wife and children are sick. They don't sound good at all. I'm willing to go, but—"

"Will, everyone's sick. I don't know of a family that doesn't have someone down. If I only sent men whose families were well, I couldn't send anyone."

"I understand that. I just hope someone will watch out for Liz and the boys."

"Ask some of the men in your company to get her set up on the west side of Locust Creek, where we plan to make our camp. Give her a blessing before you go—her and your children—then ask a sister to stay with them. But don't take all day. Get going as soon as you can." That voice of command was something Will knew well, but Brigham also grasped Will's shoulder. "You're a man I can trust to do this, Will. I'm sorry, but I need you. Put your trust in the Lord and all will be well."

"Aye. I'll leave within the hour."

"Half an hour would be better," Brigham said, but he was smiling.

• • •

Will, Jesse, a man named Jackson Bellows, and another named Mitchell Pace had ridden south all afternoon. Their two wagons were each pulled by four mules, which were faster than oxen. Will hadn't known where the border was, but he was certain they were in Missouri by now. The men had stopped at farms three times along the way, each time hearing the same answer from farmers. This early in the season, they had little fodder left for their own animals and couldn't think about selling what they had. The farmers didn't ask whether Will was a Mormon, but he felt their suspicion, and he wondered whether that made a difference in their willingness to help.

Will was beginning to feel that he was on a fruitless pursuit, but he knew what President Young had told him. He needed to seek the Lord's guidance, find fodder somewhere—and do it fast. Will had been praying silently all day, but now, as he left a farm, he called the other men to gather around him, and he prayed out loud. "Lord, we are on Thy mission," he said. "Thou knowest what we need. Show us which direction to take."

He ended his short prayer and looked at the other men. "Any thoughts about where we should go?" he asked.

Brother Bellows looked at the ground. "Will, no one's going to sell us the last of their feed."

"Thanks for that encouragement. Anyone else have anything to say?"

No one else spoke. Everyone knew, including Will, that Jackson was probably right. But Brigham hadn't told the others to follow the Spirit, the way he had told Will. So Will looked farther south. He saw a place where the road dropped into a little valley through some dense woods, but he saw no sign of any farms, and they didn't have more than two hours of sun left. "Let's just keep going south," he said. "Brigham had an impression that south was where we would find something."

So they set out again and crossed the next little valley and then another after that. At the crest of the next hill, the road forked. Will prayed to know what to do, but he didn't say that to the others. He told Jesse, who was sitting next to him, "This little road looks like it might be a lane leading out to someone's farm."

"Or it's an old cow trail. I think we better stay on the main road."

"You're probably right." But Will had his impression, so he shook the lines and turned the mules into the narrow lane.

He didn't explain, and Jesse didn't say a word, but Brother Pace shouted, "Hey, whar yuh goin'?"

Will decided not to answer. He was trying too hard to hear the Lord, and he didn't need other opinions right now. But after a mile or so, no farm appeared. He was about to admit his mistake when he saw the peak of a barn roof just showing above the oak woods in the distance. He was glad of that, though he had a hard time holding out much hope that the farmer would be any more cooperative than the others had been.

Will drove up to the farmhouse all the same. He got down from the wagon, walked to the house, and knocked on the front door. Will saw a woman look out through a curtain, but she didn't open the door. About then, however, a man came around the corner of the house. He looked to be about Will's age, and just as muddy. "What is it you need?" he said, not with any hostility, but with an all-business tone of voice.

"Hello there," Will said, and he stepped toward the man, shook his hand, and introduced himself. He knew he had to get off on the right foot this time. "I'm traveling with a company of emigrants heading west. We plan to settle out that way. The only trouble is, we started a little early, and there's no grass on the prairies yet. We're searching for hay or grain—or both—and we'll pay cash for it."

"Mormons, ain't yuh?"

"Well, that's what some people call us."

"And you left Illinois because no one wants yuh there, the same as here in this state."

Will nodded, didn't argue. He thought of walking away, of not wasting any more time, but as he glanced around, he noticed the good barn and the acreage of plowed ground in the valley just below the house. It was the sort of valley he had grown up in. "This is surely a nice farm you have here," he said.

"Yes, it is, and you need to get off it, just as fast as those mules will carry yuh."

"All right. That's what I'll do. Sorry to bother you." He reached to shake the man's hand again, but got no response. So he took a couple of steps away and then turned back. "I was just noticing," he said, "all that good, dark soil you've plowed. It makes me think of the farm where I grew up in England. The valley there was like this one—so green in the spring it was like a picture someone had painted. But I'd wager your soil is even better."

The man stared at Will, seeming confused. Finally, he said, "It's good land, all right."

"The thing is, in England I never could have owned land. Only the nobles and rich people have land over there. That's one of the things I liked about coming to America—I could maybe buy my own piece of land. It's pretty much the only thing I've done in my life—farming. Did you grow up on a farm yourself?"

"Of course I did."

"Where was that? Not here, I'm thinking."

"Listen, I don't have time for this. I told you to get off my land, and I want you to do it. I've heard what's going on. You people have a whole army just north of here, and you mean to build yourself a kingdom out in the West, and do the bidding of your madmen leaders. I want nothing to do with you. I want you out of here before it gets dark and you run off with some of my cattle."

"People say a lot of things about us that aren't true. Most of us in Nauvoo were farmers, like you, and a farmer doesn't steal another farmer's cattle. It's just not anything we could do. We work sunup to sundown, we raise our families, and we worship the Lord on Sunday. Take a look at me. Do you think I'm a thief?"

The man tried to hold his gaze, tried to stay as firm as he had been all along, but he finally shook his head. "No, I don't suspect you are. You may be a good man, for all I know. But you—"

"You ought to see my wife. She's a beautiful woman. She almost died crossing the ocean. She was carrying our first baby, and maybe we shouldn't have set out on a voyage like that, but we wanted to come to America. The baby—a little girl—came too early. She died about two weeks after she was born."

"There's no reason to tell me all this. Like I said—"

"My wife had to stand on the banks of the Mississippi and say good-bye forever to that little girl, who's buried on a hillside outside Nauvoo. Right now she's looking after our two little boys, and they're both sick." He hesitated, and then he added, "Do you understand what I'm trying to say? We're just people like you. Have you ever had a child die?"

The man nodded.

"Well, then, you understand. You're right that the people didn't want us in Illinois, so we left, and we had to leave too early, and now we're making our way as best we can, but our animals need feed. And the only way we can clear out—the way people want us to do—is to find enough fodder for our oxen and mules. If you have anything at all you could sell us, we would pay better than a fair price, and we'd give you hard cash for it."

The man had thrust his hands deep into his pockets. He was standing stiff, his face not seeming so harsh as before. "I think you might be a liar," he finally said. "The story you tell ain't the one we've heard around here."

"But you know better, don't you? You know what I'm telling you is the truth."

The man stared into Will's eyes. Finally, he said, "I put up a lot of hay las' year, and then I had to sell some of my cattle to buy provisions for the winter. So I have a little more hay than I need, what with the grass likely to come back soon. What would you pay me for it?"

"You tell me what you would sell it for."

"I'll sell you a wagonload for eight dollars, not a penny less."

"All right, then. That's a steep price, but we'll pay it. What about corn? Do you have any of that you could sell us?"

"I guess I could sell you a wagonload of ear corn, too."

"How much?"

The man was thinking again. And he was still looking Will in the eye. He nodded after a time, as though he had settled the matter in his own mind. "Ten dollars," he said.

"For a load of corn?"

"No. Ten for both. That's a fair price."

"Aye. It is. The Lord will bless you for this, sir."

So Will and his men loaded their wagons, and when they had finished, the man—who turned out to be named Sebert Myers—told them they could sleep in the barn. And then his wife came out and invited them into the house, where she fed them a good supper.

When Will finally wrapped himself in the quilt he had brought along and pulled some hay over himself, he was comfortable—and he was satisfied. He had listened to the Lord, and he had accomplished the mission that Brother Brigham had sent him out to do.

Jesse told him, "Will, I should na' ever question ye when yer lookin' to the Lord for guidance. You allus lead me right."

Will certainly didn't think of himself that way, but he felt sure the Lord had guided him to the right farm and told him what to say to Mr. Myers. He drifted off to sleep feeling better than he had since he and Liz had crossed the Mississippi.

And then he awakened with a start.

He didn't know if he had dreamed it, or where the idea had come from, but he suddenly knew that something was wrong. He sat up and tried to think what it was he knew. It seemed as though he had actually seen Liz holding little Daniel and crying. He listened for words, for the Lord to tell him what to do.

"What's wrong, Will?" he heard Jesse ask.

"It's Liz. Or Daniel. Or both of them. Someone's sick."

"You knew that when you left, Will."

"But something's happened."

"What do you mean?"

Will didn't answer. Before he knew he was going to do it, he was praying out loud. "Lord, not again. Please, don't take my sons. Don't take Liz."

But it sounded so weak. He remembered what Liz had once told him to do. He got to his feet and raised his arm to the square. "Elizabeth Lewis, in the name of Jesus Christ, I command you to live. Daniel Lewis, I command you to live. Jacob Lewis, I command you to live, too. Lord, touch them now. Take the fever away. Save them." He stood for a time, listened for an answer, and then he added, "Please."

· · ·

Daniel had been quivering even though the evening was not nearly so cold as the last few nights had been. Liz feared that he was chilling, and, beyond that, his cough had grown raspier. Ellen had stayed with her until quite late, but then had gone to bed with her own children in a tent just inches from Liz's. Liz liked having someone there, but it didn't really change anything. She had not been so frightened since she had lost little Mary Ann. She tucked Daniel in close to her and let Jacob snuggle up to her back. She tried not to cough but couldn't stop herself at times.

After a time, Daniel seemed to absorb her warmth and settle down. Liz told herself not to sleep, but she had slept so little lately. She didn't know she had fallen asleep until she realized, somehow, that time had passed. What she did know before she was fully conscious was that little Daniel, at her breast, was extremely hot. She grasped him and pulled him away from her, then felt his face and forehead. She had never felt such a burning fever.

"Help me, Ellen," she gasped.

"What. What is it?" Liz heard from the other tent.

"Daniel. He has a fever. A raging fever."

"Unwrap him. Give 'im air. I'll be right there." In only a few seconds, she was pushing her way through the opening in the tent. She dropped to her knees, felt for Liz, and then touched Daniel's head. "Oh, my!" she said. "I'll wet a rag."

Jacob stirred and let out a little whimper, then a cough. Liz twisted around to touch him, but Jacob wasn't hot. "It's all right, Jakey," she told him. "Go back to sleep."

In only a minute or so, Ellen was back. Liz had left Daniel's clothes on, as usual, to keep him warm, but now she pulled his shirt up and bared his chest. She felt the cold when Ellen kneeled next to Daniel and wiped the wet cloth over his head and face. Liz couldn't see her very well, but she knew that Ellen was washing it over his chest as well.

Daniel started his barking little cough again, but he didn't seem to wake, didn't cry. Liz wished that he would. She feared that he was sinking, that the fever was already taking him. She touched his face again and found it was hot as ever, even though it was wet with the cool water.

"What can we do, Ellen? What else can we do?"

"We have to cool him, that's all."

"Let me try." Liz took the cloth from Ellen, pulled Daniel's shirt over his head and off, and bathed his chest, then his neck and head and face. The cloth was cold in Liz's hand, but she didn't think his body or head had cooled at all.

But there was nothing more to do. She prayed out loud, pled with the Lord, and kept wiping him. "Danny, can you hear me? Can you talk to Mummy?" she kept asking. And then, again, "Oh, Lord, save him. Please don't take him from me. Please."

She realized that Ellen was praying too, not merely pleading, but pronouncing a kind of blessing, telling Daniel to be healed.

The two continued for a long time, but Liz could feel no change in Daniel, and she got no response from him. She remembered that terrible night on the ship when Ellen had lost her baby, and now Ellen was praying for Liz's baby with all the same love and concern.

Liz remembered what she had told Ellen then, and she told herself she would have to accept whatever came. She would have to be just as strong.

And then something changed. Liz looked around in the dark. She thought she had heard Will's voice, thought she had heard him speak gently in her ear. She didn't know what the words were, but she felt peace, calm.

Daniel began to cry. "No, Mummy. Cold, Mummy." Liz touched his head and felt the change, but she had known already. The fever was letting up.

• • •

As Will finished his command, his prayer, he dropped back to his knees and waited for some indication that his petition had reached the Lord. What he felt was peace. Maybe that only meant he had accepted the Lord's will, but he thought it meant his family was safe after all.

CHAPTER 11

It was late on Thursday evening, April 9, when Will and Jesse arrived back at their camp at Locust Creek. Will's nervousness kept mounting as he crossed the middle fork of the river and looked about for his family. It was hard to trust the inspiration he had been so sure of the day before. But then he saw Liz waving at him, and her smile was bright enough to end his worries. She told him her story first, and then he told her about the blessing he had proclaimed, standing in the hayloft.

"The Lord was with us, Will," Liz said. "He's blessed us again."

"Aye. It's what I feel too." And then he held her in his arms for a long time before he looked for the boys, who were sitting close to the fire, the evening being cold again. Jacob and Daniel, when they spotted him, ran and jumped for him, and he caught them both up in his arms. Then he sat down on a log by the fire with them. He was relieved to hear how much better they both sounded—and Liz was doing better too. Will had the feeling things would be all right now. As they bedded down in their tent that night, he prayed with his family and asked the Lord to stay the elements, to grant the refugees some days of good weather so the camp could make better progress. He went to bed feeling more optimistic than he had been in a long time.

And the next morning, another storm blew in.

Will was deflated for a time, but Liz laughed and said, "It's just a little rain. Nothing we haven't seen before."

Will smiled. "Aye. But I feel like Job. What's next? All our animals dying off?"

"We have our boys, Will. Let's not worry about a few troubles along the way."

Will nodded, and then he went to the tent, drove the stakes in deeper, and scraped a trench to divert the runoff from their bedding.

• • •

The rain did clear later in the day, but more cold came after that. Still, the entire Camp of Israel had finally gathered in one place, there by Locust Creek, and finally some warm spring days did come—before more stormy ones returned. It was not until April 16 that the camp was able to move forward again.

What Will was beginning to believe—and most of the men he talked to were of the same opinion—was that the Saints would never make it to the Rocky Mountains this year. The rains would surely let up sooner or later, but too many provisions had been used up. The animals were too worn down, and so were the people.

Will knew that Brigham and the Apostles were considering all these same matters, but so far, no announcement had been made, and Will didn't think it was his place to press his opinion. The one thing he did cherish now was the President's good opinion of him. When Will had returned from Missouri with the feed for the animals, Brother Brigham had said to him, "The Lord took you to the right place, Will. You've learned to listen to His voice."

"Sometimes I do," Will said. "I've still got a lot to learn."

Brigham nodded, spat on the ground, and wiped his mouth with his hand. He often said that he was going to quit chewing tobacco, but so far he hadn't been able to do that entirely. "Yes, yes," he said. "So do we all. I give a sermon and it sounds like I'm swinging a sledgehammer. I've never learned to move the Saints along with gentle nudges."

"That may be so," Will said, "but when we're stuck in the mud, we need a little more than urging. We need someone who's not afraid to tell us to repent. And what we appreciate most is that after you admonish us, you wade out into the mud and help us push our wagons."

Brigham wrapped his arm around Will's shoulders. "Thank you, Brother Lewis. And thank you for bringing back that hay and grain. Grass will soon be growing, but you've saved our animals for now."

A week had passed since then, and the grass *was* coming up. As the camp moved northwest toward the head of the Grand River, the grass got longer every day, and the animals were able to graze. The good weather was holding for now, and everyone seemed cheered by that. The entire camp moved along better on drying roads, and when the wagons arrived at a point that had been scouted ahead of time, it turned out to be a beautiful ridge with plenty of timber and a large, open valley. Brigham named it Garden Grove. With the hills turning green and all the trees budding out, the name seemed right.

Brigham let the Saints rest again for a couple of days, allowing all the wagons to catch up to the first company. Then, on Sunday, he spoke to the entire camp, telling the people that they would stop here for a time and plow fields and build log homes for those who would come later. Some of the camp would stay for the winter. They would cultivate the crops and welcome the Saints who would be arriving all summer and fall. He praised everyone for their perseverance, but almost in the same breath he chastised them for their wastefulness. He told them he would try to procure more food, but they would all have to be careful with what they had.

Brigham also announced that he had a new plan. Some of the emigrants would continue on and establish another way station. Others would go on farther, to an area called Council Bluffs, near the Missouri River. But then he and the Apostles would take one hundred men and cross the plains to the Rocky Mountains this summer. The chosen men would have to be young and strong, and they would have to be prepared for a hasty trek of a thousand miles. They would plant crops and begin to ready a place where the main body of the Saints could join them in the following years.

Brigham then assigned one hundred men to start splitting rails for fencing, forty-eight to fell trees and build houses, twelve to dig wells, and ten to build bridges—all to start Monday morning. Will was assigned to build houses, and he liked that. It was work he felt confident about doing.

When the meeting ended, Will was walking away with Liz and his boys when Brother Clayton stopped him. "Will, Brother Brigham wants to talk to you," he said.

So Will let Liz take the boys to their camp while he turned back to find President Young, who was talking to some of the brothers.

Will waited, and when Brigham finally had a chance, he turned to Will and asked, "What did you think of what I said today about taking a small company on ahead this season?"

"It sounded right to me. We can't keep all these women and children going on this way. They're used up. So are our teams."

"That's right. But that's not what I'm asking. When we leave for the West, I want you to go with us. I want you to serve as one of my captains. Will you do that?"

Will felt the question like a thump on his chest. He couldn't think how he could possibly leave his family now. Liz had managed to get along all right during his missions, but she had been in a warm home, with neighbors around to help her. This would mean a longer absence, and he would be leaving her in a wilderness. "Would we have time to build houses for our families first, or—"

"Probably not. But I'll assign brothers to help the women who are left behind. I don't know all the details just yet; those matters will be dealt with later. But that wasn't what I asked you. I want to know whether you'll go with me—and I don't think it's something you should have to think about."

"Aye. I *will* go with you."

"Good. That's what I thought. We'll speak more of this later."

Will nodded, and he shook Brigham's hand. But he was sick at heart. He knew Liz would accept this new hardship, as she had done before, but he also knew what it would cost her.

• • •

The good weather had seemed a little too good to be true, so Liz was not surprised when the rains returned on Monday morning. The men went about their work all the same—felled trees, split rails, and dug wells as the rain soaked their clothes. Will worked in off-and-on storms for four days, and Liz tried to dry his clothes by the fire each night—often with rain still falling. But Friday was better.

On Saturday evening, May 2, Liz was sitting with some of the sisters from her company at the crest of the hill, all of them gathered around a campfire. No one was crowding the fire the way they had back at Sugar Creek, and no one was covered in cloaks to protect against the wind and rain. It was, in fact, a lovely evening. It was a little cool still, but clear, and all the evening sounds of spring were coming on: crickets and night birds and breezes in the trees.

The children were calling back and forth, playing Old Cat with a stick and a ball of rolled-up cloth on the broad meadow just down the hill from where the women were sitting. The men were walking over the land in little groups. Liz knew they were judging the moisture in the soil, deciding which areas could be plowed first—and probably guessing when they might be able to begin. Liz was reminded of so many other springs when that had been Will's great concern.

The women had become less than enthusiastic about this place when the men kept finding nests of rattlesnakes as they cut timber. Several horses—and one boy—had been bitten. But the beauty and peace of Garden Grove were enough to satisfy most hearts, and above all, the people needed these good days to rest.

Since leaving Nauvoo, one thing had become obvious to Liz. The leaders of the Church had extended plural marriage to a few more of the men, and the fact of their living with more than one wife was no longer kept secret out here on the trail. The principle was not preached or even acknowledged, but the life was obvious. The Young family and the Kimball and Taylor families had been traveling together during the crossing of Iowa, and such families were clearly made up of several wives and many children. They made up whole companies, with their extended relatives, but as far as Liz knew, the men in their own company each had only one wife.

Margaret Johns was sitting next to Liz. "Can you get the mud out of your children's clothing?" she asked.

"No. Nor my dresses, either, or Will's trousers. I've boiled them time and again, and used soap. The mud is gone, I suppose, but the color of it is left behind."

Sister Johns had taken off her bonnet, and Liz could see her face better than she could most days. Margaret had been a plump little woman at one time, but her face was thin now, and there was weariness in her eyes. "My boy Evan fell 'n hit his head on a wagon wheel.

He bled like a stuck pig. That's yet another stain that's in his shirt to stay. Can we get any material for sewing out here?"

"Not likely," Sister Bellows said. "If we have anythin' left ta bargain with, it has to go for food."

Another woman from the company, Sister Gifford, said, "Brigham tells us to help the poor, an' I want to say, 'An' who am I? If I ain't poor, who is?'"

"We're all poor," Liz said. "So we all have to make the best of things."

But Liz had never said those words to herself before. She had known that she and Will had struggled to get by during these years in America, but she had never really thought of herself as poor. She had merely trusted that she and Will would prosper in time. But she wondered now. Was there any way to live well out in the West? She knew she would never leave the Saints the way the Winthrops had done, but she wondered what a life of poverty would do to her, and to Will and her boys. She knew how tired she had been until these easier days had finally come; it was difficult to imagine that she would ever do anything but work hard all her life. She could do that, she supposed, but when she thought of all the miles still ahead, she wondered whether there would be anything left of her, and she wondered how she and Will could find the strength to start over again.

But it never helped to think of the long road ahead. She had to concentrate on this day, even this hour. Her life in England, her chatty days with her sister—all that seemed a distant world now. What she hoped was that this effort would matter someday—to her boys, to whatever other children would come, and to the generations that would follow.

There were a dozen or so women around the fire. Most of them were mending clothes, using the last light to see their stitches. When the conversation quieted for a time, Sister Lamborn, a woman

Liz had known in England, began to sing an old hymn that Liz remembered:

> *Prayer is the soul's sincere desire,*
> *Uttered or unexpressed;*
> *The motion of a hidden fire*
> *That trembles in the breast.*

Sister Lamborn had a wonderful voice, full and mellow, and she sang with a pure pitch and a pure heart. Liz had never expressed such "sincere desire" in her prayers as she had these last two months, so the words of the song sounded right to her. She could see that they touched all the sisters. A calm seemed to settle over the entire valley.

"I'm sorry," Sister Lamborn said. "I thought of the motion of the fire, and those words came back to me, but I don't remember the other verses."

But Liz remembered. She continued the hymn, and everyone soon followed:

> *Prayer is the burden of a sigh,*
> *The falling of a tear,*
> *The upward glancing of an eye*
> *When none but God is near.*

By the time the women had finished the second verse, more people, mostly women, were gathering from other campfires. They joined in on the third verse:

> *Prayer is the simplest form of speech*
> *That infant lips can try;*
> *Prayer, the sublimest strains that reach*
> *The Majesty on high.*

Those were the only verses Liz remembered well, so she stopped and let the quiet take over. She knew that everyone must feel what she was feeling. They had prayed so hard to survive the rain and the mud, and the Lord had been there with them. Their test was anything but over, but they knew they had continued on when they were tempted to give up. Liz couldn't hold her tears back, and she saw that the other sisters were wiping their eyes too.

And then Liz heard a man's voice—a voice she knew. "Sisters, I've written a new hymn. I wrote it back when we were camped on Locust Creek. It's called, 'All Is well.' If I may, I'd like to teach it to you."

"Oh, yes, please do," Sister Lamborn said.

It was William Clayton who stepped inside the circle and stood by the fire. "Those from England will know the tune. Maybe you all will. It's one that's often sung in the public houses." He began to hum the melody, and most everyone picked it up immediately. "Yes, you know it," he said. "Now let me say the words, and you sing it to that tune."

Brother Clayton nodded to Liz when he saw her. She thought he seemed a little self-conscious in front of so many women, but he recited the first line, and everyone sang it back to him: "Come, come, ye Saints, no toil nor labor fear."

He continued to announce the lyrics, one line at a time, as the women sang the entire verse.

> *But with joy wend your way.*
> *Though hard to you this journey may appear,*
> *Grace shall be as your day.*
> *'Tis better far for us to strive*
> *Our useless cares from us to drive;*
> *Do this, and joy your hearts will swell—*
> *All is well! All is well!*

Never had Liz heard a hymn that applied so directly to her—
and to all the sisters around her. They had passed through so much
"toil" and "labor," but she told herself it didn't matter. Those were
"useless cares." Everything really was all right.

The next two verses emphasized the idea: they need not mind
the hardships they were facing; they would build a better place "far
away in the West, Where none shall come to hurt or make afraid."
Liz thought of George Samples, who had threatened her and her
children. She felt certain she would not have to fear such men again.

But the final verse touched something deep in everyone:

> *And should we die before our journey's through,*
> *Happy day! All is well!*
> *We then are free from toil and sorrow, too;*
> *With the just we shall dwell!*
> *But if our lives are spared again*
> *To see the Saints their rest obtain,*
> *Oh, how we'll make this chorus swell—*
> *All is well! All is well!*

Liz thought of people in their company who had lost their loved
ones—especially babies. She understood something that she hadn't
known before her baby daughter had died. Peace could come to a
mother after a child was lost. She had received that peace. But she
also knew that discouragement could not be thrust aside by a few
pretty words. She knew William Clayton. He sometimes became
resentful of all that Church leaders asked of him. She had heard
him complain about his treatment. There were clearly times when it
didn't help him much to claim that his troubles were actually a blessing. But the hymn called upon the Saints—and Brother Clayton—
to take courage, to think of their larger purpose and not focus so

much on current difficulties. On this mild night, Liz could do that. She hoped she could when harder days came again.

· · ·

On Sunday, Brother Brigham preached to the camp again. He asked the Saints to bear one another's burdens, but then he chastised some who were taking their rest in Garden Grove and not working as hard as others. He organized a stake presidency for the settlement, and then he announced to the camp that most of them would move ahead that week. They would establish another way station nearer to the Missouri River—another place to plant crops for the members who would follow.

An advance group moved out the next morning, and all the other companies, including Will's company of ten, followed on Wednesday. But just as everyone was setting up camp in a hickory grove that night, a wild storm struck, with thunder like cannon fire and rain so hard that it was difficult to stand up in it. Everything was soaked through, and that meant another night in wet clothes and wet bedding. In the morning, almost everyone was searching for animals that had been scattered by the angry storm.

One more day was lost as the companies retrieved teams and waited for roads to dry. Will tried to remember the words to Brother Clayton's hymn, but he found himself thinking that God had chosen never to let up on this company, to batter them over and over. Still, better weather followed again, and his resentment faded one more time. The Saints reached the new campsite in four more days. Parley Pratt had been in the advance company, and he had given the place a name already: Mount Pisgah. Brother Parley had thought of Moses, standing on that mountain, looking out across the promised land. The settlement was to be established on a ridge overlooking a large valley, even more extensive than the one at Garden Grove.

Will and the other men again felled trees, put up shelters with dirt floors, split rails for fences, and began to plow the land. But the rains soon returned, and plowing was once again delayed. Creeks ran so high that much of the men's time was occupied with bridge building. Still, it was a beautiful place, and at the end of two weeks Will had moved his family into a log cabin he had helped to build. He thought he might like to stay here for the winter. But Brigham asked him and his party to move on to the Missouri River. So, once again, they broke camp and headed farther west.

The wagons rolled down through a Pottawatomie Indian village and then on to Mosquito Creek, near the Missouri River. Brigham told his captains that here on the Missouri, a major camp would be established, and most of the Saints would winter here—but he didn't know exactly where. He would have to negotiate with Indian agents. So, for now, Brigham moved on ahead to a place called Council Point, leaving most of the companies at Mosquito Creek.

Will walked over some of the land, looked out on the Missouri, and was eager to get another house built—a more permanent one this time—so his family would be warm this winter. If he had to leave, he wanted Liz and the boys to have a safe, warm house to live in. But time kept going by, and Brigham was still telling men to wait, not to establish any settlements until the Saints had permission to do so.

Will was assigned to work with a crew of men who were building a flatboat that could be used to ferry people and wagons across the river. Will knew nothing about boat building, but he could fell trees, so he set about that work again. And once the lumber for the ferry had been supplied, he worked with a gang of men who were splitting rails. Each night, after Will returned to his camp—the light lingering until late this time of year—he would fell a nearby tree and cut it to length. He didn't know where he could build his cabin, but at least he wanted to have logs ready so that he could put something up quickly if Brigham called for him to start west.

• • •

Will had finished his breakfast on June 30 and was sharpening his axe before heading to the woods when he saw some American soldiers in blue tunics riding toward his camp. There was an officer in the lead, with five soldiers and a wagon following behind. This worried Will. Word had spread through the camps that the United States government might be sending troops to stop the Saints from continuing west, or to drive them off Indian lands. These men might be the ones sent to warn the Saints, and a company of dragoons might well be coming behind them.

The soldiers kept riding toward him, and Will held his ground. They finally halted their horses a few paces off, and the officer dismounted, handed his reins to one of the soldiers, and walked toward Will. He was a round little man, anything but stately, but he said, "Hello there," in a friendly voice. "Do you know where I can find Mr. Young?"

"Why do you ask?" Will said, not about to give such information until he knew a little better how it would be used.

"I'm Captain James Allen," the officer said. He pulled off his leather glove and held out his hand.

"Will Lewis."

The two shook hands. "Mr. Lewis, I've ridden here from the settlement you call Mount Pisgah. I met with some of your leaders there and made an offer that will be good for your people. But I was told by Mr. Kimball that I must speak to Mr. Young. I need his support before my proposal can be seriously entertained."

"What sort of proposal?"

"I should talk to Mr. Young about it first. Can you tell me where to find him?"

"I'm one of his captains. You can tell me, and I'll carry the word to him."

Captain Allen smiled. "I don't want to repeat myself too many times. I'm hoping Mr. Young will call all you men together, and I can explain the . . . opportunity . . . just once. The truth is, I think he'll be very pleased to know I'm here."

The captain seemed good-natured, but Will was skeptical. "I'm not *exactly* certain where you'll find him."

Captain Allen laughed. "You're not going to tell me until I explain the offer, are you?"

"Let's say, that's your only hope. But I might not tell you even *after* you explain."

"All right, then. I'll see if I can't change your mind." He pulled his other glove off, tucked the pair under one arm, and then he took his hat off. The morning was getting warm already. "Mr. Lewis, you may not be aware of it, but our country is now at war with Mexico. There's a dispute over the boundary with Texas, and war has been declared. We're recruiting a battalion of soldiers—five companies of a hundred men each—to join General Stephen W. Kearny's Army of the West and march to Santa Fe and then on to Upper California. You're on your way there anyway, but we'll pay you and feed you, and that will help some of you reach your destination."

Will shook his head and laughed. "So you want us to fight, maybe die, for a country that refused to protect us when mobs killed our people and burned our homes. Sounds like a fine offer, indeed."

"I know how you feel about that. The men at Mount Pisgah—"

"You might as well know right now, there's not one man here who will take any interest in your offer. They might prefer to fight for Mexico."

"But this is an attempt to come to your aid. A Mr. Little, a relative of Mr. Young, negotiated with President Polk, and this opportunity came as a result of that."

"I'm sorry, sir, but I have a hard time accepting that. We're leaving the United States, in case you haven't noticed, and we're doing that because our rights were stolen from us."

Surprisingly, Allen was smiling again. "I believe Brigham Young will have a different opinion. May I know where he is now?"

Will thought for a time and then decided on a compromise. "Why don't you speak to John Taylor? He's my leader, and he's camped nearby." Will pointed a little farther up Mosquito Creek. "Ride up to those tents you see grouped together. His is the largest one."

"Thank you, Mr. Lewis." Captain Allen reached his hand out to Will again. "When your leaders call for volunteers, I hope you'll join our force. You look like a man who could throw an ox on his shoulder and walk a mile, and you sound like a man who is resolute in his beliefs. You'll want to be with us—and help your people."

But Will knew something Allen didn't know: John Taylor was about as angry with the United States as any of the Saints were. He would tell these soldiers to recruit the devil and his angels—and where he would have to go to find them. "I think I'll look after my wife and children for now," Will said. "We don't have so much as a shelter to sleep in."

"I don't blame you for wanting to do something about that. But we'll talk again."

Captain Allen walked back to his horse, and he rode away with his soldiers. Will laughed at the idea that he would sell John Taylor or Brigham Young on his proposal. But it didn't matter anyway. No matter what anyone else thought, Will would never consider leaving his family to go off to war—not for the country that had turned its back on the Saints.

CHAPTER 12

Liz had been getting her boys up for the day, helping them put on their boots, when she had heard men's voices and looked out to see who was speaking. She had seen six men, all American soldiers, and she picked up a little of what one of them was saying— something about fighting a war in Mexico. She heard Will say that he was not about to go off and fight Mexicans, but she couldn't imagine why anyone would think to ask him such a thing. She got down from the wagon and then helped Jacob and Daniel down. "What did those soldiers want?" she asked Will.

Liz was on her way to the fire circle, where coals remained from the night before. She hoped she could add some kindling and stir the coals enough to get the fire going again.

Will sounded angry when he said, "They think our men should go off and fight for the United States."

She stopped and looked back. "Fight over what?"

"It's some sort of border dispute."

"Will anyone go?"

"No. Of course not. They say that Brigham will want us to join

155

their army, but that's a lie if I ever heard one. We're not about to leave our families to bother about a line someone's drawn in the dirt hundreds of miles from here."

"Will, you can't do it, even if Brigham does ask you."

"I know that. But don't worry. Brigham won't agree to such a thing. And from what I'm hearing, he's given up the idea of anyone going west this season. It looks to me like I'll be here with you this winter."

But Liz wondered. It had been the way of things since she and Will had come to Zion. Every time life settled down a little, the Church asked him to leave. She had always accepted that. She had wanted him to serve the Lord even when it was difficult. But war was different. She wouldn't let Will go off and get himself killed in a war with Mexico.

• • •

A day passed, and Will heard nothing more from Captain Allen. On the following morning, he ate his breakfast and then sat down once again to sharpen his axe. He could tell that another hot day was ahead. The air already felt like steam. Will had also decided that Mosquito Creek was named correctly. The night had been full of mosquitoes. Jacob and Daniel had apparently kicked off their bedding and gotten themselves chewed up. They had welts on their arms and faces, and both were scratching themselves. Daniel had scratched so hard that he had opened a sore on his face.

Will set his axe down and walked over to the boys. He picked up Daniel and asked him, "Did the mosquitoes bite you?"

Daniel nodded, still scratching.

Jacob said, "Me too, Daddy."

"I know. They got all of us," Will said. "Come with me. I'll fix it so you don't itch so bad."

But Liz said, "Oh, Will, don't get them all covered with mud."

"It helps, Liz. I swear it does."

She laughed. "Well, then, bring some back for me," she said. "I'm bitten on this whole side of my neck—even in my hair."

It bothered Will to see the red marks on Liz. After all they had been through, it seemed sad that one more little plague had to fall upon them.

"We need to get a cabin built," Will said. "I wish Brigham would tell us where we're going to settle."

What Will hoped was that he could build a good little house here, with a decent fireplace that drew well, and they could settle in for the winter. Some talked of Indian trouble, but the Indians he had seen were mostly beggars, not warriors. A winter spent inside, out of the weather, was what he and Liz—really, all the Saints—needed.

Will thought of sleeping in a bed at night, keeping Liz and the boys safe and warm, having time to read the Book of Mormon each day, and having Liz in his arms at night, just the two of them. For four months now they had been crowded up with their little boys in the wagon, usually cold, often wet, and always facing a hard day ahead. Life simply had to offer some comfort sooner or later.

Will took the boys down to the creek and daubed mud on their mosquito bites. It made a mess of their faces, but it cooled the itch for a moment, and, more than anything, it kept them from scratching. "Do I look funny, Daddy?" Jacob asked. "Daniel looks like a dog. He has spots."

"Aye. You're two fine-looking puppies. Let's hear you bark."

Jacob barked, and then Daniel did, and then they ran back to the camp, barking all the way. Jacob told Liz that they were dogs, and they barked at her. Will followed behind with a handful of mud. "Should I put some on you?" he asked.

"Does it really help?" she asked.

"Look at the boys. They're cured."

"Put a little on me, then." She pulled her collar back. Today would be a day for a bonnet, with the sun so bright, but she hadn't put hers on yet.

"I'll tell you what helps the most," Will said, and he bent and kissed her neck.

"Oh, that's a nice treatment," she said, teasing him with a smile. "But I think mud might do me more good at the moment."

He daubed the mud on her neck and cheek. He was still smoothing it out when he heard a wagon coming up the road. "Oh, my," Liz said, and she hurried away. Will knew she would rather wash—and feel the itch—than be seen with mud on her face.

Will could soon see that it was Brigham Young approaching, riding in a carriage and joined by several men on horseback. Some of the Twelve were among the riders—Wilford Woodruff and Heber Kimball. But so was Captain Allen.

Brigham stopped his carriage and called out to Will, "Where's your company?"

"All camped nearby, here along the creek," Will called back.

"The men are all called to meet at ten thirty. Have them assemble at John Taylor's camp, there by the bridge."

Will knew in an instant what this was, and he didn't like it. But he walked around to each of the wagons and told the men to remain in camp this morning, and then to meet at the Taylor camp at ten thirty.

But it was Liz he had the hardest time telling. "They're going to ask you to join the army," she said. "Brigham has agreed to it, for some reason."

"It could be. But I won't be pushed into it. You don't have to worry about that."

She didn't say what she was thinking, but he saw the doubt in her eyes, even sadness, and he knew she was expecting the worst.

Will and Jesse and some of the other men walked to the Taylor camp a little before the appointed time. Men from the other camps along Mosquito Creek were beginning to assemble. The Church leaders were all inside Brother Taylor's tent, and Captain Allen was apparently with them. When they came out, Brigham took Captain Allen around and introduced him to the men. Will shook his hand again and said, with anything but warmth in his voice, "Aye, I met him yesterday."

Captain Allen chuckled. "Mr. Lewis told me to ride away and not look back," he said. "He wants nothing to do with our war."

Will nodded his agreement, but he glanced at Brigham, who smiled a little and said, "I understand that, Will, but hear us out before you make up your mind."

Will felt sick. But he knew just as surely as he had the day before that he would *not* join the army.

The men kept gathering, dozens of them. Will saw the confusion in their eyes when they spotted Captain Allen. One man whispered, "Is he here to stop us from going west?"

"No. It's something else," Will said, but he wasn't about to say anything more. He would let Brother Brigham do that.

President Young finally stepped up on the bed of a wagon that was stopped close to Brother Taylor's tent. "Boys," he said, "I want to give over some time to Captain Allen. And I want you to listen with an open mind to the offer he's bringing to us." Will heard that voice of authority that all the men knew so well. Brigham let his gaze pass around the crowd from one set of eyes to another. "Last year I asked Jesse Little, president of the Eastern States Mission, to speak with President Polk and see if we couldn't get some help moving west. I was willing to set up trail stations on the way to Oregon—for all the people migrating out that way—or carry mail, or do whatever was needed. I knew we were going to have to leave Nauvoo, and I knew we were awful short on cash and provisions for such a hard trek. President Polk has responded with a good offer. Captain Allen will tell you about it."

So that was it. The Saints needed money. Well, fine. Maybe some of the young men—especially the unmarried ones—could go. But Will would not.

Allen was so much shorter than Brigham that he struggled to look dignified as he clambered up on the wagon. But he smiled at the men and said, "I'm happy to have a chance to speak with you." There was something good-natured in his voice and manner.

What Captain Allen described was what he had told Will the day before—with more detail. The men would be paid regular army pay, and they could send the money back to their families and Church leaders. They would be leaving in ten days, and if he couldn't get five hundred volunteers, he didn't want any.

Brigham Young thanked Captain Allen, and then he said, "Brethren, here's what it comes down to. The Lord is in this. It may not sound like anything you want to do—and I don't blame you for that—but I tell you, it's an answer to my prayers.

"The government will not only pay you a monthly paycheck for your march, but each volunteer will receive forty-two dollars. That's to fit you up with a uniform, but the fact is, you don't need a uniform. Anything you do need—your musket and ammunition, canteens, and such—will all be furnished by the army. The money you receive will help your families get fit out for the long migration beyond the Rocky Mountains. And if we pool the money—more than twenty thousand dollars—and share it all around, all the Saints will have adequate supplies and you won't have to worry about finding a way to feed your families. What's more, the poor and elderly will be looked after."

"Where's this war going to be fought?" one of the brothers asked.

"It may be fought in Texas or in Mexico. But that will not be your concern. You will march to Upper California and all the way to the West Coast, where Mexico has few citizens and is not likely to put up much of a fight."

"What do you mean, 'march'?" Will asked, and his voice made it clear how skeptical he was.

"You would be infantry soldiers, not dragoons," Allen said.

"In other words, this is all on foot," Will said.

"That must be two thousand miles!" someone in the back of the crowd said.

"Yes. Around that," Captain Allen said. "But it's where you're going anyway—or at least close to it."

Before Will had left Nauvoo, he had studied a map of the continent, and he remembered that the Mexican territories of New Mexico and Upper California—all of the West, except for the Oregon country—were mostly made up of deserts. He would have to be a fool to march out there for forty-two dollars and a few dollars a month for pay.

"You're asking the wrong questions," Brother Brigham said. He had spoken softly before, but now his voice took on some power. "Now, listen to me." He drew in some breath, and his chest expanded. "We asked for this, and God has sent the opportunity to us. We need this cash, and we need to demonstrate our loyalty to the United States of America. We—"

"*Loyalty?*" someone said. "I've heard you say it yourself, President Young—our government turned its back on us."

"Now, wait just a minute. What was done to us was done by mobs. But now President Polk wants to make up for some of that. If we embrace this offer, we will have the United States to back us as we move west."

President Young was singing a different tune from the one Will had heard before. But Brigham was surely aware that turning the government down at this point would seem like disloyalty, and the Saints would be labeled enemies. Brigham was wise about such political matters, but that didn't change Will's mind about his own responsibility. Others could go if they wanted, but Will would not.

"Brethren," Brigham said again, "I just told you that the Lord wants us to fulfill this call, and I promise you, if you turn your back on it, you'll regret it all the days of your life. I've talked at length with Captain Allen. He'll be Colonel Allen as soon as this battalion is filled out, and he'll be your leader. He's promised me that you'll be treated well, and I believe him. A few of the officers at the top will be experienced men, regular army, but many of the officers will be appointed from your ranks."

No one spoke. Will felt duly chastened, but he knew he would have to walk back to his wagon and face Liz. He was absolutely not going to tell her that he was leaving her here by the Missouri, almost out of food, and without so much as a roof over her head.

"How long would we be gone?" Jesse asked.

"You would sign up for one year," Allen answered.

"Yes," Brigham said, "but I promise you this. We'll bring your families with us next year, and we'll look after them while you're gone."

Will knew there were many more questions, but no one asked them. He could see the worry in all the faces, not the enthusiasm Brigham was hoping for.

"It's a simple matter," Brigham said. "The Lord has asked you to serve his people—*save* his people. I won't apologize for Him. We must *not* turn our backs on the Lord. Five hundred men will go. I don't know who they are yet, but I can tell you that if you stand here and worry about every detail, and refuse to enlist, you'll be taking the first step to apostasy."

President Young let that sink in, and then he said, "Let me say this another way. The day will come, many generations from now, when the Latter-day Saint people will honor your names, and they'll say, 'It was our grandfather who accepted the call to serve at a time when it was almost impossible to do so—and he saved our Church.'" He paused and seemed to look directly at Will. "I've asked some of you to leave your families and go west with me in our pioneer company. But I release you from that now. This is more important."

Will looked down at the ground. He tried to understand what he was feeling. It was shame—just what Brigham intended—but there was also some lingering anger. He didn't want to be pushed into this.

Someone else asked the question Will had been wondering about. "Will there be time to get houses built for our families—to get them inside for the winter?"

"No," Brigham said. "We have no permission to settle on this Indian land so far. But that's part of why we have to raise this army. Captain Allen has promised us that if we get our five hundred volunteers, he'll see to it that the government grants us permission to set up camps on both sides of the Missouri."

A man from Heber Kimball's camp—an Englishman—said, "Brother Brigham, my wife is sick. So are my children. As far as that goes, so am I—and so are lots of others in our camp. How much more can the Lord ask of us?"

"I know what you're saying, Brother Miller. It's something I've thought about all night. But I want you to know, I left my wife when she was deathly ill, and I crossed an ocean to *your* island. Had I—and the other Apostles, who were just as sick as I was—not accepted that call, however much we feared to respond to it, not one of you English Saints would be in the Church today. The Lord asks hard things sometimes, but when you answer His call, He blesses you. That's all I can tell you."

"I'll go," one of the men said, and then three more.

Will's anger was gone, but his frustration was mounting. He would probably have to do this, and the idea sickened him. He didn't look at Brigham, didn't speak. He told himself he would have to talk to Liz. He would only go if she felt he should—but he hoped she wouldn't.

"How many more are willing to sign up?" Brigham asked.

Will glanced to see a few hands go up, but not many.

"Brethren, you'll sit in this camp, ashamed of yourselves all winter, if you refuse to accept this call."

"Give us a little time to think on it," Brother Miller said. "And time to talk it over with our families."

"Brethren, it's not thought, and it's not talk, that is needed. It's faith. It's humility. And it's courage. Now let me see how many hands will go up—without another moment's thought."

More hands did go up—but not half. Will was relieved he was not the only one holding out.

"All right. Those who are willing, step up here and we'll write down your names. We're going on to Mount Pisgah, and we'll see how many true Saints reside there. We'll give you your time to *think* and *waver* and feel sorry for yourselves. But be careful. I wouldn't want to be in your shoes if you deny the Lord."

It was a powerful argument, but to Will, it sounded too much as though it came from Brigham, not from the Lord. Brigham could be a hard man, and Will came close to telling him so. He said nothing, though, and he told himself the Lord would not punish him for thinking things over, for talking to Liz, for trying to get his own answer as to whether the Lord was "in it."

• • •

Liz had walked with her boys to the Taylor camp, just as many of the women had done. She had stayed back where Will couldn't see her, but she had heard every word of what President Young had said, and she was furious. She was at least as mad at God as she was at Brigham, but the truth was, she didn't like Brigham Young very much right now, and she didn't like the way he had used God to make the men feel guilty.

She walked back to their own wagon ahead of Will and waited for him there. As he approached, she could see in his eyes what he was feeling. He had dared to defy Brigham just a little, but now he was contrite, and he was coming to tell her that he had to join the army.

"No!" Liz said when Will was still several strides away. "When the Lord asked you to go preach the gospel, I told you to go—and I did my best to get by without you. But I don't believe God wants you to shoot Mexicans—or get shot by them."

"It's not the war that matters, Liz. It's—"

"It *is* the war. It's America grasping for land. Don't ask me to support you in something like that. God doesn't hate the Mexicans, and he doesn't sanction all this fighting over *dirt*. It's always the same with men. They have to expand their borders, conquer weaker people—make themselves more important. That's why Brigham tried to make you think you would be a hero."

Will didn't answer. But she knew that he had changed his mind, and in the end, all her anger would mean nothing. He would enlist, and he would leave her. "What did you tell me this morning, Will? You said you wouldn't go. Absolutely wouldn't. You said you owed nothing to the government."

"It's not that, Liz. You know it isn't. The Saints need the money. Brigham said the Lord had opened the way and we couldn't turn it down."

"Forty-two dollars? You want to throw your life away for forty-two dollars?"

"It's forty-two multiplied by five hundred, Liz. It will feed a lot of people, buy teams and wagons. It's what we need right now."

"We have teams."

"I wouldn't do it for us. If I went, I would do it for everyone. Brother Brigham is our leader, Liz, and you heard what he said. If I refuse, I'm turning my back on all these people who don't have enough food to make it through the winter. How will I feel if five hundred men walk away and I stay behind? I'll be ashamed of myself."

"And what do I do with these two boys? Where will we sleep? How will I feed them?"

Jacob and Daniel were clinging to Liz, each having taken hold of one of her legs. She looked down at them, and she saw how frightened they were—not because of the war or Will leaving. They were frightened because she was raising her voice, sounding angry with their father, and they had never heard anything quite like that before. She cupped her hands against their cheeks and pulled them closer to her. "Will, I'm sorry. I don't mean to sound this way. But nothing about this feels right. I don't know how we'll get by this winter. I don't know—"

"Brigham will assign someone to look after you. Other men will rally around you, build you a house, and make sure you have food."

"What men, Will? If five hundred leave—five hundred of the young and strong—who will be left? Old men and sick men, that's who. Brigham told us in Sugar Creek that the Lord would be with us as we traveled, and all we've seen from the Lord so far is rain and mud and misery. Brigham can promise all he wants, but he can't take away the hardship we'll face if you leave."

"Liz, Brother Brigham says hard things sometimes, but he's true to the Lord, and when it comes to getting this people as far as we've come, I suspect he's been better at it than Joseph ever would have been."

Liz knew all that, had said it herself. But she wasn't ready to let go of her anger. "I'm not so terrible as Brigham says I am. I'm tired of him telling us how sinful and worthless we are. You know what he says when he preaches to us."

"He only means the ones who—"

"Never mind, Will. There's no use talking. I can hear it in your voice—in everything you say. You aren't going to listen to me. You're going to leave us."

"I don't know that yet, Liz. I really don't. I'm just trying to think how I'd feel if I didn't go."

"You know what men are? You're little boys. That's all you are. You can't let anyone else be stronger or braver or . . ." And then she broke down and cried. She even let Will take her in his arms. And she told him the rest. "Will, I'm expecting another baby. I'm sure I am."

He took hold of her shoulders and held her away from him, and he looked into her eyes. "I'll stay, then. I can't leave you now."

"No, you won't stay. You'll go. You know you will."

He didn't disagree this time, and she knew for certain what he would do. But she also saw in his eyes how sorry he was—how much he hated that he had to do this.

• • •

The next week was busy. Will did everything he could to get his wagon repaired, to buy flour and corn and meat, to fell more trees and begin to notch the logs. He felt lucky that he still had a few dollars that he could use to set things right, as much as possible. What broke his heart was that he couldn't start building a house. He wouldn't feel quite so bad if he could just get his family inside before he left. But he talked to Brother Pendleton, who had been assigned as bishop to look after the women in his company. "I've cut some logs, and I've notched some of them. I'll fell more trees if I get the time. All you need to do is notch the rest and assemble them. Will you promise me to do that?"

"Of course."

"The summer won't be so bad, sleeping in the wagon—or in a tent—but you must get her inside before the cold sets in."

"I know. I won't let you down."

But Will wondered. The man looked more like a bookkeeper than a builder. He was small and delicate, and even when he had promised Will, he had never really looked him in the eye.

Jesse had gone through all the same conversations with Ellen, but he had also agreed to go, and he and Will were both listed as members of B Company. In the next two weeks, four companies were completed, but E Company was very slow to fill. By the time Brigham and the other leaders returned from Mount Pisgah, and then talked hard again with the men around Council Bluffs, most of the young, able-bodied men had enlisted. There were fewer and fewer left who would even be capable of making the march. Many a man had taken Will's attitude and vowed not to fight for the United States, but most of those gave way to Brigham's arguments. Some of the last one hundred came from those just arriving from their trek across Iowa; others were the ones who had to be pressured the most. But there were also those who were sick, or who saw their families as being so destitute that they simply couldn't leave them. In the end, most of the final hundred were enlisted, but age limits had had to be extended, with boys and older men signing up, and even some who were sick and just hoped they would recover in time.

A young man named Thomas Kane had arrived from the East. He was not a Church member but a friend to the Mormons who, as it turned out, had helped Jesse Little negotiate the deal with the government. He was a gentleman, and well educated. Above all, he was confident that the Saints would benefit from gaining the support of

President Polk. He was also one more voice in the recruiting as it became ever more intense.

A day was finally set for the men to follow Captain Allen and begin the march.

The night before the departure, an evening of dancing was held. Pitt's Band played, and people tromped out their quadrilles in the dust and dirt along the banks of the Missouri under a makeshift bowery. Brigham gave a grand speech, thanking the men and calling them heroes. He even promised that no one would die from enemy fire if they obeyed the commandments and conducted themselves as true Saints. Will felt a little better after that.

But the next morning he had to say good-bye.

He held Liz in his arms. She and the boys were crying, and Will cried too. He hadn't sobbed so openly since he was a boy. He was scared for her, scared for his children—for his boys, but also for the baby who would come while he was gone. He was scared he would never see any of them again. He knew how many people had died since the Saints had left Nauvoo, and surely, in a trek this long, others would die along the way, whether fired on by enemies or not.

A year. How could he leave Liz for a year? He knew that missionaries had gone much longer, and he didn't want to pity himself. But this was different. If he had been going to gather souls, he could see the infinite worth in that, but this was for the money. However much he might be helping the Saints, he still didn't picture himself as doing anything truly noble.

"I won't cry the whole time, Will," Liz was saying. "I promise you, I won't. I'm sorry for all the things I said to you. I'm proud that you're willing to go—and I'll be as brave as you."

But Will couldn't say a word. He didn't want to let her out of his arms. He had lain awake all night, holding her, asking himself whether he weren't a fool to take the chance that he would never see her again.

CHAPTER 13

One morning in February Jeff told Abby that he and Malcolm had to make a run to Quincy that evening to pick up some cabinet hardware and some lighting fixtures for a job they were trying to get finished.

"Couldn't Kayla and I go with you?" Abby asked.

"I thought about that, but we can't get all the kids in one car, and I hate to drive both cars all the way down there."

"What if I find a babysitter? You guys never take us out anymore."

"Well, we—"

"We could stop and eat at Steak 'n Shake."

"Hey, now you're talking my language." Jeff and Malcolm both loved the big hamburgers and milk shakes at Steak 'n Shake.

So Abby found a sister in the ward who would take all the kids, and soon after Jeff came home from Fort Madison that day, they all set out for Quincy. For Jeff, it was a great evening away from his moonlighting job and a nice chance to talk to his friends. What was beginning to bother him was that the weeks kept going by without his seeing any possible way to stop working both jobs. Malcolm really needed his help with all the work they had taken on, but Abby hadn't found any prospects for a job that offered benefits.

Life seemed to be on hold right now, all their big plans delayed, and besides that, Jeff truly wasn't putting enough time into the class he was taking this semester. He was taking another course with the same professor, but his first paper had in reality been a first draft, and Dr. Woodbury had called him out on it. He had written at the bottom of the paper that the writing was sloppy and the thinking not thoroughly developed. Jeff hated more than anything to do less than his best at something as important to him as this class was, but he had no idea how to squeeze more time out of his schedule.

Jeff and Malcolm had also been feeling as though they were letting their assignment with the elders quorum slide. They tried to do as much as they could on Sundays. They visited people they were worried about, did interviews with their elders, and got to their meetings. But that meant little time at home on the one day they had away from work, and it also meant that they weren't helping as many people as they had at first. Jeff was worried that they had been doing too much of that kind of thing themselves anyway, and needed to involve all the elders more, but the truth was, most of the men in the ward had lives entirely too much like Jeff's and Malcolm's.

But Jeff didn't want to think about all that during their "date" to Lowe's, the home improvement store. He really needed to have a few hours when he wasn't feeling either guilty or overwhelmed. He drove down the river to Hamilton but decided to take the long way, through Warsaw. "I want to show you something," he told Abby. "Malcolm and Kayla have probably already seen it."

Warsaw was a pretty little town, but the downtown area had failed to compete with all the big-box stores on the Iowa side of the river. It looked rather sad, with lots of storefronts boarded up. In the middle of a block, Jeff pulled the car over to the curb and pointed across the street. "See that store that's caving in over there? Look what the printing on the window says."

"Warsaw Signal," Abby read out loud. She was sitting in the back, behind Jeff, and Malcolm was sitting up front.

"Do you all know what that is?"

"That's the paper Thomas Sharp owned," Malcolm said. "He's the one who got the people all riled up against Joseph Smith."

"That's right. According to Dr. Woodbury, someone tried to turn that little shop into a museum at one time, but the actual press was down on the corner. But right here on this block was where old Tom Sharp issued his newspaper and called for people to rise up and start killing Mormons."

"That seems so weird to me," Kayla said. "I mean, I know some of the reasons people didn't want us here. But they didn't need to *kill* anyone."

"No. They certainly didn't. But it's hard for us to think the way people did back then." He continued to look at the shop front. He was trying to imagine the scene he had read about recently. "Here's what's interesting to me. My ancestor who lived in Nauvoo, William Lewis, came here that next winter after Joseph had been murdered. He wanted to see what he could do to end all the troubles. He thought he might be able to change Thomas Sharp's attitude. So he walked right into the office of the *Warsaw Signal* and asked to see the boss."

"How do you know this?" Kayla asked.

"Grandpa Lewis wrote about it in his life history. My aunt has been transcribing it and sending me pieces as she gets them finished."

Malcolm bent over to look past Jeff and across the street, as though he wanted to picture the scene himself. "It took some guts to walk into a place like that," Malcolm said.

"It really did. He's lucky he didn't get himself drawn and quartered."

"Did he get anywhere with the guy?" Abby asked.

"I don't think so. He just says they talked for a time and then Sharp told him to get out. But he said something that's interesting to me. He said he felt inspired to make the effort, and, at first, when it didn't seem to do any good, he felt as though he hadn't been inspired after all. But over time, he decided, he had given Sharp a chance to hear another point of view—and a chance to change his course of action. It was something he needed to do."

"I guess," Abby said. "But it seems like you have to consider the risk against the possible gain."

"That's certainly true. You have to admire his nerve, though. I picture him walking into that office—right in the middle of the town where most of the people *detested* the Mormons—and then trying to find the right words to stop all the hatred. I'd sure like to know what he said to Tom Sharp."

"If he was anything like you," Kayla said, "I'll bet he gave the guy a big old handshake and told him he wanted to be his friend."

"It's funny you say that. Grandpa Lewis said the Saints should have tried harder to make friends when they first came here. Separating themselves so completely was probably the first thing that made the old citizens so suspicious."

"But they weren't just suspicious. They *hated* us," Malcolm said.

"I know. But I think now, we sort of like that idea. It's our heritage. We love that image of ourselves: the outcasts. You know, hated for His name's sake."

Jeff pulled the car ahead and resumed the journey toward Quincy. After a time, he said, "This little town up ahead is called Lima. That's how they pronounce it, like 'lima beans.' Lorenzo Snow lived here at one time, and his sister Eliza lived with him and taught school one winter. The Morley settlement was just off to the east from here. That's where the anti-Mormons started burning houses and driving the Saints into Nauvoo. They killed a Mormon named Edmund Durfee. It was the beginning of the end, really, before we agreed to leave."

"Let's see. Where do we get the idea that we're hated?" Kayla asked.

Everyone laughed.

"But Grandpa Lewis was still right. He tried his best to end the hostility."

• • •

When the four reached Quincy, they ate at the Steak 'n Shake first, then stopped at Lowe's. While the men picked out the things they needed, Abby and Kayla looked at appliances. A man in an apron approached them and asked, "Can I help you ladies?"

He was a middle-aged man who filled out his apron a little too roundly. But he was grinning, as though calling them 'ladies' had been his way of teasing. Abby, especially, still looked younger than she was. He probably thought she was single. So Abby went a little out of her way to say, "No, thanks. Our husbands are picking up some things. We're just looking around."

"Oh, I see. So do you both own your own homes?"

"Kayla does," Abby answered. "We're still renting. Sort of." He looked a little confused by her response, so she added, "My husband is fixing up a house. We get free rent for doing the remodeling."

"Well, he must be pretty handy if he can do that."

She smiled and glanced at Kayla. "Well, *fairly* handy. He depends a lot on *her* husband."

About then, Jeff and Malcolm came down an aisle pushing a basket full of the items they had picked out so far. "Oh, I know these guys," the man said. "The great fixer-uppers. Why didn't you tell me you were married to such industrious young fellows?"

Jeff laughed about that. Then he said, "Abby, we need your help. Will you look at these colors?" He handed her a color wheel and pulled a paint chip out of his shirt pocket. "Which of those shades of blue matches the chip the closest?"

"The ladies always have a better eye, don't they?" the clerk said.

"That one does," Kayla said. "She's trained. She has a degree in decorating."

"Are you serious?"

Abby glanced at him and nodded, but she had no idea why he seemed so surprised. Maybe he thought she was too young to have gone to college.

Abby compared colors and offered Jeff her opinion, and Jeff gave Malcolm a nudge with his elbow. "See, I told you," he said.

"Hey, I never claimed to be a—"

"Do you live here in Quincy?" the clerk asked Abby.

"No. Up north of here. In Nauvoo."

"Oh." But he looked like he still had something in mind. He tucked his hands in his pockets and leaned back a little with a thoughtful look on his face.

"Why?"

"Well, we get lots of decorating questions, especially about drapes and blinds and all that sort of thing. We had a decorator working for us for quite a while, but she quit last month and we can't find anyone with that kind of background. How far is Nauvoo, anyway?"

"It takes about an hour to drive there." Abby was suddenly interested.

"The thing is, the woman didn't come in every day. She would come in and work with clients a couple of times a week, and then she would go out to their homes and give them decorating ideas. She also worked from home a lot, answering questions on the telephone and by email."

"Is it full-time?"

"I don't know exactly what her arrangement was."

"What about benefits? Did she get insurance?"

"I just don't know. But I'll find out. Are you interested?"

"I might be if I didn't have to come down every day—and if insurance came with it."

"Yeah. I don't know about all that."

The possibility didn't really sound very promising, and yet, Abby had a feeling about this. She had been praying constantly that something would open up for her, and it seemed serendipitous that she had come down with Jeff tonight. So Abby gave the man her contact information.

And three days later she had a job.

She had talked to the manager, Jay Waddups, by telephone, and she had driven down for an interview. Lowe's hadn't hired the last woman full-time and hadn't offered benefits, but the store really needed someone who could help customers coordinate textures and colors and fabrics. Mr. Waddups told her she probably wouldn't put in actual full-time hours, but he thought she would more than pay for her own salary with the sales she would make. He didn't offer her an awful lot of money, but he did say that the store would provide insurance for her.

There were all sorts of things to work out, but Abby didn't say that she needed time to think. She didn't want Jeff to talk her out of this. She accepted the job, and then, as she drove home, found herself worrying about the complications to her life she had just created. Kayla had already said she would take William on the days Abby was away from home, but getting by with one car was going to be difficult—maybe impossible—and yet she saw no way they could afford another one.

She decided not to call Jeff, but to wait until he came home so that she could talk everything out with him. He had arranged for a ride to work that day with a man who lived downriver, so she didn't have to go after him, but it was one of his eat-and-run nights, and he always tried, during the few minutes he was home, to play with William as much as he could on those days. So, when he asked her how the interview had gone, she told him she thought it had gone very well and she would talk to him more about it when he got home that night.

That turned out to be after eleven, and he looked beat when he came in. She waited until he'd had a chance to shower, and then she broke the news. She watched him light up at first about the full-time pay for less than full-time work—even if the salary was nothing to get all that excited about—and he slapped his hands together with joy when she said the boss had offered her benefits. "That's great," he said, and she knew what he meant.

"You may not want to give notice just yet," she said. "We maybe ought to try it for a few weeks, just to make sure it will work out."

"Well, yeah. That's probably smart."

"And I need a car."

"Oh." That one stopped him. He tucked his fingers into the pockets of his old bathrobe and thought for a time. "Yeah. I don't see how we could get by with one car—even after I leave my job in Fort Madison."

"Maybe we can find an old clunker that—"

"No," Jeff said. "We've got one of those already. I was just thinking, we better buy something that's still in decent shape. I don't want you driving that far in a car that could break down. We can afford a car payment now."

"Even after you quit your job?"

"Yeah. I'm starting to think this business can turn into something pretty big."

"How could it get any bigger? You two can't handle any more than you're already doing."

"I don't mean the remodeling. I'm talking about the web site. I had this amazing email today. A guy wants to advertise on our web site. I haven't even tried to find clients, but my blogs are starting to get popular. I'm getting dozens of new hits every day. Once I have more time to work on it, the web site will be our real business, and remodeling will be something to keep us in the know."

Abby was skeptical. "Will they pay you much money to advertise on a site like that?"

"I'm not sure. This first guy just asked me what I would charge. I have to figure that out. But here's what I'm thinking. We need to do a whole lot more about home décor on the site. Those two blogs you did are getting a lot of hits. Women are the ones who get online and try to figure this stuff out. If you were doing the blog once or twice a week, I think we would really increase our followers."

It was late, but the talk didn't end soon. Jeff and Abby scribbled down ideas that she could write about, and they talked about the way their lives would change if he didn't have to drive to Fort Madison every day. It was after one thirty when they finally got to bed, and even then, Abby couldn't sleep. She finally whispered to Jeff, "Are you awake?"

"Afraid so," he said, and he laughed.

"The Lord opened a door for us, didn't He?"

"That's what I was thinking," Jeff said.

"Why don't you give notice right away?"

"Really? Maybe we should—"

"Jeff, you're too conservative. We have to dive into this thing."

They both laughed. Then Jeff said, "Okay, then, let's go for it."

"All right. But don't forget about the car."

"What car? Did I say anything about a car?"

She poked him in the ribs, and they laughed again. Abby felt good about this. She didn't want to work very long, but she was glad she could help Jeff move more in the direction he wanted to go.

• • •

On the following Sunday, Bishop Harrison stopped Abby in the hallway of the church after sacrament meeting. "Could I talk to you after church today?" he asked.

"Sure."

"Bring Jeff, okay?"

Abby couldn't think what that would mean. She only knew that she loved teaching Sunday School and hated to think that he might want to call her to do something else. But she had little time to think about that until her class was finished, and then, during Relief Society, she told herself just to wait and see what he wanted.

Abby was too happy today to worry very much. She wasn't starting her job until Monday, but she and Jeff had driven to Quincy on Saturday and bought a used Camry that had only forty thousand miles on it. That meant a serious car payment each month, but she had been pleased by how quickly the loan had gone through. She had been able to tell the salesman that she was going to be working almost next door, and that she and Jeff each had incomes. So she now had a bright red Camry that looked almost new, and Jeff was telling her that it was her car. He would still drive their old car to work—until he was finished there—and once he was working full-time with Malcolm, his trips would not be so long.

All that was exciting, and Abby felt a kind of comfort she hadn't known in a long time. The Lord seemed to be on her side these days. After all the worry of the past couple of years, the direction of their lives was turning. Jeff had not been this happy since—actually, she didn't know when—probably since they had first gotten married. He talked nonstop about the web site and all it could be, and he saw himself as finally having time to take his class at Western Illinois more seriously, and to do his elders quorum job the way it needed to be done.

Today Abby had seen Jeff after her Sunday School class and told him about the appointment with the bishop. "He probably wants you to be the Young Women president," he had told her.

The thought had already occurred to Abby, and it made her nervous. She knew what a big calling that was, and the bishop didn't know that she had just taken a job. She could see why Bishop Harrison might think of her for something like that, but she knew she couldn't do it. She would have to explain to him what she was doing now, and once he knew, he would probably let her off the hook. But another thought kept coming to her: the Lord had blessed her so much lately. How could she tell the bishop that she wouldn't accept a calling?

When Bishop Harrison opened his door and asked them to come in, he seemed his usual calm self, but rather more upbeat. He smiled and asked Jeff and Abby to sit down. "How are things going for the two of you?" he asked.

"Actually, we're pretty excited," Jeff said. "Malcolm and I are doing really well with our remodeling business." Jeff was holding William on his lap, but the boy was already starting to squirm. He never liked to be in one place very long. Jeff held onto him and talked about his plan to give notice to quit his job the next day, and he described the success he was starting to see with his web site.

"That's all good news to me," the bishop said, "because it means you'll be around here for quite some time yet."

"Maybe forever," Jeff said. "We really might."

"One thing he didn't tell you," Abby said, "is that I start working tomorrow. Jeff and Malcolm are doing well, but I just felt we needed insurance." Then she told him how the Lord had blessed them to come across a job in Quincy—and what the job would entail.

As she saw his face change, she told herself it was good she had explained their situation to him. He needed to know all this before he extended a call.

"So you'll be going down there kind of on a part-time basis?" he asked.

"In a way. But it's a full-time job."

"But working from your home quite a bit?"

"Yes. I'll be driving down to Quincy fairly often, though, calling on clients at their homes. But I'm just so lucky that Kayla can take care of William. I think William loves her as much as he loves me, and I know her daughters will give him so much attention he won't want to come home."

Bishop Harrison nodded. He was looking thoughtful now, and Abby could tell that he was reconsidering what he had planned to ask her. She watched his glance go down to the desk for a few seconds, but when he looked up, he said, "Abby, I want to call you to be our Relief Society president."

"*Relief Society president?* Me?"

"I didn't know about this new job, but I feel quite certain that the Lord put your name in my mind. I told Him you were too young and inexperienced, and I told Him you would feel overwhelmed—and a bunch of other things—and He just kept telling me that the women in our ward need your love and your good attitude. So many of our women are feeling beaten down these days, and you've passed through a very hard time and come out of it positive and faithful."

"But would I have time, if I'm working?"

"No. But then, no one has time. Most of the women in the ward work, and most all of us are way too busy these days. There's no way in the world I have time to be bishop, but I do it—and it seems to work out."

Abby still couldn't think. She knew she couldn't do the job. She had no preparation. She was one of the youngest married women in the ward. She didn't even know all the reasons she couldn't do it; she only knew it was impossible. "Bishop, I've only been in the Church a few years. I don't know . . . anything, really."

"Yes, you do," Jeff said. "You know how to love people. You know how to teach. And you're very organized. You'll figure out the rest—and you can choose some good counselors who will help you."

She looked at Jeff. Strangely, he looked pleased. She had no idea what to say. She shut her eyes for a moment, tried to calm herself, and when she opened her eyes she looked at the painting on the bishop's wall. It was a picture of Jesus Christ looking calm and reassuring. All she could think was that *He* had helped her work things out, had guided her to this job, and now He was asking more of her. She couldn't say no. And yet she felt breathless as a weight seemed to press down on her shoulders.

The bishop said, "I'm sitting here asking myself, should I take this back? I know I'm asking a very great deal of you. But the Lord knew you were looking for a job—knew you had found one. He didn't tell me that, but He told me you were the right woman for the calling, and I just have no question about that."

Abby stared at him. She didn't even know exactly what the calling involved. She only knew how busy Sister Lawrence had been when she had helped Abby through her crisis the year before. And yet, it was thinking about Sister Lawrence that changed Abby's heart. How could she turn the Lord down after all that the sisters in the ward had done for her?

"All right," she said. "I guess I can try."

The bishop looked at Jeff. "How do you feel about this?" he asked.

"I'm excited for her," Jeff said. "She'll be great."

Bishop Harrison smiled and looked back at Abby. "I think that's right. It's not a death sentence, you know. You won't believe the joy this calling will bring into your life. Both your lives. Jeff has done so much, working with the elders, and now you'll be able to work with him on a lot of things. I feel that the Lord sent you to our ward. We needed both of you."

Abby let herself cry, and she made a decision. She wouldn't think too much about this. She wouldn't feel sorry for herself. She would simply find a way to make it work.

CHAPTER 14

Will was leaning back against a wagon wheel with his legs stretched out in front of him. Rain was beating down on him so hard that there was no way he could sleep. He had shifted his broad-brimmed hat down over his face so the water was running off it in a little stream, and now he was merely waiting for morning to come. He had started the night rolled up in a blanket under a makeshift shelter he had built with tree limbs and brush. He had slept all right for a time, but eventually he had felt the rain dripping onto his face and, worse, running on the ground into the shelter. That was when he had crawled over to get under the Company B baggage wagon, but most everyone had come up with that idea ahead of him. There was no room to crowd his way under. So he had moved around to the side of the wagon that was away from the wind and had taken up his position against the wagon wheel. But his blanket was soon soaked all the way through, as were his clothes, and the swirling winds kept sending the downpour in one direction and then another in cold blasts.

But Will was feeling something worse than mere cold. He had

begun to shake as chill after chill passed through him. This was the same kind of fever and chills he had experienced when the ague had struck him back in Nauvoo. He hoped he wasn't getting sick again, not with this long march only just begun. Quinine powder had helped him before, but he doubted he would be able to obtain any now.

Will had experienced some dark periods in his life, but all this—the cold and the misery, the sickness and the homesickness—was pushing him to some sort of edge. He had been walking all day for two days, and his feet were already a mess. He had needed good boots for such a long hike, so he had purchased new ones, but that had been a mistake. When he had pulled them off the night before, his stockings had been soaked with blood, the blisters having broken open and the skin having torn away. He knew he would wear calluses on his feet in time, but he had no idea how he could walk all day, every day, month after month.

An entire winter—a lifetime, it seemed—would have to pass before he would see Liz and the boys again. He had wondered almost incessantly since he had left them: What were they doing now? Was anyone looking after them? Were the boys upset about him leaving them?

Will hoped that Daniel Johns could be of some help to Liz. But the man had been deathly sick when the Battalion—the "Mormon Battalion," Colonel Allen was calling it—had marched away. Brother Johns had actually tried to volunteer for the force, feeling ashamed not to go, but he had been turned away. And yet, others were sick and had only hidden their illnesses better. Will knew more than a dozen men who had started out very ill, and he couldn't see how they would make it all the way to the West Coast. One man, Samuel Boley, was so ill that some were saying he wasn't likely to last another day. It was pitiful enough to think that he could die not yet a hundred miles away from his family, but worse to think that he might have survived had he not put himself through this march in the sweltering heat—and this torturous night in the driving rain.

One of the problems was that the men had not wanted to take food away from their families, so they had marched away with few provisions. The army had promised to supply the men with food, and supplies were supposed to be on the way from Fort Leavenworth, but so far, they hadn't arrived. Hunger had set in for many on the very first day. Will and Jesse had brought enough bread and dried meat to last a couple of days, but they had finished what little was left the night before. They had no idea what they would do now.

Will wanted to trust that the Lord would watch over this little army made up mostly of priesthood holders. He had heard Brigham Young's promise—in the name of the Lord—that no one would die from enemy fire *if they were righteous.* That had seemed inspiring at the time, but some of the men had hardly gotten out of the sight of the President before they began to behave like worldly young fellows, not God's chosen. Will had heard them curse and use the name of the Lord in vain. He had heard them wrangle with one another about the available food. And worst, he had watched some of the men steal from farms along the road.

The justification was obvious enough. These men were United States soldiers on their way to war, and the army had no food for them. If they had to grab some eggs—or even a hen—they considered themselves justified. But they had wiped out whole cornfields near the road, actually destroyed farmers' crops. They had plucked ears that weren't fully ripe and parched the kernels or made mush. Will had even heard one man brag about stealing a cow, milking it once, and then trading the animal for whiskey. The soldier didn't seem to worry at all about the farmer who needed that cow for his family—or what he had been taught about drinking hard liquor. Will wondered what would become of the promise of safety if the men couldn't control themselves any better than they had done so far.

What also worried Will was that the men were not trained as soldiers. They had played at war a little in the Nauvoo Legion, but they knew almost nothing of battle tactics, and they were showing already that they knew nothing of the military way of doing things. Colonel Allen seemed a good man, but he had become upset already at the lack of discipline and military courtesy. Privates complained to officers about the length of the daily march, the state of their feet, the lack of food. When reprimanded for any of their actions, they defied their own officers by either ignoring orders or arguing about the commands. Will didn't particularly like the military way of thinking—the separation of officers from the troops and the superior treatment for those of higher rank—but he sensed that if this gang of men, and that's what they seemed so far, went into battle, the results might be disastrous.

As Will lay on the ground, waiting out the night, he thought of Liz's question. Was he throwing his life away for forty-two dollars?

At some point, with dawn probably not far away, all Will's discouragement seemed to coalesce into an emotion so powerful that he couldn't stand it anymore. He simply knew that he couldn't do this. He couldn't abandon his family, and he couldn't walk all day and sleep on the ground every night. He couldn't sacrifice his life for so little return. Suddenly he knew what he had to do. He kicked the wet blanket off himself, pushed back his hat, and stood up. Only one thing made sense: he was going back to Liz. He knew that was desertion, and he could be shot for that. But he didn't care. He would go after his family, and he would take them away somewhere. He would hide out if he had to. Who would bother to look for him if he headed into the wilderness and then met the Saints in the West somewhere?

But the night was overwhelmingly black. He took a couple of steps, feeling the pain in his feet and the mud under his boots. He realized he could never find the road and wouldn't know how to stay on it if he did. And in that same moment, the impulse passed. He had made a commitment. How could he show his face back at the camp if he returned there?

He stood for a time, realizing gradually that the wind had let up. The rain wasn't beating down so hard as it had before. He knew he still couldn't sleep. He thought of walking enough to get his blood flowing, but there was nowhere to go, and his feet hurt too much, so he sat back down in the mud, hunched forward with his arms on his knees, and once again waited. He wanted to cry. Or maybe scream. But he did neither. He just waited, and after a time he realized that the sun was coming up and the rain had actually stopped.

When Will could finally see, he found Jesse, who was just as soaked as Will was. "I got under the wagon," he said, "an' it wasn't so bad in the beginnin', but then a flood of water filled up my blanket. There was nothin' to do but wait out the storm—an' the night."

Will nodded, but he didn't bother to describe what he had done. "How can we do this, Jesse?" he asked.

"They say we're to receive tents at Fort Leavenworth. Then thin's will na' be so bad, I think."

"Aye, and some food would help. But we'll have muskets to carry after that, and ammunition."

"I know that. I know all of't. But last night, in the dark, I tol' meself, Jesse, do na' think on all the days ahead. It will kill ye if you do. On'y think about this day, right now. Make it through this 'un. Then worry 'bout tomorrow, tomorrow."

"I've been telling myself the same thing, but it's my head sayin' it, and my heart won't believe the words."

"I know. But we must keep sayin' it, and then a week will go by, and then a month, and after that yet another month, and we can make't through."

Will nodded. He didn't mention that he was doubtful he could walk all day with the bottoms of his feet so torn up. He didn't even point out that they had no food for breakfast. He merely limped with Jesse to a campfire someone had gotten started. The heat felt good for now, and it was a chance to dry their clothing a little, but Will knew the day would soon be hot and sticky after the rain, and he knew the Battalion would be marching along the Missouri River southward toward the Zion the Saints had once given up in Independence, Missouri. That meant they were getting ever closer to another people who hated Mormons.

A brother named Charley Buttars, a private like Will and Jesse whom Will had known in the Nauvoo Legion, was hunched down by the fire. He was rather short and stout, but there was something childlike in his features, in his large, dark eyes. He had mixed a little flour and water and wrapped the dough around a stick, which he was holding over the flame. He looked up and said apologetically, "This is all I have. But I'll share it with you if you like."

"No. You needn't do that," Will said. It was not enough to fill one man, let alone three.

But a young man Will didn't know had set an iron pot close to the flames. "There'll be corn mush ready here before long. If you have nothin' better to eat, you're welcome to have some of this."

Will glanced at Jesse. They had vowed not to steal any food, but now it seemed likely they were being invited to eat some of the corn the men had been nabbing along the way. "Hey, it's manna from heaven, my friends," the boy said. "As I walked past a field, it volunteered. If I remember right, it jumped the fence and dropped inta my knapsack." He was grinning. But then he added, more seriously, "We're goin' off ta fight for these people who don't want to share their food with us. I asked a farmer for a few potatoes, an' he pointed a pitchfork at me and tol' me to get off his land."

Will tried out the justification in his own mind and accepted that there was some truth to it. What seemed obvious to him, besides, was that he couldn't walk all day with nothing in his stomach.

"My name's Philander Gray. But mos'ly jist 'Phil.' Me an' my brother Josh signed up together." He pointed to his brother, who was standing close to the fire. The boy nodded, but he didn't say anything. Will figured that Phil couldn't be more than nineteen or twenty, and Josh was surely younger. They were both fair-skinned boys, but they looked tough and lean as young coyotes, with maybe some of the same bite to them.

Will and Jesse introduced themselves.

"Sounds like yer from England," Phil said. "Me and Josh was from Maryland afore we come to Nauvoo. Our pa had a dream one night about men of God comin' to our house, and then they come, lookin' jist the same as in the dream. Thass how we joined the Church. Me and Josh was jist boys then."

Jesse laughed. "An' what is it you be now?"

"Soldiers. An' we kin both shoot good. Jist give us a rifle an' we kin do as good as anyone in this here army." He grinned.

"In this war," Will said, "you may do more walking than shooting."

"We kin do that, too. Don' worry 'bout us. We'll hold up jist fine, and do whatever needs ta be done." He grinned again. "Like *discoverin'* food, when that's what's called for. You ready for some mush?"

Will glanced at Jesse, and Jesse nodded. They each ate a bowl of the mush, and then another.

The men were still gathered at the fire, not yet having been called to morning muster, when Will saw Lydia Hunter walking toward them. One of the odd concessions Captain Allen had allowed the Mormons as he had worked to recruit them was permission for a number of women and children to travel with the Battalion. Men who had served in the army said that it was not out of the ordinary for a military unit to include laundresses, who were then paid by the soldiers, but it was not the normal way of things to include whole families. The men with families had agreed to pay all the extra expenses, and eighty civilians—women and children—had set out on the journey. Will wondered how that might affect the progress of the march.

But Lydia Hunter was looking surprisingly fresh and clean after such a bad night. Will knew that she had ridden in her husband's wagon most of the time so far, and she had probably slept in the wagon, too. But with all the heat, and the miserable storm the night before, it was hard to believe she could look so confident and at ease this morning. "Men," she said, "Captain Hunter asked me to tell you that we have provisions in our wagon. We'll ration out as much food as we can until the wagons from Fort Leavenworth reach us."

Will knew what she was saying. Captain Jesse Hunter was the company commander, one of the Mormon leaders chosen by Brigham Young. Brother Hunter had been direct in telling his men not to raid the farms along the way. The intent of his wife's message was to take away any justification for thievery. Will immediately felt ashamed that he had given way to his hunger.

Phil Gray sounded defensive when he said, "But you ain't got enough to feed us all—not for long, anyhow."

"I think we can manage," Sister Hunter said. "The wagons should reach us today, or at least by tomorrow."

Will was impressed with how pleasant she sounded. She was a

young woman, not much over twenty, Will thought, and not exactly pretty, but quick to smile, and quick to make conversation with the men. She and Melissa Coray, the eighteen-year-old newlywed wife of Sergeant William Coray, might have stayed in their wagons and shied away from a company of a hundred men. But both seemed to accept their situation and perhaps even like it, as though they thought they were setting out on a grand adventure.

What all the men in the company knew was that Jesse Hunter had left his first wife, Keziah, along with his younger children, at Council Bluffs, near the Missouri River. Lydia was his second wife; the two had been married shortly before leaving Nauvoo. The captain had also brought along William, his oldest child, who was fifteen and serving as a musician with the company.

Melissa Coray had been married for only six weeks. She had told Will, "I didn't want him to go without me. Why should women stay home and worry about their husbands when they could just as well march beside them?"

Will had agreed with her, and he had wondered since then whether he shouldn't have arranged for Liz and the boys to come. He could have brought his wagon and oxen, and he could have put by some provisions, but he knew that this march would have been impossible for Liz, expecting their baby. The boys needed to rest this winter, and Liz needed to rebuild her strength. Still, every time he looked at Lydia or Melissa, he was jealous that his own wife was not with him. Neither woman was half so pretty as Liz, but they were young and strong and optimistic, which raised the spirits of the men.

"I won't eat stolen corn again," Will told Jesse.

"No. Nor I. It tasted foul in my mouth, no matter I was hungry. If we want the Lord with us, we must do right, no matter what."

Will believed that. In the night he had been ready to break

almost any rule to escape the misery of his situation, but he was well aware that he had made promises to his wife, to President Young, and to the Lord. He knew he wanted to return to Liz next year as worthy as he had been when he left her.

• • •

Liz was lying in her wagon. A week had passed since Will had marched away, and she had been sick the entire time. She knew it was the sickness she had known before, with a baby coming again, and she knew that watching Will march off with the other men— her eyes straining to see the cloud of dust as it disappeared down the river road—had left her broken inside. But this illness was something more. She felt almost as sick as she had been on the sailing ship four years back, crossing to America. There were all sorts of illnesses going around. Some said there was typhoid fever, and ague was on the rise again. Liz didn't know what she had—she hoped it was only a summer fever of some sort—but she did know that her courage was already waning.

The remains of Will's company of ten were still camped near Mosquito Creek on the east side of the Missouri River. No one knew yet where a permanent camp would be set up. Will had left Liz enough food to last for a time, and even a little money. But she doubted she had enough of either to get her all the way through the winter. She would have to rely on Brigham Young's promise to look after the wives of the Battalion members even if it shamed her a little to think of taking help.

Liz did not want to just lie in her wagon, and yet, every time she tried to get up, she began to vomit again. She knew her one great blessing was that she had Ellen, who had been watching her boys, and she had Ellen's children, who liked to play with Jacob and Daniel. Jacob had felt the loss of his daddy and had cried each night, asking when he would come back. But in the day, with other children to keep him busy and Ellen's watchful eye to keep him safe, he had held up all right. But Liz was worried about the load Ellen was carrying. Brother Johns was still very ill, and Ellen often looked after the Johns children, too.

Liz told herself she had to climb out of the wagon; she had to do her share of the chores. She sat up. But as soon as she did, she felt a wave of the sickness again. She dropped back and took long, deep breaths. And after a few minutes, she fell asleep. It was mid-afternoon, when the heat was stifling under the wagon cover, that she heard Ellen's voice. "How are you feeling, Lizzy?" she asked. "Any better at all?"

"Maybe a little," Liz said, only because she didn't want to admit how sick, and how sick at heart, she actually felt. After all, Ellen was facing a year alone the same as she was, and she seemed to be willing herself forward better than Liz.

"There's someone here to see you," Ellen said. "Brother Pendleton."

Liz raised her head and saw a slight little man with a balding head peering through the opening in the wagon cover. She had seen him before, but she hadn't known his name.

"Hello, Sister Lewis," he said in a thin, raspy voice. "Sister Matthews tells me that you're ill."

"Yes. A little." She wanted to say, "Why do you want to look at me when I'm like this?" but she held her tongue. She only hoped he would soon leave.

"Brother Brigham has asked me to look after you," he said. "I'll be your bishop when we start a settlement somewhere."

"That's good," Liz said. "Thank you. But when will that be?"

"No one knows. We plan to cross the river at some point, or so I'm told, and we'll set up a camp for winter. That's what Brigham has told some people, but I don't think he has permission just yet—at least, not *official* permission. It's all Indian land on that side of the river."

"What will we have there, Brother Pendleton? Will we build houses?"

"Oh, yes. Long before snow flies. We'll build log shelters, and I'm to make certain that you're cared for and that you stay warm through all the cold months. Brother Lewis showed me the logs he cut before he left. We can haul those over the river and build you a good little house."

"That's good. I'm not quite so worried now. Thank you."

"All right, then." But he had begun to cough. She looked up again and realized for the first time how very pale he was. "I'm sorry," he said. "I'm not well either. I'm not . . ." And then his head disappeared.

"Are you all right?" Liz heard Ellen ask. Then Liz heard a bump, as though Bishop Pendleton had fallen against the wagon. "Oh, my," Ellen was saying. "Liz, he's sunk to the ground. I think he's passed out. I'll run and get him some water."

Liz forced herself up. She felt the dizziness again, but she didn't let it stop her. She was dressed, except for her shoes, so she climbed down from the back of the wagon in her bare feet. She found Brother Pendleton on the ground, his eyes open but looking dazed. "Did I . . ."

"I believe you fainted, Bishop. You must be very ill."

"I have been for a few days, but I thought I was doing better today."

"You coughed so hard, I think you took your own breath away."

"Yes. I think that's what it was."

He rolled onto his side and seemed to be ready to get up to his feet, but Ellen was back by then, and she said, "Brother Pendleton, stay down another minute. I have some water for you."

The water was some that had been dipped from the river in a bucket and allowed to settle, but it was always brackish and nasty tasting. Liz hardly thought it would be refreshing to the poor man. But he sat up and took a few swallows from a tin cup. "I'm all right now," he said, handing the cup back to Ellen, "but I need to get back to my camp, just up that way. Could you possibly walk with me?"

So Ellen took his arm and walked with him, and Liz decided to stay up. In her concern for Bishop Pendleton, she hadn't thought of herself, and now she realized that she wasn't feeling quite so weak. She could see her boys playing with the Matthews children nearby, and just up the river she could see a man chopping on a tree. She hoped he had in mind to build a cabin, but maybe he was only cutting logs for firewood. Still, the sound of chopping had a familiar ring to it. It had often been the sound of Nauvoo when Will and so many other men had been felling trees, building cabins, making Zion. Somehow this place would have to be their temporary Zion, and Liz had to get up and do her part.

Ellen was soon back, looking concerned. "Are you all right, Liz?" she asked. "Should I help you back into the wagon?"

"No. I'll stay up now."

"Everyone's sick, Liz. I talked to one of the Taylor sisters, up at their camp, and she said there wasn't one of them who wasn't sick. She's been down herself and is only up now because someone has to do for the others."

"What's making everyone so sick?"

"We're wore down, Liz. We're too tired out from all we've come through to get here, and we do na' have proper food. People can na' live on cornbread an' corn mush an' parched corn . . . an' every other kind of corn. There's mostly no meat now, an' how long since we had a onion or a turnip—or anythin' from a garden?"

Liz knew all that was true, but she also wondered about the water. So many bad diseases struck people along the river. The people needed wells, needed fresh water to drink.

"At least our children seem all right," Liz said.

"They are na' too bad. But my Mary cries at night with achin' legs. If we do na' find better food for the children, we'll be seein' the black canker again, an' all the other things babies died from in Nauvoo."

Liz refused to think of that. She had to find berries in the woods, or vegetables from farmers somewhere. She had to get up, had to get to work, had to think of her little boys—and of her baby.

"So where do you think Will and Jesse be?" Ellen asked. "I wonder ever' minute how they're holdin' up, marchin' all day in such dreadful heat. Jesse's always been healthy, but he do na' stand the heat good. It was ne'er like this in England, was it?"

"No, it wasn't." Liz thought of cool days in Herefordshire, even in summer. "And we had good food to eat. Do you remember how we walked to the market in Ledbury, how we picked out the nicest carrots and leeks, how we had apples in the autumn and fresh fish from the vendors in town? It was all so wonderful, and we didn't know it."

"I did na' walk to the market, Liz. You town people was the ones what did that. But we had such a garden at our farm, and fruit trees. I picked cherries from the trees an' tossed 'em in my mouth to see if they was ripe yet. I'd give 'most anythin' for the taste of a cherry now, or a good ripe apple."

"Did you make shepherd's pie?"

"Aye. We did. Here, people eat beef and mutton, but they do na' know the joy of good puddin's, good pies."

Liz felt tears come to her eyes. She decided to say no more. She couldn't start all this—remembering what once was. She had a year ahead of her, and then some time after that before she saw Will again. She didn't know where that would be, and she didn't know what she would have to go through before the day came, but for now, she had to make the best of her days, stay strong, and keep her children safe. And then the day would come when she could look back on all this and know that she had done her best and shown some courage.

But still, she thought of those walks with her sister Mary Ann to pick up a few items for the cook. They had visited with friends and strolled back, and then Liz had sat in her parlor and read a good book, or she had played her pianoforte, and she had waited for a nice dinner to be placed upon her dining-room table—a lush dinner with such a variety of dishes, and tea, and often cakes or sweets. She knew it had been an empty life, in its way, but she couldn't resist wishing that she could have just one such day now.

CHAPTER 15

Levi Hancock's sermon had already lasted an hour and a half, with no hint that it would ever end. Will was struggling to stay awake. It was August 9, and the Battalion had been camped at Fort Leavenworth for over a week. The morning had been warm, but now the sun was high, and the heat was sapping Will's strength. His shirt was soaked through with sweat.

"Now, brethren, there's one more matter I must speak of," Brother Hancock was saying. "I asked Brother Pettegrew to speak to all of you at your tents, and I believe he's received promises from you never again to indulge yourself as you did last night. I only hope you meant what you said. I pray that your shame has driven you to your knees to call mightily upon the Lord for forgiveness."

Will's jaw tightened. He would repent for his own sins, but he didn't have to be admonished for something he hadn't done. A few men, all of them in Company A, had gotten drunk and made fools of themselves the night before. There was something in Brother Hancock's accusing voice that reminded him of the preachers he had grown up with in Ledbury—preachers who never stopped talking about sin and hellfire. Levi Hancock was one of the presidents of the Seventy—the highest Church authority with the Battalion—and he surely felt responsible for the conduct of the men, but in Will's opinion, the man took himself much too seriously. When he preached, his mouth turned down in a grim frown, and he shook his head and waved his finger as though he were talking to naughty children.

"One of our men is locked up in the guardhouse right now," Hancock was saying. "A holder of the Holy Priesthood, and he filled himself up with whiskey and with Satan last night. He was not the only one, either. But what do you say to me? You've walked a hundred miles; you've trained in the hot sun. You were in need of a little refreshment. I say, go to your tents and kneel down, let the God of Israel heal your wounds and lift your spirits. The devil himself is in a whiskey bottle, and no man of God ever needs to touch the stuff, let alone intoxicate himself."

Brother Hancock dropped his head for a time, as though he were saying his own prayer of contrition. When he raised his head, he looked at the men for a long time and finally, in a softer voice, said, "We acted as badly as those Missouri troops camped just beyond us. And here's what I fear." Again, he lowered his head for a time. "I marched with Zion's Camp back in 1834. Some of the men became fractious and disobedient. Joseph Smith promised in the name of the Lord that if they didn't repent, a scourge would come upon us. And the scourge came. Cholera struck the camp, and more than a dozen of our men died. Now, listen to me. I warn you in the name of the Lord, the same is awaiting you—all of you—unless you repent. We've buried one brother already—dear Brother Boley. I don't want to see any others buried out on this prairie, with nothing but a blanket for a coffin."

Will hated the implication that Brother Boley's death was some sort of punishment—but still, he felt Brother Hancock's sincerity, and he felt a sense of dread come over him. He hadn't drunk any whiskey and never would, but he had been harsh in his judgment of his officers; he had expressed some hard opinions of Colonel Allen when he had kept them marching so many hours each day on their way to Fort Leavenworth. He had even felt dark feelings toward Brigham Young for pressuring him to join this army.

Will knew he had to humble himself. He would never survive a march of two thousand miles if he didn't. He had been sick again lately, chills and fevers returning. He knew he would need the Lord's help if he was going to keep up the daily march. Brother Hancock was right about a lot of things. The men did need to improve their behavior. As he glanced around, he saw the soberness in the men's faces, and he thought many were feeling their own regrets.

Will wondered whether most of the troops weren't feeling what he was: that they weren't prepared to be soldiers. Here at Fort Leavenworth the men had learned to march in company formations, and they had fired their weapons, but there had been little time for anything approaching military training. By the time the troops had reached the fort and survived three thunderstorms, at least half of them had come down sick, and everyone was exhausted. Now the Battalion was about to set out across the Santa Fe Trail into Mexican territory, and Will had no idea what he—or any of the men—would do if they actually faced an enemy. Everything was about speed, getting west as fast as possible, but no one seemed to worry that the Battalion was not ready for battle.

One of the promises Colonel Allen had made the men when he recruited them was that they would receive muskets they could keep at the end of their hitch in the army, but the old 1816 models they had been issued were hardly worth having. Will had heard that they weighed nine and a half pounds, but he would have sworn that his weighed closer to twenty. And yet, that was what he would carry as he left the fort. He also had to carry a leather cartridge box on a strap slung over one shoulder and a bayonet in a scabbard slung over the other. A three-pint canteen would hang from another strap, and a canvas knapsack would fit on his back, with a blanket rolled up and tied on top of it. He would also carry his daily ration of food in a canvas haversack, strung from his belt. The men had learned that they could pool their money and purchase a company wagon to haul the knapsacks and blankets, but the rest they would carry each day of the march. Will wondered how heavy all that would feel after a long day in the sun.

As promised, no actual uniform was required. Some of the men had dyed their trousers and shirts blue, but the colors had come out so variegated that there was nothing to identify the men as a unit except for the white leather shoulder straps that crossed over on their chests, and white belts. Most of the men also wore broad-brimmed felt hats.

That week the men had also lined up and received their forty-two-dollar allotment. By then, John Taylor, Parley Pratt, Orson Hyde, and Jesse Little had arrived to collect that allotment and carry it back to the main body of the Saints.

How much of their pay the men gave to the Church was left up to them, but the decision was not easy. Will and Jesse were now sharing a tent with four other men: Charley Buttars, Josh and Philander Gray, whom they had camped with on the way to Fort Leavenworth, and an Englishman named Abner Clark. As the men had stood together in the paymaster's line, Will had heard the Gray brothers say that they weren't about to give up all their money for the poor when no one was any worse off than their own parents.

Will didn't know what to think about that. After Will and Jesse signed their names and received their money in coins, they walked around to the shady side of the headquarters building. "What are you going to do, Jesse?" Will asked. "Are you giving all your money over to the Brethren?"

"I do na' think so, Will. I've talked to the men, and 'most ever'one says the same. They left their wives with nothin' to go on, and they can na' see sending everythin' to other members when their own children do na' have food on their table."

"I know. But I talked to Brother Taylor. He says that if the leaders have our money, they can go to St. Louis and buy goods for the winter—at a good price—and then see that everyone gets a fair share."

"I can na' say that's wrong, Will. But I must think of my own children first. There's people what have more than enough, and crossing Iowa, they did na' do a thin' to help those who was starvin'."

Will knew that. But he also remembered the covenant they had all taken at general conference to be sure that the poor were taken care of. If some were going to make it to the West, they all had to make it, and that meant they had to care for one another.

"I'll tell ye what besides," Jesse said. "I'm not agoin' to starve mysel'. I do na' see any way that the army will carry provisions enough to feed us all the way to Santa Fe. I want to buy myself a li'l somethin' if I have to, and ne'er again get caught hungry the way we did on the way down here."

Will had been thinking the same thing. "So how much are you going to keep for yourself?"

"On'y a few dollars. But somethin'."

Will thought that might be right, but he considered long and hard before he parceled out his money. He finally decided to keep only two dollars for himself, and he sent ten dollars with the Brethren to be given directly to Liz and his boys, but he passed thirty dollars on to be used for the poor. Still, before the Brethren left, John Taylor told Will that he was disappointed. Less than six thousand of the twenty-one thousand was going back to Brother

Brigham. President Young was not going to be pleased about that. He had expected to have much more than that to feed his people.

• • •

Liz was sitting up front in her wagon, waiting in line. She had told the boys to stay in the wagon with her, out of the sun, but the heat in the wagon might have been worse. Getting to the river was taking hours. The ferry could take only two wagons at a time, and a rope was used to pull the flatboat across. It was a tedious process. Liz still wasn't feeling well, and sitting so long in the heat was almost more than she could tolerate. She had vomited after breakfast, and now she felt weak from keeping so little down the last few weeks since Will had left.

Ellen had continued to be a strength to Liz, but her little Mary and Jesse Junior were both sick now, and that left Ellen busy just trying to take care of her own family. The Johnses' wagon was in line for the crossing, too. Daniel had been able to get up and around that week, but he was suffering with fever and chills again, and so was Eliza, the Johnses' daughter. Liz had also learned something else that worried her: Ellen was expecting another baby and was just a little farther along than Liz. Ellen had worked so hard to help Liz and to look after her own children at the same time, and all the while, she couldn't have felt well herself. Liz had to wonder about all the months ahead, with both of them pregnant. She hoped that Brother Johns would be doing better before long, and she hoped Bishop Pendleton really would be able to help them get some cabins built. But the bishop was as sick as anyone. Some wondered whether he would even live much longer.

So it was a difficult day, and Liz and her friends didn't make it across the river until well into the afternoon. The plan was to camp in a large settlement that had been divided into lots. It would be called Winter Quarters. Brigham Young had promised the local Indian agents that the settlement would serve as a temporary waiting place, to be used only for a winter or two.

A man led Liz's oxen off the ferry, and then he guided Liz to a lot in block 32, close to the river. She had been assigned a spot in Bishop Pendleton's ward, as promised, and so had Ellen and Brother and Sister Johns. They all knew they would be sleeping in their wagons for now and cooking over campfires. What no one knew was how long it would take to start building cabins.

As soon as Liz had stopped her wagon at her assigned lot, she unhitched her oxen and took them to a fenced-in pasture that had been set up for everyone. She did the same for Ellen while Ellen looked after all the children, and then she lugged enough sizable rocks to make a ring in the middle of the three wagons. Jesse Junior said he felt well enough to make a trip to the woods by the river for firewood. He brought back some sticks and dead branches, but the effort wore him out, and Liz had to make two more trips to find enough wood to make a cook fire.

Liz wished she had a chicken or a cut of beef to feed everyone, but she was already down to a bushel of corn, a sack of flour, and a small cut of bacon. The others had similar supplies, but for tonight, Liz used her own food to cook for everyone. They had become accustomed to sharing what they had. She parched some corn in a frying pan, and she cut thin slices of bacon. She did decide to use a little of the tea she had left, just to lift everyone's spirits.

"I can say this," Ellen said. "A lord in his manor ne'er eats any better'n us. The trick is all in the hunger. Hunger makes parched corn taste as good as a fine roast of beef."

Liz had to laugh. "I'm so hungry, I could eat *anything* right now, but I have to say, that doesn't make parched corn taste like anything but parched corn—a little burnt, a little gritty, and about as tasty as dirt."

"Shut your eyes and say it's pheasant or a nice suet pudding."

"Oh, please. Don't speak of such things."

Jacob was sitting next to Liz, and Daniel was on her lap. The boys were eating the kernels of corn one at a time. Jacob said, "We could catch a fish. I saw some in the river. Big ones."

"Now, that's right," Ellen said. "There's catfish, big as a young calf, and they swim right up to the banks of the river. Maybe Jesse Junior can take Jacob tomorrow, and they can catch one for us."

Liz worried about that. Jacob was not yet four, and she didn't want him falling in the river. But Jesse Junior was good about looking after him, and he was eight now. She doubted they could catch a fish, but she knew how much Jacob would like to tag along and try.

Liz continued to parch more corn, and the Johnses came to the fire, all but Eliza, who didn't feel up to it. They ate the corn and bacon as though it were a real meal, and Brother Johns sipped on the tea and said it was what he had needed. "I'm getting stronger," he told Liz and Ellen. "Better each day. I'll try to help more in coming days. I'll see what I can do about cuttin' more trees for cabins. We need to start as soon as we can and do a little each day. As hot as it is now, it won't be long 'til the nights be cold."

Liz longed for the day when she had a house to live in. She wished for a bed, too, but doubted that was possible.

The light lingered rather long on these August evenings, but tonight Liz was actually looking forward to dark so she could go to bed in her wagon. It has been a tiring day, and she knew the boys were worn out too. But a little breeze had begun to blow, and the temperature was finally easing off a little. There was hope that in another month or so, days would be milder. The only problem was, as the sun disappeared, Liz began to hear mosquitoes buzz around her head.

"Squitoes," little Daniel said, and he began to slap at the sound of them.

"Let's go to the wagon," she told her boys. "We can hang a blanket over the opening and keep them out." But that meant no air coming through.

"That's what we best be adoin'," Ellen said. She laughed. "Them mosquitoes is big enough, maybe we can pretend they's geese and stuff 'em and bake 'em."

Liz tried to laugh too. Then she stood up with Daniel and said, "Come on, Jacob."

"I don't want to go to bed," he said.

"I know. We won't go to sleep yet. We'll just get in the wagon."

"Will you tell us a story?"

"Yes."

"A long one?"

"Very long."

Liz was looking past the fire and down toward another camp. A man was walking with a woman, seeming to lead her along. The woman looked tired, as though every step were an effort. But she also looked . . . familiar. There was something in her way of walking, of holding her head, that reminded Liz of someone she knew.

As the man and woman came closer, Liz could see that the young woman was bedraggled. Her dress was made of a fancy fabric and adorned with a beautiful lace collar, but the skirt was dirty and torn, and her bonnet was limp. It was as though a wealthy lady had set out to walk to church and had gotten lost and wandered in the woods for many days.

The two seemed to be heading for Liz's campfire, and now everyone in the camp was watching them. And then, as the fire lighted the face of the woman, Liz finally admitted to herself what she had been seeing from far away.

"Mary Ann!" Liz called. She handed Daniel to Ellen and ran to her sister. "Is it you?"

"There's not much of me left," Mary Ann said. But when she smiled, it was the smile Liz knew. Liz reached for her sister. Mary Ann dropped into Liz's arms and began to cry.

• • •

Company B had been marching down the Santa Fe Trail for almost two weeks since leaving Fort Leavenworth. During the time at the fort, Colonel Allen had become seriously ill and had not been able to lead the men as they began their march. Brother Jefferson Hunt—Captain Hunt—had been assigned to command the Battalion for now. The soldiers had liked Colonel Allen, and they hated to leave without him, but at least one of their own was leading them now. The only problem was, Captain Hunt was not going easy on them, brother or not, and they were covering many miles each day.

At first, the men had stepped briskly, in formation, with fifes playing "The Girl I Left Behind" and a drum beating out the cadence. But gradually the men had forgotten about keeping step and had strung out, some trudging along slower than others. The August heat and humidity were oppressive. The companies started very early each morning, and the first few hours weren't bad, but as the day wore on, the men slowed without meaning to, and they used up their canteens of water. The trail rolled across green hills, thick with timber, but somehow it seemed to Will as though they were always climbing another hill, with little time allowed for any sort of rest.

All that was hard enough—but on top of it, Will was sick. His fever was burning hotter than the sun that was beating down on his head. On his worst days, Will had reported to the Battalion doctor and had been allowed to ride in a "sick wagon," but he tried not to do that very often.

On August 26, word had arrived from Fort Leavenworth that Colonel Allen had died. With that information came a letter explaining that a new regular army officer, Lieutenant Andrew Jackson Smith, was being sent to command the Battalion. All the Mormon officers and men felt sorrow at the loss of Colonel Allen, but most of them were downright angry about the decision to send Lieutenant Smith. Colonel Allen had promised Brigham Young that a Mormon officer would replace Allen should he, for some reason, not continue as their commander.

The Battalion camped and waited a few days at a place called Council Grove. When Smith arrived, he had a physician with him named Dr. George Sanderson. Both men seemed a little too "military" in their manner to Will, but he had no chance to get to know them. Enlisted men were not included in the meetings that soon took place. Still, it was the enlisted men who were furious when they heard the results of the discussions. The rumor had been that the Mormon officers were going to hold the army to its promise and keep Captain Hunt in his position of leadership, but the announcement was made that Lieutenant Smith was now in command. And when, for the next few days, he marched them harder and longer than before, all the talk among the men was that they had been lied to by the army again. "But then, who cares what we think?" Will kept hearing the men say to each other.

Will gave little thought to such matters. He was too sick. He was thankful for the days of rest, but when the march began again, he felt weaker than ever. He trudged along for a few days, but early one morning he was pushing forward as best he could when his vision began to blur. And then he was plummeting toward the ground face-first. His musket rolled from his grip, and he felt a flash of pain on the side of his head. He was only vaguely aware that time had passed when he felt water splashing on his face.

"Will, Will," Jesse was saying. "Can you hear me?"

Will grunted, "Aye. Help me up."

"Not yet. Stay down a minute. We're taking you to the doctor."

"No."

"You can na' walk another step, Will. We have to get you on the sick wagon."

"I won't take calomel. Brigham told us not to."

In the last few days, the medicines Dr. Sanderson had been giving the men had become a big issue. Dr. Sanderson followed the standard military procedure, which was to dose the soldiers with calomel for almost any ailment. But Alvin Smith, Joseph Smith's older brother, had died from a dose of calomel when Joseph was only a boy. Church leaders had learned from Joseph a revulsion at the idea of taking such medicines. Brigham Young had told the men to use gentle herbs, or to heal one another with blessings, but to avoid the medicines army doctors might try to administer to them.

"You must do what the doctor says," Jesse told Will. "It's that or die out here on this road."

Will didn't want to accept that, but he also couldn't do anything about it. Four men hoisted him off the ground, two reaching under his arms and two more grabbing his legs. They carried him forward, called for the doctor's wagon to stop, and then set him down in the shade.

Will felt the world swirl again, and when he opened his eyes, Sanderson was bent over him. "You're used up," he said, "and burning like a fire. I have something for you to take, and then we'll let you ride for a time."

"No. I won't take your medicine."

"Don't start with that. I've heard what your Mr. Young thinks about calomel. But you're in the army now, and that is the medicine prescribed."

"No."

Sanderson was holding a big spoon with rust marks on it. He was pouring liquid into it from a bottle.

"No. I won't take it."

"That's just fine. Get up and march, then. But you won't ride on the sick wagon unless you're willing to accept standard treatment. I'm doing exactly what I'm required to do."

Will realized that someone was behind him, holding him in something of a sitting position. He rolled away from the man's grip and onto his side. And then he fought to get up to his knees. He held there for a moment. He could see now that the man who had been holding him was Jesse. "Take the medicine," Jesse said. "You must."

"No." Will straightened up on his haunches and then used one hand to brace himself as he struggled to his feet. He was wobbling, but he pulled himself to full height, took a long breath, and then stepped forward—and went down again.

He was lost in a haze for a time, but when he got his eyes open, Jesse was holding him up again. "Take the medicine, Will, and then we'll help you to the wagon."

Will knew by then what he would do. He opened his mouth, took in the liquid, and pretended to swallow. As soon as he did, Charley Buttars got under one of his arms and Jesse under the other, and they raised him up to his feet. When the Gray brothers came around him, as though to grab his legs again, Will shook his head and took a step. So Jesse and Charley braced him, and Will walked with their support. The sick wagon had stopped behind the doctor's wagon, so it wasn't a long walk.

As they rounded the back of the sick wagon, Will gathered his strength and stepped away from his two supporters. He bent and spat the medicine out on the ground. But just as it hit the dirt with a splat, Will heard a booming voice behind him. "I knew very well that's what you had in mind to do."

Will kept his balance on his own, but he didn't look back at Sanderson.

"I followed you down here just to be sure you really swallowed that medicine. But you think you know better than I do, don't you?"

Will didn't speak.

"You think you know better, don't you? Answer me."

"Aye. I do. I won't take that stuff. A better man than you told me not to."

"Fine. I don't care what happens to you. You walk the rest of the day—that, or sit down and die, for all I'm concerned. But you will *not* get on that wagon."

"I'll walk."

"No, Will," Jesse said. "You can't do it."

But Will turned around and took a couple of tentative steps. He found his balance and set out. He was sick to his core, and weak, so weak that his knees wanted to go out from under him. But he kept walking.

The company was already well ahead of Will and Jesse and their tent mates. There was no way to catch up. But Jesse stayed with Will, and so did the other men. And they kept going the rest of the day, sometimes two of them holding Will up when his legs began to give way. When they finally reached the camp, Will collapsed. The other men raised the tent and set about building a fire. Will didn't help, but he actually felt a little better. Ague had a way of coming and going, and he believed he would be able to march better in the morning. More than anything, he was glad that he hadn't taken any of the poison Dr. Sanderson had wanted to give him.

CHAPTER 16

Mary Ann hadn't been able to stop crying that first night she had arrived in camp. She had collapsed into Liz's arms, and Liz had barely been able to hold her up. "Help me," Liz had called, and Brother and Sister Johns had hurried to her. "This is my sister," she explained. "Let's get her into my wagon. She's exhausted."

"I can walk," Mary Ann said, but she leaned heavily on Liz as the two walked to the wagon. "I'm sorry," she kept saying. "I'm so tired. I'm *so* tired." She curled up on the quilts in the wagon. "I need to sleep."

So Liz pulled Mary Ann's shoes off—the broken remains of her shoes—and pulled the lightest of the blankets over her.

"I came to Nauvoo and you were gone," Mary Ann mumbled. "I was so scared."

"Just sleep now," Liz told her. "We'll talk about everything later."

Mary Ann had slept all that night and all the next morning. Liz had put the boys to bed next to her, and Liz had slept underneath the wagon. In the morning, the boys had not been all that quiet as they had roused and climbed from the wagon box, but nothing had awakened Mary Ann.

Liz had recently received ten dollars from Will, which John Taylor had brought to her. On the morning after Mary Ann arrived, Liz walked to Sarpy's Point, the ferry station and supply store on the river. She used some of the precious coins to buy a chicken and some vegetables. She stewed the chicken and the carrots and onions all morning. She knew that Mary Ann needed nourishment. In England she had always been soft and rounded, but in Liz's arms the night before, she had seemed nothing but bones.

Jacob and Daniel were curious about this aunt they had never known. They had looked in the wagon many times that morning. Finally, Liz heard Mary Ann's voice. "You're my nephews, aren't you?" she said. "I know your names. You're Jacob and Daniel." Jacob giggled. "Do you know my name?" she asked.

Jacob said shyly, "Aunt Mary Ann."

"Yes. And now I want to kiss you."

Jacob bolted when he heard those words and ran toward Liz, who was standing at the fire. Daniel ran right behind him, but they were both laughing.

"Jacob," Liz said, "go back and give your aunt a kiss. She's the one who wrote us such nice letters—and always sent kisses for you. She's my sister, and I love her ever so much. You must love her too."

But the boys stood their ground. Liz noticed, however, that Mary Ann was climbing down from the wagon. She looked even worse than she had the night before. The filthiness of her clothing was more obvious, and her hair was a tangled mess.

Mary Ann tried to straighten her hair a little. "I don't blame you, boys. I wouldn't kiss anyone who looked so ghastly as I do."

"You look wonderful to me," Liz said. She went to Mary Ann

and held her in her arms for a long time. "I can hardly believe that you're here. Why didn't we know you were coming?"

"I wrote a long letter to you and told you I was about to sail. I thought it would get to you in time. But now I know, as I was sailing from Liverpool, you were long since gone from Nauvoo."

"Was the voyage a hard one?"

"Oh, Liz, there were terrible storms, and coming up the Mississippi River, the weather was ever so hot. I was sick the whole time. I thought, if I could just make it to you in Nauvoo, I would be all right. But you weren't there, and I was all alone in the world."

She was weeping by then, and so was Liz. "I'm so sorry," Liz told her. "If only I had known." Liz led Mary Ann to a grassy place in the shade of the wagon. They sat together, Mary Ann still leaning against Liz, who was holding her with one arm.

"What did you do when you couldn't find us?" Liz asked.

"Everyone was leaving. There were lots of empty houses, and I needed to rest, so I stayed at a nice brick house where there was a good bed. I had some money that Mum had given me, so I was able to eat all right. People were kind to me, but everything was so strange. Everyone said, if I stayed long, the mob would come and chase me away."

"How long did you stay?"

"A month, I think. Or a little longer. But more were leaving every day, and, sick or not, I didn't dare stay. I joined some people— a family named Hicks and one named Gould—and I gave them most of my money so they could buy supplies for all of us, and then I walked almost the whole way. Brother Hicks said he couldn't let me ride and wear down his mules." Her voice broke. "I don't mean he wasn't nice to me, but he didn't know how sick I was."

"Are you still sick?"

"I don't know, Lizzy. I'm just so tired, and it's been so hot every day that I can't get my breath. I brought lots of clothes from England, but we couldn't haul them with us, so I left them behind and I wore this same dress and . . . oh, Liz, everything's so different here. I don't know how to do anything. I was no help to anyone."

"But you made it this far. You did well."

"They had to help me sometimes. They were kind to me—especially the sisters were—but Liz, they didn't like me. I heard one of them say that I thought I was a 'fine lady.' But it wasn't true. I didn't think I was better than they were. It was my way of speaking they didn't like, and how *foolish* I am. I didn't know how to cook, or how to drink water from a stream—or so many other things. We had to walk into the woods for privacy, and there were so many insects, and so many . . ." Mary Ann was crying again.

"Still, you got here. We didn't grow up doing hard things. But you can learn."

"I don't want to learn hard things, Liz. Every day I would have turned back and gone back to Mother, but it was such a long way, and I couldn't face the river and the ocean again. I would have quit a thousand times, but I didn't know how."

"You'll get your strength back, love, and you'll learn how to do the things we have to do here. If I have learned to get by, you can too. And maybe you'll find a husband here—someone to give you love and comfort."

"Will's gone with the army, isn't he? When we made it to one of the settlements across the river, we found a man who knew you were here, and he said that Will was marching to Mexico to fight in a war."

"Yes."

"How long will he be gone?"

"At least a year."

"Oh, Liz, what will happen to us?"

Liz took Mary Ann in her arms once again. "You'll gain strength, little sister. That's what will happen. By spring you'll be ready to travel again. You'll just do what you have to do. That's what we all learn, in time."

Mary Ann pulled back and looked at Liz. "You're not Liz anymore. I'm glad you've learned to do so well on your own, but you don't look the same, and you don't sound the same. You're like these women now—the ones who didn't like me."

Liz smiled. "That might be true. But I do love you. And it's time to start restoring you. I've stewed a chicken this morning. You need to eat, and you need to build some muscles."

"Muscles? Liz, who are you? I don't want muscles."

"Then write to Mum for money. Tell her you want to sail back to her—and sit with her in her parlor the rest of your life."

Mary Ann turned her back and looked away from Liz. For the first time, Liz saw the old Mary Ann. The journey had worn her out, but it apparently hadn't changed her nature. She pouted after that, and when Ellen and Margaret came to meet her, she showed little interest in getting to know them.

After Mary Ann ate, she came a little more to life, but she stayed in the shade all day, and she seemed to like being taken care of. Liz heated water for her and hung blankets to create a private place by the wagon. She even helped her clean herself up and wash her hair. And then Liz gave her the only other dress she had, a calico that was better suited to the weather than the dress she had come with. But it was obvious to Liz that Mary Ann didn't like it.

Liz struggled not to be irritated most of that day, but then Mary Ann began to play with the boys, and that reminded Liz of the playful, fun side of her sister. "I came across the ocean on a big ship," she told Jacob.

"With sails?"

"Yes. Big, white sails. And when the wind would die down, I would stand on the deck and fill my cheeks full, like this." She puffed out her cheeks. "And then I blew the sails with all my might, and that's how I got to America." She blew the air out of her cheeks. "I blew so hard that I made the wind that brought me here. Do you believe that?"

"Yes."

"You do?"

"No." But he was laughing, and Liz could see that Jacob liked Mary Ann. She looked rather pretty now, with her hair clean and her face brighter. She was too thin, but her figure would be nice enough when she gained a little weight. Liz thought maybe some young man would take an interest in her—if she learned to do something besides tell funny stories.

• • •

The march to the Mexican town of Santa Fe from Fort Leavenworth was more than nine hundred miles. It had begun in hill country and had gradually leveled into vast, flat prairies. And after the grasslands came desert country, dry and prickly. Steamy days had given way to dusty days, and nothing was worse than marching behind the wagons. Men spread out to avoid the dust, but that didn't relieve the pounding pain of walking all day long.

Will had recovered from the worst of his ague attacks. He was still feverish at times, but he had settled into a routine he could live with. Reveille was sounded at sunrise, which was still early on these late summer days. Every man had to report quickly for roll call. Each mess group of six men cooked their own breakfast over an open fire, struck their tents, and looked after their animals, and then they set out in their company units. The drums and fifes were mostly forgotten now. The march had become an endless slog through country that was beautiful in its way, but empty compared to all that the men had known in their lives. Some days there were reasons to stop—rivers to cross or wagons to repair—but most days the troops covered twelve to fifteen miles, and sometimes as many as twenty. And each night they had to set up camp again and build fires, sometimes with nothing more than buffalo dung to burn.

The families of the soldiers had started out riding in wagons most of the time, but the mules and oxen had suffered in the heat. So women and children had had to get down and walk with the men. What had started out as an adventure had turned into an arduous task, and Will often heard children whining that they couldn't keep walking—and he heard impatient mothers scolding them. A violent storm that had torn down every tent and drenched everyone's bedding had taken some of the starch out of all the marchers, but it had especially discouraged the families.

When Colonel Allen had led the Battalion, he had been strict, but he had also been understanding and likable. Some had been disappointed when Jefferson Hunt took over and seemed to try to please the regular army officers more than they thought he should, but they knew him to be a good man, and most of the soldiers liked him. As it was turning out, no one liked Lieutenant Smith. He made no attempt to explain anything to the men, and he demanded more of them than seemed reasonable. When he made the decision to take the "Cimarron cutoff," the more direct route to Santa Fe, the troops knew it would save them many days of walking, but word soon spread that Colonel Allen had sent provisions to Fort Bent, and the Cimarron route would bypass that area. The cutoff was known to be a sandy, desolate march along a mostly dry riverbed, with little drinkable water. That was discouraging enough, but when word came that rations would be cut, anger spread through the ranks.

Lieutenant Smith made another important decision at that

point. He didn't believe he could take all of the eighty women and children across this cutoff, nor could he march them all the way to the West Coast. He had learned of a group of southern Latter-day Saints who had set out for the Great Basin when they had thought Brigham Young was departing that year for the same destination. Once these "Mississippi Saints," as they were called, learned that Brigham's excursion had been delayed, they had decided to winter in a little settlement called Pueblo. Lieutenant Smith decided to send Captain Nelson Higgins and twelve soldiers who were too ill to continue, along with more than forty of the women and children, to join these Saints in Pueblo. Needless to say, the soldiers who had been told they could take their families with them to the end of their march were upset.

And then Alva Phelps had died after accepting a dose of Dr. Sanderson's medicine. When John D. Lee and Howard Egan arrived the next day, sent by Brigham Young, something close to an insurrection was taking place. Lee quickly made things worse. He demanded that Colonel Allen's promises to Brigham be kept, that Captain Hunt be reinstated, and that Dr. Sanderson stop his autocratic domination of the sick. He made his demands in a language and with an attitude that insulted Smith, who only dug in his heels. Some of the men were put off by Lee's blustery approach, but they still believed that he was right.

Brothers Lee and Egan had another mission. They had come to pick up the soldiers' pay and take it back to help feed the members still camped along the Missouri River. As it turned out, however, Lee and Egan learned that there would be no pay until the Battalion reached Santa Fe, and they would have to continue on to that point.

What mattered to the men more than any of this, however, was that Lee and Egan had brought mail from the main body of the Saints. To Will's great joy, he had received a letter from Liz and one she had sent forward from his mother. He was anxious to know something of his family even though Liz's letter had been written weeks earlier. Liz wrote that she was preparing to cross the Missouri River and settle in a place that would be called Winter Quarters. She had clearly made the best case she could for everything being all right, but Will could feel her fear and worry. She said that she had been promised help in getting a cabin built, but she also spoke of the illness that was so rampant in all the settlements, and she admitted that she wasn't feeling well herself. She did say that the boys were doing better. Will knew that the pregnancy was probably the source of Liz's sickness, but he also knew that if she were seriously ill, she wouldn't say so. Will finished the letter still worried and wishing that he knew more.

Will's mother, as always, also tried to put a good face on conditions at home in England, but she admitted that Will's father still struggled with his bad knee. More than that, he had suffered from a catarrh the previous winter and was still coughing up phlegm. Daniel had taken over the farm entirely, and he had married Molly and brought her to the farm. Sarah had also married, and she had moved away, and Josiah had joined the navy, so they managed to have enough room in the house. Will knew that in truth they had very little living space, but he was glad that both Daniel and Sarah had been able to marry, even though he knew they wouldn't have much to live on. Esther was nineteen now and, according to Mum, "very pretty." A young man in the Church was "happy to greet her each Sunday." Edgar was fourteen, and Solomon, twelve. Will longed to see how they looked now and what sort of young men they were turning out to be. He hoped all of them could live with him in Zion someday.

As it turned out, all the Battalion officers gathered to talk with Brother Lee and decide what stand they wanted to take, but once again the enlisted men were left to wonder what was being said. Will used the time to catch some extra sleep, but when the meeting broke up, he happened to be crossing the camp, and he ran into Jefferson Hunt. "What happened, Brother Hunt?" Will asked. "Have you been reinstated?"

"No, Private Lewis, I haven't been. I voted with most of the other officers to keep Lieutenant Smith in his place."

Will was taken aback by Brother Hunt calling him "Private," but even more by what he reported. "What about the promise to Brigham Young? Colonel Allen told him that—"

"Brigham Young asked us to enlist in the *army*. We're soldiers, and it's about time our men understood that."

Will couldn't think what to say.

Brother Hunt continued, "I wondered the whole time I was the commander what I would do if we got into the war. I'm not well enough trained to handle something like that."

"But Brigham said that no one would die from—"

"Private Lewis, we need to become an army. Our men don't want to follow orders. They complain about everything. Someone has to teach them some discipline, and they never would have accepted that from me."

Will was trying to take all this in, to consider whether he had been thinking all wrong about these matters. He grabbed onto one thing he was sure of: "Brigham told us not to take calomel. I followed the will of a prophet, not the orders of a quack doctor."

"Dr. Sanderson is an officer, Will, and he was following military procedures. You could be shot for disobeying him. We can't run this Battalion if all of you men ignore orders from your officers. Armies can't operate that way."

"We're not like other people, Brother Hunt. We follow the Lord."

"Stop right there. I've studied the maps between here and the Pacific coast. Between Santa Fe and the Pacific, everything is either desert or mountains. If we make mistakes in the desert, we'll die out there. So don't ask me to lead you. I don't know how. Lieutenant Smith is a hard man, but he's experienced. It's going to take him— or someone like him—to keep us alive. So don't complain to me again."

Brother Hunt walked away.

Will was astounded. And yet, he had seen the confusion in his company. He knew that the men thought they were only serving the Church, answering Brother Brigham's call. It was chilling to think that they might have to change their ways if they wanted to survive this march.

In the following days, word came that General Kearny expected the Mormon Battalion to arrive in Santa Fe by October 10. He and his troops were leaving for the coast, and he needed a battalion close behind for support. There was no way the entire force could make it to Santa Fe that fast, so Lieutenant Smith asked his officers to form an express unit, fifty from each company, to push ahead and report their arrival in Santa Fe by the deadline that Kearny had set. Officers could then outfit the Battalion for the next leg of their march, and the slower soldiers—along with the remaining wives and children— could catch up by the time they pushed off again.

Will wasn't sure that he was one of the stronger men at this point, but he had been asked to go on ahead with the express group, and he didn't want to stay behind. He was certainly getting stronger, and he wanted to be with Jesse, no matter what. But the march through the sand dunes along the Cimarron, the most desolate country they had seen so far, turned out to be brutal. Animals foundered as they tried to pull through the sand, and the men were all eating half their usual ration, then grubbing holes in the sand of the dry riverbed in hopes of finding water, however muddy. Still, it took them only a week to reach Santa Fe, and when they got there, they had a few days to rest.

Will was not impressed with the little settlement of Santa Fe. There was a handsome sandstone cathedral there, but otherwise, only a scattering of low adobe houses. The people lived in dirt and poverty. The big news the men received was that they would have a new commander to replace Lieutenant Smith. He was Colonel Philip St. George Cooke, an experienced officer who had been serving in Kearny's Army of the West. He was said to know the western region well. He cut a fine figure—six feet four inches tall, with hair and beard the color of the desert sand they had been looking at every day. He was a Virginian and well educated, but he seemed stern, even austere.

Cooke told his officers that he saw too many broken-down men, sick and weak and unable to walk across the great western deserts. He was also shocked to be told that families, not just laundresses, were still with the Battalion. He was convinced that women could not survive the country they were about to face. He now ordered all remaining women and children, along with men too weak to make the trek, to form another detachment and travel north to Pueblo.

After some discussion, some able-bodied men were allowed to travel with their wives and families to provide protection, and that meant that 91 men and more than 30 additional women and children would be departing. The Battalion was cut to about 375 soldiers, all of them healthy enough to make the march.

Many men were angry, including John Lee. They argued that Colonel Allen had promised that the Battalion would never be split apart. But Will thought Cooke had made a good decision. Will couldn't forget what Jefferson Hunt had told him. Since then, he had worried about families making their way across the desert. He liked the women with Company B, Sister Hunter and Sister Coray, but he hated to think of what the march would do to them. As it turned out, Cooke held to his decision. He sent the detachment away, and he prepared his men to move south along the Rio Grande.

Will and Jesse had heard Lydia and Melissa talking, and the two women were insistent they were not going to let Cooke send them away. The men had laughed at their strong words, and Will had told Jesse, "This should be good. We'll find out whether ol' Cooke is as tough as he thinks he is."

That night, after the men in Will's mess had eaten, they sat by the fire for a time. The sun was going down much earlier these days, but Cooke no longer allowed the bugler to wait for sunup for reveille. That meant it was always better to bed down with the sun. But tonight the talk had turned to the green places each of them had lived in earlier in their lives. Jesse told them, "You should all sail to England one time in your life. You would do well ta see the hills of Herefordshire, where Will an' me was from. We keep our sand at the sea's edge where it belongs, not spread across the land like it is out here. An' our farms is green as emeralds."

A little debate followed as the Gray brothers talked about the beauties of Maryland and Abner Clark told them about the Lake District of England.

"As I see it, Jesse," Phil Gray said. "You've only seen Illinois and this country out here. The East is not like any of this, where little prickly things have to fight for a drop of water and then manage to live on that drop for a year or two."

All the men laughed at that, and Josh Gray said, "Phil and me, we was given our own calves when we was li'l fellers, and we growed 'em and sold 'em off each year. An' the calves growed so big we had to lead 'em out of the barn after a month or two so they wouldn't bust the roof off. One of them beeves, fully growed, would feed all this army two year, maybe three."

Josh, who was usually quiet, had sounded serious, and Will had been drawn in at first. Now he said, "That's a mighty steer, all right, but we do na' seek mere size in England. We grew lambs so tasty that many a man swooned from the flavor. We had to warn strangers not ta let the taste knock 'em off their feet."

And now the tall tales really began to fly. Jesse told of deer in the woods in England that appeared on the doorstep waiting to be butchered and smoked for winter, and Phil claimed to have seen geese fly into his kitchen, pluck themselves, and jump into a boiling pot. Finally Charley Buttars said in a quiet, deep voice, "You mean that goose didn't even gut itself? We wouldn't have put up with such rascals where I lived in Virginia."

The men liked Charley's claim, probably because he had never seemed one to joke as much as the others. Charley was built hard, but there was a softness about his manner. He seemed about Will's age, and he had a wife, Rebecca, whom he sometimes talked about. He also had a little boy, Andrew, who was not yet two. All the men missed their families, but Charley seemed to find more pain in his separation, or at least he admitted to more of it than most of them did.

The men were still laughing when Lydia Hunter and Melissa Coray came walking toward their little circle. "What's all this laughing about?" Melissa asked. "Colonel Cooke will think he hasn't marched you long enough if you still have the breath to laugh at the end of the day."

"The Colonel actually laughed once," Phil said. "It was thirty or forty years ago, from what I've heard."

"It's true," Lydia said, "but his mother had to tickle him and say, 'Goo-goo, my fine, fat boy.'"

"No. He was never fat," Phil said. "He was shaped like a arrow when he was born. His mother wrapped him up in a blanket and couldn't find him for a month."

"So what did he tell you two?" Will asked the women. "Is he sending you away?"

"No, he's not," Lydia said. "We told him we're staying with our husbands. Five of us told him that. If the army doesn't want us as laundresses, it matters not a whit to us. We're going the same way he is, and he can't stop us."

"What did he say to that?"

"He fumed and fussed and swore, and then he said, 'All right. But you'll pay your own way. And you may have to walk most of the way.' I told him, 'I don't mind walking, but last I noticed, you're the one riding 'round on a big white mule.'"

"Oh, my," Jesse said. "I'd wager he did na' like that."

Melissa said, "He turned the color of them red rocks we've been seeing lately. And then he walked away. But five of us women is goin' forward, no matter what he thinks about us. An' I'll tell you this much: we won't ever slow you down."

"And we'll do our share of the work," Lydia said. "If we need to push the wagons through deep sand, the way we did out on the cutoff, then we'll push with the rest of you. And we'll cook and carry water, and we'll even wash clothes if anyone still wants us to. Philip St. George Cooke may think he's the strongest man who ever came west, but he's never met the likes of us."

Will smiled as he listened. Lydia and Melissa certainly had done well so far, and he liked their pluck. He only worried that everyone—both men and women—may not feel quite so confident before this march was finished. And there was something else that worried him. Melissa Coray was just a girl, really, and she was built strong and sturdy. Will thought she probably could keep up with the men as they crossed the desert. But Lydia seemed pale lately, and one morning he had seen her walk away from camp. It was only natural for the women to seek a place of privacy away from the men, but she had been in a hurry, and Will had wondered whether she was feeling sick. He thought she might be expecting a baby. If that were so, how would she manage the worst of the trek? And what if Melissa were to become pregnant along the way? He just hoped the women weren't making a mistake to continue on with the men.

"We'll promise you this," Will said. "If you ever need help, we'll be ready to offer a hand." Lydia shot a quick glance at Will, and he thought she knew what he was thinking about her condition. So he added quickly, "The same as soldiers do—one helping the other."

Lydia nodded. "We'll manage all right," she said. "I'm sure we will. But thank you, Brother Lewis. We all have to look out for each other."

Will also nodded, but his thoughts went to Liz, who would be swelling with their child all this coming winter. He hoped someone would offer the same kind of help to her. He also thought about the things Brother Hunt had said. Will wasn't sure that any of the soldiers, and certainly not these women, understood the kind of country they would be marching through—or what battles might lie ahead. It all frightened him more than he liked to admit.

CHAPTER 17

Abby was on her way to Quincy, driving a little too fast. She had to stop at the hospital in Carthage on the way, but she had an appointment at ten o'clock, so she would have to make her visit a quick one. She didn't have any details yet, but she had had a phone call early that morning. A young woman named Sierra Farr—one of the high school girls Abby had taught in Sunday School—had been in a serious car accident the night before. The woman who had called Abby had talked to Sierra's mother, Melanie, but she hadn't known very much. The car had rolled somewhere south of Nauvoo as a carload of Nauvoo kids were on their way to an event at Warsaw High School. Sierra had been seriously hurt, it appeared, but even the mother hadn't been certain about the extent of the injuries. A home teacher had been called and had gone to the hospital to give Sierra a blessing, and Sister Farr had said to him, "Could you let the Relief Society presidency know?"

That had seemed right to Abby. Sister Farr was a single mom with three kids, all teenagers, and surely she would need help. What Abby didn't know was exactly how that all went. What was she supposed to do? If the mother was going to be at the hospital, maybe someone needed to look after the two younger siblings: a sister who was probably fifteen and a younger brother who was still a deacon, maybe thirteen. Abby knew what the Relief Society had done when William had been in the hospital in Quincy; she simply didn't know how everything had been organized. Abby had been president for over a month now, but this was the first real emergency that had come up. As Abby had hurried down River Road, she had thought about calling her counselors, but she decided she had better get more information first.

Abby's mind was racing. She had drawn up some decorating ideas for a house in Quincy, and she had conferred once with a client—Mrs. Phelps, a wealthy woman with a classic old house on Maine Street. Mrs. Phelps was remodeling her house extensively and needed guidance on redecorating. Abby had given her a few ideas, which the woman had liked, but today Abby was supposed to have a detailed plan worked out. And she had done it. The trouble was, she could hardly think at the moment, and she had to make a presentation that would sound well prepared and authoritative. She tried again to remember what she had planned to say, but nothing was coming back to her. She knew she would have to dig out her drawings and swatches and get everything back into her head once she left the hospital. But saying that to herself only brought back that other issue: what was she going to say to Sister Farr?

At Memorial Hospital, just outside Carthage and close to the highway that would take her to Quincy, Abby pulled into the parking lot and then hurried inside to the information desk. She learned that Sierra was in intensive care and Abby wouldn't be able to visit, but the woman at the desk called the station, and in a moment she said, "Mrs. Farr is going to walk outside to talk to you. If you continue down this hallway, she said she would meet you by the atrium."

So Abby hurried in the direction that the woman had pointed, and she saw Melanie walking toward her. She looked disheveled, probably having sat up all night. Her blonde hair, which she kept short, was tousled like a young boy's, and her shirt was rumpled. But what Abby noticed more than anything was her eyes: red from crying, and no doubt from lack of sleep, but there was also an intense, narrow focus in them that looked like panic.

"Oh, thank you for coming," she said, and she threw her arms around Abby. "It's been so lonely all night, waiting." Melanie was twice Abby's age and seemed twice her size, too. Abby felt like a child trying to give comfort to a grown-up.

"How bad is it?" Abby asked.

"They don't know yet. She's got broken bones—in her right leg, her ribs, and her clavicle—but, Abby, she can't move her legs. They don't know if that's permanent. They just don't know anything for sure." Melanie was crying by then. "They're thinking that they might fly her to Peoria, but they're not even sure about that yet."

"Do you know what happened?"

"Not really. There were a bunch of kids in the car, and Brandon Cox, from our ward, was driving. He must have been going too fast, but I don't know what made the car roll. All the kids were hurt, but Sierra's the worst—by far the worst. She didn't have a seat belt on, and she got thrown out of the car."

"Are you—"

"Abby, she *always* wears her seat belt. She has since she was a little girl. I won't even start the car unless the kids buckle up. I think there were too many in the car, and not enough belts, and kids just don't think about what might happen." She was breaking down, and Abby reached up to take her in her arms again.

Melanie clung tight for a time, but finally she pulled away and said, "I have to stop doing this. It doesn't do any good to cry. I have to start thinking what to do."

So the two sat down in the atrium, and Abby asked, "What did your other kids do last night?"

"They managed on their own. They're old enough. But I talked to Sasha a little while ago, and she was a wreck. She couldn't sleep. She worried and prayed all night. She just went to pieces when I told her Sierra couldn't move her legs."

"Is she going to school today?"

"I think so. I told her to go. And Dallas, too. I told them both to get themselves something to eat for breakfast, then to take the bus to school. It won't do any good to sit around the house all day and worry. But Sasha wants to come here after school. I can run over to Warsaw and get her, I guess, or maybe—"

"We can do that for you. I'm coming back through here—or I'll find someone to do it. Don't worry about driving over there. And we'll take dinner to the kids. If they decided to fly Sierra to Peoria, when would that happen?"

"I don't know. This morning, I think."

"Would they take you, too, or—"

"I just don't know. Maybe I'll have to drive there. And I don't know if I'll have to stay, or . . . Abby, I just don't know anything, and I can't think straight."

"It's all right. We'll be with you. If you fly with Sierra, one of us can come and get you when you need to come home. Sasha can help us pick out some clothes, and we'll bring them to you, or bring you your car, or whatever needs to be done. You just keep your mind on helping Sierra, and we'll make sure everything else is taken care of."

"Can you stay a while now, or do you have to go?"

Abby suddenly felt sick. "I . . . well, yes, I can stay. Or . . ."

"No, Abby. I can tell you have to leave."

"Let me make a call, Melanie. I'll change an appointment. Then I will have to leave for a while and run down to Quincy, but I'll come right back."

"No. I didn't mean that. I'll be fine. There's nothing you can do, really. I just thought, if they decide to take her, then you would . . . I don't know. But there's no reason to stay. I'll just call you—or I could call Sister—"

"Melanie, I'll make that call, and I'll try to stay until you know what's going to happen. But I'll also call my counselors and your visiting teachers. Someone will be here with you. We won't leave you alone."

So Abby walked down the hall a little way and called Mrs. Phelps in Quincy. The woman was very nice about changing the appointment when Abby told her that she was with a friend whose daughter had been injured in a car accident. Mrs. Phelps even offered to change to another day, but that worried Abby. She didn't know what her boss would think. He knew about this appointment, and he knew Mrs. Phelps. He would be asking about the way things had turned out.

Abby stood for a moment after she ended the call. She stared at her cell phone and tried to think whom to call first, how she could get everything organized. What bothered her most was that she wanted to stay with Melanie today herself—not just because Melanie needed someone, but because Abby wanted to be that someone. But that wasn't the right way to think about this, and she knew it. So she made a few calls and involved some of the other women in the ward.

Abby stayed another hour after that, and by then Melanie had had time to talk to the orthopedist who had been called in to treat Sierra. He told her that trauma to the spine could cause temporary paralysis. An MRI had revealed no break in any of her vertebrae, so he was hopeful that bruising or inflammation was the cause of the trouble, and that it would clear up after a time. For now, they would set the broken bones and possibly operate to attach a rod to Sierra's femur.

Having more information seemed to help Melanie get herself under control. "The doctor isn't going to send her away," she told Abby. "They'll treat her here, at least for now. And I talked to Sierra. They kept her sedated all night, but she's awake now, and she sounded better than I thought she would."

"Melanie," Abby said, "I called Sister Lloyd. She's on her way over here right now. I'll have to leave before long and take care of something I have to do in Quincy, but I'll be back this afternoon."

"Abby, you don't have to come back. I'm a grown-up. I can manage now. I was just having trouble figuring things out."

"I know. But we want you to know we'll help in every way we can. I've got a meal for you and your kids arranged for tonight. I think you need to go home and sleep tonight."

"And take a shower," Melanie said, and she smiled.

"Just be honest with us about the things we can take care of for you. I know what it was like to sit in a hospital and wait when William was first born, and I know how many sisters helped me get through that time. We'll do the same for you."

. . .

Abby continued on to Quincy, and she got there in time to sit in the car and review her decorating plans. Turning over some of the responsibility for Melanie to other sisters had cleared her mind a good deal. Maybe she would figure out the job one step at a time, mostly just responding to the needs that arose. But somehow her decorating ideas seemed less exciting than they had when she had first worked them out. Mrs. Phelps had a lot of money and was perfectly willing to spend it, but right now Abby had to think that there was something to be said for simplicity. Nothing else seemed to matter very much when a mother's child could be paralyzed. Being with Melanie seemed infinitely more important than deciding the color of drapes or choosing new floor coverings for a fancy house.

Still, Abby felt some renewed enthusiasm when she presented her ideas, and Mrs. Phelps—who wanted to be called Sue—was thrilled with Abby's design. As it turned out, that felt good too.

• • •

Jeff rolled over as gently as he could and let his feet slide out of bed and onto the floor. He had told himself he would get up at 5:30 a.m., and it was only 5:00, but he had awakened early—even though he hadn't been in bed very long. He knew he couldn't really rest until he finished the job that he and Malcolm were working on. Another client was threatening to cancel if they didn't get started on his house before the weekend.

When Jeff stood up, his legs felt dead. It was still dark outside, but there seemed to be a deeper darkness in his head. The worst was, he could have lain back down and rested another half hour, but he knew he would only feel the mounting tension. Once he was up and going he would wake up, and maybe he and Malcolm could make good time and move their tools over to the other house by late in the day—and quiet the man's worries.

"What time is?" Abby asked.

"I'm sorry. I was trying not to wake you."

"But what time is it? It's still dark."

"It's about five. We've got a ton to do today, so I thought I'd head over to the job early."

"What time did you come in last night? I didn't even hear you."

"I know. It was late. We've got to have this job done today." He sat back down on the bed, reached in the dark, and touched Abby's shoulder.

Abby rolled over and took hold of his hand, and she gave it a kiss. "How late, Jeff?"

"I don't remember. After midnight."

"I looked at the clock after one o'clock and you weren't home yet."

"I know. It was close to two, I guess."

"You can't do that, Jeff. You can't live on three hours of sleep."

"I know. But for one day I can."

He wanted to go back to bed with Abby, just roll up next to her and hold her in his arms. He hadn't seen her much at all lately. But she needed to go back to sleep too. She always needed more sleep than he did, and she hadn't had much lately.

"It's just this one job," Jeff said. "It's taken us about twice as long as we expected. After today, things will be under control."

"You always say that."

"I know."

Jeff had finally quit his job in Fort Madison two weeks back, but he had been worried about having enough income and had been a little too aggressive on a couple of bids—and too optimistic on some promises he had made about completion dates. He had assumed that he and Malcolm, working together, could cut their time on a job in half. That had certainly sounded reasonable. But every job had a way of becoming more complicated than he expected. Materials would come in late, or a pipe or wire would show up behind a wall where Jeff and Malcolm hadn't expected one. There was always something, and Jeff knew he had to start assuming that delay was the norm, not really an anomaly.

"William walks around the house saying, 'Daddy. Daddy.' It's like he thinks you're hiding somewhere."

"I'll do better, Abby. I really will. I haven't gotten us into so many jobs this next month."

"I know, Jeff. I'm not mad at you. I just worry what's happening to us."

"I'm thinking that you better quit your job."

"Oh, sure. That ought to make a good impression. Work a few weeks and then quit. I don't think so."

"It doesn't matter what kind of impression it makes. I'm just saying the same thing you are. We can't keep going on this way."

Jeff lay back on the bed, his head close to Abby. He knew he had to get going, but he also knew that he had to talk with her for a few minutes before he ran off again. He was afraid that by quitting his job he had made a real mess of things.

"Jeff, the whole point of my going to work was to get a regular paycheck until you guys are sure you can bring in enough for two families. And you know we have to have the insurance."

"Yeah, I know." But Jeff didn't say what he was thinking. He really had wondered lately whether Abby had done the right thing to accept the calling as Relief Society president. Looking back on it, maybe he should have told the bishop that she just couldn't handle the assignment right now. Jeff had felt good about it at the time, and Abby certainly hadn't wanted to say no, but the calling had come at the worst time he could imagine. It was filling up Abby's days and all the free moments she might have had. Even more than that, it was filling her thoughts. The two of them had intended to do some work on the web site, and Abby had promised to write some blog entries on decorating ideas. Jeff wasn't getting time to work on the site himself, hadn't written anything lately, and Abby kept saying that she would write something "one of these days," but he didn't see how she could possibly do it.

The worst was, he worried that it was little Will who was paying the price. It hurt Jeff to think of him wandering about the house asking for his daddy. He had always thought of himself as the guy who would be the world's greatest dad—the kind who played ball with his kids but also taught them all about the world and the gospel. He had taken a walk with Abby and Will a few weeks back, out on the nature trail in the state park. Jeff had tried to get Will to say "bird" and "tree," with little luck, but it wouldn't be long until he could teach him the difference between a hickory tree and a black locust, and show him goldfinches and blue jays. He wanted his son to *see* the world, to notice all the subtleties and variations of God's creation. That concept really mattered to him, and yet, if he kept going the way he was now, the boy wouldn't even know his dad, let alone the world around him.

"Well, we'll figure everything out," Jeff said. "Things are just a little too chaotic during this transition."

"Jeff, I'm really worried about Sierra."

"I know. But didn't you say that the paralysis was probably just temporary?"

"I said it might be. But I talked to the doctor myself yesterday. He can't see any vertebrae broken, but that doesn't mean that the spinal cord wasn't damaged. He said he's getting no response at all in the nerves in her feet. She really might not be able to walk—ever again."

"But there's no reason to assume the worst, is there?"

"No. But Jeff, what if it turns out that way? How do we get Sierra through something like that? And Melanie? I just don't know what advice I can give them. I'm not that much older than Sierra, and Melanie's twice my age. How do I give advice to people like that?"

"It's not about *advice*. It's just looking after them, helping them figure out each decision they have to make—as it comes."

"But, Jeff, I don't know how to do that. I didn't grow up in the

Church. I don't *know* what comes next, and I have no idea how to figure out all the money issues, and insurance, and . . . I don't know what else. Melanie started asking me yesterday how she was going to manage everything. She has insurance, but she doesn't know how much it will cover. She's trying to think about ramps for a wheel-chair and remodeling and . . . everything else."

"You know that Malcolm and I would do that kind of stuff, but you're the Relief Society president, not her resource for every issue she's dealing with. Right now, just give her emotional support. And as questions occur, use the Lord's storehouse—all the resources of the members. There are people who know about everything that will come up—or know where to go to get the answers."

"Maybe. But I feel like I'm in over my head. I should have been a counselor or the secretary. I should have gotten to know how Relief Society works. Someone else should be president."

Her voice broke, and he heard her twist and bury her head in her pillow. He turned and pulled himself up next to her, ran his hand over her hair. He let her cry for a time, and then he said, "Abby, when the Church was organized, Joseph Smith was twenty-four years old, the same as you. But the Lord called him—not some older, more experienced person. The Lord knows what we can do, and He calls us to serve so that we can grow. This will be a great experience for you."

"Okay. But I need you to help me figure things out."

"I will. And I'll make sure I'm not working so many hours just as soon as I can."

"Okay."

Jeff got up and walked to the bathroom. He took a shower that lasted about a minute, with the water only really warming by the time he was finished. He decided he should shave, too, since he hadn't the day before, but he took some quick swipes at his face and wasn't sure he hadn't left big streaks of stubble. In any case, in less than ten minutes he was dressed in the same work clothes he had worn the day before.

He walked to the kitchen and poured out a bowl of Honey Nut Cheerios and sloshed a little milk on them. He needed more than that, so he grabbed a couple of slices of bread and four cheese sticks, and he headed out to his car. He held his breath as he turned the key and was relieved when the starter engine kicked in and his old car started. He didn't know whether it was his battery or the starter engine that was failing him sometimes, and he hadn't had time to find out.

As he drove up Warsaw Street and turned west on Mulholland, he was still thinking about Abby. The poor girl really was carrying a huge burden. But the thought brought an image to his mind, and he felt a weight hanging over him and Abby both. He had never known that life would be like this, that he would be pushed to the limit just to put bread on his table, and that he would find no time for his wife and little boy. He wondered how long this day would turn out to be, and whether he would see Abby before bedtime again that night. The thought seemed to crack something in Jeff's chest, and tears began to run down his cheeks. He knew he could never let Abby know how burdened he felt, but there was some solace in admitting it to himself.

The sun had not fully risen, and down the street he could see the temple, still lighted. There was a glow from a distance, and then, as he passed the Bank of Nauvoo, the full glory of the temple was before him again, the beautiful curved east window lit from within. He knew that the light came from the celestial room, and he tried to let the peace of that space come into him.

"We'll be okay," he said to himself. "We'll get this figured out."

Abby had thought she wouldn't be able to sleep after she had talked to Jeff, but she soon drifted away again. The sun was shining brightly into the bedroom from the west window before she awoke. She was shocked to realize that William wasn't making a fuss yet. So she got up quickly and walked to his bedroom. He was already stirring, and when he saw her, he stood quickly and reached for her.

Abby pulled him from his crib in his fleece sleeper, and she held him close. "How's my boy this morning?" she asked him.

He didn't answer, but he tightened his grip around her neck. And then he said, "Daddy?"

"He's gone to work, honey. But he gave me kisses for you." She kissed him on the cheek and neck over and over until he giggled.

CHAPTER 18

William wasn't sure that he liked Colonel Cooke, but the man certainly knew what he was doing. Cooke had been ordered to reclaim the heavy wagons that General Kearny had had to abandon along the Rio Grande south of Santa Fe, and then to make a wagon road all the way to the coast. The colonel planned accordingly. He fitted up his extra mules with saddle packs and bought all the cattle and long-legged Mexican sheep he could afford. That way much of the food for the Battalion was "on the hoof." Money was scarce, since the army hadn't supplied officials in Santa Fe with enough cash to finance Cooke's excursion. That meant he had to use his limited resources wisely to obtain all the supplies he could. The problem was, everything depended on the Battalion's marching all the way to the ocean in sixty days, and Will couldn't imagine how that could happen. Cooke admitted that the distance was about eleven hundred miles and that most of the territory they would cross had never been traversed by ground troops. It was October now, and not as hot as it would have been had they crossed in summer, but Cooke was honest with the men and let them know that days would still be warm in the desert.

Colonel Cooke was clearly savvy about his duties. Will soon learned that he could be a harsh disciplinarian as well. A few days out of Santa Fe, Captain Jesse Hunter had spent too long, in Cooke's judgment, searching for a mule that had wandered off. Cooke gave him a blistering reprimand in front of the men, and then he had him tied to the back of a wagon and forced him to march in the dust all day. On the one hand, Cooke proved immediately that he would not favor officers over enlisted men, but to the men of Company B, their leader had only done what he needed to do—whether he had gone against orders or not—and such humiliation seemed far too severe.

All the men were being treated with a similar severity. Cooke had ordered the wagons to go first, in front of each company, and the men were ordered to walk behind, breathing in the dust all day. Will, however, thought he knew what was going on. He remembered what Captain Hunt had told him about the Mormon recruits needing to act like soldiers. Cooke seemed to be establishing immediately that he was in charge and that the men must follow orders, whether they liked them or not.

As November came on, nights were becoming cold, and the men still carried only one blanket each. The only salvation was, under Cooke's command, reveille was blown so early that the coldest hours didn't matter much. The men were up long before sunrise, building fires. What they didn't receive was adequate time to sleep. Will heard men grousing every morning, worn out before the day had begun.

As days passed, the dust was of less concern. The new difficulty was sand. The old Mexican trail—the Camino Real—followed the banks of the Rio Grande, where the sand was sometimes deep. The challenge was bad enough with the wagons the Battalion used, but when Cooke retrieved the heavier wagons that General Kearny had left behind, the daily march turned into grinding work. At times the big wagons had to be hitched to three or four teams of mules, and men had to help the mules by pushing from behind. In spite of the harder work, Cooke wasn't letting up at all on the pace of the march. When miles were slower and more difficult, he merely kept the men going longer.

And then things got worse.

The Battalion reached the area called "the dunes." It was a spot where a ridge extended close to the river and created a long, steep—and sandy—hill. Will had seen the outcrop ahead and wondered how the troops would get past it. When Company A reached the spot, Cooke rode back on his mule and commanded Company B to march forward and help the soldiers get the wagons over the top. Will was tired, but he was getting his strength back after his illness. He had always taken pride in what he could do when heavy work was called for; he felt sure he was stronger than most men, no matter what the ague had done to him. He hurried up to the first big wagon, which was hitched now to four teams. Setting his musket and cartridge box aside, he threw his shoulder into the task. The wagon inched forward, but the mules were soon bogged down in the sand and unable to get much traction. For half an hour the mules and men continued their effort, making little headway. When some of the soldiers tried to drive the mules harder by whipping them across the haunches, the mules brayed wildly and fought against their harnesses, more intent on escaping than on pulling the wagon.

Colonel Cooke was in front of the mules. Will heard him shout, "Back off, men. Back off." And then, as the soldiers stopped the whipping, Cooke shook his head and muttered, "This will never do."

Will was surprised when the colonel stepped up to the lead mules, patted their heads, and talked to them to calm them down. He was a strange sight, this tall, thin man. He was dressed in a full dark-blue uniform with gold epaulets at the shoulders. He also wore sideburns that bent across his cheeks and connected to his mustache. He could seem arrogant, and he sometimes talked to the men as though from on high, and yet, here he was consoling the mules with soft pats, whispering into their ears.

Cooke turned to the two men who had been whipping the mules. "No more of that," he said. He raised his voice so everyone could hear. "I want more of you to get around back of the wagon or on the wheels, ready to push. We need to help these animals all we can."

Men gathered around the wagon wherever they could find a spot. Will kept his place at the back.

"We'll all push at once," Cooke said. "The mules have to know they can move ahead or they won't bother to pull. Once we get the wagon going, keep pushing, and if we can, let's make it over the top without stopping. All right now, get ready."

When Cooke gave the command to push, Will gave his full effort. Everyone else did the same. The mules struggled ahead, and the wagon moved forward a few feet.

"Don't let up. Keep pushing," Cooke shouted.

The wagon creaked as it picked up just a little speed and moved forward maybe twenty yards, but the incline was increasing at that point. Will heard the hard breathing of the mules, the sound pitching higher with each effort.

"Don't let up. Keep it moving," Cooke was shouting.

But then Will heard something close to a squeal. He looked up just as the lead mule threw its head back, stood stiff for a moment, then collapsed in its harness. It hung there for a moment, held up by the mule next to it, but then both animals dropped to their knees, as did the mules harnessed behind them.

"All right, men," Cooke shouted. "This won't get us there. We're killing these animals."

All the men stepped back. They were breathing hard too. Some of them dropped down on the sand themselves.

Cooke helped to unhitch all the mules, and he let them rest for a time before he tried to coax them onto their feet. But the lead mule couldn't get up, and it was still breathing hard, wheezing.

"There are ropes in the supply wagon," Cooke said. "If we push from behind and get enough men on each rope, we can pull the wagons over the top ourselves."

Jesse had come up next to Will. "The mules get themsel's a day off," he said. "An' Cooke makes mules outa us."

"He's right, though," Will said. "It'll be a hard go, but it's the only way we can get this wagon to the top." But Will was surprised by what he was feeling. The sudden effort had sapped his strength much faster than he had expected. He didn't feel powerful the way he always had. He had never doubted that he could make this march—and he still didn't—but the painful wail of the lead mule had unnerved him. There were limits to what muscles and even determination could do. He pushed the thought away. He was a young man, and the Lord had blessed him with strength. He would do his share, and more, all across this desert march.

"We're o'er our boots in sand, Will," Jesse was saying, "and the wagon's in up to its axles."

"I know. It's going to take every man we can get on those ropes."

"It's a fool's errand, I say. We've got a thousand miles ahead of us. How many days like this'n can we manage?"

"I don't know. I was wondering the same thing. Let's hope this is the worst of it."

"We're on our way to a desert, Will. Cooke will kill us just ta bring these wagons along. He wants ta look good ta General Kearny. He do na' care about us."

"That may be so. But we're in the army, Jesse. Cooke has his orders, and he passes them on to us. It's not as though we have a choice in the matter."

"Aye. And what if we're worn down so we can ne'er walk another step, an' then we fight the Mexicans? What then?"

"The Mexicans are defeated already—at least the ones in Upper California where we're going. If we can make it through these next couple of months, we'll have things easy after that."

"So they tell us. But do you believe't?"

Will laughed. "Maybe. Maybe not. No one knows much of anything, and people believe what they want to hear. But Captain Hunter believes it, and he said he got it from Cooke himself, so who knows? Maybe we'll have us a swim in the ocean and then choose a big tree to sleep under the rest of our time."

"Or we'll get oursel's killt for no good reason. I ha' no quarrel with any Mexican. If he wants this empty land, he can take it all. The on'y way they farm here is to dig ditches and block the water in the puny streams."

Will had seen that sort of farming—irrigation, it was called—back in Santa Fe and in some of the little towns they had passed by since. "But it works all right," he said. "Things grow in this sandy soil, if they get some water to it."

"Aye. An' think of the soil we left behind in Herefordshire."

"I do think of that. But who owned the land we farmed back then?"

Jesse didn't answer for a time. Men were attaching long, heavy ropes to the front of the wagon. But Will noticed that Jesse was looking out across the sand. "You may be right, Will. You think better'n I do about such things. I let mysel' get worn out and dreary. But it's hard not to think about Ellen and the little ones and wonder what it is I'm adoin' here when it's my family that needs me more. I ne'er knew when we sailed away from Liverpool that I'd see land like this. Maybe it's all we'll have to farm, Will, if we're lucky enough to be alive in a year."

Will was surprised by the loud report of a pistol. He turned to see that Cooke had shot the used-up mule. It took a throng of men to drag the animal off to the side. The ropes were then stretched up the hill, and men trudged up the incline and found a place to grab on— all the men from two companies who could join in. Will decided he could put more force into the work if he stayed where he was, behind the wagon. And so he got ready, with Jesse next to him. And then Cooke, in his reedy voice, called out, "All together now, *pull!*"

Will thrust his shoulder into the back of the wagon, and the men pulled from up the hill. Slowly, the wagon dragged through the sand. It didn't roll on its wheels; it only scraped along on the box's underside. The wheels were holding the wagon back more than helping, but the men managed to move it forward about ten feet. Cooke called out, "That's good. Take a breath, get a foothold again. All right now. Are you ready?"

Then Will saw something he never would have predicted. Cooke walked to one of the ropes, grabbed it not far from the front of the wagon, and when he called out, "Pull!" he followed his own command.

Higher on the hill, the sand was not so deep, and progress accelerated. When the wagon finally crested the hill, the men cheered in relief. But getting the wagon down the other side was not as easy as Will had expected, the sand deep again toward the bottom of the dune. Still, that was not the thought that was filling Will's head. What he knew was that they had gotten only one wagon over the top. Not all would be this heavy, but there were thirty-one in all, and the men were almost spent already.

And so the men worked all day, trading off with other companies so no one had to stay at the job the entire time. The lighter wagons were not so much of a chore, but muscles weakened as the day went on, and there came a time when Will, who had chosen not to rest even when he was told to, was becoming aware that he was no longer much help. But he wasn't going to sit in the shade and let the others work.

Still, he was gratified when Philip St. George Cooke himself, in his erudite style, slapped Will on his sore shoulder and said, "You stayed with us all day. I appreciate your effort."

"Aye, sir. But I was giving out at the end. I've been sick for most of the march so far. I'm only now getting somewhat better."

"Are you English?"

"Aye, sir."

"And what is your name?"

"Private Lewis, sir. William Lewis."

"Did you leave a family behind, back at Council Bluffs?"

"Aye, sir. A wife and two boys. And a child to come."

Cooke hesitated and then asked, his tone curious, "And how did you come to . . . all this?"

"You mean, come to be a Mormon, sir?"

"Yes."

"A man of God taught us. And I believed."

Cooke nodded as he looked carefully into Will's eyes. "They told me you were all wild fanatics. But most of you seem to have your feet on the ground. You're not trained as soldiers, and you question me as though you never learned the military way of things, but when I give a command, you throw your shoulders into it. I've never met better behaved men."

"Not all have done what we're taught. There's been some drinking and swearing and—"

"Do you have any idea what most soldiers are like? I watched you people in Santa Fe, and I expected everyone to get drunk and chase after the women. But I saw none of that."

"That's so. Or at least, for the most part."

"Well, thank you. Now rest yourself. You, more than anyone, deserve a good night's sleep."

Will did appreciate the kind words, and his attitude toward Colonel Cooke changed a good deal. He was also pleased when an extra portion of meat was served that evening. Or at least, until he tasted it. It was like cutting into a plank of wood and then trying to chew it.

"It's the mule," Phil Gray said. "The one we killed off this morning."

"No doubt it is," Jesse said. "I can na' eat such stuff."

But Will said, "Chew it a little longer, and it goes down, Jesse. You need to fill your stomach. Don't pass up the chance."

"Cooke should na' give us our own mules to eat."

"I have a feeling we'll eat plenty more before we're finished. And it might be the only thing that gets us through."

Jesse stared at the meat for a time, but then he sawed off some more and began to chew.

• • •

Liz was worried. It was November, and nights were getting cold. She was still sleeping in the wagon, she and Mary Ann and the little boys all close together under the quilts, but Liz knew this couldn't last much longer. They needed to get inside, needed some sort of shelter with a fireplace.

Men had stopped by a couple of weeks ago long enough to throw some logs off the back of a wagon—the same logs that Will had cut to length for a cabin. But most of the timber was not yet notched. "We'll be back," one of the men had said. "We're working our way around the settlement, building as fast as we can."

But they hadn't come back, even though a good deal of building was going on. Brigham had promised that the wives of the Battalion men would receive help, but he surely hadn't counted on so much sickness. Liz knew that Bishop Pendleton, for one, was deathly ill. Some said he was not likely to last much longer. With most of the strong young men gone to the war, there were few who could do all the work that needed to be done. More Saints were arriving all the time, and they were camping on both sides of the river, little settlements getting started everywhere, but as new families arrived, the first thing they had to do was get their own children inside. Winter Quarters was the largest of the settlements, and the most organized, but it was also the place where the most women without husbands had been assigned to live.

Daniel Johns had also promised Liz some help with the cabin, but he was down again. A fever—maybe cholera—had struck his family, putting all of them on their backs in a single day. Their daughter Mary had been sick and weakened before the fever struck, and the poor little thing was now fighting to stay alive. Margaret was not as sick as Daniel, but she was broken down by all her family had been through. She fed her children as much as they could hold down, but she looked distant and emotionless. Some were afraid to help the Johns family, fearing the fever, but Liz and Ellen cooked for them, carried the food to their wagon, and carried away their chamber pots. Margaret thanked them, staring as though she hardly understood what was happening, and every day Brother Johns promised that he would be back up the next day, ready to help. But Liz thought he was unlikely to be up and around very soon, with the ague attacking him again as this new fever was abating.

One morning, snow began to fall—not heavy, and not for long, but for Liz that was enough. She couldn't wait any longer for someone to take care of her. After cleaning up the tin mush bowls from breakfast, she told Ellen and Mary Ann, "I watched Will build our cabin in Nauvoo. I know how it's done. I've never tried to build one myself, but I know this: I will not wait for the men in this camp to do for us what I have the ability to do for myself."

"I have an idea of't too," Ellen said. "I'm not good at choppin', but I say we at least get started."

Mary Ann was looking shocked. She had only the calico dress that Liz had given her, and it offered her no protection against the cold. She wrapped herself in quilts and stayed as close to the fire as possible. But there was simply not enough firewood to keep the fire going strong all day, so she spent much of her time in the wagon with quilts stacked over her.

All that was understandable, but what worried Liz was that Mary Ann, who had always been so cheery and talkative, was withdrawing into herself. She was finding nothing that made her happy, and when she said anything at all, it was usually a complaint about the lack of food or about the cold.

"I cannot chop wood," Mary Ann said. "I don't have the first idea about that."

"Mary Ann," Liz said, "I couldn't chop wood when I arrived from England. I understand how you feel. But you are not in Ledbury now. You will have to do the things a woman does here."

Mary Ann didn't answer, but Liz could see in her unyielding expression that she wouldn't give the work any effort. But Liz told herself she had seen enough self-pity from the girl. It was time for Mary Ann to start doing her share.

Still, Liz would have to deal with her later. "Ellen," she said, "where do we want this cabin? It won't have a floor, so we must put it where the water won't run into it when rain falls or when snow melts."

And so the two talked about that, and they chose a site. They drew a line in the dirt and then dragged a log to it. Some of the logs appeared to be two feet shorter, so the little cabin would only be ten by twelve, but Liz understood what Will must have been thinking. A small cabin would be easier to heat. Of course, he surely must have thought that only Liz and the boys would live in it—but Liz knew she and Ellen could never build two cabins. One would have to do. And at least for now, they may have to invite Daniel and Margaret and their children to join them.

Liz thought she could do the notching, but she also understood that the house would need an opening for a door, and another for a fireplace. She had seen people build chimneys from sticks and mud, and she wasn't sure how that would go, but she told herself that if she at least got started, she could get something done, and then she might find men to help her finish the work.

Liz and Ellen had already been chopping wood for their fire, and they each had hand axes in the side boxes on their wagons. They got those out now, and Liz stood over the log that they had set in place. "All right," she said, "let me teach you what I know." She knelt in her skirt on the damp earth. "We have to notch each end of the logs, and the notches all have to be the same distance from the end. Will always did this." She set the axe on the log and used the blade as her measurement, and then she chopped a mark into the back. "You can see how wide Will has made the notches that he cut for us. It's just a matter of chopping down almost halfway through the log and split-ting off the wood until there's a flat place for another log to fit into."

Liz raised the axe and struck the log with more force this time. She wanted to cut the log in the same place she had marked, but she missed by an inch or so. This was not a good beginning.

"Liz, you cannot do it," Mary Ann said. "You're about to make a mess of these logs, and someone will have to bring us new ones."

"There's no making a mess of them. The notches don't have to be perfect. They just have to make room for another log, notched the same way. If the fit isn't perfect, we'll daub in mud to fill the hole."

"And where do we get this mud? From the river? Is that something we have to do, too? Wade in the mud and get cold and filthy?"

Liz stood up. Without meaning to, she pointed the axe at Mary Ann. "Yes, Mary Ann, we may get ourselves muddy. Would you rather spend the winter outside?"

"I'd rather die. That's what I'd rather do. I'm sick of everything here."

"There's a good spot over there on the ground, Mary Ann," Liz said. She pointed a few paces off. "Lie down right there and get it over with. If the weather turns cold, we might not be able to bury you until spring, but we'll do the best we can—without your help."

"Liz, I don't know you anymore."

"That's right. You don't. But I'm going to be alive when spring comes, and you're going to be frozen stiff on the ground."

The two young women stared into one another's eyes. But it was Mary Ann who finally got tears in hers. "Liz," she said, "I'm not strong. I want to help, but I have no idea how to do it."

"Well, I *am* strong. And do you know how I got that way? I winched water out of the well and carried the heavy bucket into the house. I milked our cow. I hoed the garden. I chopped wood, churned milk, and made butter. You won't get strong lying in the wagon with quilts piled on you. You'll get strong when you *work*. Now watch what I do and then try to do it. You won't be very good at it—no better than I am—but we'll both get better."

Liz knelt down again, and this time she brought the axe down harder. A patch of bark flew off. She kept slamming the log, first at one end of the notch and then the other. And finally she used the blade of the axe to pry a layer of wood away.

"Let me try it," Ellen said.

Ellen started tentatively, the way Liz had done, but she slowly deepened the notch. Liz knew that Will had made much faster progress, had struck the log with resounding power, but it didn't matter. If they notched only one log today, that was one more than they had started with that morning. She even found herself hoping that no man would come along to tell her that she was going about things incorrectly. She wanted to build a cabin and then ask Brother Brigham to drop by and see what women could do.

Liz and Ellen took turns on the first notch for what seemed half the morning, but they finally had what they wanted.

"All right, Mary Ann," Liz said. "You trade off with us on this next one. I'm getting a blister already."

"A blister?"

"Yes, and you'll get one too. I hope you do, anyway. You chose to come to this land, and now you're going to find out what it takes to live here."

Mary Ann did not look pleased, but she knelt, with the quilt still wrapped around her, and she made some weak little chops. The blade bounced off the bark without leaving much of a mark. "I told you, Liz. I can't do it," she said. "I'm sorry, but I—"

"Don't push the axe. Swing it. Use your wrist."

Mary Ann made a better swing, but not with much effect.

"Here. Give me that quilt." Liz grabbed the quilt and pulled it away from Mary Ann. "You'll get warm when you start to chop harder. Now take a real stroke."

"I hate you," Mary Ann said, but in her anger, she swung the axe with fury, and it cut into the bark.

"All right. That's the idea," Liz said. "A little hatred seems to be what you needed."

Ellen laughed, and then Liz did. And finally Mary Ann smiled— a little—and she took another serious crack at the log.

CHAPTER 19

As the Mormon Battalion turned from the Rio Grande and headed west across the southern desert, water became much more difficult to find. The farther west they traveled, the more they encountered a land of mesquite brush, prickly pears, and dried bunch grass. In the distance, a jagged blue line of mountains loomed, but close by were only rocky hills jutting up among long stretches of wasteland. Will felt a deeper sense of foreignness here than in the yellowed grasslands north of Santa Fe. This didn't seem a suitable place for anything to live—at least, not any form of life Will had ever known. There were hints of green in the brown and gray, but there was nothing lush or bright or satisfying. The heat that filled up the air and rose from the pale earth baked the men in the daytime— and yet, the nights were very cold.

The troops kept walking every day, mostly without speaking— just plodding forward hour after hour. They had walked through August, September, October, and now into November. They had come four hundred miles since leaving Santa Fe. After crossing the dunes, they had followed the Rio Grande for another three hundred miles, had eaten more of the mules that they had worked to death, and had gotten by on rations that had been reduced by half. But now it was water they wanted and had to ration, and that, for Will, was a greater test. He tried to think how he could keep going this way. The Battalion still had at least six hundred miles to march, and most of it would be through land as dry as this. He couldn't think how his feet, his legs, or his mind could continue.

Gradually, however, the terrain did change. When the troops reached the Guadalupe Mountains, they finally found plenty of water, but they faced even colder nights. Nine men were sleeping in each tent by then, and their tents were being held up by their muskets. Cooke had gotten rid of tent poles in order to reduce weight in the wagons. Three men had been added to Will's mess: Ephraim Hart, John Tinney, and Job Steele.

What all the men resented was Cooke's dogged determination to take the wagons through. As they crossed the summit and began to descend, they came to cliffs that were simply too steep for wagons. Will had thought that Cooke finally had no choice; he would have to give up the heavier wagons. But instead, he roped them and had the men lower them off the cliffs. And then they had to lead the animals down steep, dangerous paths.

In the next few days, however, there was some good news. The soldiers began to come across herds of cattle roaming the desert. These, they learned, were the remnants of herds abandoned by Mexican settlers who had been run off by Apache tribes. The cows were wild and underfed, and the meat on them was tough and stringy, but the men were hungry enough that they didn't complain about that. Will knew, however, that a diet of mostly lean beef was nothing to build strength on. It was no wonder the men were losing more energy each day.

The march continued on to the San Pedro River, and then the

five companies camped and rested a little. One of the men shot a bull, and other bulls, enraged by the smell of blood, attacked the Battalion. The animals thundered into the encampment, gored one soldier badly, and broke another's ribs.

When all the dust had finally settled, the men had their first story of bravery in the face of battle. Corporal Frost, in A Company, had stood his ground as a great black bull had charged down upon him. He had waited until the last second to fire his weapon, and the bull had tumbled to the ground at his feet. Levi Hancock wrote one of his many poems about the "battle," and the men sang it to a familiar tune. Of course, the troops saw the irony in their only battle having been fought with beasts rather than enemy soldiers, but they still praised God that no one had been killed.

As the men left the San Pedro, the scouts warned them to carry as much water as they could and to use it sparingly. Water would be scarce again. Rumors also abounded that their first actual battle might occur in a Mexican settlement called Tucson. As it turned out, however, the Mexican soldiers, scared off by the size of the Battalion, put up no defense, and the soldiers marched through unopposed.

What the troops faced now, however, was a desert that seemed designed to cause misery for humans and mules alike. Melissa Coray told Will and some of the other men, "God must have decided to protect his children from thorns. He stuck everything that's prickly together in one place—and hoped no one would be dim enough to cross such land."

Melissa seemed older than she had a few months back, but she had never stopped laughing—and laughter was helpful these days. She and Lydia Hunter were also smart about conserving their water and food, eating their rations in even parcels, and they often walked around to the campfires at night and tried to teach the men to do the same. Both of their husbands were busy with their duties and often left the two women to fend for themselves, but they seemed to have no trouble with that. They had set out never to trouble the troops, and, as it turned out, they were doing the opposite: they were helping the men, cheering them, washing and sewing for them at times, and offering good advice. Melissa had taught Will a good trick. When water was short, she sucked on a little pebble, and that brought saliva to her mouth. Will found that it worked, and he shared the idea with Jesse and the other men in their mess.

Melissa was right about this prickly desert, too. Will had known nothing of cactus in England, but now he was seeing all kinds. Some types were shaped like trees or bushes, some like globes or cones, and others had thin, twisted arms—but all of them had thorns. The soldiers' clothing had been wearing out before this, but now their trousers were being shredded by the thorns. For poor Lydia and Melissa, the walk was a torment. They rarely rode in wagons these days, and the thorns tore at their skirts, ripped pieces away, and even jabbed through the leather in their shoes.

Everyone tried to watch where they stepped, but the mules sometimes jammed their heels into the prickles, and then they went wild from the pain. They bucked, or balked, and it was all the men could do to pull them along and help them avoid the worst of the hazards.

Will's boots had been falling apart. He used a bit of rope to tie a piece of canvas around each sole, and that delayed the disintegration, but he feared the day when he would face the thorns and the deep sand without any shoes at all. The sand was already working its way inside his boots and scraping his skin raw. His shirts were also falling apart, worn through at the shoulders where the straps crossed, and ripped in various places.

One evening he was able to cut the hide from the legs of a bull that had been butchered and eaten. He used the natural curve of the knee to convert the leather into a sort of moccasin. It relieved his feet considerably the first day he tried it, and the hide gradually stretched and molded to his feet at the bend of his ankle. He cast his boots away and told Jesse he would make some moccasins for him. Will had talked to Robert Harris, the butcher from Company E, and Harris had promised additional hide when he butchered more cattle.

It was the evening of December 18, 1846, when Captain Hunter approached the men in Will's mess. "You need to know," he said, "we start tomorrow across a stretch of desert with very little water. Or I guess, to be honest, probably no water at all."

"And what is it you have in mind when you describe a 'stretch'?" Abner asked, sounding very English. "How many miles would that be?"

"It's from here to some Pima Indian villages—where we can get plenty of food and water. The scouts say it may be seventy miles."

"Did you say *seventy?*" Jesse asked.

Captain Hunter nodded. "Yes, I did."

"That's four days, probably five, at the rate we've been moving lately. We can't go that long without water."

"We simply can't be out there that long," Hunter answered. "We have to carry all the water we can, and we'll have to make the march in three days, at most."

Will's first impulse was to tell Captain Hunter he was crazy. The men had pushed themselves as hard as they could. There was no way they could walk that far without water—and move faster, not slower. But he didn't say anything. He only stared at the captain, as all the men were doing.

"We have no choice," Hunter said. "We can't sit out here and die. We'll have reveille very early, at four in the morning, and then we'll have to walk all day and keep walking into the night—get thirty miles or so behind us. We'll rest a little and do the same the next day. Two very long days may get us close, at least, and we can finish on the morning after that."

"I take it we're finally going to give up on the wagons," John Tinney said.

"No. I'm sorry. We have to get some of the wagons through. We've left some that broke down, and we'll leave a few more here. But we've got to keep the rest of them going. You might have to push at times, to help the mules. They'll be working without water too."

"The mules will die out there, Captain Hunter," Will said. "Some of the men will too."

"No. Not the men. Let's make up our minds right now to get everyone across. Use your water as carefully as you can, and if some men fall by the wayside, try to help them along. You can put your muskets and ammunition on the company wagon. That should help some."

Will saw the sadness in Captain Hunter's eyes. Like all the soldiers, he didn't seem the same man who had set out on this march the previous summer. He had given up on shaving some time back, and his dark beard was shaggy, his hair long, his skin deep brown, and his clothes as shabby as Will's. More than that, though, he looked used up. He had lost maybe thirty pounds, and his eyes were sunken behind skeletal facial bones. The man knew as well as anyone that they were facing something close to impossible, but he had no choice but to pass along the order.

"Captain," Will said, "some men are worn down too far already. And some are sick. They can't—"

"Private Lewis, there's nothing else to say. We start early. Let's get some rest now, and let's do what we have to do to make our way to those Indian villages. Just remember, we'll have some days to rest there. We'll be there for Christmas."

It was a strange thing to say. Will wondered what kind of Christmas could happen out here in this desolate place.

Captain Hunter walked away, off toward another campfire. The men at Will's camp were still staring, but Will knew they were looking inside themselves now. Jesse said, "I swear, Cooke has gone crazy. How can we get wagons across this sand—and cover seventy miles in three days?"

But Will saw the greater danger. He had started it by saying that some would die. He had to keep the men from thinking that way. "We'll just do it, that's all," he said. "We'll pray for help, and then we'll keep thinking about the food and water at the end of the march. I'll tell you one thing: I'm not going to die. I'm going to get to the Pacific Ocean, and I'm going to dive in for a swim. And next year, I'm going to see my wife and children again. Let's all promise each other. We'll get through together."

The men nodded, but they didn't say much. They started getting up to head for their tent. But Charley Buttars stopped Will. He said, softly, only to Will, "I can't die. I have to get back to my wife."

"That's how we all feel, Charley. That's what keeps us—"

"But I made a promise. Rebecca was sick—really sick—when I left her. I made her promise to stay alive, and I promised to do the same. Every day I think of that—and pray for it. I have to see her again. And see my Andrew."

"We'll all help each other, Charley." But Charley was still waiting for something, so Will added, "I'll keep *you* alive, Charley. You do the same for me."

The two shook hands.

• • •

Will was not even sure that he had slept when the reveille bugle sounded. For two hours he had wanted to get going, just to take advantage of the cold night air. He noticed that all the men were up quickly, seemingly as anxious as he was.

The troops set out more resolutely than they had in recent days. The prickly pears and other cacti were not as dense in this area, but the sand was deep. The day gradually got warm, but not hot, and the marchers did well all morning. As the day progressed, however, Will felt himself slowing down. His moccasins worked fairly well, but his feet sometimes sank into the sand, and it was all he could do to tug them back out. That extra exertion was sapping his strength, and by midafternoon he could feel himself longing for the usual chance to stop and set up camp. He had taken only sips of his water, and fortunately he wasn't sweating as he had back during the heat of summer, but thirst was a constant presence, almost the only thing he could think about.

Evening came early this late in the year, and Will didn't mind the cool air. The men stopped briefly and ate a little beef, and then Captain Hunter came around again. "All right, men, we're moving out. We think we've come over twenty miles so far—that's good, but it's not nearly enough. We'll keep going as late as we have to and see if we can't make thirty."

No one groaned. No one asked questions. Men simply stood up and waited for the command to move out. Jesse turned to Will. "Can we fill our canteens?" he asked. "From the barrels?"

"Not yet. That's for tomorrow."

"My canteen is empty, Will."

"You drank *all* your water?"

"Back an hour ago or so, I come near passin' out. I drank too much. But I do na' think I would have made it this far, had I na' done't."

"All right. I'll give you half of what I have left. But we can't start using the barrels yet."

"No, Will. I can na' take yor water."

"I'm fine. Give me your canteen."

The truth was, Will could hardly fight down the anger he felt toward Jesse. The man never should have indulged himself that way. Every drop of water Will poured into Jesse's canteen seemed to drip like blood from his own body. But Charley, without saying a word, put his hand on Will's arm and stopped him before he had poured out very much. He dribbled some of his own water into Jesse's canteen. Will thanked him, and the three set out together. Will, by then, was talking to himself. He had to fight back his resentment toward Jesse. Jesse was his brother, his best friend in this world.

They walked steadily for over two hours. Will had no idea what time it was or how far they had come, but he realized after a time that his vision was blurring. He stopped Jesse and Charley, took a sip of water, and bent over long enough to give his back a short rest.

"Are you all right?" Charley asked Will.

"Aye. And what about the two of you?"

"I'm managing," Charley said, but Jesse didn't answer, and Will could see in his face that he hardly knew what was happening.

They set out again, but Jesse didn't go far before he stumbled and sprawled in the sand.

Will dropped down next to him. "Are you all right?"

"Aye. I on'y tripped on somethin'. That's all." Will helped him up. By then, however, Jesse was saying, "The sole tore off my boot. I've walked right through't."

"Can we tie it up, or—"

"No. I done that all I can. Help me pull 'em off. I'm better off barefoot."

Will and Charley helped Jesse get rid of his boots, and they pulled him up. The three set out again, Jesse limping badly. Will had no idea how long they would have to keep going. He guessed that somewhere ahead Cooke would choose a camp where men could sleep a few hours before taking up the march again, but for now, Will's only worry was Jesse—and trying to help him avoid stepping on thorns. They kept walking, kept taking breaks, sipped a bit of water, and finally saw some fires ahead.

They stumbled into the camp, and Jesse collapsed on the ground. Will could think only of water. He drank the last of what he had and felt a little surge of satisfaction. He wondered where the wagon was with the barrels of water, wondered where Captain Hunter might be. But already, now that they weren't walking, the cold was setting in. Will pulled loose the blanket that was tied to Jesse's knapsack. "Wrap up in this," he said. "The best thing we can do is sleep for a while."

He pulled off his own knapsack and was untying his blanket when he heard a voice that he recognized as Captain Hunter's. "Private Lewis, can you go back with me?" he asked. "Some men have given out, and we need to go back and help them in."

Will's muscles strained as he pulled himself up. "All right, then," he said. "Let's go."

"Take a drink of water first," Hunter said. He handed Will his canteen.

"No. That's your water. I can't—"

"They found a bit of water in this dry riverbed by digging down deep in the sand. We filled some canteens."

Will nodded. But he took only a swallow of the gritty water. Then he gave Charley and Jesse each a little drink.

Will and Captain Hunter walked back and found men who were down on the ground, unable to go on. They gave them water and helped them to their feet. Those who got up locked arms with others who were just as exhausted, and the pairs stumbled on toward the fires. In time, Captain Hunter had accounted for everyone in his company, so he and Will turned and made their way back to the camp themselves. By the time they dropped down on the ground, Will knew it must be almost morning, but he wrapped himself up and slept a little.

No reveille sounded. Captain Hunter simply came around and said, "We need to head out again. I have water for everyone. We gave some from the barrels to the mules, and we have enough to give you maybe half a canteen. You'll have to be more sparing with it than you were yesterday."

"How can we—"

"It's all we have, men. Just keep going today, whether you think you can or not. Let's stay alive."

No one set out with strength this time. Everyone was in pain. Will kept an eye on Jesse, but he also watched other men around him. When soldiers sat down to rest, he stopped to be sure they were going to be able to get up again. And then, midmorning, he saw Lydia and Melissa, walking arm in arm. As Will came alongside them, he could see the bulge under Lydia's dress—which had become more obvious the last couple of weeks.

"Sisters, how are you holding up?" Will asked.

Lydia looked at him, and he saw a hint of a smile. "We were just saying what a lovely day it is for a walk," she said. "Don't you love the scenery?"

For the first time since leaving Tucson, Will laughed a little. "Sounds like you're doing fine," he said.

But Melissa said, "No, Lydia's not fine at all. Her legs keep giving out. But we're going to make it."

And on they went. Will tried to stay close enough to watch the women in case they needed help. But there came a time late in the day when the numbness in Will's body seemed to fill his brain. He feared he had allowed himself too little water. Jesse had portioned his water better today, but his mind was drifting at times. "How are you doing?" Will would ask Jesse from time to time, but Jesse would only glance his way and not make the effort to answer.

Will had wrapped Jesse's feet with canvas that morning, tying it with ropes. This helped him avoid being stuck by thorns, but he seemed not to know where he was stepping. Will finally had to take his arm as Melissa was doing with Lydia, and he marched Jesse around prickly pears and past taller cacti. Charley stayed close too, and he eventually took Jesse's other arm.

Night came again. At one point Colonel Cooke came by on his mule and called out, "We've set up camp a few miles ahead. We have a little more water left. And we'll have some bread for you. Don't give up."

But "a few miles" never seemed to end. There were times when Will sensed that he had slept as he walked, and he was stumbling almost as badly as Jesse. But they kept going, with Lydia and Melissa just ahead. Will also kept watching for fires. The land was flat, and a fire would show up well ahead, but he could see nothing but stars that seemed to sit on the desert floor and then reach upward like a great tent over the land.

And then Jesse began to sink toward the ground.

Will and Charley tried to hold him up, but his weight pulled all three of them down. Will rolled over, intent on helping Jesse, but for the moment he couldn't find the strength to pull himself up. He lay there for a time, taking long breaths, getting himself ready to make the effort.

Then he heard Lydia's voice. "Jesse, open your eyes," she was saying. "We have water." Will managed to get his own eyes to open. "They've brought some water back to us. Sit up, if you can. I'll give you some."

"All right," Jesse said. But he didn't move. Will raised himself up enough to help Jesse. They held the canteen to Jesse's lips, and he took a nice long draw on it. Then Lydia let Will and Charley take a drink.

"Jesse, are you all right?" Will asked.

"Aye. It was my legs what quit. But I'll go again. I haven't given up."

"Eat a little bread," Lydia was saying to Jesse. "They brought us bread, too." She gave a slice to Jesse, and then to the other men.

. . .

Liz loved the smell of the mutton cooking at the fire, but the house was full of smoke. The women had built most of their log cabin before men had finally joined in to help them. It was a drafty little structure, and the fireplace, made from mud and sticks, did not draw well. Smoke hung in the house and filled up everyone's lungs. All the same, Liz and Ellen and Mary Ann were inside now, fairly warm most days.

Mary Ann had helped to build the house—as best she could. She had chopped away at the logs until her hand had been so covered in blood and blisters that she cried when she took her turn. But Liz had gotten her angry, and that had fired up her stubbornness. She had started to take pride in staining the hatchet with her own blood. Liz had also seen something else happen. As the cabin had taken shape, not only had Mary Ann learned to use the axe with a bit more skill, she had seemed to take pride in the idea that women could build a house for themselves. Liz felt the same way. By the time a man had asked if he could help, she had told him, "We'll do just fine without you, Brother."

He had looked rather shamefaced and said, "I'm sorry, Sister. There's just so much to do. We'll get the roof on for you and help you build a chimney. Those are the hardest parts of the job."

The truth was, Liz had been worried about the roof. She was

relieved—and a little ashamed of herself for being so curt with the brother.

But now it was Christmas Day, and a good sister had brought them some mutton. They had wheat flour for bread, too, and a few potatoes. The children were excited by the smell of the food, and Mary Ann had taken it upon herself to make certain they understood that Christmas in old England was a special day—and was going to be for them from now on. She had hiked out into the woods and found some evergreen boughs, which she used as decorations. There were really no mantels, no windowsills, no cabinets—or anything else to adorn—but she had pounded some sticks into the mud between the logs, and she had hung the limbs as best she could. Now she was playing games with the children. There was no room for Fox and Geese, and most of the children were too young for word games, so she had managed to lead them in little circles in a game of Follow the Leader, and she had taught them London Bridge Is Falling Down.

Part of the joy for the children was that they finally had a little room to play. The Johns family had lived with them for the first couple of weeks after they had moved inside, but the same brothers who had put the roof on this house had helped Daniel Johns build a little cabin for his family. And the great joy in that house was that Eliza had survived her fever and was doing better every day.

Liz finally said, "It's time to sing Christmas songs, and then we'll read the story of Jesus from the Bible. And after that, what?"

"Christmas dinner!" Jesse Junior shouted, and Liz knew how difficult life must feel for these children, with such meager provisions and so little variety in what they had to eat.

Everyone was still singing Christmas songs when a knock sounded. Mary Ann unlatched the ill-fitting door and pushed it open. Liz saw that it was Bishop Pendleton standing outside in a heavy blanket coat. "Is it Father Christmas?" she asked the children.

Bishop Pendleton stepped in. "I guess I'm as close to Father Christmas as you'll see today. But I do have something for the children."

He opened a burlap sack, and from it he pulled out little toys. They were not wrapped, and there were not enough of them for each child to have his or her own, but there were a hand-carved toy horse, a "Jacob's ladder," a rag doll, and a little sack of marbles.

The children were delighted with the surprises, but they were wide-eyed when Bishop Pendleton said, "I also have this." He pulled out another little cloth sack. "This is molasses candy, made by my dear wife herself. There's one piece for everyone, but be sure to eat your dinner first."

All the children were nodding, saying they would do that, and little Jacob said, "Thank you, Bishop. Thank you *so much*."

The words brought tears to Bishop Pendleton's eyes. "I'm sorry I haven't done more for all of you."

"But you've been so sick," Liz said.

The bishop still looked pale, even skeletal, but he said, "Yes, but I'm finally getting better. The Lord's been good to me."

"To all of us," Liz said.

And when they prayed over their food, Ellen prayed that Jesse and Will were feeling as well as they were on Christmas Day.

• • •

Will and Jesse were eating watermelon. The Pima Indians had provided them with a beautiful dinner. Will had never seen such melons in his life. He and the other men ate them as though they were candy. All that water, all that flavor: it seemed too miraculous to be real. The Indians knew nothing of Christmas, but the soldiers were all aware that this was Christmas Day, and every single man—and woman—had made it to the Pima villages alive.

The troops had made it into the second camp, having walked almost all night. They had rested for an hour or so, eaten a little, drunk very little, and then limped ahead another few miles to the village. All that day the companies had straggled in, but those who made it first had had a good drink and then had gone back to find those still under way.

Now, a few days of good eating had brought the entire group back to life, and there were many prayers of thanks on Christmas Day.

CHAPTER 20

Jeff got home about nine o'clock. He and Malcolm and Larry had held a presidency meeting on Wednesday evening, and then they had called on a couple of families they were concerned about. Jeff and Malcolm had actually intended to return to a job they had been working on, but the visits had gone a little long. They decided they would go home and then start earlier than usual the next morning.

When Jeff came in from the garage, he found Abby at the kitchen table with drawings spread out in front of her. She seemed surprised to see Jeff. "Wow. You're home early."

"Yeah. We didn't go back to the job."

"Hey, that's a first. I just got home about an hour ago. Sister Becker got a call from her son's mission president today. I guess Jordan's about to give up and come home. She was able to talk to him, but she doesn't know if he'll stay or not."

"What can you do about that?"

"Nothing. But Sister Becker is really worried, and she doesn't have a husband to talk things out with. I just went over and spent a little time with her."

"What's happening with Sierra Farr?"

"The news is pretty good. She's getting more feeling back in her legs. She won't be up and running around very soon—but her mom gets more confident every day that she's going to be able to walk."

"You call her every day, don't you?"

"Not always. But she calls me quite often. She's another one who needs someone to share her worries with."

"Did you tell her you have the same problem? No husband around to talk to?"

"I actually did say something about that." Abby smiled. "I told her you quit your job in Fort Madison so you wouldn't be gone such long hours, and now you're spending all the more time working with Malcolm."

Jeff knew that was mostly true. He was home a little more, but he was spending most of that time working on the web site or studying for his class.

"Jeff, you can't help it right now. I'm not complaining. But let's go to bed early for once. I can't concentrate on these plans anymore tonight."

"Okay. I need to check a couple of things on the web site, but it won't take too long."

She let her eyes roll, and he knew what she was thinking.

"No, really," he insisted.

"Well, don't take too long, or I'll fall asleep before you ever get to bed."

Jeff understood what she was saying. It had been that way more often than not lately, the two of them hardly ever finding time to be together. So he decided to hurry.

Abby stood up and said, "I'm going to take a shower."

"Okay. Give me just a few minutes." Jeff found his laptop in the living room and brought it to the table where Abby had been sitting. He turned it on and had a look at the blog article he had started the night before. He needed to post it on the site soon, and yet, when he looked at it, he saw that there were facts he needed to check, and the writing seemed awkward now that he read it again. He didn't intend to do much with it, but he did a search for articles on the same subject and soon found that he needed to know a lot more before he started sending out advice. The article was on techniques for hanging doors, something he had done before, and something a lot of people might want to do on their own, but he realized that getting a door exactly square and in perfect balance was important—and a little hard to explain.

So he gathered the information and then noticed that almost an hour had gone by. It wasn't really late yet, but it might seem late to Abby, who was always up early with William. So he shut down his research and was about to close out his computer when it occurred to him that he ought to check the messages on his site. He discovered something he hadn't expected. There were two new requests from people wanting to know how much he charged to advertise on the site. He had gotten several of those lately. Jeff decided he had better confer with Malcolm about raising their prices per ad, but he was excited when he walked to the bedroom.

"Hey, Ab, guess what?" he said.

But he got no answer. He knew he had blown it again, taking so long. He stood for a moment, thought about waking her, but knew it was the wrong thing to do. Just as he was turning to leave, though, he heard, "Jeff, did you say something?"

"Yeah. But it's okay. Go back to sleep."

"I'm sorry."

"It's okay. I just wanted to tell you, I have more people wanting to advertise on our site. I need you to post some more articles. If we could get the decorating angle going stronger, this thing might really take off."

Jeff waited, but he could only hear Abby breathing steadily.

And that made him angry—not at Abby, but at himself for not coming to bed sooner. He was tired of the way life kept going, no matter how hard he tried to get his schedule under control.

Jeff was not sleepy now. He went back to his computer and fiddled with the article for a while, but he couldn't seem to keep his mind on it. He finally stood up, thinking he really should go to bed. But then he decided to walk outside. He just wanted to feel the air. It was April now; the nights were still cool, but the breeze felt mild, and the smell of life was in the air. Jeff had smelled so much wood and sawdust lately, not a bad smell, really, but he needed more of this: the damp earth and the hint of something acrid in last year's leaves as they aged in the woods. There was something sweet, too, maybe lilacs.

He hadn't intended to walk across to Grandpa Lewis's property, but he found himself strolling in that direction. He pushed through the brush and made his way into the clearing where he had stood many times before in the last two years. "I don't know what I'm doing right now," he said out loud. He didn't know if he was telling Will Lewis or if he was speaking to himself.

"I wanted to get out of my job, and I'm glad I did. But I'm in over my head now. Malc and I work too many hours. I don't see Abby. I don't see Will. I just work." And then he said what he had never admitted to himself: "I can't be a carpenter all my life. I just can't."

Jeff regretted the words as soon as he said them. They sounded arrogant, as though he thought he was too good to do ordinary work—the work Jesus had done. But he knew it wasn't the work itself that bothered him. "The thing is, I'm not myself. I've invented this new guy to fit my situation."

He stopped himself. Maybe he was exaggerating. He didn't want to be dramatic. He reminded himself that he loved that feeling when a job was completed and the owners of the house were excited and happy. He also loved being around Malcolm. He thought of Grandpa Lewis, farming from sunup until sundown. The man surely wouldn't feel sorry for Jeff. "Never mind," he said. "I shouldn't say things like that. I just need to survive this time we're going through, while we're getting everything going, and then I'll be all right. Really, these requests for advertising space might change everything."

Will laughed at himself. He wondered what Grandpa Lewis would have thought of the Internet or of making a living by selling ads in cyberspace.

But he couldn't seem to get rid of the discouragement he was feeling. Lately he had found himself remembering the guy he had been in high school. He hadn't known exactly what he would do with his life; he had merely known that he would do something well. Teachers had told him how smart he was, how interesting, how full of ideas. He had always thought he would use all that to do something significant, something satisfying, and into that life would fit a family and Church callings, and all of it would somehow blend and make sense. But that confidence seemed to be slipping away from him now, and the loss of it was frightening.

Still, he didn't want to think himself into some corner. "Grandpa, I'm just letting off steam," he finally said. "I've just got to stick it out."

And then he walked back across the street. He slipped into the bedroom, sat down quietly, and took off his shoes.

"Jeff?"

"Yeah."

"Where did you go?"

"You fell asleep, so I—"

"I'm sorry. Come to bed with me now."

"Just sleep. I know how tired you are."

"No. I need you to hold me."

That was what Jeff had wanted to hear.

• • •

When Abby woke up in the morning, she wasn't surprised to realize that Jeff had gotten up early and was already gone. For a while she had been hearing William babbling in his bedroom, but now he had begun to cry. Abby took a deep breath, and then she rolled over and slipped out of bed. "I'm coming, William," she called, and she grabbed her terrycloth robe from a chair near the bed. She pulled it on and pushed her feet into some fluffy slippers on the floor, and then she walked into William's room. "Hello, my big boy," she said. "Did you think I wasn't going to wake up this morning?"

He stopped crying. He was reaching for her, and when she reached for him, she saw the delight on his face. As she pulled him from the crib, he grabbed her around the neck and hugged her.

"I love you, William. Do you know that?" she said, and he grasped her even tighter. What she knew, however, was that she had to drop him off this morning. He sometimes fussed a little when she first left, but he loved Kayla, and the girls were like sisters to him now. So it wasn't a terrible trial to leave him each day, but it was not what she would have liked.

When Abby gave William a bath, she loved the touch of him, loved his personality—the way he seemed to accept what life brought him and rarely "complained" about anything. The scar on his chest was hardly noticeable now, and he seemed to have no deeper scars.

What she felt in herself was a touch of sorrow that she would be away from him all day. She hoped he didn't feel abandoned.

Abby was still feeling the warmth and closeness to Jeff from the night before. She was glad she had awakened and had had that time with him. But she thought again of what he had told her. Lying in bed, nestled together, she had said, "Are you okay, Jeff? Is this remodeling thing what you want?"

He had not answered quickly. When he did speak, he only said, "I was thinking about Grandpa Lewis tonight. I don't think he indulged himself in such questions."

"Maybe he did. You don't know that," she had told him.

"Maybe. I know this, though: we both married women we fell in love with. He said more than once in his life history that the greatest blessing of his life was to marry his Liz. And I feel the same way. I have you and Will for eternity. Next to that, nothing matters very much."

She had held him after that, but she knew that he never had answered her question.

But now she had to hurry. Her hair needed work, and she had to dress up a little because she was meeting with a client in Quincy. It would have been much easier if Jeff didn't leave so early most mornings, but at least William was good about sitting in his high chair and feeding himself Cheerios while she called to him from time to time from the bathroom.

By the time she had him ready, though, and took one last look at herself, she realized she had the remains of wet Cheerios smudged across the shoulder of her shirt. She sponged that off and then hurried to get William into his car seat. By the time she got to Kayla's she was realizing she might have to make a call to her client to move her appointment back half an hour. But she hurried in with William and found Kayla looking much less put together. Abby envied her that she could still be in her robe and seemingly at ease with her day.

"Did I leave William's sippy cup here last time?" Abby asked Kayla. "I couldn't find one when I was getting ready to leave."

"I think I've got a couple of his. Or at least I've got some that are clean that he can use."

"I brought some apple juice, but I was reading, maybe I shouldn't be giving him sugary juices. Do you let your kids drink juices, or—"

"I probably don't worry enough about stuff like that. I just don't let them get too hooked on any one thing."

"That sounds balanced. That makes sense."

Kayla laughed. "It makes *perfect* sense as long as you don't think too much about it."

"Well, listen, I've got to run. I got a speeding ticket on my way to Quincy last week. Jeff was really nice about it, but I just can't drive like that anymore. I feel like I never stop running."

Kayla pushed her hair back behind her ears. "Oh, Abby, I've got the easy end of this job. I'm glad I don't have to drive down there as often as you do."

Abby nodded. She suddenly felt her dread in making the same trip again, but she said instead, "It's not so bad. Are you two doing all right?"

"Yeah. Mostly. I'm relieved that we figured something out. We have more money than we ever did when Malcolm was with the tire shop, and he likes the work. He just gets frustrated that every job seems to take more time than he expects—and his clients get mad at him."

"The guys are still putting in way too many hours, aren't they?"

William had already run off to the toys in the girls' bedroom. Abby could hear little Sophie talking to him. "Listen to her," Kayla said. "She thinks she's William's mother." But then Kayla returned to the subject: "I don't like that Malcolm's gone so much, but I think they'll get past that pretty soon. Even the way things are going, Malcolm's still happier than when he was working at his old job."

Abby had moved toward the door, but now she stopped. "I'm glad to hear that," she said. "But, Kayla, I don't think Jeff's very happy. I thought that when he quit his job across the river he'd be in seventh heaven, but I don't see it yet. I knew Jeff in college, and it's like the guy I knew back then has ceased to exist."

"Jeff still has too much on his table—with the web site and the class he's taking. Malcolm doesn't have all that."

"Maybe Jeff should give up taking classes for a while," Abby said.

"Are you kidding? That would kill him."

Abby really needed to get going, but Kayla's words had taken her by surprise. "What do you mean?"

"Malcolm says that's what Jeff loves to talk about when they're working together. He's never known anyone who loves to learn as much as Jeff does. He comes back from that class he's taking with all these thoughts about how Americans think, and how Joseph Smith had to be born in America . . . or something like that. Malcolm loves to hear about it. But I'm sure you and Jeff talk about it too."

"Not really, Kayla. He tries sometimes, but . . ." She couldn't think how to end her sentence. Yes, they were both busy, but maybe Abby didn't show the same interest that Malcolm did. She wondered whether her job and her Church calling weren't filling up all her thoughts, leaving nothing for Jeff.

"Well," Kayla said, "I'm the last person to give someone as smart as you advice, but I'd say, you better talk to him about those things. I think that's probably the college guy you've been missing."

Abby nodded, thought for a time, and then said, "Yeah. I think you're right." And then, on the way to Quincy, she thought about the Jeff she remembered, the young man who loved more than anything to share what he thought. And she had been much the same. That was part of what had caused the two of them to fall in love. Now they were talking about who could run to the grocery store tomorrow, since neither one had any time. Maybe something like that happened in all marriages. The last thing she wanted was to start whining, "We don't talk enough anymore," especially since most of the problem was probably her fault. What she wanted was to get things right. She wanted Jeff to learn again. It was becoming obvious that he couldn't live without that.

• • •

It was three o'clock in the afternoon, and Jeff was home. At noon, when Jeff and Malcolm had sat down to eat a sandwich, Malcolm had suddenly said, "Jeff, you need to get out of here."

"What?"

"I've been thinking about this all morning—ever since you told me about those new requests for ad space. As long as we're getting paid a price for each job we do, there's no way to expand from there. We'll just work ourselves to death, get old, and hope we can keep up with the cost of living. It's the web site and the advertising that we need to build up."

"I know. That's true."

"So why are you working on this job with me? Go finish that blog you've been working on. Fill up our site with all kinds of stuff that people are searching the Internet to find out."

Jeff could hardly believe this. That morning he had cut a length of floorboard too short and had to run to Keokuk to replace it. That had put them way behind. How could he take off this afternoon? "But we've gotta finish this job today," he told Malcolm.

"I know. But here's what I was just thinking about. We keep saying we should hire someone, but we don't do it. Maybe it's time. Do you know Ed Ewell in our ward?"

"Sure."

"He's out of work, has been for a couple of months. He's not a carpenter, but he does all the fix-up stuff around his house. I'll bet he'd jump at a chance to come and work with us." Malcolm reached into his back pocket and pulled out his cell phone. "I'm calling him right now. If he can help me finish this job, you're going home."

And it had happened. Ed *had* jumped at the chance and said he could be over in half an hour. Jeff had been more than happy to go home and work on his blog. And he had gotten a lot done. The change of routine had charged him up, and writing while his mind was still fresh, rather than late at night, was surprisingly fun.

But then his phone rang. When he dug it out of his pocket, he heard a voice say, "Jeff, this is Ed Ewell. You need to run back over to the job. Right now."

"Why? What's happened?"

"Malcolm's cut a slice in his leg with the Skilsaw, and I can't get him to go to a doctor. But it needs to be sewn up."

"I'll be right there."

Jeff ran for his car and hurried back to the house where Malcolm was working. He found Malcolm down on his knees finishing the floorboards in the kitchen. But Jeff could also see that Malcolm's jeans were stained with blood.

"Malc, what are you doing?"

Malcolm didn't look at Jeff. He merely said, "I think that's pretty obvious. I'm trying to get this job finished."

"Ed said that—"

"It's not that bad. I slapped a big bandage on it and taped it up really good. I'm okay."

"Let me look at it."

"No."

Ed walked into the kitchen. "The guard on his saw stuck, and he brought the blade right back against his thigh. It cut a bad gash. It's downright dangerous for him to stay here and work."

"Come on, Malcolm, let's go," Jeff said.

"It's not that deep. Ed's making too much of it. And we have to have this job done tonight. The family's coming home in the morning, and I promised we would be out of here by then."

"Malcolm, that's nuts," Jeff said. He walked over and put a hand on Malcolm's shoulder.

But Malcolm's reaction was the last thing Jeff expected. He reached back and pushed Jeff's hand away, and then he stood and faced him. "I'll tell you what's nuts," Malcolm shouted into Jeff's face. "What makes no sense whatsoever is the way you bid these jobs. You don't have the slightest idea how long it takes to get a project finished. That's why we're always in a mess."

Jeff stepped back from Malcolm's rage. He couldn't think what to say.

"I'm sick of it, Jeff. I can't keep up this pace. And I can't work with a guy who's *clueless* about the work we do."

Jeff still hadn't taken a breath. He was staring into Malcolm's face, thinking this couldn't be happening. He finally muttered, "Sometimes I—"

"Not sometimes. *Every* time. You live in the clouds, Jeff. You never land on planet earth. You don't think of all the things that can go wrong on a job."

"I guess I—"

"I'm going to tell you the truth, Jeff." His voice had lost some of its heat, but Jeff heard bitterness in his tone. "I sent you home today because I want you to start doing the web stuff—and maybe that will make us some money. But I don't want you to bid anymore, and I don't want to correct all the mistakes you make. I think Ed can do a better job. I'm sorry, but that's just way I feel."

Jeff stood for a long time. He was utterly deflated. He tried to think what all this would mean. But then he looked down at Malcolm's thigh and saw the wet blood that was seeping through his bandage and coming out around the rip in his jeans. "You've got to get that stitched up," he said.

"I know."

"Come on, then. I'll drive you."

Jeff looked at Ed and said, "Do what you can. I'll be back as soon as I can get here."

Jeff drove Malcolm to the clinic on Mulholland, but the two didn't say a word to each other, and Jeff didn't go in with Malcolm when the receptionist took him back to an examining room.

Jeff waited for well over an hour, the whole time trying to think what he would do now. He couldn't just keep up the web site and remain some sort of silent partner with Malcolm. It had all been about friendship—about Zion—and that was dead now. What hurt more than anything was the realization that he had failed. As it turned out, he had been letting Malcolm down the whole time, and it had taken a crisis to get him to admit it.

When Malcolm finally came out, he looked pale, tired. He took care of some paperwork at the desk, and then he nodded to Jeff, as if to say, "Let's go," but nothing more. It was back at the car that Malcolm said, "I need to talk to you, Jeff. Don't say anything. Just listen to me for a few minutes."

Jeff didn't start the car. He just stared out the windshield at the rusty back end of an old white pickup.

"When I cut myself, all I could think was that I had to finish the job, no matter what. Ed started pushing me to go to the doctor, and that made me mad. He didn't have the first idea how hard we've been trying to get that project done. I told myself I could keep working, but I knew I couldn't, and that started making me madder and madder. And then, in my head, I started taking it out on you."

Jeff didn't say anything. In a way, he didn't want to hear this. Maybe too much had already been said. How could Malcolm take it back?

"I told you back at the house that I was going to tell you the truth, but I didn't. I just popped off. It's definitely true that you don't allow enough time for the jobs. But I probably wouldn't do any better. It just always looks like things will be simpler than they are. I'll have to admit, when I told you to go home, I was thinking that Ed would be a little faster than you and maybe get things right the first time more than you do, but I don't know that for sure. I do know that what I told you was right. You need to work on our web site and make us some money."

"But do you still want to—"

"Jeff, you're the best friend I've ever had in my life. Yes, I want to be partners with you. I can't believe I said some of those things."

"It's good you did. I know I'm not much of a carpenter. I—"

"Jeff, you're doing the wrong work. It's just not who you are. Let me do the bidding. You track the ordering and the bills and all that, and make that web site into the best part of our business. Plus, you also need to put more time into the class you're taking. You can't give up that part of your life."

"I know. I won't give that up."

"You need to go to grad school, my friend." The final words came out with a little sob. "I'm sorry, Jeff. I really am."

They didn't look at each other, but Jeff said, "I love you, Malc."

Malcolm didn't respond for quite some time, but finally he said, "Yeah. I'm trying to say the same thing."

CHAPTER 21

Will was working on a pair of moccasins. Brother Harris had given him the hide from the legs of another bull, along with the sinew Will could use to lace the opening shut. He had given his own pair to Jesse, whose feet were so bad now that it was all he could do to walk. It was well after dark when Will finished his sewing, pulled the makeshift boots on, and then tied them with a bit of rope around his ankles. But when he stood to test them, he felt all the pain: in his ankles, his knees, his lower back. And the soreness in his feet was simply part of life now, always expected.

"It's going to be bad," he said, not really to anyone except himself. "Two more days without water."

But Jesse said, "I hope I can make it. I have a feeling some won't."

"We can't say that, Jesse. We'll carry people if we have to, but we'll get everyone through."

"I can't carry anyone, Will," Jesse said, and Will didn't argue with him. What bothered Will more was that he was not sure he could carry anyone either. The ague had taken his strength in the beginning, but it was the desert that was depleting him. He was not sure that any of the men had enough life left in them to do more than trudge forward on their own.

Jesse walked off to the tent, and Will was about to follow, but he could see a man moving through the dark, toward the fire. "Private Lewis, are the boys in your mess ready for another hard day?" a voice asked, and Will recognized that it was Captain Hunter.

"Ready as we can be," Will said.

Captain Hunter stood close to the fire and looked across it at Will. He looked troubled. "Will," he said, "Lydia says she's all right too, but I don't know how she could be. I'm wondering if you could watch out for her tomorrow."

"Sure I will. But couldn't she ride in a wagon for a day or two?"

"That's what I want her to do, but she's stubborn. She tells me that our animals are too worn down to pull the extra weight. And there's something to that. But I know the truth. She doesn't want Colonel Cooke to see her riding in a wagon. He made too much of her not being able to get across this desert. She wants to show him he's wrong."

"Well, I'll stay close to her. Is Melissa holding up?"

"She is. And my son tries to help them, but he's nothing but skin and bones himself now. The problem for me is, I'm back and forth, looking out for all the men, and I can't be with them the way I'd like to be."

"Don't worry. I'll do what I have to do to keep her going—even if I have to hog-tie her and put her in a wagon."

"You'll never manage that," Hunter said, and he smiled. "I'll stop by as often as I can. But I'll feel better if I know you're staying with her. I'm . . ." His voice caught for a moment, and Will realized just how much this meant to him. "Will, I'm worried about her. The baby's only a couple of months off. I'm scared that I'm killing her— her and the baby both."

"It's not you, Captain Hunter. She wanted—"

"I shouldn't have let her come. I knew better. But she wasn't taking no for an answer."

"It's all right. We'll get her through. Don't worry."

"I appreciate your help, Will. You've been good to her all along." Captain Hunter stood for a time, looking into the flames. "Have you heard anything from your wife?"

"No. Not since Brother Lee brought those letters. But she was sick when she wrote—had been for a while—and she's expecting a baby, too."

"Do you worry about her?"

"Of course I do. I'm not sure that Lydia isn't safer out here than she would be with the folks back in those sickly camps."

"No. I doubt that. I'm sure Brigham looked after all the wives. Your wife is safe in a warm house this winter. Trust in that."

Brother Hunter left then, but his words lingered with Will. It was six months since Will had seen Liz and his boys, and he had no way of knowing what had happened to them. He wasn't sure at all that they had a decent place to live. He worried every day about that, but tonight, with so much to face again in the morning, his anxiety was worse than ever. He wanted to help Lydia Hunter if he could, but his hope was that someone was looking after Liz. He kneeled down and asked, as he did every night, that the Lord would keep her safe.

It was only as he got back up on his feet and turned toward the tent that he realized that Charley Buttars was sitting close by, just outside the entrance to the tent. "What are you doing, Charley?" Will asked.

"I don't know. Just thinking about things."

"You're holding up fine. You'll be all right."

"It's not that, Will. I heard what you told the captain. I'm worried about the same thing you are."

"We can't assume the worst, Charley."

Charley got up. Will couldn't see his face in the dark, but he had heard the despair in his voice. "Rebecca's never been strong. I asked too much of her when we made that trip across Iowa. She was not just sick, but worn down. I wish I hadn't left her. Our leaders shouldn't have made this whole thing—all this marching for nothing—so important. I should be with Rebecca, taking care of her."

"The Lord will bless you, Charley. You answered a prophet's call, and you'll be blessed for it."

"That's all fine to say. But it doesn't always work out that way. Two of our men have died already. And some who went off to Pueblo probably won't make it. And think how many died coming across Iowa."

"I know." Will looked into the dark, felt the weight of all the terrible days the Saints had experienced since leaving their homes. "I don't mean to say that nothing bad will happen. But the Lord gets us through, no matter what comes."

Charley didn't respond, and Will sensed that he took no solace in his words. Charley merely turned, bent down, and entered the tent. Will followed, and he wrapped himself up in his blanket. He needed to sleep.

It was January now, and the men were crossing the Imperial Valley of California. They had been marching for six months and they were badly weakened, but tonight they had been warned again to carry all the water they could. There might not be a new source for forty-eight hours or more. Since leaving the Pima villages in Rainbow Valley, nothing had been easy. At first, the troops had followed the Gila River close enough to have water each day, but food had become ever more scarce, with fewer wild cattle to kill and no game to hunt. Colonel Cooke had tried to save the mules from pulling so much cargo. He had sent some of the Battalion supplies down the river on a raft. But the raft had lodged on a sandbar, and a good deal of the food had been lost. Cooke had had to further reduce the rations at about the same time that the men had had a good many sandy hills to cross. That meant more pushing, more roping, more fatigue. And there was always mesquite and ironwood brush to cut, a road to make through all this barrenness.

Mules had been giving out almost every day, and the carcasses did offer food for the men, but it was tough, unsalted meat, and there was little else to go with it. The rice and beans and flour were mostly gone. The January afternoons were warm most days, but the nights and mornings were cold, and the men were nothing but bones now, vulnerable to these changes in temperature. Will noticed how haggard everyone looked, their clothes hanging off them in shreds, their beards grown long. And he saw the dull, lost look in their eyes when they set out each morning. He knew that everyone was looking inside for strength. Will kept telling himself that one day he would see Liz again; he would hold her in his arms, and he would see his boys and his new child. He would laugh with them and play with them, and all these days in the desert would be only a dark memory. And yet, it was all very hard to imagine. There seemed no other world now, only mesquite and creosote bushes, barrel cactus and yucca and a strange plant with spindly arms that Colonel Cooke called ocotillo. And sand. When he shut his eyes at night he saw sand.

Not only the mules but the wagons were breaking down. There had been more than thirty wagons when the march had begun, but only seven had made it beyond the Pima villages and the Colorado River crossing. Cooke, however, was not about to give them up. He absolutely would get a few wagons through. His assignment was to build a wagon road, and he couldn't claim he had done that if he brought foot soldiers to the coast with no wagons.

Cooke was a determined man, sometimes unreasonably so, and

at times it would have been easy to hate him. And yet, Will had actually come to think rather highly of him. The man refused to spare himself. He never seemed to sleep. He was always moving up and down the line on his big white mule, finding ways to solve problems, taking care of those who were sick or injured. He was a taciturn man, and harsh at times, but he seemed to understand that he could never be soft, that he had to expect the most of his men. He had admitted to the officers, and word had gotten around, that he regretted that seventy-mile march without water. He had not expected that ordeal to be quite so destructive as it had turned out. He might have taken a longer way and stayed closer to water—but he had known that supplies were giving out, and he had gambled that some sources of water might be located along the way. He also regretted the food he had sent down the river; he had sent men back to try to locate it.

The men had finished crossing the Colorado on January 11. That had been a long ordeal, mostly spent waiting for rafts, but at least it had meant a couple of days of rest from walking. There was so little food for the surviving mules and sheep that men had picked mesquite seeds and fed them to the animals. The next stop had been at a well that General Kearny had dug, but after a march of sixteen miles, they had found very little water, and in the pool they had found rotting wolf carcasses. Some men had been sent forward to dig more wells, and a little water had been available, but so little that it took most of a day for the men to fill canteens and for the animals to drink.

After that, Colonel Cooke had sent an advance company on mules about twenty miles ahead to dig wells at a place called Pozo Hondo. The troops had followed, marching two days to get there, thinking of the water they would have when they arrived. But the news had been bad when they reached the well. Only a little muddy water had been extracted, and the men were allowed only a pint and a half each for their canteens.

It was at Pozo Hondo that the scouts had arrived with fresh mules from California. The mules were wild, however, and would need to be trained to pull wagons. What was worse was that news from the battlefront was not good. Kearny's troops had fought a bloody battle and lost some men—dragoons Cooke knew as friends. The colonel seemed to feel a greater need to get to the battle, and he knew nothing good could come from resting in this place with such a pitiful well. He spread the word through the officers that the men should sleep a few hours, and then they would set out again very early. But Will had given up his shoes to Jesse by then, and he didn't think he could make it across this next stretch if he didn't find some way to protect his own feet. So he had spent the evening making a new pair of moccasins, and now he had to face more days without water.

At three o'clock, drummers sounded the signal to arise. By four, the Battalion was marching again, under the starlight. The moccasins helped, and Will felt some renewed energy after getting a little sleep. But the sun gradually changed from pleasant to hot. Will stayed close to Lydia and Melissa all day. In fact, all of the men from his mess stayed together, and Will noticed that everyone was keeping an eye on the two women. Melissa still tried to joke a little, or at least converse, but Lydia was moving awkwardly now, straining to keep her balance and walk in the sand. She seemed to need all her concentration just to keep up a steady pace.

Will called on the group to take breaks more often than he normally would have, and then he helped Lydia to her feet when they all set out again. He tried to use as little water as he could stand to get by on. And once, when Lydia didn't notice, he had taken her canteen, which she had set down beside her, and poured in a little of his own water.

It was well after dark when Captain Hunter called for a halt. He came by to each mess group and told the troops that they should eat something, rest for a few hours, and then set out again at one o'clock in the morning.

"How can we do that?" Will heard a man ask.

"How can we not?" Hunter answered. "We have no water here. We have to make it to Carrizo Springs. There's plenty of water there, and then we can give you a longer rest."

"How many miles?" Phil Gray asked.

"I'm not sure. Maybe twenty."

Phil said nothing. No one complained. No one speculated. They only sat quietly in the sand. But Will knew what everyone was thinking. This would probably be the day when some would die.

Captain Hunter sat down by Lydia for a time and spoke to her quietly. Before he left, he came over to Will and whispered, "She's held up all right so far. But this next push will be worse."

"I know. I'll take care of her."

Will sat down next to Lydia. "How are you feeling?" he asked.

"Not so bad," she said. "Thank you for looking after me all day."

"I didn't do anything. You did it all on your own."

"Not really. I prayed every minute, and the Lord kept me going. And you made sure I got some rest."

"We all needed rest. That's all."

Lydia leaned back a little and stretched, her hands pressing against the small of her back.

"Are you in much pain?" Will asked.

Lydia laughed. "We're all in pain," she said. "But you surprise me sometimes, Will. Most men don't ask about a woman's pain when she's . . . in my condition. What makes you the kind of man you are?"

Will was embarrassed. He looked away. "I'm not sure I know what you mean."

"My husband asked you to help me. I know that. But you've

been doing that from the beginning. More than any of the men. Why?"

"I only . . . I don't know. I haven't really done much."

"You've always been ready. I've seen that."

"Aye. That I was. But I had the feeling, way back before we reached Santa Fe, that you were in a family way. And so is my Liz. I've worried about her the whole time, and I suppose that made me worry about you."

"Liz is a lovely woman. You must miss her terribly."

"Every minute of every day."

"You're such a good man, Will."

"No. I want to be a good man, but it doesn't come natural to me. I'd rather knock a man down than forgive him, and I haven't the faith of a gnat."

Lydia laughed again. "I'm sorry, but I don't believe that. What I do believe is that you'll make it through this, and one day you'll have your Liz back."

"We'll all make it through."

"Yes. I hope we do."

But when she glanced at him, he could see worry in her eyes.

Everyone ate a little after that, and then they rolled up in their blankets around the fire. Will built up the fire with mesquite brush. Then, locating Lydia's canteen again, he poured a little more of his water into it, and he covered her with a second blanket—his own.

Will found a place as near to the fire as possible and fell into a deep sleep. He was still there when the drums sounded again, and not exactly awake when he pulled himself up. He stood for a time and tried to get his balance, get his mind straight. He knew that this would be the hardest day of his life, but he told himself it was just one more terrible day, and then there would be water. He shut his eyes and tried to see Liz's face, tried to concentrate on why he had to survive. But as he tried to walk, he felt the weakness in his knees. Jesse was next to him, along with Charley and the other men from his mess. All of them were putting one foot in front of the other, moving rather slowly. Will told himself not to think, not to doubt, not to worry, but just to keep stepping. They let Melissa and Lydia, along with young William Hunter, set the pace, and they followed behind them.

The heat kept coming on, and the day stretched longer than any day Will ever remembered. Gradually the formations fell apart as some men couldn't keep up and others dropped back to help those who were staggering, even stumbling and falling.

The troops stopped to eat a little dried meat at noon, but they were so hungry by then—and so thirsty—that some cut strips from their belts and chewed the leather for the bit of nourishment they might obtain, as well as for the saliva the chewing might create. Will had tried doing that himself, but he found that there was no saliva left in him, and even the chewing had seemed an effort. He had long since spat out the pebble he had once sucked on, the thing having become an annoyance against his swollen tongue.

Will didn't know how far they had come or how far they had to go. It was better not to guess. He was impatient waiting for those who were still sitting on the ground. Finally he said, "Let's go," and the men began to pull themselves up. Will helped Melissa and Lydia up, and they all set out together again.

Lydia told Will, "Don't worry about me. I feel much better now."

He wondered how long she would feel that way. As it turned out, the long afternoon was full of pain. The new moccasins had become creased across the top of his foot, and the hide bit into his skin with each step. But many were in worse shape than he was. He saw men down on the ground along the way, but never alone. Always, someone was kneeling by the man, talking to him, helping him adjust the burlap on his feet or offering some other sort of help. Mostly men stayed with the troops they had tented with for six months. This was an army, a battalion, but mostly now it was teams of friends keeping one another going.

When the sun started to go down, Will realized that he had lost all track of time. He was glad that the heat was diminishing, and he figured, having started in the middle of the night, they must have come many miles. He kept telling himself that water couldn't be more than a few more hours ahead.

But something was happening to him. It had been coming on gradually all afternoon. At times he felt confused, unclear as to where he was, as though he were dreaming—and walking in his dream. Even his pain had turned into a kind of nausea all through him. He had begun to say, "Step, step," as though his body would forget if he didn't remind it. Then finally, without warning, his knees struck the sand, and he felt himself wheeling forward, his face smashing into the sand.

When he knew what was happening again, he was looking up, toward the stars, and voices were asking him if he could hear. He could, but he couldn't say so. Someone else was saying, "It's over, Will. They've brought water back to us from the springs. We're almost there." A canteen was before his eyes, and then someone was holding it for him so he could sip at it. It was good water, clean and cool. He shut his eyes and swallowed, loving the sensation, then sipped again.

"You've been pouring water into my canteen, haven't you?" Lydia was asking. "Yours is empty. How long has it been that way?"

Will didn't try to answer. He knew he had been out of water most of the day. But that wasn't the important thing. What he liked was hearing Lydia's voice, still sounding strong. In his foggy state, it seemed to mean that Liz was well.

• • •

Snow had been falling for two days, and the wind had been blowing. Liz had seen a few blizzards in Nauvoo, but nothing like this. The snow was piled so deep against the door of the cabin that the women could no longer open it. They knew they would have to get out sooner or later, but they had decided to let the children use the chamber pot for now—really just a tin pail—until the worst of the storm passed. They thought they had enough wood to last through the night, but they would have to use it sparingly.

The trouble was, no matter how much they built up the fire, it was never big enough to keep everyone warm. The wind seemed to blow right through the cabin, and the only place that was warm was very near the fire. The children tried to get in as close as they could, and then, of course, they soon became too hot. It was a matter of changing off, taking turns being the hot one and then one of the cold ones. That had been all right during the day, but during the previous night, no number of quilts could keep anyone warm. Liz had slept with her boys tucked in against her, and still they had shivered and even cried, especially as morning came on.

Another evening was coming now, and still the storm wasn't letting up. The children were getting cranky. "It's my turn," Jacob complained to Mary.

Mary was old enough to look after the little ones most of the time, but she was clearly tired of all that today. "I only just got close, Jacob," she said. "You stood here for *ever* so long, and I waited for you."

Jacob turned to his mother. "She's lying," he said. "She's been close for *hours*."

Liz laughed at Jacob. "I don't think you know how long an hour is, Jakey. She's only been there a few minutes."

"I *do* know." And then he began to cry. "I'm cold, Mummy."

"Oh, go ahead," Mary said, and she stepped away from the fire.

Liz pulled Jacob in front of her, but the truth was, Liz had never taken a turn to be truly close, and the cold on her back had seemed to work its way all through her. Liz tried to tell herself that this was merely one more hardship, and it would pass like the others.

It was January now, 1847, and spring was still far away. What Liz didn't know was how anyone could stock up enough food to set out again on the western trek that Brigham often talked about.

The summer illnesses—ague and typhus and typhoid fever—were gone now, but the lack of good food was causing other problems. Black canker was taking lives again. Measles had gone through the settlement too, along with mumps and whooping cough. Word passed through the camps almost every day that another child had died, another grandmother, or even a strong adult who had left Nauvoo in good health. No one knew how many had died, but Liz guessed that it had to be hundreds. So far, her children and Ellen's had done pretty well. But Liz worried about Ellen's baby, who would be coming soon, and her own, due in the spring. It couldn't be good that she and Ellen were not eating any better than they were.

Liz knew how to plant and tend a garden, but she wished she had Will to plow a little plot of ground when spring came. And she worried, if companies set out for the Rocky Mountains, how she and Ellen and Mary Ann could manage to join them without Will and Jesse.

But Liz had learned some things about herself. She could do many things that she had always considered "men's work." She had driven oxen a few times now, and if her animals got through the winter all right, she figured she could make her way to the West.

What Liz tried not to think about was Will being in a battle somewhere. She thought he was strong enough to hold up, no matter what the march demanded of him, but she hated to imagine anyone shooting at him. He was a little too likely to be brave in battle, not because he wanted to fight for more land for America, but because he would want to protect his brothers. It was very difficult in this remote place to get news of the war, but some had heard of battles in Mexico and in Upper California.

Mary Ann was standing next to Liz. She suddenly stepped away from the fire and said, "All right, that's enough quarreling. We're going to play some games."

"It's too cold to play games," Mary said, and Jacob mumbled that he didn't want to play. But Mary Ann didn't listen. "Come on, Mary, Jesse, boys, it's time for Follow the Leader. We haven't played that for *such* a long time."

"We play it every day," Jesse Junior said.

"Well . . . maybe. But I have some new tricks you children have never tried. I doubt you can even follow me this time."

"I can do anything you can," Mary said, and the game was on.

Mary Ann cavorted rather wildly around the room, and soon the older children were imitating her. Little Daniel could not kick up his heels quite as well as the others, but he tried.

The children seemed to warm with the activity, and Liz took the chance to move a little closer to the fire for a few minutes. The laughter was wonderful and lifted her spirits.

Mary Ann stopped after a time. "I have another idea," she said. "The Johns children must be tired of being alone. Let's go to their house and show them what merry souls we are in our house."

"We can't get out," Mary said.

"Ah, but listen."

All the children listened. "What is it?" Jesse Junior finally asked.

"It's the sound of no wind. Do you hear it?"

"There's no sound of *no wind*," Mary said.

"That's exactly right. But that's the sound I'm hearing. Let's try to open the door again."

So Mary Ann pushed at the door, with the children helping. They made a small opening, pulled back, and pushed again. On the third try they had opened the door enough to step out. Mary Ann used a shovel to push back some snow, and after a time, they worked the door all the way open. It was a big job to dig a path out through the snowdrift, but everyone took turns.

When they finally shut the door behind them, Liz and Ellen were happy to have the fire to themselves. "Maybe we can haul in some wood now," Ellen said.

"Yes, let's let them open a path, and then we can go out and try to dig our way to the woodpile."

But for now, the women listened to the children outside working and laughing, and later, when they returned, they had stories to tell of leading the whole Johns family in a game of Follow the Leader.

"They liked having us come," Mary said. "It was so much fun."

"They can't follow as good as me," Jacob said.

"But you've practiced more, Jakey," Liz said. "You can show them how to do it when they make a visit here—maybe tomorrow."

"I'll show them how to hop," Jacob said, and then he hopped all the way around the room before he stopped, looking very pleased with himself. By then, Daniel was trying to hop too, but he wasn't very good at it. Still, he had everyone laughing, and that was nice.

And what was even better, with the snow letting up, Bishop Pendleton made a visit to their house with new supplies of potatoes and flour and even a few turnips. With a good supper and a bigger fire, everyone was much happier.

CHAPTER 22

Will was sitting in a hot spring in the San Felipe Valley of the Sierra Nevada Mountains. He was at the Warner Ranch, the first large non-native settlement established in the southern part of Upper California. The Battalion troops had eaten their fill since arriving at the ranch. The food was still mostly beef, but it was fattened beef, not the tasteless meat they had eaten for months now—and there had been plenty of it. They had also eaten plenty of the pancakes made by local Indians. The search party Colonel Cooke had sent back to find the stranded raft on the Gila River had also arrived. As it turned out, four hundred pounds of wheat flour had been salvaged. Will had eaten bread all his life, but he hadn't known that it could taste as good as it did now.

The days without water were behind the men now. As it had turned out, Corrizo Springs had not offered the plentiful water Cooke had promised, but the soldiers had drunk what they could and filled their canteens, and then they had pushed ahead one more day. They had rested at a place called Palm Springs, where they had drunk all the water they wanted. But the next day had brought one more trial. They had had to climb all day before they reached a narrow passage out of what they called "Box Canyon." It had been necessary to use crowbars, picks, and hatchets to widen a passage through solid rock so they could bring their wagons with them. But once beyond the canyon, they had reached a beautiful valley, and from there they had pushed on to the ranch, which seemed a green paradise to them.

Will was basking in the water now, and the layers of scaly dirt were coming off him. What he wished was that he had decent clothing to put on. He had patched his shirt and trousers as best he could, but the patches mostly just pulled the threadbare fabric apart. He knew he was lucky to have anything at all that he could wear. Some of the men were nearly naked. One man had fashioned something that looked mostly like a skirt from a canvas wagon cover. Others had bartered for a little rawhide from local Indians. They looked more like trappers than soldiers.

Will knew it would be difficult to move out again after these days of luxury, but he was thankful for the energy that was pumping back into him. What was best, however, was the news that the rebel *Californios* had been quelled, and little or no fighting was expected.

On the night before the Battalion was to take up its march again, Levi Hancock called all the men together. They sat in a grassy area, and he stood on a little prominence above them. After a prayer and a hymn, Brother Hancock spoke to the men in his big, coarse voice. "Brethren, we have been blessed," he said. "Not one of us died out there in the desert when hell itself seemed to open up and attempt to pull us all down. And now we hear that no battles loom before us, and President Young's promise has been fulfilled."

It was not like Brother Hancock to sound so hopeful. Will was glad that he shared the men's gratefulness. But then the man's voice doubled in volume.

"Aren't you deeply pleased to have received rich blessings that you know very well you haven't earned? I say to you now, as I've said before, repent, brethren, or God's judgment may yet strike us to the ground."

He looked about, as if to assess the reaction to his words.

"And where have you sinned? Is there a man among you who hasn't cursed, hasn't used the Lord's name in vain, hasn't spoken evil of a leader or quarreled with a brother? How many of you drank whiskey when you had the chance, and how many more would have, had there been any to obtain in the desert? And do you think I don't know that some of you chased after harlots back in Santa Fe? Why God didn't cut you down on the spot, I'll never know.

"But worst of all is your pride. I've heard your self-praise since we've basked here in this garden place. I hear you telling one another how you triumphed, how you got here on your own. If that's what you think of yourselves, your pride will only lead you to a great and calamitous fall. I say to you, end your gluttony, stop your haughty boasting, resist your self-satisfaction. Repent this day before we take up our march again.

"Remember this. No one has died from enemy fire, but some have died of sickness. If you want to see your families again, repent before you end up buried with them."

He wasn't finished. He talked for another hour, but mostly he only repeated his accusations and admonishments. Will listened to it all, and he admitted to himself that he had used some hard words at times and had been angry with some of his brothers. He told himself he did need to guard against pride now that the worst of the hardships might be over. But he was troubled by Brother Hancock's opinion of the men, who, it seemed to Will, had conducted themselves well considering all they had been through. He had watched the men serve one another, even in the most extreme circumstances, and he thought Brother Levi might have mentioned that.

When the meeting ended, Jesse, who had been sitting next to Will, leaned closer and said, "I didn't chase any harlots. Did you?"

Both men laughed. "The only thing I chased," Will said, "was a rabbit I never did catch. But if I'd caught up to him I might have committed the sin of gluttony—so it's good I couldn't run fast enough."

Jesse, however, sounded serious when he said, "An' what think ye? The ones who died along the way—or in Pueblo—was it their sins what killt 'em?"

"No. I don't accept that. I know Brother Hancock means well, and I know I'm not what I ought to be, but the men who died were not being punished for their sins. And they weren't taken from this earth because of the sins of others in the Battalion. I refuse to believe that."

"Thanks for sayin' it so. I was wonderin' if I was the one who was thinkin' wrong." He lowered his voice even more and added, "There's many a way to show pride. It can e'en come out in the way a man preaches."

Will nodded. "But let's leave it at that. I know I need to be careful of pride. And let's let him answer for himself."

"Aye. It should be so."

Will spent that evening with his friends, eating more fattened beef, finishing the last of their bread, and preparing to march again the next morning. But he ate less than he might have, and he did think it was wise not to indulge too much.

As it turned out, the night was cold, and Will felt the bite of it more than he had for a time. He was actually relieved to get up when the sun rose in the morning. In fact, all the troops were up early and back in formation. They marched west, through the mountains and gradually downhill toward the coast. But a storm blew in that night and lashed the men with wind and a hard downpour of rain.

Will had been asleep in the tent when he heard the rain begin to strike the canvas, and then, a huge burst of wind ripped the tent stakes loose and brought the tent down on top of the men inside. One of the muskets they used for a pole struck Will a glancing blow across the side of his head, scaring him more than hurting him. The men were all in a jumble, each fighting the canvas out of his own face and trying to make some sense of what was happening to them.

There was nothing to do but keep the canvas over them for now and let the storm blow itself out. But water was running under them already, and soon their blankets were soaked. Will felt the cold work itself into him again, and he lay there thinking, "It never ends."

It was Job Steele who said, "I think maybe Levi Hancock was speaking the truth. God isn't finished with us yet."

Job had spoken in a joking voice, and the other men laughed, but Ephraim sounded more serious when he said, "Not every hard thing is over. That's certain. Pride could still bring us down."

Will knew that was true, but he thought back to the terrible storm that had struck the second night out from Council Bluffs. He had sat in the rain, soaked through, and he had almost despaired. Now, half a year later, he and the men had suffered worse things than they ever could have imagined, and they had survived them all. He lay there thinking that he could withstand anything for a few hours. Morning would come, and the storm would end sooner or later, and the Battalion would keep moving forward. The important thing was, the wait to start his return to Liz was now cut in half.

So he shivered in the cold, and he listened to the rain beat down on the canvas over his face, and he hoped it would soon stop. But it didn't stop. The men got up with the first light and did what they could to provide themselves with a little breakfast, and then they marched in the rain all day. By late in the day, the rain finally ended, and they dried out as best they could by a fire that night, and then they slept very cold one more time.

But they were descending from the mountains, and the next day they entered a valley that seemed a paradise. Tall grass, almost up to their knees, grew in green meadows. Wild cattle roamed about, and Will saw birds and waterfowl of kinds he had never imagined. Mustard plants and clover added a spray of yellow and white to the rich green that was everywhere. Even more, a change had come into the air. There was a mildness, a soft, moist touch on the skin, and steady, temperate breezes.

The men ate more beef that night, but they added mustard greens and savored every bite.

The following day, January 27, 1847, the Battalion reached the abandoned mission of San Luis Rey. It was white and gleaming after the rain. The men stopped long enough to eat another meal, but they knew that they were almost to the ocean—the goal of their march for all these months—so they pushed on. About a mile past the mission, they climbed a little prominence. As Company B hiked up the rise, Will could see that the men of Company A had stopped. They were staring out toward the west. "It's the sea," someone close to Will said, and the men moved faster, breaking their formation.

And then, there it was.

Will caught a glimpse as he worked his way around the men in front of him and found a spot where he could get a full view. It was almost too much to believe. All those days, out in the desert, he had thought of this scene, this ocean, and at some point it had come to seem a delusion, something he had conjured up to keep himself going. Even now it didn't seem quite real. He whispered, "We did it. We're here," but it was more than he could comprehend. Had he really walked two thousand miles? Had he really suffered everything that was still filling up his head? How could it all be finished?

Will had crossed an ocean once, had been tossed on its waves, but he had never seen anything like this. The sea looked flat from this height—smooth as a pool. The color was intensely blue, and it was set against the green of the hills. Low, gray clouds on the distant horizon hung against the water, but the sun was bright above, and every breath Will took brought him peace. It was as though he had arrived in heaven, and he felt God very close, His Spirit filling up all his senses.

Jesse walked up next to Will, threw an arm over his shoulder, and said, "We made it."

"I had no idea," Will said, but he wasn't quite sure what he meant. He had had no idea the Pacific would be so beautiful. But mostly, he had had no idea he would feel this fulfilled, this relieved. He began, silently, to pray. He thanked the Lord to be alive and to have made it out of the desert, but he was also feeling something else: it now seemed worth all the misery to experience this moment, to feel so strong and humble at the same time, and so blessed.

The Battalion stayed at the spot for quite some time, with all the companies crowding to have a glimpse. Men began to move about and shake hands, congratulating one another. But they kept their voices hushed, as though they had entered a temple. And all the talk was about the thankfulness they felt.

Will saw Lydia Hunter standing next to her husband, and he walked over to the two of them. He shook the captain's hand and said, "You've been a good leader, Captain Hunter. Thanks for getting us here."

"You've been our strength, Brother Lewis," Hunter said.

Will was looking at Lydia. She appeared happy but very tired. "How are you feeling, Sister Hunter?" he asked.

She smiled. "Never better," she said, but her voice seemed frail.

"I don't know how you did it."

"I boasted that I could do as well as you men. I had to prove it. But I'm not boasting now. It was God who brought us through in the end. Every one of us."

"Aye. It's what we all feel today. But I want you to know, I looked at you a thousand times, and I told myself, 'If she can keep going, in her condition, I can do it too.'"

"And I looked down at my 'condition' and said, 'Little one, I will not fail you.'"

Melissa Coray and her husband, Sergeant William Coray, were walking toward them now. The two women embraced, held each other a very long time. Both had begun to cry. Will had watched Melissa become lean and hardened, but he could see that she was coming back to herself a little, ragged as she looked in her tattered dress.

Sergeant Coray shook Will's hand, then Jesse's. But he couldn't get any words out. Will could see the emotion in his eyes. It was Melissa who said, "We're not the same people we were when we started."

Will nodded. He knew what she meant, but he wondered whether anyone who hadn't been with them would ever understand.

The Battalion moved on and camped that night close to the ocean. Will had promised himself he would swim in the ocean when he arrived, but he was surprised by the power of the water. He walked to the edge, but he didn't walk in. He merely stood and listened to the waves, watched them crash on the shore. He wondered at himself, that he had once called upon God to still such waves. What he knew now—that he hadn't realized then—was that he was like the foam that the waves tossed about: powerless, even insignificant. But God cared about him all the same. He had kept him going and brought him to this place, and that gave Will hope that God would also carry him back to Liz and his family. He didn't know whether they had survived the winter, but it was consoling to trust that God knew—and God cared.

For two days after that the troops continued their trek, but it was pleasant going. Walking all day was what they were accustomed to, and doing it in such mild weather was a joy. The ocean was often visible from the road they followed, and it was a wonderful change from cactus and mesquite.

The troops camped near San Diego Bay, at another mission, which they tried to clean up and rid of fleas, but they found that they still could not obtain any clothing for sale or trade, and people looked at them as if they were impoverished vagrants.

Once the satisfaction of reaching the coast settled in, the full weight of the men's weariness seemed to come down upon them. Will found himself tired in some way that he had never experienced before. His limbs ached and his feet throbbed when he lay down at night, but more than that, he felt as though all his reserves had been used up. He was allowed to sleep much longer each night than he had in months, but he awoke tired and felt that way all day. It seemed as though he had aged, that he was no longer a young man and never would be again. He would recover, he kept telling himself, but so far, his body couldn't believe it.

• • •

Liz had been feeling labor pains. What worried her was that the pains were coming too early, and she remembered too well what had happened before. She hadn't eaten as well as she knew she needed to, and she wondered what that might have done to her baby. She also wondered whether she would have enough milk for the little one when it did come. But Ellen had given birth late in January, and

her new little boy was thriving. She had named him Cyrus, after her
father, just as she and Jesse had agreed before he had left. Adding a
baby to their tiny cabin had made things a bit more crowded and
complicated, but life was feeling better now, with spring not far away.

Some lovely days had come in February, and the children had
been able to go outside and run and play. No word had come from
the Battalion for many weeks, but Liz liked to think that Will was
at the ocean now, where the weather was said to be beautiful year-
round. Reports were that Upper California was conquered. Most of
the news of the Battalion that was received in Winter Quarters concerned the sick detachments in Pueblo. Some of the wives had received word of their husbands dying there. It was frightening to think
that the Lord had not protected the soldiers against every danger, but
Liz knew mortality didn't work that way, and she also knew that anyone could be struck down. All the same, she believed Will was alive,
and she believed she would see him again before the year was over.

Brother Brigham sometimes expressed his exasperation with the
Saints. He spoke of thievery, gambling, drunkenness, negligence of
the poor, slothfulness, even lasciviousness. Liz supposed there were
such sins being practiced among the members. People were weak,
and temptations were always present, but Liz had seen none of this.
She had felt lonely at times when winter had kept people indoors,
but she had also felt loved, especially by the sisters. Always, when
her supply of food had run short, someone had appeared with a little
flour or a sack of beans—something to keep her and Ellen and the
children surviving. Patty Sessions was always about, caring for the
sick, and she had followed the progress of Ellen's and Liz's pregnancies. Dear Eliza Snow also called the sisters together from time to
time, and they blessed one another, praised God in hymns, even
spoke in tongues. The spirit of those meetings lifted Liz and touched
Mary Ann more deeply than Liz would have expected.

What Liz did hear from time to time was the grumbling of those who were discontented. One morning in March, with the orange-limbed willows along the river just beginning to bud, Liz was returning from the outhouse that was shared by some other nearby families. She was up earlier than anyone in her household, earlier than almost anyone in the settlement, it seemed. Sleep had become difficult with the baby so near, and staying down had become tedious. She loved being out in the morning air. There were no mosquitoes now, no smoke from prairie fires, as there had been in the fall.

Liz was strolling slowly toward the house when Sister Boardman, who lived in the same block of houses, came striding up from the river carrying a bucket of water. She stopped when she reached Liz and set the bucket down, clearly needing to take a rest from the weight of it. "Sister Lewis," she said, "how are you feeling? Ellen Matthews told me your sickness was coming too early and you were staying down these days."

"I'm afraid so," Liz said. "Mother Sessions thinks I should stay off my feet as much as I can. But nothing tires me out so much as lying in bed."

Sister Boardman laughed. She put her hands on her hips and stretched her back a little. She was a woman of at least forty, who looked even older. Liz had known her in the Female Relief Society back in Nauvoo, where she had been busy, always doing good about the town. But she looked tired now, as though she had aged many years, and, like most of the Saints, her face looked drawn. "I'm glad I saw you this morning, Liz," she said. "There's something I need to tell you. I'm afraid that as soon as the weather allows us, my husband and I are pulling out, going back to Indiana, where we're from."

"Why, Sister Boardman?"

"This is no way to live, Liz. Brigham's led us out here in the

middle of nowhere without enough food to eat, and without a no-
tion as to where we're going."

"But we're going west, to the—"

"Yes, to the Rocky Mountains. And what's out there? Nothing.
What kind of life will we have in that wilderness?"

"I think, in time, we'll build up a—"

"I don't want to hear it, Liz. I've listened to Brigham's promises
long enough. He never stops tellin' us what a sinful lot we are, but
he needs to look to himself and ask whether God speaks to him the
way he did to Brother Joseph."

"But will you leave the Church?" Liz asked.

"We'll give up the one Brigham preaches. But there are people
trying to bring the Saints back together."

"James Strang?"

"He's one. And if you've heard him preach, you might not sound
so surprised. He's a man like Joseph. He's had visions. Some say he's
been called to lead the Church in this time."

Liz knew that missionaries from the Strangites had been holding
meetings among the Saints here along the Missouri. She had also
heard that some members were thinking of joining Lyman Wight,
who had led a group to Texas, or banding together with those who
were waiting for the day when Joseph Smith III was old enough to
take over for his father.

Liz wanted to remind Sister Boardman of the day the mem-
bership had voted for the Twelve to lead the Church—the feeling that had been in the meeting that day—but she could hear in
Sister Boardman's voice that she was in no mood to listen to such
arguments. "We'll miss you, Judith," she said. "You've been a great
strength to the sisters. How soon will you leave?"

"As soon as we can cross Iowa again—and this time not in mud
up to our necks."

"I'll pray for you to change your mind before then."

"You do that. But I'll pray that you will join us, Liz. We're not the only ones getting ready to leave. There are *hundreds* leaving, quietly. For the most part, they only speak to each other about it."

That all might be true. Liz had no way of knowing, but she felt disheartened as she walked back to her house. She understood how discouraged people were after what they had been through all this last year. What she witnessed every day, however, was the simple truth that hardship had its benefits. She remembered Ellen, back on the sailing ship crossing the ocean, when the loss of her child had almost destroyed her. Ellen was strong now, stronger than Liz ever could have imagined.

But the miracle was Mary Ann. During this hard winter she had gone out into the biting cold and chopped wood that was frozen hard as stone. She had never cooked in her life, but now she was cooking over a fire that filled her lungs with smoke and burned her eyes.

Mary Ann had always known, the same as Liz, that she had been an indulged child, but since that day she had first tried to notch a log, she had taken more and more satisfaction in carrying her share of the load and being someone the other sisters could rely on. And now that Liz was down most of the time, Mary Ann had done even more to look after the children and take care of chores.

Liz only wished that she could also be up and doing. But for three more weeks, she stayed down most of the time. She could often see through the open door what glorious days had come. One day she was lying in bed, thinking how much she would like to walk outside, when something blocked the bright sunlight in the door. The stocky figure was only a silhouette, and yet she thought she knew that shape. She hesitated, however, not quite certain.

"Sister Lewis, I was walking through the camp and I met your sister outside. She told me you were down in bed."

The voice was not one to mistake. "President Young, it's so good of you to stop by."

"May I come in?"

"Yes, of course."

He walked to her bed. "How are you feeling, Sister Lewis?"

She held out her hand to him. "I'm fine, President."

"Your sister told me about your confinement. She's a cheery girl, isn't she?"

"Yes, she is," Liz said, and she decided not to tell him that Mary Ann had not always been so happy with her situation. "It's been a blessing to have her here with me while Brother Lewis is gone."

"What have you heard from him?"

"Not anything for many months."

Brigham's head dropped a little. She couldn't see him well with the light behind him. "I know what a trial this has been for all the wives left behind."

"We've managed."

"I was told that you built your own house."

"Not entirely. Bishop Pendleton was sick when the men brought us the logs that Will had cut before he left. I suppose we were a little impatient, so we did the best we could to notch the logs and put them up. But men came and helped us finish the job. We never could have put the roof on by ourselves."

"I doubt that's true. I think you can do anything you put your mind to. And so can many of our women. But I want you to know, I'm sorry we haven't looked after you better than we have. There was so much sickness, and people just kept arriving—without much in the way of provisions. It was very hard to find the food people needed—and to make certain everyone had a place to live."

"But it's been a blessing for us to make the best of things. We had enough to eat, almost always."

"But sometimes, I know, only corn, three meals a day."

"It filled us up."

"You've held on, Sister Lewis, and you will be blessed through all eternity for your faith. Lots of folks are angry with me. They're jumping like rats off a sinking ship. I've had men threaten to kill me, and women tell me I sent their husbands away to their deaths. I don't know what to tell them except that I'm doing my best. It was God who gave me this job. I didn't go looking for it."

"Better days are ahead, President. That's what we all should remember."

"It's good to think so, Sister Lewis. But we'll face plenty more tests before easier days come."

Liz knew that was true, but the sorrow in Brigham's voice was unnerving. She felt sorry that he had such a load to carry.

"May I give you a blessing?" he asked.

"I would like that very much."

Brigham walked outside first and asked the family all to come in. He told the women that they were noble sisters, and he told the children he was proud of them. "It's people like you who will pass your strength down from generation to generation. They'll use that strength to build a kingdom that will never be thrown down." Then he blessed Liz that her baby might be well and healthy and that Liz would recover quickly and be ready for the great trek ahead. And he prayed for her husband, William Lewis, that he would be led by angels back to his home and family.

CHAPTER 23

The men of the Mormon Battalion only spent three nights in San Diego, and then word came that they would return to the mission at San Luis Rey. They had been impressed with the valley it rested in, so they didn't mind setting up camp there, but now they were back to marching. Some complained about the sudden change of plans after such a short rest, but most men simply accepted the decision, and another three-day march began—with no wagons to worry about. What the men longed for most, however, was clothing to cover themselves, and boots. Many were marching barefoot, and their feet were in terrible condition.

The men were also disappointed not to have better supplies of food. They had started from Santa Fe with only sixty days' worth of supplies—some of which had been lost on the Gila River—but their trek had lasted almost twice that long, and no new provisions were available. Colonel Cooke promised to resupply the companies as soon as he could, and the men were able to fish and to pick good fruit to eat, but they longed for bread more than anything.

When the troops reached San Luis Rey, they were told to inhabit some old barracks just outside the mission. That meant more cleaning and delousing. They were also ordered to clean up as best they could, to shave and cut their hair. That was one order Will was only too happy to comply with.

On the morning after their arrival at the mission, Colonel Cooke addressed the Battalion. He issued a printed statement, which he then read to the men, all of them standing in formation:

> The lieutenant-colonel commanding congratulates the battalion on their safe arrival on the shore of the Pacific ocean, and the conclusion of the march of over two thousand miles. History may be searched in vain for an equal march of infantry. Nine-tenths of it has been through a wilderness where nothing but savages and wild beasts are found, of deserts where, for lack of water, there is no living creature. There, with almost hopeless labor, we have dug deep wells which the future traveler will enjoy. Without a guide who had traversed them, we have ventured into trackless prairies where water was not found for several marches. With crowbar and pick and ax in hand we have worked our way over mountains which seemed to defy aught save the wild goat, and hewed a passage through a chasm of living rock more narrow than our wagons.

Will liked all this, however flowery the language was, and he liked the conclusion of the statement: "Thus, marching half-naked and half-fed, and living upon wild animals, we have discovered and made a road of great value to our country."

When Colonel Cooke finished reading the formal document,

he spoke to the men personally. He thanked them for what they had accomplished and the kind of men they were.

The soldiers answered by shouting three cheers for Colonel Cooke and tossing their hats in the air.

That night, before the men went to bed in their tents one more time—their new quarters not yet inhabitable—Jesse asked Will and the other men in their mess, "What do you think of ol' Cooke now? It seemed a li'l as if we all loved the man today—after not thinkin' we did for all these months."

Charley Buttars laughed. "He said somethin' good about us, after cursin' us since we set out from Santa Fe. It sounded so good, we had to holler for 'im."

But Ephraim Hart said, rather solemnly, "I'll never love the man. He's too hard, and he's too profane. But I'll remember all my life, he wouldn't let us die. That's what we have to thank 'im for."

"Aye," Will said, "but here's what I want to know. Why did we do it? Is that road so great a thing to pay such a dear price for?"

All the men let the question sink in. The fire they had cooked on that night had mostly died away, and the sun was almost gone. Will only could see shadows, not faces. But he knew these men had all been asking themselves whether making the long march, and sinking so near to death, had been worth the effort.

"The road might do some good, I guess," Phil Gray said, "but that's not why we come here. We did it 'cause Brigham asked us to. He needed any money he could get his hands on."

"That's so," Jesse said, "but we might ha' worked in Missouri or some'eres, and maybe brought in as much. An' how far away are we e'en now from where the Saints will coom? We may walk another thousan' mile afore we join 'em."

Silence fell over the group again. Finally Will said, "Here's what I think. I say it was not worth it—not for a road, and not for the dollars we sent back to the Saints. The cost to our bodies, and the cost of leaving our families so long, was just not worth it."

"But Brigham told us hisself," Josh Gray said, "the Lord was in it. It's what we had to do."

"I know. I've thought long and hard about that. We needed to find a way to feed the Saints, and our pay helped some with that. But the Lord could've found another way."

"So did Brigham make a mistake in sending us?" Jesse asked. "Is that what yer meanin'?"

"No. I'm saying this. When you keep going until you can't go anymore, then go on anyway, you come out of that a different man. We've learned things we couldn't have learned any other way."

"It mighta made some men worse, not better," Jesse said. "And it killt some more."

It was Charley who said, "People died in Nauvoo, too, and crossin' Iowa. People get sick. But the way I see it, we gave up everything—and none of it was for ourselves. The Lord will bless us for that."

"I don't know, Charley," Will said. "We still have hard times ahead of us. But there were times in the desert when nothing else was real except God and me—and you men around me—and I turned to the Lord in ways that I had never thought I could. That's what I mean when I say I've changed. I trust God, and I know all of you trust Him too. The Church needs men—and women like Sister Hunter and Sister Coray—who will keep goin' in the hard days ahead."

All the men were quiet, but Will felt their agreement.

"I feel a little sorry for Colonel Cooke," Will added. "He still thinks we were out there to build a road."

• • •

Conditions gradually improved as the soldiers settled in and a daily schedule continued to allow them enough sleep. Even though daily military training had begun, both morning and afternoon, that seemed child's play compared to the marching they had become accustomed to. Flour was eventually delivered, and the men had bread to eat.

Still, when Captain Hunter called his men together and told them that Company B was to return to San Diego, Will was actually not sorry to hear it. He had liked San Diego, and the daily schedule of drill at San Luis Rey had already become a little too routine. Captain Hunter said that a small force was needed to occupy San Diego, and the men could help with certain local projects there: they would build needed structures and work with the local people to establish a new government. The other four companies would also be leaving. They would march north to Pueblo de Los Angeles, where they would build a fort.

The return march to San Diego was not as enjoyable as the first one, now that the men had grown used to the plant life and had looked out on the ocean so many times, but they were stronger now and could walk with less effort. Will's rawhide moccasins were still his only footwear, but they had shaped themselves to his feet and were actually quite comfortable. Lydia Hunter and Melissa Coray rode in a wagon this time. Will could see that Lydia's time was not far off, but she and Melissa seemed happy these days. They sang hymns and other familiar tunes as they rode along, and some of the men joined in with them.

Company B arrived in San Diego on March 17, 1847, and for a time there was plenty of work to do. An attempt had been made earlier to build a well on a bluff that overlooked the bay, and now the men set about to deepen that well. San Diego was a tiny settlement built around a fine church and a plaza. The few houses were built from unbaked brick and looked slouchy to the soldiers. General Kearny's men had taken over the mission rooms now, so Company B set about to build a small enclosure for a fort. For the present, it was back to living in tents.

Life had changed, however. The men soon found themselves following the schedules of the local people. They didn't rise as early as they had under Colonel Cooke's watch, and although they worked rather hard all morning, they rested during the midday, often taking a siesta in the shade of a tree. They talked more than anything of the day they would be mustered out of the army, and they speculated incessantly about where the Saints were, and where they would finally meet up with their wives. But they didn't march anywhere.

• • •

When Liz's pains finally came on strong, she was no longer worried that the baby was early. She didn't make a fuss—didn't want to alarm the children—and she waited for morning, but very early on March 18, she whispered to Mary Ann, "I think you should take the children outside. They won't want to get up yet, but I can't wait much longer."

"Is it your time?"

"Yes. No question."

So Mary Ann got up, got dressed quickly, and said, "Children, it's a wonderful day. We're going to have a visitor."

The children didn't share her enthusiasm, and they took their time responding, but she kept after them, and finally it was Mary, old enough to understand, who said, "I think a new baby will be coming today."

The children did take more interest in that, and Jacob showed some excitement. "Where's the baby?" he asked his mother.

"In heaven, my dear," Liz said. "But he wants to come to us

today." She knew Jacob understood that there was a connection between her shape—her loss of lap—and the arrival of the baby. But the idea remained a mystery to him, and she thought it just as well that he not know too much about what was coming for her that day. Above all, she didn't want the children to know about the pain she would suffer. So Ellen and Mary Ann helped the little ones get dressed, and they took them all outside. Liz knew that it was rather cool still, but she trusted that Mary Ann could get them busy and moving about.

All this had been planned, and it was agreed that Ellen would help with the birth while Mary Ann tended the children, including little Cyrus. Mary Ann had admitted that she didn't want to know what childbirth was like—until she someday found out for herself. "And if I end up an old maid, I might never have to find out anyway," she had told Liz.

So Ellen helped clear bedding away, and she used canvas from the wagon cover to put under Liz. And then she sat with Liz and held her hand, even gave her a rolled-up piece of cloth to bite down on, but Liz never allowed herself to scream. This baby was more difficult than the ones before—so much larger. But the labor progressed quickly, and it was not yet ten o'clock when Liz finally felt the release, and Ellen said, "Oh, Liz, it's a little girl. And she's just fine."

Liz heard a plaintive little cry from the baby and, at the same time, Ellen calling, "Mary Ann, come in now. I need some help."

Mary Ann was there almost instantly. "Is everything all right?" she gasped.

"Yes," Ellen said, "but hold the baby while I cut the cord. And then clean it up. I need to finish things off with Liz."

This too had been agreed upon before. Mary Ann grabbed the clean flour sack they had set aside for that purpose, and she cradled the new little girl as soon as the cord was cut and tied. She was about to carry the baby away when Liz said, "Let me see her first."

"She's not a pretty sight right now," Mary Ann said. "Let me get some of this . . . mess . . . off her first."

"No. I want to see her now."

"Really? I hate to tell you, Sister, but she's ugly as a little suckling pig. I was hoping for something much better."

"Oh, Mary Ann, don't. That isn't funny. Bring her to me."

So Mary Ann brought her to Liz, wrapped in the flour sack, and she let Liz take her in her arms. "She *isn't* ugly," Liz said. "She's beautiful."

"She's the color of a bruise, and she's covered in something pukey."

"Mary Ann, I told you to stop. Look at her. Look how pretty her face is. Just like her sister who had your name." Liz began to cry. "And she's so strong and healthy."

"All right, then. We'll keep her if you really like her. And I'll fix her up as best I can."

· · ·

April had come and was mostly gone. Will and a group of his friends from Company B had been working on an adobe building that would serve as a city hall for the new government in San Diego. Will and Jesse were taking their noontime rest one day, and some of the men were sleeping, but the Gray brothers and Charley Buttars had joined the work team, and the old friends were discussing their favorite topic—almost their only topic. "I think by now," Will said, "if the weather's decent at all, the first company of pioneers must have left the Missouri."

"Heading where?" Phil Gray asked.

Will thought he knew. "Some of the men here think they'll head all the way out here to the Pacific. Either that, or more north, to the Oregon country. But none of that's true. When we get mustered out, Brigham will have started a settlement out by that big salty lake in the Rocky Mountains—or somewhere not too far from it."

"And why are you so sure about that?" Phil asked.

"John Taylor always praised that region in the *Times and Seasons,* and I know why. I have a friend—an Englishman—who knew everything that was going on, and he sometimes let me in on things."

"That would be William Clayton," Jesse said. "I know you talked to him all the time."

"I don't admit that he was the one. And I've kept what the man told me a secret until now, but I say, they're on their way to the Great Salt Lake Valley. Or soon will be."

"What sort o' country is that?" Jesse asked. "Is it like the desert we walked over?"

"No, it's not barren desert. It's in the mountains, and there's snow in winter. It won't be so green as Nauvoo, but it can be planted."

Jesse was leaning against a tall palm tree. He was wearing better clothing now. The army had finally suited the men up in old uniforms, scrounged from some camp. Not everyone had received trousers or shirts that were a good fit, but they made do, cinching up belts and even cutting and sewing as best they could. At least everyone was covered now. Boots had been supplied too, even though finding the right fit had been next to impossible.

Will was sitting with his legs stretched out in front of him, his arms braced behind him, and the Gray boys and Charley were lying on their backs. Phil had an arm over his eyes to shade himself from the sun. But the weather was perfect. Some mornings were gray until the mist cleared away, and rains came from time to time, but even then the temperature was never severe.

"What if a man wants to do something besides farm in that valley?" Josh asked. "I've plowed enough in my life. I'd like to try some other way of living."

"There will na' be anythin' else at first," Jesse said. "What can there be?"

"But Brigham will try to get some kind of industry started," Will said. "That's how he thinks. He'll start factories of some sort."

"And sell the products where?" Charley asked.

"Everything will have to be hauled overland a thousand miles, either back to the East, or on here to the coast, once more people are living here."

Jesse laughed. "See, Will, we can start our hauling business. Would ye na' like to drive oxen back and forth, a thousand mile?"

"I'll have to think about that one," Will said. "I'll farm until I find some other way. But I'm still going to build Liz a fine house. I don't know how I'll do it, but I shall. It's what she deserves, and it's what I promised."

Will had noticed someone walking toward the men. He realized that it was Sergeant Coray, from their company. He looked as though something had upset him. He didn't greet the men. He stood before them with that same look of distress on his face. The Gray brothers both sat up. Everyone surely knew that something had to be wrong.

"Lydia Hunter had her baby back a couple of weeks ago," the sergeant began. "I guess you knew that."

"Aye," Will said. "Has something happened?"

"She got an infection. They tried to help her, but it just got worse and worse. She died last night."

"Lydia? She's dead?"

"I'm afraid so."

Will couldn't move, couldn't think. This couldn't be true. He

326 • DEAN HUGHES

fought the impulse to cry, but tears ran from his eyes all the same. This simply couldn't happen. Lydia had faced everything.

"The baby lived," Brother Coray said. "A little boy."

Will was seeing Lydia out there in the desert, taking whatever came, she and Melissa arm in arm. This *couldn't* be.

Will saw Josh drop down on the ground. He covered his face, but his chest was shaking. Charley was staring straight ahead, the color gone from his face.

"It's breaking Melissa's heart," Sergeant Coray said. "I can't seem to console her. She's in a family way herself and isn't feeling well anyway."

There was nothing to say, nothing to compensate. Will wished that he could be angry, but it wasn't in him. "The pain in this world just never stops," he thought to say, but he didn't say it. He knew he couldn't speak without the other men hearing his emotion.

"It's not right," Charley said, and there was anger in his voice. "How could God let her walk all the way across that desert and then take her now? She deserved better than that."

"She's in a better place now," Jesse said. "Think on that."

"And what about her husband? What place is he in?"

No one tried to answer that. The men were all silent until Jesse finally asked, "What will Captain Hunter do?"

"I don't know," Brother Coray said. "He doesn't know anything yet. I tried to talk with him, but I couldn't think of anything to tell him—and he had nothing to say."

Will thought of himself, of Liz. Lydia and Liz had been wrapped together in his mind for such a long time. He had tried to help save the one he could, and now she was gone. What did that mean for Liz? Did all his prayers matter? Surely Captain Hunter had prayed, and now this had happened. Will didn't even know whether he had another child yet, didn't know about his boys, didn't know whether

Liz had survived the winter and the birth. He only knew that terrible things happened in this world, and he was powerless to do anything about that. He had felt so confident lately that God was in his life, looking out for him, but his old doubt was back now, and he felt the fear. His own bad news might be on the way.

• • •

Lydia Hunter was buried at the cemetery at Point Loma, near San Diego Bay. All the men in the company attended the burial. Melissa Coray was helping Jesse Hunter look after the baby. Lydia had named him Diego before she had died, and so far, he was doing all right. But the men were changed by this death. Lydia had become a symbol to the troops. They had all drawn from her strength and stamina. Now, strength didn't seem to mean so much. Resolve didn't hold up against the forces that powered the universe.

Army officers were beginning to talk to the men about staying in the military for another year, since an occupying force was still needed, but Will knew he would never do that, and he doubted that any of the of the men would. All anyone could think of was returning to their wives.

• • •

In May, mail finally came. When Will's name was called, and he grasped a letter from Liz, he had no idea how long it might have taken to reach him, but he felt the tremendous relief at seeing her handwriting, knowing she had been well enough to write at some point. Will hurried to a private place on the shady side of an adobe building where he could be by himself. He opened the letter quickly, nervously, and he read:

Dearest Will,

    I have wanted, ever so long, to send you a letter, but I had no opportunity until now to write something that I thought might reach you. I've written some others that I will let you read when you are back with us, but for now, I must send you this news: you have a daughter. She's beautiful, much like our first little Mary Ann, and she is healthy. I feel strong now, too, and I have plenty of sustenance for the baby. She feeds herself like a hungry little lamb. I wish you could hold her and see how perfect she is, but at least I have hope now that you will see her before too much longer. I want to name her Mary Ellen, if that sounds all right to you. It combines the names of the women I love most in this world, and reminds me that I almost have my little Mary Ann back.

Will put down the letter and tried to take this all in. He took a long breath, drew in as much of the good, soft air as he could, and then he prayed, "Oh, thank you, Lord. Thank you." But the relief and joy were too much for him. He dropped his head down and let the tears come. All he could think was that he *would* see Liz again—and they finally had the little girl they had wanted.

When he was finally composed enough to go on, he read:

    Will, I pray every day that you are safe. We hear some things, but we know nothing for certain. We have heard that your battalion has not had to fight any battles. We know that some men have died of illness, but we only know of those who wintered in Pueblo. You are said to have reached California, but even that is only rumor. I would give anything to know that you are well. Can you find a way to send me a letter?

I have another surprise for you. My sister has come to America. She joined us here in Winter Quarters and has been a great help to me. She was distraught when she first arrived, worn out from crossing the ocean and walking so far across Iowa, but you will never believe the change in her. She chops wood, carries water, and entertains all the children tirelessly.

You won't believe this, either, but we women built our own cabin—or at least a big part of it. It's a shabby little house, about the same as the first shack you and I moved into in Nauvoo, and winter was harsh on the Missouri. So nothing has been easy. I won't complain, however. We are blessed to be alive and well, with winter over, and all our illnesses behind us.

Will had a hard time hearing this. Brigham had said he would make sure the Battalion wives were provided for. Why had they had to build their own house? But Liz added:

Some things couldn't be helped. It was difficult to care for everyone. But now we must get ready for the next great effort. Brother Brigham has departed, leading a pioneer company to the West, probably to the valley of the Great Salt Lake. Other companies will follow before the summer passes. We have been told that some of the soldiers' wives will be among those in the companies, but many will not start the migration for another year. I cannot say for certain that we will be among those departing this year, but we hope we will have the opportunity and that we will be there by summer's end. We also hope that once you leave the army, you and Jesse will be able to make the long trip to the same place.

I know all this is still indefinite, but it's what I pray for every day, that before this year ends, I will hold you in my arms again. I long for the day when you will see our baby, and our two strong boys, who are growing fast. Ellen is well too, as are her children, and she has a new son named Cyrus. Margaret and Dan Johns were very ill, but are also well at this time. We all feel blessed.

Will, you and I have loved one another since we were little more than children. But back then, I only thought how handsome you were. How little I knew you then. I know much more of mankind now, and you are a man among men, a great spirit, and the kindest man I know. Once I have you back, I don't ever want to let you go again, forever.

> Your wife and friend,
> Liz

Will put the letter down. There were so many things to think about. He knew he wanted to read the words over and over and draw every detail out into some kind of understanding of who Liz was now and what she had experienced. But mostly, he thought of holding her in his arms. He thought if that could ever happen again, he could face anything.

CHAPTER 24

There was much to do in the Missouri River settlements to get ready for the new challenges the season would bring. When milder days finally came with the spring, Liz felt the renewed life inside herself, too. Brigham Young and his vanguard party of pioneers departed for the West soon after general conference, which was held in Winter Quarters on April 6, 1847. The migration to the West was now begun, and many of the Saints were getting ready to follow later that season.

Liz knew that more would stay behind than would make the trek this year. President Young had warned the people that conditions in the West would be primitive at first, and most people should wait, plant crops, rebuild their strength, and not think about making the trek until 1848 or later. But Liz wanted to be among those who departed soon. She wanted to meet Will this year.

Liz had received a letter from Will, and with it, some money. He had reassured her that he was fine now, that the long march had been "difficult," but he was in good health. He only wished his release from the military could come much sooner than July 16, the date when his year would be up. Will told Liz, "If it's too hard for you to drive a wagon and look after three children, please stay where you are, and I'll come for you. But if you and Ellen can join together and receive the help of some of the brothers, I would hope that you would come this summer. I will make my own way to whatever place Brigham Young chooses, and I will start my journey on the day I am set free from the army.

"If our oxen are still healthy, you may want to sell them and buy a team of mules, or two, if you can afford them. They are not as steady as oxen, but they move along faster, and they are easier to drive while sitting in the wagon.

"Above all, don't put yourself in danger, and be sure to care for little Mary Ellen. I will walk to the Missouri and then bring you back, if that is what is needed. I've learned to march this year, if nothing else, and with no road to build, no wagon to push, I can cover many miles in a day and rise up and walk just as far the next day. I have better boots now, and enough clothing to cover me."

Liz didn't know much about this last part. She had never heard that he had been short of clothing. There were so many things she didn't know. But she was convinced that she and Ellen and Mary Ann could manage, and they could make the journey this year.

Spring had not been easy for Mary Ann. She had admitted to Liz during the winter her hope that when better weather came, people would be out and about more often, and she might get to meet some of the young men in camp. She had been excited about attending her first general conference, but Liz knew very well it was not her interest in the sermons that caused her to curl her hair as best she could and to do some repair on the silk dress she had worn when she first arrived at the camp the year before. But during the big outdoor gathering, Mary Ann had gazed about a good deal and then whispered to Liz, "They're a sorry lot, Liz. I could never love any of them." And Liz had to admit that the young men did look rather ragged and sallow after such a hard winter.

When the meeting ended, Liz and Mary Ann had walked back through the muddy streets of Winter Quarters. They had been trying to avoid the puddles and the manure when a man's voice had sounded behind them. "Hello there, sisters."

Liz and Mary Ann both turned back to see that a tall, thin man had greeted them. His face was as lean as his frame, his cheekbones and forehead protruding over deep eyes. "My name is Isaac Elder," he said. "Or Elder Elder, as some have called me." He seemed to consider that a great joke. He laughed in a tight voice. "I understan' that you, Miss Duncan, come over from England not so long back."

"Actually, I came last year," Mary Ann said.

"Ah. So that's it. But I only seed you the first time jist a few days back."

"I didn't wander about much this winter when the snowdrifts were higher than my head."

"I know what yer sayin'. My head sticks up a little more, but I ducked it inside most days too. I got me six children to look after, all by mysel', an' that keeps me at home most of the time. But I'll be bold and speak the truth. If I'd got me a glance at you, sister, I never woulda forgot it."

"Six children! You best hurry back to them right now. I would think they miss their papa after such a long meeting."

"That's so. No doubt about it. But what they long for most is the touch of a softer hand."

"I know what to do about that," Mary Ann said, and Liz saw Brother Elder's eyes widen with interest. "Try rubbing a little cream from the milk pail over your hands. That's the trick women use."

"But I wasn't meaning—"

"Have a lovely Sabbath, Elder Elder. Enjoy those children." And Mary Ann picked up her pace.

Liz had to hurry to catch up. She was trying not to laugh, but she couldn't help herself. "You know what Mother always told us," she whispered to Mary Ann. "Looks aren't everything."

"Oh, Liz, he'll be showing up again. It's the same everywhere I go. I inspire the deepest love from the shallowest of men. He must be *fifty*. Does he really think I want to bed down with him in some dark little shanty—and mother his six children?"

"He was simply passing the time of day, Mary Ann. Don't read so much into his intentions. And I'd say he's closer to forty than to fifty." But she was still laughing.

"He knew my name, Liz. He knew I was a 'Miss.' No doubt, he's been asking about me. He'll be wanting to walk out with me before a week goes by."

"I doubt that, Mary Ann. You made it quite clear that you weren't interested in his attentions."

"Men like that aren't smart enough to know when a woman has no interest. Mark my word, before I'm finished, I'll have to be rude with him, and even then he'll stick to me like molasses."

"Look at it this way, little sister. You do attract men. One of these days it will be the right one."

"Oh, Liz, I've only met one man I could love—and you married him. I wish I had been the older sister and as pretty as you. I'll never find a man like Will."

"That's certainly true. But there's someone right for you. And maybe this is the year you'll meet him."

"What I'll do this year is walk across this whole land. That's not exactly the best way to search for a husband."

"Maybe not. But we'll keep looking."

"Where? Under all the rocks along the way?"

"No, dear, not under the rocks. There are great men in the Church. You'll find one of them."

"I won't do it the way some girls do. I won't marry a man who already has a wife. I'm not playing second fiddle to another woman, no matter how many girls think that's a fine way to get themselves a husband."

Mary Ann had heard about plural marriage before she had sailed to America, but she had been surprised, all the same, to see some of the large families of the Church leaders. Liz had tried to tell her how happy and comfortable Vilate Kimball was with her sister wives, but Mary Ann had said, "That's fine, if she's happy that way. But if I find a man, don't ask me to share him with *anyone*. I'll carry a big stick around and use it on any woman who looks at him—or use it on my husband, if I catch *him* looking."

Liz had laughed, but she understood what Mary Ann was saying. She still felt the same way herself.

• • •

For Will, the months in San Diego had been almost restful. True, he had worked most days, but the pace of the work had been easy. He and the men of Company B had also done much good. They were well thought of and appreciated by the local people. They had also been paid for their work, which had given Will money to send to Liz. When they had originally shown up in San Diego, their ribs had been showing, but now they had filled out some. They looked rugged, and as the time for their mustering out of the service came, they were increasingly happy.

The army made an all-out effort to convince the men of the Battalion to sign up for another year, or even six months. Occupation troops were needed and were hard to come by, and the Mormon men had gained a good reputation with General Kearny and other military leaders. Some of the men decided to sign up for another hitch in the service, but most of the troops could think of only one thing: getting back to the Saints and to their families.

One day, after laying adobe brick all day, Will and Jesse walked down to the San Diego Bay and dug a mess of clams to go with their dinner that night. When they reached the barracks, the Gray brothers were sitting outside on the grass, each reading a letter. "There's mail," Phil shouted as Will and Jesse approached.

Will hurried to Phil and dropped down on the grass next to him. He sorted through the letters and found one from Liz. He opened it with some apprehensiveness, as always, but he could tell from the beginning that there would be no bad news in it. The only disappointment was that Liz couldn't tell him anything about her plans. She didn't know whether she would be included in the wagon trains coming that summer, and she still couldn't say for certain where the Saints would settle in the West. But the boys were doing well, and little Mary Ellen was growing. Liz made light of Mary Ann's search for a husband, and the various suitors she had rejected. "But I do hope she can find a good man—like you," she had added, more seriously.

Will finished his letter and was about to start reading it all over again when he thought to ask, "Did Charley get mail?"

Phil was engrossed in his own letters. He had three, all open before him. He was apparently reading them a second time. "Charley got two letters," he said. "He took them and walked away. I think he's scared what he's going to hear."

"Where did he go?"

"I don't know. I didn't notice."

But Will knew. Charley had found a clearing among some lush palms and ferns. He liked to go there and be alone. Will closed his letter and hurried back toward the bay. When he entered the clearing, he saw Charley sitting with his back against the trunk of a palm tree. He was staring straight ahead.

"Is everything all right?" Will asked, but he already knew the answer. Charley didn't move, didn't seem to hear the question. Will approached carefully and sat down next to him. "What's happened?" he asked.

"What I always feared would happen," he said flatly.

Will knew what Charley meant, but he didn't ask. He just waited.

"I told John Taylor I couldn't go with the Battalion," Charley said. "I told him Rebecca was sick and too weak to manage on her own. He said not to worry, that the Lord would look after her. Well . . . she's dead now, so I guess the Lord has His own idea about what's good for her. And for me."

Will wished Charley would shed some tears. But he sounded too broken to cry, even to be angry, although that was clearly what he was trying to be.

"Out in the desert," Charley said, "you kept telling me, 'We have to stay alive. We have to keep going so we can get back to our families.' Now I wish I'd died."

"But you still have a son, Charley. You have to get back to him."

"My wife's sister has him. He's better off with her." Charley leaned his head back and shut his eyes. Will had no idea what to say. Finally Charley said, "I don't care about anything anymore, Will."

"You will though, Charley. When we lost our baby girl, I thought—"

"That's not the same." And now he did sound angry. "You have Liz. I had less than a year with Rebecca. And like a fool, I gave away this whole last year. Don't tell me God will heal my wounds, because God takes no interest in me. I've prayed every day for just one thing—that I'd make it home to her. Well, the good Lord must've had other matters to worry about 'cause He didn't take time out to listen to me."

"I know it seems that way, but—"

"Leave me alone, Will. I don't want to hear it."

Will said no more, but he didn't leave Charley alone. He stayed with him that day and night, and he led him along after that, not preaching to him, not trying to justify, but walking him through the steps he had to take each day.

Will continued to stay alongside Charley—he and Jesse and the other men in their mess—as they marched to Pueblo Los Angeles and received their release from the army. There had been a good many decisions to make, but Charley hadn't cared about any of them, so Will had made sure he was included with his friends in a company that would make the long march back to the Saints.

When the soldiers left Los Angeles on July 16, they didn't travel as a single unit, but they organized as they had in crossing Iowa the year before, in companies of fifty. What they did finally know was approximately where they were going. Word had come that Brigham Young would be somewhere close to the Great Salt Lake or perhaps in the Bear River Valley, just as Will had predicted. One company, under Jefferson Hunt, planned to march close to the coast as far as Monterey and San Francisco Bay, and then to head east toward Sutter's Fort. A few had decided to head back into the desert, and then northward to the Great Salt Lake, but most of the men, including Will and his friends, formed into three companies of fifty that marched inland across the Sierra Madre mountains and into the Central Valley of Upper California. Sutter's Fort was also their planned destination. Sutter owned a huge ranch far north of Los Angeles, and it was there that the men could outfit themselves to cross the Sierra-Nevada Mountains and the northern desert to the Rockies. There were no wagons to carry provisions this time, but the men had purchased their own pack animals, and at first they had driven cattle along with them. So many of those animals died in the mountains, however, that the remaining cattle had to be slaughtered and the meat dried.

No one had ever experienced the kind of heat they were passing through now. They had crossed the Sonoran Desert and the Imperial Valley in winter, when the heat was moderate. They had also known the moist heat of Nauvoo, but what they were facing now was dry, scorching heat that dragged the strength out of their bodies and left them limp at the end of a day of walking.

Will had been chosen as a captain of ten, and most of the men in his group were the same ones who had shared a tent the year before. One night, as they were resting in a little valley near a trickle of water that was sometimes a stream, James Pace, the captain of their company of fifty, approached on foot. "Just wanted to let you know," he said, "the next two days could be hard ones. The scouts just came back and said there's no water in this stretch ahead—not for thirty miles or so."

"I guess we've made it through worse than that," Ephraim Hart said.

But Jesse said what everyone knew: "Not in heat like this."

"I know," Brother Pace said, "but we can do this. Make sure your pack animals are well watered, and fill your canteens. We'll try to get some people up to Kings River on mules. They'll bring some water back to us. But we'll have to make it most of those thirty miles before they reach us."

"How early are we starting?" Will asked.

"Let's say two in the morning. We'll stop, if we can find some shade, in the middle of the day, and then we'll wait for sundown and start again. We can't walk all day in the sun."

When Brother Pace left, the men were quiet. Will knew that

they were all stronger now after eating well for a few months. But he didn't know whether they could reach inside themselves so deeply as they had last winter. What he knew, personally, was that he had never expected to have to do that again. He prayed for help, and then he talked to himself, tried to get himself ready.

"Just remember," he told the others. "We're all together. We'll all help each other the way we did before."

The men were nodding, agreeing, but Will saw no reaction from Charley Buttars. The man had rarely spoken these last two months. He no longer expressed his anguish; he had simply turned inward. But Will saw the real problem in his eyes: he didn't care about anything.

Will actually wished he could start now and walk all night, until the heat came on in the morning. The problem was, everyone was worn out and thirsty from the day they had just put in. Will knew it would be better for everyone to drink as much as they could, and then to sleep for a while, but he didn't sleep well, and he didn't think the others did either.

When the company set out in the dark, Will and Jesse were together, as always, and they kept Charley between them. They talked to him from time to time, but he said little. They walked all morning as the heat came on ever stronger. Sweat pulled all the water from them, and their canteens emptied out, but they knew enough not to drink deep, only to let a little swallow trickle into their mouths from time to time. Captain Pace eventually found a washed-out draw in a little canyon, with just enough chaparral to provide a bit of shade. He called a halt, and the men rested, but they continued to sweat. And then, when the afternoon light was angling low, they set out again.

They walked late into the night. By then, no one had any water, and some of the men began to break down. Will kept putting one foot ahead of the other as he had done back in the Imperial Valley, and he kept watching Charley and Jesse—and the rest of his men— but no one spoke now. They had learned where their power came from, and Will knew they were all seeking it now—and taking one step at a time. Time and again, he thought of Lydia Hunter, and he told himself to be a strength to the men around him, as she had been the year before.

What Will realized was that Charley wasn't going to last much longer. He had begun to stumble at times, so Will had taken hold of his arm, and Jesse had done the same on the other side. But more and more, Will could feel Charley's weight, and he knew that he and Jesse were keeping their friend up.

The night went on and on. Will had no idea how far the company had walked. Logically, he knew that they must have covered most of the thirty miles, but emotionally, he suspected that there was no end to the ordeal. As the night wore on, he had begun to struggle himself.

"Are you all right?" Jesse asked him.

Will gave his head a shake to clear his mind. "Yeah. We must be . . ." He couldn't think exactly what it was he had started to say. He glanced up and saw that the morning light was a hint in the east.

Will kept stepping, stepping, but Charley's weight was getting harder for him to bear. He could also see now that Jesse was battling his own difficulties. His feet had never been the same since the great march across the deserts. He was hobbling now, obviously in great pain.

Then Jesse said, "I can see someone coming. Maybe they have water."

Will saw two men walking toward him—just silhouettes in the dim light, but they were leading pack animals. As they approached, one of them said, "I can't give you men any of this water. We have to get to the ones who are farther back. But you have only a couple of miles to go. Just make it over this rise, and then you'll drop into the river valley."

Jesse asked, "Couldn't we have just one quick drink?"

"I'm sorry. Brother Pace said there's men who've gone down. We have to help them first."

"It's all right," Will told Jesse. "We can make it."

The men with the pack mules walked on past, and Will and Jesse kept trudging ahead. Will thought they might have gone half a mile when Charley's weight suddenly fell full on his arm. Charley slipped from Will's and Jesse's grasp and went down.

Will and Jesse both dropped down next to him. They grabbed him under his arms and tried to hoist him up, but his dead weight was too much for them. They sank back to the ground.

"Let go of me," Charley said. "I can't do this."

The words seemed to wake Will, fire his determination. He glanced at Jesse but couldn't see him well. "We'll get him there," he said to Jesse. The other men gathered around, and together they lifted Charley to his feet. Will and Jesse began to drag Charley. They stumbled forward until they fell, and then the Gray brothers took over for a time. All the men took turns, finally four at a time carrying Charley. When they began their descent into the river valley, the going was a little easier, but Will couldn't see the end in sight, and he didn't know how many more steps he could take.

The last mile might have taken an hour. Will had lost almost all sense of time. But finally the men saw the river and picked up their pace to get there. They fell down at the bank and used their hands to scoop water into their mouths.

Will drank more than he should, he feared; then he filled his canteen and got down next to Charley. He and Jesse rolled him over, and Will dribbled water onto his face, forced some between his lips. Will heard him cough and then saw him begin to swallow.

"Don't," he finally coughed out. "Don't."

"Drink some more," Will told him.

"I don't want to do this," Charley said. "Just let me . . ." But he didn't finish his sentence.

"You will not die. We won't let you do that." Will shook Charley, gave his face a sharp slap. "Drink some more," he demanded.

Charley did take another drink.

• • •

Liz was sitting in a wagon, holding the reins, watching the rumps of two tall mules as they swayed with each step. The company had reached the high plains beyond the prairies and the Platte River. Liz knew that the Rockies would not come into view for a few more days, but she watched for them anyway. This trek had been easier than the one across Iowa, but harder than she had expected.

Back in June she had heard about companies being organized for the migration west, and she had gone to Will's old friend Charles Rich. "My sister and I, and Sister Ellen Matthews, have a good wagon and two teams of mules. We want to join a company. Could we sign on with yours?"

"I'm full up, Sister Lewis," Brother Rich said. "Too many want to go this season, but they would be better off to wait another year. Life is going to be hard this first year out there."

"But Will's on his way to meet me. I want to be with him."

Brother Rich took off his broad-brimmed hat, as though aware that with it on, he towered over Liz. He rubbed his hand over his hair, pushing it back, and he seemed to give her request some thought. But then he said, "Sister Lewis, I think you should let him get there and get a house built for you. I know you had a rough winter here, but now you have a house, and you can tighten it up for another winter. That tiny daughter of yours would be better off here than she would be in a wagon all summer."

"My baby is doing fine," Liz said. "She'll be just as healthy in a wagon as she would be here among all the sickness along the river. Everyone says the air is better out west."

"That may be, but it won't be easy going for three women and a pack of little children. Just wait another season."

"Brother Rich, we three women *built* our own house when no man could spare the time to help us. I think we can do for ourselves in a wagon just fine. Brother Brigham promised the wives of the Battalion that he'd help us get to our husbands this year. I think it's about time *someone* remembered all those promises made to us when our husbands were being recruited."

"Back then, no one realized that—"

"No one knew a lot of things, but that doesn't change the fact that our leaders promised to take care of us, and we've mostly taken care of ourselves. They promised to get us to the West, too, and I'm not even asking for that. I'm just asking that we have a chance to join a company so we can make it on our own."

Brother Rich laughed. He set his hat back on his head. "All right," he said. "I'll make room for you, and I'll assign some of my leaders to keep an eye on you. But I really do think you're facing much harder things than you might be ready for."

And that had turned out to be true. The early part of the trip had not seemed difficult. Liz had been told to expect Indian attacks, but the tribes along the way had actually been quite welcoming. As they reached the dry heat of the West, however, the lumber in the undercarriage of Liz's wagon had split apart. It was the sort of thing she had no idea about, and it had only been the help of some of the leaders that had kept the wagon together. Mules were cantankerous animals as well, and Liz had learned that she wasn't dealing with docile oxen. She had to let the mules know who the boss was, and she had had to use all her strength to fight the big creatures at times. Twice she had awakened to find her mules gone, even though she had tried to halter them and stake them to the ground. Once again, men had had to help her search for them. Liz felt humbled by all that, and she had become aware that she wasn't quite so strong as she liked to think she was.

But the greater test was the daily task of breaking camp, moving ahead, breathing dust all day. Mary Ann was a big help with the children. She tried to keep Jesse Junior—with Jacob and Daniel tagging along—from exploring too many streams or carrying too many snakes into camp. But the journey gradually became less of an adventure for the boys and more of a trial. All the children wore down, and they became cranky with one another. There were always little mishaps, too: the children chasing after one another and falling in the dirt, scratching elbows and tearing trousers and dresses.

Worst, however, was caring for little Mary Ellen and for Ellen's baby, Cyrus. Mary Ellen had been four months old, and Cyrus almost six, when the company had moved out, and the children had loved to play with the babies and take turns keeping them company. But as everyone grew tired, the fun of entertaining fussy babies lost all its appeal.

Every day something seemed to happen to keep the forward progress of the company from being quite what the leaders hoped. Wagons broke down; people hurt themselves; and someone was always sick. Captain Rich's mother suffered terribly and seemed very near death at times.

One day Mary Ann was driving the mules, telling the animals what miserable, cursed beasts they were, and Liz was walking alongside the wagon. She had sat in the wagon long enough to nurse Mary

Ellen, but then she had been able to put her down in the back of the wagon and take a turn walking. She felt bedraggled, her skirt ripped and tattered, and the elbows splitting out of her blouse. She had washed her clothes as often as she could after perspiring so much during those hottest days, and the cotton fabric had worn thin.

It was a fair day, and early enough that the children were walking rather resolutely, not bothering each other, and Liz was able to think about Will. She tried to imagine how much he had changed, and she wondered where he was now. She also wondered whether he would be disappointed when he finally saw her. She certainly wasn't as pretty as she had once been. She had aged, and weathered, in the last year. Maybe his youthful passion for her would wane now. Maybe taking a second, younger wife would appeal to him. But she pushed all those thoughts aside as much as she could, and she tried to imagine herself with him again, able to talk about everything they had experienced in the last year. She didn't know what sort of bed they would have, in what sort of shanty, but she wanted to lie next to him at night again, hear him breathe, feel her hand touching him.

And then Liz tripped. She didn't know whether it was a gopher hole or what, but something caught her foot, and she went down. She felt her knee twist, and she cried out. Mary Ann pulled back on the lines and stopped the mules. In only seconds, Mary Ann and Ellen, even all the children, were gathered around Liz. Her knee was hurting badly, but she tried not to let everyone know. "It's not so bad," she kept saying. "I'll be fine."

But when the women helped her up, she soon knew that she couldn't walk anymore that day.

"We're holding up the company," Liz said. "Let me drive the mules again. I'll be fine if I don't have to walk for a little while."

"You'll drive the mules all day," Mary Ann said. "I can walk. I don't need to ride—ever."

"I like your spirit, Sister Duncan."

Liz twisted to see that John Wade, their captain of ten, had come up behind them. He had apparently come back to see why the wagon had stopped. "Don't worry about us. We're fine," Liz said.

Liz glanced to see that Mary Ann was blushing. But she was smiling, too. "I'm stronger than I ever thought I was," she was saying to Brother Wade.

"Well, it's been a fine thing to see you women do so well," he said. "I'm sure your husbands will be proud of you."

"*My* husband will be busting his buttons," Mary Ann said.

And now it was Brother Wade who was blushing. And smiling. "I didn't mean you, Sister Duncan. I know that you're not married." But he was quick to change the subject. "Let me help you up on the wagon, Sister Lewis. If you like, I could send back one of the older boys to drive your mules while you rest your leg a little."

"Just help me up. I'll be fine."

But Liz was taken by surprise when he gripped her at the waist and lifted her easily. She thought she might be blushing herself when she thanked him.

Liz shook the lines and called to the mules, "Gid-up." But after a few minutes, Mary Ann, who was walking close to the wagon, said, "He's *very* strong, isn't he?"

Liz didn't like the tone of that at all. "Yes. And he's very handsome. And he's also very *married.*"

"I know that," Mary Ann said. But she looked away, and then she took up her walk a little farther away from the wagon.

CHAPTER 25

Abby was driving home from Quincy, pushing the speed limit a little, worried that she had been leaning on Kayla way too much lately. The agreement with her boss had been that she would drive to Quincy only twice a week normally, but lately, now that summer had come on, lots of people were interested in updating their homes. Abby had been seeing clients in Quincy and surrounding towns four of the five days this week, and next week looked to be even busier.

And now her phone was ringing—again. She didn't like to drive and talk, but she picked up the phone and saw that the call was from Alice Evanson, a woman in her ward. She instantly felt guilty. She had been letting too many responsibilities with Relief Society slide lately, and Alice, who had been president a few years back, still had strong opinions about how things ought to be done.

Abby was tempted not to answer but decided she didn't dare do that. At least she had an excuse to keep the conversation short. She swiped her thumb across the screen of her smartphone and said, "Hello."

"Hi, Abby. Did I catch you at a bad time?"

"Well, no. But I'm driving and I don't like to—"

"I won't keep you long. But there's something you probably ought to know—if you haven't heard by now."

"What's that?"

"It's Sister Marshall. You know Maggie Marshall, don't you?"

"Yes."

"Well, she had a miscarriage this week. Did you know that?"

"No."

"That's what I was afraid of. I talked to her last night, and I told her to call you, but she said she knew how busy you always are and she didn't want to bother you."

This felt like a stab. Abby couldn't think what to say.

"I mean, I know how it is, Abby. You have an awful lot on your table, but Maggie's miscarried twice before, and this time she was fifteen weeks along, so she was feeling like everything was going to be all right. She's *very* upset. I tried to talk to her about it, but she—"

"I'll call her just as soon as I get home, Alice, and I'll go see her tonight."

"Well, that would be good—if you have the time."

"I'll make the time, Alice."

"You sound upset, Abby. I didn't mean to point fingers. I just thought you'd want to know."

"I'm fine. Thanks for letting me know. I'll go see her tonight." Abby's thumb was hovering over the "end" button.

"Just let me say one more thing. I know you've never served in a job like this, but I have, and I know it's hard to keep track of everyone. But if the sisters feel they can't get hold of you, they—"

"Alice, listen to me. I'll go over there tonight. I don't know what else I can tell you." But now she had lost control of her voice.

There was a rather long hesitation on the other end of the line. Then Sister Evanson said, "All right. But, Abby, you need to know that a lot of women in the ward are getting tired of this. They try and try to reach you and you're *never* home—and your cell is turned off. You need to show the sisters you actually care about them or you'll lose their trust. And once that happens, you—"

Abby pressed the "end" button, and then she instantly wished she hadn't done that. She was crying by then and actually needed to pull off the road—but she didn't have the time.

• • •

That night Abby got home from visiting Sister Marshall before Jeff got home. She tried to work on some drawings she needed to do, but she couldn't get her thoughts straight. When Jeff finally came in, she said, too abruptly, "Jeff, we need to talk."

"Okay," he said, and she saw the concern in his face.

Abby sat down on the couch, but when Jeff came to join her, she said, "Sit in the chair, okay? I want to be able to look at you."

"All right." He sat down and waited.

"I had a call today," she started, keeping her voice steady. But then she realized she didn't want to get into the whole story about Sister Marshall. "Sister Evanson called me. She said the sisters in the ward can never find me home and they're losing trust in me."

Jeff grimaced. "Wow. Really? But Alice has a way of—"

"It is hard to get hold of me, Jeff. I *am* too busy. And so are you. We keep saying things will get better, but nothing's ever going to change if we don't start putting first things first."

Jeff bent down and pulled his shoes off, and then he stretched his legs out and slid down in his chair. She could see the frustration, maybe even irritation, on his face. Finally, he said, "Abby, I actually do know the answer. Will you listen to me and not just reject what I say until you hear me out?"

But he was taking on his "wise husband" voice, and that bothered her. Still, she said, "Yes. Of course I'll listen."

"Okay. You need to quit your job in Quincy. You've only been working there a few months, but you've done a good job for them and I don't think it will ruin your career forever. Just tell them that driving back and forth from here is too demanding for you. I still think Jay would write you a great recommendation if you needed it someday."

He hesitated, as though he expected an objection, but she had promised to hear him out, and she was going to do it. It was just that she knew something he didn't, and it would make a difference.

"I know that insurance is your big worry, but I've been looking into that. Malcolm and I, as small business owners, can buy insurance for all our employees, which, of course, includes ourselves. We can get into a group program. That's expensive, but the costs become a business expense."

He was still watching her, as though he expected an argument, but Abby actually liked what she was hearing.

"And here's the real point: Abby, we're starting to make some decent money. These last couple of weeks the number of advertising clients we've taken on has snowballed. The more traffic I get on the site, the more interest I generate, and the higher prices we can charge people who want to buy ads. You really don't have to work. I was going to talk to you about this, but I've just been waiting for the cash flow to start showing up so I could show you the books and reassure you that we're okay."

"What about maternity insurance?" Abby asked.

"Sure. That would be part of the package. We'd be covered."

"But is there a time limit?"

"Probably. I don't know if it's a year, or just nine months, or how they work that."

"But it can't be a preexisting condition?"

"I'm not sure. The laws have changed, and I think . . ." And then he realized what she was saying. "Are you pregnant?"

"Yes." She watched for his reaction. "Jeff, I thought I might be, so I took a test when I got home today, and it was positive."

"Then we better worry more about *life insurance*. Your mother's going to kill me." But he was coming to her now. And he looked happy. She had worried all evening whether he would feel that way.

"We'll figure this out," Jeff said. "I'm sure we can get coverage. Don't give notice until I talk to an insurance guy, but whatever it takes, we'll work it out." He was kneeling in front of her. He took hold of her hands, kissed each one.

"I thought you might be upset," she said. "We didn't plan for a baby right now." She had begun to cry again.

"Hey, it's great," he said. "Will needs to have someone to play with. We talked about not waiting too much longer."

Abby was still holding onto Jeff's hands. She was relieved and even a little hopeful. "Jeff, I've got to be a better Relief Society president."

"Maybe so. But you need to remind Sister Evanson that all the sisters can help each other. That's what visiting teaching is all about. Everything doesn't have to come back to the presidency."

"I know. I've thought about that. But they have to be able to reach me when they really need me."

"I know. This will be great for you—finally to have the time to do the job."

Abby was nodding, but one other problem did cross her mind. "I'm not going to tell Mom for a while," she said.

"Hey, I'll take care of that. I have a diplomatic way of explaining things to your mother."

Abby laughed and wiped at her tears. "I think you better leave it to me," she said. "But thank you, Jeff. I'm so glad you're happy about it."

He pulled her close, and Abby felt that she could finally breathe.

• • •

Jeff and Malcolm had finished a job late one afternoon and decided that before they called it a day they would take care of a few things in a kitchen they had been redoing in another house. The house was in Sycamore Haven, a road that ran along the north end of Nauvoo, directly along the river. Will loved this hidden part of town that most of the tourists never discovered. He loved to watch the sunset as it reflected off the ripples of the river. And even though he wanted to get home, he liked having some time with Malcolm again.

Pulled up in front of the house, the two remained in the truck, engrossed in a conversation they had begun. Malcolm had caught Jeff's interest by saying, "I think it's time to hire another guy besides Ed, or maybe two—men who can think for themselves if I'm not there every minute. Ed could be the foreman. Maybe, after that, we could get a second foreman and a second crew. Our biggest problem is that we disappoint our customers too often by running back and forth from one job to another and coming in late on both jobs. But maybe the answer isn't to take on less work. Maybe it's to hire more workers."

"Have you figured out the overhead, though? We'd have to buy equipment and probably have to get another truck. And we'd have Workers' Compensation and benefits and everything to worry about."

"I know. But if we had two crews, we could put a few more guys to work. We both know men who need jobs. I could keep doing the bidding and maybe take over the buying, and you could put all your time into the web site and the blog."

"It doesn't take *that* much time. And I want to stay involved.

It seemed good today to spend a little time with a hammer in my hand."

"I know what you're saying, but actually I have something else in mind." He looked over at Jeff. "I've made up my mind about one thing. I've got to start college again, and do it for real this time."

"I thought you said you wanted to wait."

"But I'll keep waiting forever if I'm not careful. I need to do what's best for Kayla and the kids. And I need to know more about that stuff you were asking about—overhead and benefits and all of that. I've gotta take some business classes so I know what I'm doing. Actually, what I want is a business degree—so I start to have some options in my life."

"So would you start school this fall?"

"Yeah, I think so. If I had a foreman, I'd have more time to run down to Keokuk and take classes. I don't think I'm ready to turn the whole thing over to other guys quite yet, but I've gotta stop working sixteen hours a day."

"That all makes sense, Malc. The business could even pay your tuition and books."

"Okay. That's great. But that's only half the plan I've been thinking up. The other thing is, you need to go to school too."

"I'm taking a class again this summer."

"Yeah. But you need to move ahead. You really need to go to grad school."

"I can't even apply yet. I need more undergraduate credits in history first."

"That's right. So here's my plan. You register in Macomb—or wherever you want to go—full-time this fall, and then get your applications in to Princeton and all those places you've talked about. Wherever you go, you can take that laptop of yours with you, and you can run the web site and make us rich."

"Actually, I've thought about doing something like that. But I want to stay close to this area, partly so I can keep doing research with Professor Woodbury on the old Mormon settlements around here. I could maybe apply to the University of Iowa, or over in Champaign, at the University of Illinois. I want to be close enough that Abby and I can run over here on weekends. I need to stay connected to the business so I know what kind of stuff to put on the web site."

"All right. Let's do it. If you want, you could stick around here this year and just commute to Macomb, but there's really no reason you couldn't get the credits you need at one of those big universities—and sort of get your foot in the door for graduate school."

"Yeah, well, I'd have to think about all that."

"Don't think. Let's just do it."

Jeff could feel wood putty on his hands, dried and crumbling now. He knew that he liked getting his hands dirty, that he would miss that kind of work if he went away from it entirely. "But I do have a few things to figure out," he said. "You're not the only one who's been thinking about all this stuff, Malc. I've thought for a long time that I wanted to be a professor, but I don't know anymore. Working with my hands has been good for me—even if I'm not that good at it. It's brought me down out of the clouds. Sometimes professors get into all this esoteric, theoretical stuff and—"

"Hey, wait. I don't even know what that means."

"I'm just saying that historians, in my opinion, are moving too far away from telling stories. I think I want to write books that normal human beings would enjoy reading. And you know what? I hate the idea of leaving Nauvoo."

"I'm glad to hear you say that."

"If we could keep running the business—both the building end of it and the web site—maybe we could make enough money to support us, and after grad school I could come back to Nauvoo and help keep the business going but spend a lot of my time writing."

"So you would come back here and stay?"

"Yeah. That's what I'm thinking. And I know Abby would love the idea."

"Let's go talk to Abby and Kayla about all this. I don't want to work on this kitchen tonight. Do you?"

"Never did. Just didn't want to tell you that."

"Okay." But Malcolm didn't start the truck immediately. He was looking straight ahead, not at Jeff, when he said, "I just wonder, do you feel like you want to keep working with me?"

"Sure I do. My only worry is that you might cut your leg off one of these days if you don't have me around to take care of you."

But Malcolm didn't laugh. "I wish I'd never said that stuff that day."

"Actually, it was good. It got us both thinking where we were going with this thing. I feel like we've got the right idea now."

"I guess good friends can get mad each other once in a while."

"No question. Abby gets mad at me fairly often, and I'm still good friends with her."

Malcolm laughed, and he finally started the truck. "Call her now. If she hasn't started dinner, we can take the girls out tonight—now that we're claiming to be so rich."

"Okay."

And then Malcolm stuck his hand out, and Jeff wasn't exactly sure what it meant, but the two of them shook hands. And that seemed to be all that needed to be said.

But when Jeff called Abby, she said she had started dinner already and also didn't know what she and Kayla would do for baby-sitters on such short notice. "Just tell Kayla to bring whatever she was cooking and come over to our house," she suggested. "We'll put everything together and make some sort of meal for all of us."

So Malcolm called Kayla, and an hour later the men had each stopped home long enough to shower, and the families were together.

• • •

Abby was happy to have the McCords over, and especially happy that Jeff wasn't going to work all evening. But she was curious about what it was the guys wanted to "talk over," as Jeff had suggested.

So Liz and Kayla got the kids fed first, and then they sent them in to play in the living room while the adults sat down at the kitchen table together.

"Okay, what's this 'meeting' all about?" Kayla asked.

"We have a proposal to make," Malcolm said, and Jeff was pleased that Malc was the one who was ready to do the talking.

"Yes, we agree to stay married to you," Kayla said. "Or at least we'll sign up for another one-year hitch."

"Okay. That settles that," Malcolm said. "I don't know why we were so worried." He smiled at Jeff and began to pass a bowl of green beans around.

"It's always good to worry just a little," Abby said, "just to stay on your toes."

"Okay," Malcolm said, "so here's the deal. And this is serious business. We both want to quit working and go to college." He hesitated, smiled, and then said, "Well, not exactly. Actually, we both want to *keep working* and go back to college."

"And when and where do you propose to do this?" Kayla asked.

The four were sitting on the four sides of the little wooden table in the Lewises' kitchen. Abby loved their kitchen now, with its beautiful cabinets and sparkling appliances, and she loved having her friends there with her. She also had the feeling this was one of the most important moments of her life, however lightheartedly Malcolm was presenting it.

"Okay, here's the first part of that answer. Jeff can keep the web site running from anywhere, so he could go to school wherever he wants."

"But I'm thinking we would want to stay close to Nauvoo," Jeff said. "I want to look at the universities that are here in this area. If we were in Iowa City, for instance, we could get down here a lot."

Abby began to laugh.

"What's so funny?" Jeff asked.

"Nothing. Go ahead and tell us your ideas, and then Kayla and I will tell you what we think. We've been talking too."

"Well, the only other part to this," Jeff said, "is that I don't think I want to teach. I'd rather get my degree and then keep running the web site, with Abby's help, but continue my historical research. As much as anything, I'm looking for a way to spend my life here, so we can serve where we're needed and in a place we love so much."

He looked down at the table. Abby still couldn't stop grinning, and Kayla was looking across at her and beaming too.

Jeff added, "As much as anything, I want to spend my life with our best friends. And I want to keep splitting things down the middle, so everything we do is for all of us."

Abby reached across the table and took hold of Kayla's hand. She asked Kayla, "Should we tell them?"

"Yeah. I think it's time."

"Okay. But before I do, have you guys figured out the whole insurance thing?"

"Pretty much. We—"

"Do you two even know that we're *both* pregnant?" Abby asked.

"Yeah," Malcolm said. "I told Jeff about our baby today. And I'm pretty sure he knows about yours, Abby. But yes, our company will pay for the insurance, and Jeff is getting things worked out with our insurance guy."

"Excellent," Abby said, "but here's what you need to know. Kayla and I have been talking about all these same things for weeks, and we had already made up our minds to present our plan to the two of you one of these first days."

"And what is the plan?" Malcolm asked.

"Need you ask? It was basically the plan you just described. Even the part about staying close to Nauvoo."

The men were smiling, looking very pleased by all this. Abby said, "It's not just logical. I think it's what we're supposed to do. God's been helping all of us figure it out."

Abby watched everyone's face become more serious. Jeff nodded to her.

Kayla said, "A year ago, everything was such a mess. Malcolm didn't have a job, and you two were talking about leaving. I just can't believe that so many good things have worked out for us since then."

"It's not just that our little business has taken off so well," Jeff said. "What feels good to me is that I finally know what I want to do—without making a mess of Abby's life in the process."

Abby felt that too. She had wanted Jeff to soar, but she had also wanted to feel safe. This plan, of course, was not without its dangers. The web site might not develop the way they hoped, or remodeling might not always be so much in demand. Who knew? But God seemed behind the choices they were making, and that was the security Abby needed. She also knew that she would miss being Relief Society president when they left, but she had learned from the experience. And someday, no doubt, she would have another chance to serve her sisters.

CHAPTER 26

W ill and Jesse and Charley had crossed the Sierra-Nevada
Mountains and were now in the middle of another desert. The climb
through the mountains had not been easy, but water had been plentiful, the scenery beautiful, and the temperatures pleasant. While
still in the mountains the men had run into Samuel Brannan returning to California from a visit with Brigham Young. Brother Brannan
had led a group of Saints who had sailed around Cape Horn and
landed at San Francisco Bay. What he reported to the Battalion men
was that the pioneer party of Saints had arrived in the Great Salt
Lake Valley and now intended to stay there. But Brannon saw no
way that anyone could survive in such a desolate place.

"Frost can come every month of the year in those mountains,"
he told the soldiers. "Grains will start to grow and then get frozen,
again and again. It's just no place for an agricultural people."

"What does Brigham Young say?" one of the men asked.

"You know how stubborn he is. Someone has told him crops
will grow there, and he believes it. Give him one year to see what
happens and he'll be heading to the West Coast. Mark my word."

And then he talked on and on about all the reasons the Saints should settle in California.

Brannan was enthusiastic, and persuasive, but he reminded Will of Major Harcourt, the man he had met long ago on the riverboat coming up the Mississippi. Will worried that Brother Brannan was promoting his own enterprises over the welfare of the Saints. Two days later the men met Brother James Brown on his way to Sutter's Fort to collect the payments that Battalion members had received from the army. Brother Brown had brought a letter from Church leaders, and the advice was that those without adequate means to subsist during the coming winter should stay in California, get work, and then bring their earnings to the Saints next spring.

The letter had forced Will and Jesse to make a hard decision. They did have some money, but perhaps not enough to survive the winter, and they would arrive far too late to plant crops. But Brannan had also said that a large camp of five companies was on its way to the Great Salt Lake Valley from the Missouri River settlements, and they would be arriving late in September or October. From what Liz had said in her letter, she and Ellen might be traveling in one of those companies. Will and Jesse didn't know how their families would survive the Rocky Mountain winter, but they knew they wanted to be there to help. And if it turned out their wives weren't with those companies, they thought they might want to leave immediately for Winter Quarters and then help them cross the plains the following year.

Some men had already decided they would winter at Sutter's Fort, but about two hundred had started into the mountains. Now, after reading what Brigham Young had written, about half of them decided to turn back. But Will and Jesse felt they had to go forward.

"I don't like breaking up our group," Josh Gray told Will. "Maybe we should all jist stick't out together."

"No. It's Jesse and I who might be making a mistake. You men go back and work—and stay in a warm place this winter. We'll go forward and hope to meet up with our wives."

"What about Charley?"

Charley spoke a little more often now, since surviving that night at Kings River when he had almost given up, but he rarely expressed an opinion.

Will turned to Charley. "Do you want to go on with Jesse and me?" he asked.

Charley nodded and said, "Might as well."

"Good," Will said. "That sounds best to me, too."

So about one hundred men continued on, the companies of fifty no longer organized as they had been. The men were facing another desert, but it was September, and temperatures were not so intense as they had been. For the most part, they followed the Humboldt River, and that meant they were never very far from water. They walked ten to twenty miles each day, usually closer to twenty, and hoped to make it to Fort Hall by the end of the month. Then they would turn south to the Great Salt Lake.

One morning, after the men had arisen and struck their tents, Will stirred the fire and added wood, then heated water for mush and coffee. They had slept near the river, where there was some timber, but the desert stretched out to the south, bleak and never-changing. Will hated to think about another day like the one before—and so many before that—with nothing new to see or enjoy, and fatigue setting in deeper all the time.

The food was meager compared to what had been available in San Diego, but mush was what they were accustomed to again, and at least they had enough to fill themselves.

Charley finished his breakfast, but when Jesse wasn't quite ready, he lay down again with his head on his bedroll. Charley seemed to value sleep more than anything. He always went to bed ahead of the other men, and he curled up whenever Will and Jesse took a rest along the way.

The problem now was, Jesse was in great pain again. Back in the Sierras his damaged feet had gotten worse. He had awakened one morning with his left foot badly swollen, and it seemed likely that he had broken a bone or wrenched something apart inside. He was wrapping the foot tightly with a cloth now, before he pulled his boot on, but the wrapping helped only a little.

Will helped him get both boots on, and then Jesse stood and took a few steps to test the foot, but he couldn't really put his full weight on it. "I don't see how you can walk another five hundred miles, Jesse," Will said.

"What choice do I have? You might want ta toss me away an' let the wolves eat me up. Short of that, I can na' tell ye what to do."

Jesse was laughing, but his discouragement had been deepening lately. The pain had to be nearly unbearable, but beyond that, he was losing strength and maybe hope. In the last fourteen months Will estimated they had walked close to twenty-eight hundred miles. That could be the ruin of anyone's feet—or hope—but it was the mileage ahead that was hard for Will to think about. And the same thought had to be much worse for Jesse.

"If I have to carry you on my back, I will, my brother," Will said. "Don't ever think that I will na'."

• • •

Charles Rich's company had finally left the North Platte River, reached Fort Laramie, and continued on across the high plains toward the mountains. At the Sweetwater River the companies heading west met Brigham Young and most of the Apostles, who were on their way back to Winter Quarters. They planned to lead more

Saints to the Great Salt Lake the following year, but they stopped now and enjoyed a feast with their brothers and sisters.

Liz had seen some evidence of discord between the captains in the "Big Camp," as everyone had begun to call it. She knew little about the trouble, except that the leaders had quarreled about the order of the march. The company that led out always found better grazing for their animals and less dust to breathe, so there was always competition as to who should go ahead. What Liz heard now, however, as the companies set out again, was that Brigham had taken a firm hand and instructed Parley Pratt and other leaders to end contention and share the opportunity to go first. Liz had sometimes resented Brigham Young's style of leadership, but she had learned what he could accomplish with his firmness, and she also knew, personally, how kind he could be. She hadn't had an opportunity to greet him this time, with so many crowding around him at the dinner, but she heard his speech—heard him say the valley of the Great Salt Lake was the place promised by God to the Saints—and she trusted what he said.

The companies left the Sweetwater and traveled through South Pass, across the Green River, and on to Fort Bridger. What everyone knew by then was that although not many miles lay ahead, the greatest challenge was rising before them: the Rocky Mountains that guarded the valley where they would settle. They had faced plenty of sand, broken wagons, sick animals, and accidents, but they had rolled steadily ahead, sometimes the boredom and weariness being the worst of their trials. But after they crossed the Bear River and made their way through Echo Canyon, the trail—the one established by Brigham Young's vanguard company—led up and over Big Mountain. Brigham had warned these later companies that with tired draft animals, and with the people so worn down, this climb—and the descent through the canyons that followed—would test them to the limit.

Before they had started, back in Winter Quarters, Liz had

bragged about her own strength, as well as Mary Ann's and Ellen's, but she felt little of that confidence now. What made things worse for Liz was that Mary Ann had become sick. Mountain fever, as Brigham Young had called it—and which he had suffered from himself as he had crossed the mountains—was abating now, as the hot days were ending. Liz didn't know whether that was what Mary Ann had; she only knew that the girl had a fever and a terrible headache, and that she had lost all her feistiness. Liz's knee was not bothering her very much now; it was Mary Ann who was struggling to make the steep climb, so Liz had Mary Ann take the lines and drive the mules.

The climb was tedious, the mules needing extra time to rest, and the progress slow when they did trudge ahead. But when the wagons finally reached the crest of the mountain, Liz realized that the descent would be hard, too, and frightening. Brother Rich watched as each wagon started down the long grade. At times he had drivers set their block brakes to lock the back wheels and let them slide rather than to allow the wagon to pick up speed and overrun the mules. But there were also places where the canyon narrowed and left no flat roadway. The wagons teetered on the side of the hill, and the animals struggled to keep their footing.

Liz walked alongside their wagon on the high side of the hill, carrying her baby. She could see that Mary Ann was becoming frustrated. Liz was about to ask one of the brothers to take over the wagon when Mary Ann suddenly called out, "I can't do this." Liz knew that she was not only frightened but exhausted.

"Hold right there," Captain Rich shouted to her, and Mary Ann pulled back on the lines. But she jerked too hard. The mules in front raised up, their front legs flailing, and when they came down, they shuffled to the side as though they were confused about what Mary Ann wanted them to do. By then, they had jerked the wagon sideways, and it began to tip.

On impulse, Liz tried to grab for the wagon, even with little Mary Ellen in her arms, but she couldn't have stopped it. It continued to roll over and then suddenly dropped on its side. Liz saw Mary Ann try to jump, and then she lost sight of her. When Liz ran around the wagon, she found Mary Ann down on the ground.

The mules were going wild by then. They surged ahead, dragging the wagon on its side a few yards down the mountain. Brother Rich caught hold of the mules, and Liz heard him speak to them, try to calm them. Liz dropped to her knees next to Mary Ann. She seemed to have landed on her shoulder and the side of her head. Liz was still holding her baby in one arm, but she used the other hand to roll Mary Ann onto her back. Mary Ann's eyes were closed, and there was a cut next to her eye, open but only just beginning to bleed.

Men were running from all directions toward them. Liz didn't think that her boys and Ellen's children were under the wagon. She had told them to stay behind. But she wanted to see them, to know that they were all right.

John Wade was the first to reach Liz. He kneeled next to Mary Ann and took her up in his arms. "Sister Duncan, Sister Duncan, can you hear me?" He patted her face, softly at first, and then a little harder. "Can you hear me?"

The baby was wailing, but Ellen was suddenly there, reaching for her.

"Are the children all right?" Liz asked, unnerved by the sound of her own voice, so full of panic.

Ellen took the baby and said, "They're safe. I'll get a clean cloth to put around that cut."

But Mary Ann didn't seem to be alive. Blood was running down her temple and into her hair, but her face was colorless. She didn't seem to be breathing. Liz could only think that she must have broken her neck. "Mary Ann, open your eyes," she shouted. "Wake up."

But Mary Ann still wasn't moving. She showed no sign of hearing her.

Liz reached for Mary Ann's head, spread her palms over her bloody hair. "I bless you in the name of the Lord," she said. "Come back to me, Mary Ann."

A few seconds passed, and then Mary Ann took a deep breath—as though it were the first she had taken since she struck the ground. Her eyes fluttered and then came open.

"You're all right, Sister Duncan," Brother Wade was saying. "We'll take care of you." He still had her in his arms.

Liz was already praying again, thanking the Lord. But at the same time she didn't want Brother Wade to hold Mary Ann, didn't want her sister to be embraced that way by a married man. "Set her down," she said—commanded. "We need to get that bleeding stopped."

Brother Wade kept a hand under Mary Ann's head as he lowered her onto her back. Liz pressed her hand over the wound and then looked about for Ellen.

"You're all right," Brother Wade was saying. "The wagon tipped, and you hit your head, but you'll be just fine."

"My shoulder," Mary Ann said.

"Does your shoulder hurt?" Liz asked.

"Yes. Bad."

"All right. But stay where you are. You have a cut by your eye. We need to stop the bleeding." She looked again, and this time she saw Ellen running toward her, a white rag held out in front of her.

Liz took the cloth and tried to tear it but couldn't in her frantic state. It was Brother Wade who took it from her and tore it into long strips, and then, together, they wrapped the strips tightly around Mary Ann's head and tied them.

"I'm sorry," Mary Ann was saying by then. "I scared the mules. It was my fault. Now our wagon is—"

"It doesn't matter. You're all right. But you scared me so. You didn't breathe at first."

Liz finally looked up to see that men were crowding around the wagon, getting ready to lift it up. A few things—some bedding and some cooking pots—were scattered behind the wagon on the ground. Some of the cover bows might have been broken, but that seemed to be the only damage.

An hour later the wagon had been lifted back onto its wheels and men had calmed the mules and led them and the wagon off the mountain. Liz was sitting by Mary Ann. They had found a little grove of aspen where there was some shade. Brother Rich had gone to retrieve Patty Sessions from another company and had brought her in on the back of his horse. Mother Sessions had asked Brother Wade and Brother Rich to hold Mary Ann while she pulled the joint back into place. Mary Ann had screamed with pain, but she was calm now, and Patty had sent all the men away and was applying an ointment. "This concoction will help some with the pain," she was saying. "But mostly time will fix it more'n anything else. I'll fix you up a sling here in a minute, but you hafta do what I say. Don't move that arm much. It needs to settle into place and heal." She continued to rub the potion over Mary Ann's shoulder, reaching under her dress, which was unbuttoned down the front. "Did anyone give you a blessing?" she asked.

"No," Mary Ann said.

But Liz said, "Actually, I did. When you weren't answering me."

Mary Ann seemed surprised, but as they continued to look at one another, Liz felt an understanding, a sense of warmth, pass between them. Mary Ann whispered, "Thank you."

"You'll still have to walk off this mountain," Patty told Mary Ann, "and down through the last canyons to the valley, but rest for a time now. You have two or three hard days ahead of you, and then you'll be able to recuperate."

"Mother Sessions, she's been sick," Liz said.

"I know. She's still feverish. But she's better off to walk than to get tossed back'n forth in a wagon. That shoulder will hurt with ever' bounce. Sorry, dear, but that's just how it is." She gave Mary Ann's cheek a tender pat, and then she said, "Now let's see about that cut."

Patty untied the strips of cloth and applied a sweet-smelling herb to the wound, and then she rewrapped it. "You did a good job, Sister Lewis," she said. "Bleeding in the head is dang'rous, but you got it stopped." She leaned close to Mary Ann and said, "I'm afeard you'll have a little scar on your face, but thass not a serious matter. All in all, the Lord blessed you. You coulda broke your neck, the way you hit the ground."

"I know. Thank you, Mother Sessions."

"Don't thank me too much. I'm going to give you a bill one of these days." Patty laughed, and then she walked to Brother Rich, who was waiting for her just down the hill.

Mary Ann waited until Patty was gone to say, "She's right, Liz. A scar on my face doesn't matter. No one looks at me anyway."

"Don't make light of it, Mary Ann. I'm still not breathing right. I thought you were dead for at least two minutes. I really did."

"I was knocked out, I guess. I don't remember what happened after the wagon started to tip."

"I thought I had lost you." But Liz didn't want to cry. She looked down the mountain. Other wagons were passing by, the drivers struggling to keep their wagons under control during the slow descent. Ellen and all the children had walked on. Liz had told them that she and her sister would follow as soon as they could.

"I think I remember something," Mary Ann said. "Did John Wade take hold of me—I mean, in his arms?"

"Yes, he did, Mary Ann. He was very worried about you."

"Oh."

370 • DEAN HUGHES

"He's our captain. He was looking after you. Don't read too much into it."

"I don't, Liz. I'm sure he was even more worried about our mules." She smiled for the first time, and her voice sounded lighter.

But this worried Liz. So far as Liz knew, Brother Wade had no sanction to take another wife, but he seemed to have taken an interest in Mary Ann. "It would not be wrong to thank him, Mary Ann," Liz said, "but please don't flatter him. I know you like his attention, but it isn't proper to entice him in any way."

"Entice him? Do you think that's what I'm doing?"

Mary Ann started to get up, but Liz reached around her waist and held her down. "Just rest a little longer. And don't be angry. I'm not accusing you of anything. But I've seen you laugh with him and tease him. He's clearly taken with you, and that just isn't right."

Mary Ann was obviously upset. She turned away from Liz and gazed silently off across the mountain valleys that stretched ahead. Liz wished she hadn't said anything. The girl had gone through enough for one day.

After a time Mary Ann said, in a soft voice, "You don't understand, Liz. You never will."

"Don't understand what?"

"No man has ever held me in his arms. Never once. And no man has ever kissed me."

"That will come, in time."

"No, it won't."

"And why not?"

Mary Ann looked back at Liz. Tears began to slip down her cheeks. "You felt bad when you thought you had lost me. But you shouldn't have. There's something I've never told you—something you really do need to know." She looked down, away from Liz's eyes.

"What could that be?"

"Long ago, before Will ever walked out with you, I was in love with him."

"You were just a girl then."

"I know. But I have thought about him every day since you and I were *both* just girls, even before you cared about him. He was so handsome, and he was kind to me. I dreamed I would grow up and marry him. When you treated him so cruelly, I was glad of it, because I thought he would turn away from you and I would have him for myself. But you were beautiful and I was not, and no matter how little you loved him, he loved you all the more. I will never have him, and there's no one else I want."

"I did know," Liz said. "I knew back then. But every girl loved him. I thought you had outgrown all that by now."

"I want to. I really do. But he's still the one I think of. I'm a bad person, Liz. I want what you have, and sometimes I hate you for taking him away from me."

Liz had no idea what to say. She gripped Mary Ann a little tighter, but she wondered what could come of all this. She wanted her sister to find the same happiness she had found, and she didn't know how she could give that to her. And yet, she did. An idea had come to her during the winter, and as much as she had hated the thought, it had continued to come back to her. She didn't want to think of it now, but there it was, stronger than ever. She almost said it, stopped herself, and considered again. "Lord, tell me what I should do," she said to herself, and the feeling that came to her was that she had to raise the possibility with Mary Ann.

"Could we be sister wives and sisters, too?" Liz asked.

"What?" Mary Ann turned abruptly, her face just inches from Liz's. "You mean *both* be married to him?"

"Perhaps. I'm only thinking that we—"

"Will doesn't want me. I've watched him love you with his eyes so long as I can remember."

"He does love me. But he might love you, too. Vilate Kimball told me that she loves Sarah, her sister wife, and they're happy together. We could always be together that way, and you could have what you've always longed for."

Mary Ann was still staring into Liz's face, and now tears were coming. "Thank you, Liz. Thank you so much. I never had imagined that you loved me so much."

"Of course I love you. How can I be happy if I know you're not?"

"But I'm not so good as you are, Liz. I don't want to *share* him. I want him all for myself. That's what I've felt forever, that I wanted to take him away from you. If we were both married to him, I would do everything I could to make him love me, and not love you as much. I know that's what I would do."

"And I would do the same. I would be jealous and angry every time he was with you."

"Thanks for saying that, Liz. I'm not the only evil one." She smiled even though tears were still spilling onto her cheeks.

"But I want you to be happy, Mary Ann. And I want you near me always."

"I know that's what you want, Liz. You actually offered to share Will with me. I'll never forget that."

"And I did mean it, little sister."

"I know you did. But let's never speak of it again. And please don't tell Will what I've felt—what I feel—for him."

"I won't. I promise. But there's someone else for you, Mary Ann. I'm sure there is. Don't hold Will in your heart and turn your back on every other man."

"I'll try not to. I really will."

CHAPTER 27

J esse was still hobbling forward as best he could. Will tried to help by letting Jesse lean on him when he needed to. They had often fallen far behind the other men, but they had caught up when the company camped each night, and the other men were good about cooking for them, setting up tents, making sure Jesse could rest when he finally arrived.

Charley stayed with Jesse and Will each day. He no longer seemed angry, or even sad, but he continued to stay inside himself. He said little, walked steadily, and slept whenever he had the chance.

One morning, after Will and Jesse had walked for a couple of hours, Jesse asked for time to rest. After he sat down, he said, "Will, could you help me pull my boot back off? I need to wrap my foot tighter this time."

"Sure I can."

Charley, as usual, took the chance to curl up on the ground.

Will had learned that pulling Jesse's boot off was a tender operation. He had to be careful not to yank or twist and cause Jesse pain.

He sat in front of him now and slowly worked the boot off. "How many miles do we still have afore us, do you figure?" Jesse asked.

"Less than four hundred now. Maybe closer to three fifty." Will watched Jesse nod, but he saw the discouragement. "Remember, though, what we always said. Only think about one day at a time."

"I have to think on one hour, and there's times that seems far too long."

"I know't, Jesse. But we keep makin' our way along."

"Aye. But answer me this. Will it be worth all the trouble?"

"Will what be worth it?"

"Is it worth agettin' there? What think ye 'bout the things Brother Brannan tol' us?"

"What things?"

"That the land is poor an' the weather worse."

"That's Brannan talking. He wants everyone to follow *him*."

"But it's the same kind of land we been alookin' at for a year now. When I think on the green hills 'round Ledbury, I wish at times I'd never left 'em."

"It's not like this land, Jesse. It's more like what we saw in Santa Fe."

"Aye. An' that's a far cry from England."

"Maybe. But it's in the mountains. There's snow in the winter, and good streams that run down to the valleys. We can run water out onto our land, the way we saw the Indians do."

"Brother Brannan said there's no timber. Just sagebrush."

Will knew this was the wrong time to argue the point. Jesse was struggling too hard with all the realities he was facing. He was surely wondering whether he could farm at all if he did any more damage to his feet. "Let's just trust that the Lord is still guiding us," Will said. "The Brethren have chosen a place where we can finally build up a Zion city. That's what matters."

Jesse nodded, and then he advised Will as he pulled the cloth loose on his feet and wound it tighter, and he pushed his foot back into his boot as Will held it for him. But when Will reached to help him stand up, he said, "I ha' too much time to think when we walk aw day. Thin's start to weigh on me."

"What else have you been thinkin' on?"

"We keep talkin' about a new Zion, but I can na' un'nerstan' why the Lord let the devil take the old one from us. Back in Illinois, the earth was blessed. It's all cursed out this way."

"No. Not cursed. Simply not like the land we've known before."

Charley was getting up. Will was surprised to hear him say, "The land's not so important, Jesse. You'll have your family. The rest will work itself out."

Will knew that Charley was thinking of his own plight, by comparison, and still unhappy about that, but it was a good thing that he wanted to encourage Jesse.

"Well, now, that is right," Jesse said. "Inside a month, I wager, we'll be with the Saints, and then this walking ever' day will fin'ly be over. And all will seem better when I see my family." Jesse took a couple of steps, but he still couldn't put much weight on his bad foot. He stood on one foot, maybe getting his mind ready to push ahead again. "But here's what I wonder on," he said. "Will anythin' be better this time? Out in the desert we saw men help each other. But it's na' so easy when a man tries to make his way in the world—an' wants to make thin's nice for his own family. He thinks of himsel' first when it comes to that. I question when I think on that, if Zion can e'er be what we say it is. I do na' know if we're good 'nough to live in that way."

Will had thought about such things. There was so much weakness in human nature. No matter what the ideal was, and no matter how hard their leaders preached to them, there were always some who couldn't get beyond their own selfishness. And what bothered him most was that he saw the same weakness in himself.

"I don't know, Jesse," Will said. "But we hold up Jesus Christ before us, and we say, 'That's the kind of man I want to be, and that's the kind of society I want to seek after.' Zion probably never quite happens. But I'd rather *try* to live that way than give up my belief that it can come about."

Jesse nodded, but Will could see that trust was very difficult for him this morning.

Will grabbed Jesse's knapsack and helped him get the straps over his shoulders, and then he put his own pack on. "Just remember," he said, "that night we helped Charley get to the river. We all worked together—and the men who finally got some water for themselves turned around first thing and walked back to help the others. We can all be selfish, but we can also do what's right. That's something we can remember and never give up on."

"I know. I been tellin' mysel' thin's of that sort. But Will, I'm full o' pain right now, and I'm worried about my wife and children—and our new little baby. I prayed and asked God if we should come to America, and it seemed like He said yes. But I look back on't an' what's He given us in return? Mostly death and pain and worry."

"But we've passed through hard things before, and we'll make it again. And each time we're a little better for the test we've passed. Now put your arm around my shoulder and I'll try to take some weight off that bad foot. We need to set out."

"You can't carry me along for all those miles, Will."

"I know. But I can get you started again right now."

Charley threw his knapsack up on his back, and then he stepped up close to Jesse, on the opposite side from Will. "Put your other arm around me," he said, nothing more, but Will knew that something important had happened.

"Charley, thank you," Jesse said, and he put his arm around the men's shoulders. The three set out, Jesse limping badly but moving ahead.

• • •

When Liz drove her mules out of the canyon, her wagon was barely holding together. It sounded as tired as she was. The final miles out of the mountains had taken most of the strength she had left. What worried her more, though, was that Mary Ann was near collapse. Her fever had abated, but as Patty Sessions had warned her, she hadn't been able to ride in the back of the wagon when it was tipping and tossing through the final canyon.

They had traveled down a ravine so narrow that the only way through in some spots was to drive with two wheels in the river-bed, the wagon tilted at a precarious angle. The mules had balked at times, and men had had to lead them over rocks and tree stumps, but finally the first of the wagons of the Big Camp had entered the open valley, and there before them was a broad open space with a huge glistening lake out to the west. It was the kind of country they had seen a great deal of these last few months, full of sagebrush and dried bunch grass, but it was magnificent in its way. Liz was relieved to see so much open land between mountain ranges, to be out of the frightening canyons, and to feel the clear, dry air. She even found comfort in the familiar angle of the autumn sun.

They had done it, Liz told herself. She and Ellen and Mary Ann had made it to the valley, and their children were exhausted but healthy, and the two babies seemed none the worse for all they had been through. They could all rest now, and Mary Ann could recover.

Liz halted the mules. She would have to wait now for others in their company who were still struggling through the canyon. Mary Ann stepped to the wagon and leaned up against it. She was still surveying the scene in front of her, her head turning as she looked in all directions. "Liz, tell me this isn't it," she finally said.

"But it is," Liz said. "That's the Great Salt Lake we've been hearing about."

Ellen stepped up next to Mary Ann and asked, "But how can we live here? There's no trees, no . . . nothin'."

"There are a few trees along the creeks," Liz said. She wanted to think the best of this place.

"That's willows, or maybe brush—not real trees."

"Can this land be farmed?" Ellen asked.

Liz scanned the valley again. Brigham had said that the pioneer company would plant crops as soon as they arrived, that the first harvest would come in time to provide food for the winter. Far off toward the lake she could see something that looked like rubble— piles of clay, it seemed. There were wagons there too, their white covers reflecting in the sun. And nearby was a rectangular patch where the brush seemed to have been cleared away. Maybe there was a hint of green there. Maybe something was growing.

Liz saw Brother Rich heading their way. He was walking back along the line of wagons and speaking to each of the families. When he reached Liz's wagon, he said, "You've come on through, sisters. I'll be honest, I wondered at the start if you could manage this, but you've done well. Tonight we camp in the valley, and that's the end of our journey."

"What's happened to the crops?" Liz asked.

"What crops?"

"Brigham said the pioneer party would plant crops."

"He told us back at the Sweetwater that they had put in some potatoes and some corn. I'm sure they did all they could. But they didn't get here until late in July, so there wasn't much time left for growing anything."

Liz wondered what the people arriving would have to eat. But she didn't ask that question out loud.

Mary Ann, however, was not so reticent. "I don't think anything will grow here. I came from the Malvern Hills where you could throw a seed in the ground and a plant would pop right up before your eyes."

"An' it was green," Ellen said. "Green in ever' season. Good soil is black, not gray, like what you see here."

Brother Rich laughed. "I know, sisters. I was raised in Kentucky, where the woods was thick, and the soil black. But that's the thing of it. No one wants this land. We won't have to fight anyone for it."

"I should think not," Mary Ann said. Liz knew how tired the girl was, but she hated to hear her sound so discouraged. That was the old Mary Ann—the one who had complained so much when she had arrived at Winter Quarters.

"Don't worry. We'll make something of this place. We have to trust in the Lord, that's all."

"Us women can build a cabin," Ellen said. "We done it afore. But we can na' make it from sagebrush. Where's the timber fer buildin'?"

"A good house can be built from sod."

"Sod?" Mary Ann said. "You mean dirt? We'd build a house out of dirt?"

Brother Rich laughed again. "Yes, from dirt. That's where we come from ourselves, and it's where we'll return. We shouldn't—"

"So that's it. We're going to live six feet under the ground . . . and we'll get there before much longer, I'd say."

Brother Rich had begun to walk away, but he turned back. "You're too lively to die just yet, Sister Duncan," he said. "But I think the first thing to do is to push on a little and make camp. Then rest that bad shoulder. And the next thing is to offer up a mighty prayer of thanks that we've arrived safely. The Lord hears your tongue wagging right now, and I suspect He's thinking you need to humble yourself just a little."

Liz could see that Mary Ann didn't like that remark, but at least she didn't answer it. "I do think the Lord wants us here, Mary Ann," Liz said. "It's going to take a great deal of work, but we've learned to do that."

Mary Ann didn't say a word, but Liz could see that tears were running down her cheeks. She had tried so hard to take a good attitude all this last year, but she was beaten down now, and she was in pain. She must have been thinking of her house in Ledbury, too, of golden fall days and walks to the market. Liz wanted to tell her to let all that go, but she couldn't bring herself to say the words. This big valley really did look empty of everything that kept a family alive. It would take many years, at best, to make a life here, to build a city, to have even the things they had had in Nauvoo. It seemed some sort of terrible joke that a people would strive so hard to do what was right and receive nothing for their efforts but this empty stretch of ground that was a thousand miles from civilization. Liz had learned to live in a log cabin, but how could she live in a mud hut?

But Liz knew she couldn't keep thinking such thoughts. So she told herself aloud the most optimistic thing she could think of. "Maybe Will and Jesse are here. Maybe they got here ahead of us."

"That's my thought too," Ellen said.

Mary Ann said nothing, but she looked up at Liz, her cheeks streaked with tears, her face still dusty from the trail, and her skin burnt by a summer in the sun. These last few days had been the worst, as she had clambered off the mountain, her shoulder hurting every time she moved. And now, it probably hadn't helped her to be reminded that Liz and Ellen had hope of seeing their husbands.

Right now she had very little to compensate her for all she had given up.

"Come sit by me," Liz told Mary Ann. "The trail won't be so bouncy now, and it's all downhill. The mules can make their way. Ellen, you climb up here too."

So as the wagon train moved ahead again, the three women sat side by side. Both babies were awake, but they were content for now in the boxes that served as their cradles. The older children still trudged along more quietly than they sometimes had, and Liz heard Jacob tell Daniel, "This is where we're going to live. We'll have a house again. And Dad will build it. He's going to come here."

Above all, that was good to think about.

As the wagons approached the place that Liz had seen before, where covered wagons had stopped, she could see that this was actually an encampment. There was a rude sort of fort surrounded by a fence of unbaked brick. Inside were some cabins, actually built of logs, which Liz was glad to see. Many people, however, still seemed to be living in their wagons.

Near the fort, the Rich company circled in their usual evening formation and Brother Rich told the people to make camp as they had on the trail, to sleep in their wagons or on the ground. Liz told herself she should have known that they would have to do this for a time, but somehow, all across the plains, she had been imagining a bed to sleep in when she arrived.

Liz heard young Mary ask her mother, "Where will we live now?"

"We'll build another house, dear," Ellen said. "And Dad will help us. He might be here. We hope he is."

After a time Brother Rich showed up at their wagon. "I've done some asking," he told Liz. "One small group of Battalion men has arrived here. They came up from the south. But most of the men went north and were planning to cross the Sierras and come by way of Fort Hall."

"Did you ask the names of those who are here?" Ellen asked.

"I asked about Brother Matthews and Brother Lewis, but as far as anyone knew, they were not among that first group. They'll be with those who are on their way, I would think, and if they are, they'll surely arrive before much longer. They've been under way since July."

It was October 2 now, but Liz had no idea how long it would take the men to cross the mountains and walk all the way here.

"There's one thing you need to know," Brother Rich said. "Brother Brigham sent a letter to the men. If the letter reached them, it instructed them that some should stay in California and work for the winter—so they can earn some money to bring with them. It's possible your husbands might have decided to do that."

"No. Jesse and Will will come ahead," Ellen said. "They want to be here in time to help us. They both said that in their letters."

"Well, I understand that. But Brigham told them that provisions would be scanty this year, and more men arriving would only mean more to feed. If they can bring money with them in the spring, that would help everyone."

"What's money out here?" Liz asked, her voice for the first time revealing her own disappointment. "I haven't noticed any general stores in this lovely city."

"No. But we can—"

"Never mind. We'll do our best. But our children can't live outside this winter, and I have no idea how to stack up sod and make a house out of it."

"You won't have to do that. I promise you that. I'll get help for you, if it comes to that."

Liz didn't say, "I've heard such promises before," but she thought it.

That night the women cooked the best meal they could. And then they sat by the fire. They tried to cheer themselves, not to wallow in their concerns. As they were talking, a man stepped out of the dark and approached the fire. It was John Wade.

Brother Wade said, "Evenin', sisters," and he pulled his hat off. His dark hair, which had grown long over the summer, fell across his forehead. He brushed it back and said, "Brother Rich told me you're worried about having a place to live. I want you to know, I'll help you get something fixed up. I don't know how to build a sod house, but it can't be too difficult. I'll figure it out and get something going for you if your husbands don't come along." But then he stammered a moment as he looked straight at Mary Ann. "I mean, those of you who have husbands. Not you, Sister Duncan."

This was an opportunity for Mary Ann to tease Brother Wade, but she didn't do it. She merely stared into the fire. And he was rather quick to end the conversation and leave.

Mary Ann continued to look into the fire for quite some time before she said, "I told him yesterday, I would never be a second wife."

"Did he ask you to marry him?"

"No. He only hinted. But I told him what I told you. I'm not good at sharing."

"The men from the Battalion will be returning soon, Mary Ann. Many of them are not married."

"Yes, and there's Elder Elder. I can watch for him to show up. Maybe he'll start looking better and better to me." She tried to laugh, but she didn't do very well.

Liz knew how much pain she was in—in her shoulder and in her heart. But she didn't know what she could do for her.

CHAPTER 28

The summer had passed quickly. August was almost gone, and Jeff and Abby were getting ready to leave Nauvoo. Jeff had decided to put in a full-time semester at the University of Iowa, and he was thinking he might stay in Iowa City for his graduate work as well. He had met with a professor there who was interested in the work he wanted to do.

There were lots of good-byes to say even though Jeff and Abby weren't moving all that far away. Hardest, of course, was saying good-bye to Malcolm and Kayla. And that's what they were trying to do now, sitting at the McCords' kitchen table as they had done so many times before.

"We'll probably drive back down in two or three weeks," Abby was saying. "Jeff is still going to do some work with Professor Woodbury, and a lot of the documents he wants to look at are here—so we might be coming down here quite often."

"We were thinking," Kayla said, "that we could maybe run up to Iowa City for part of Thanksgiving weekend. We could have dinner with my parents and then just head up there later in the day."

"Oh, yeah. Do that for sure," Abby said. "I really don't think we're going to be out of touch at all."

Malcolm laughed. "Jeff and I will be texting every day—or talking on the phone. We'll still have a lot of coordinating to do."

All that was true, but Jeff had a feeling that they were all trying to convince one another of something they didn't quite believe. For the next few years at least, he and Malcolm would have a hard time staying as close as they had been while they were sharing both their workdays and their Church callings. He also knew that Abby and Kayla had shared little William in a way that went far beyond babysitting.

"Well, just know that our plan is to come back and live here again," Jeff said. "If the business does well enough that we can get some money saved for a down payment, we've been talking about buying a house in Nauvoo—and then we could come here for the summers or whenever I'm doing research."

"And what if the web site *doesn't* do so well?" Kayla asked.

"I don't know. I'd probably look for a teaching job, but all that seems pretty far off right now. All I know is that I want to come back to this little Zion we've tried to create together. I don't want to lose it."

Jeff felt the sudden quiet and hoped he wasn't becoming too maudlin. They really weren't moving that far away. But he thought of Kayla and Abby, both pregnant again. The lives for both families would keep changing. It was hard to guess how many things might pull them apart.

"Jeff, I hope you know," Malcolm said, "you saved our lives. I never would have had the guts to start my own company if I hadn't had you around."

"Naw, that's not true at all. You would have figured it out. I see it the other way around. If it hadn't been for you, I'd still be working at a job I didn't like." He hesitated, and then he added, "And Malc,

I've watched the way you serve people. Sometimes I don't feel like I fit in very well with Church members, but when we're out taking care of people, I don't worry about that."

"Nauvoo was supposed to be a temporary stopover for us," Abby said, "but everything that happened to us here has reshaped us. I even feel blessed by William's heart surgery now. It's like life came into focus for us when we had to deal with that."

Jeff sensed that everything had been said, and things were about to get difficult. "Hey," he said, "let's not make a big deal out of this. We're going see each other all the time."

"Could we have a prayer together, though?" Kayla asked.

And so they walked to the living room, gathered the kids together, and all knelt down. Malcolm thanked the Lord that the Lewises had come into their lives, and he asked the Lord to bless them as they continued forward.

As the four got up, Abby said, "Well, Kayla, it won't be long until kneeling down and getting back up is going to get harder for the two of us."

"I'm way ahead of you," Kayla said. "I'm feeling some of that already." She laughed. "Have you broken the news to your mother yet?"

"Yeah, I did. She was trying to get me to say that we'd go out there for Christmas again this year, but I'll be almost eight months along by then. I knew I didn't want to fly when I was that close, so I decided I had to tell her."

"Did she throw a fit?"

"Of course. And I lost my temper and told her I didn't want to talk to her ever again. But about two hours later I called back anyway, and we both apologized, and then she said, 'Would you kindly tell your Mormon husband where babies come from?'"

Everyone laughed, and Kayla said, "Did you tell her you haven't figured that out yourself?"

"No, I said, 'They come from God, Mom. That's why we feel so blessed.' She moaned, but she knew better than to start in on me again."

Now everything really had been said, and no one wanted to utter the actual word *good-bye,* so they all took turns embracing one another, and tears came no matter how hard they tried to laugh. Jeff was excited about school, but he feared that he would be lonely in a new place—after finally finding the brother he had wanted all his life.

• • •

The Robertsons' house was sparkly clean. Abby had been working hard to leave it in good shape. Malcolm had promised to help Jeff remodel the bathroom when they were in town from time to time. Jeff said he wanted to feel that he had completed the project and left the house in great shape. But even as it was, the place did look good, and Abby felt good about the decorating she had done.

Jeff and Abby would have to make a couple more trips back to haul away everything they had accumulated, but Jeff had already borrowed Malcolm's truck and taken the baby stuff and lots of kitchen things to their newly rented apartment in Iowa City. Abby had driven along with him in Jeff's old car, also full of household things, and then they had left the car at the apartment. Now the trunk in their Camry was full, along with half the backseat.

Abby told Jeff, "I've got a few more things to do in the house, but let's try to get to bed early tonight. Tomorrow's going to be crazy. It's going to take all day, once we get up there, just to get that apartment clean enough to live in."

"I think it's clean enough for *normal* people. Just not clean enough for you."

Abby knew that was probably true, but she had noticed that although the apartment was swept and vacuumed, it was not scrubbed the way she liked a house to be. It was hard enough to keep a place clean with a toddler around, but she had no chance if she didn't get it in good shape to start out.

"Okay," Jeff said. "But before the sun goes down, walk across the street with me. We've got to say good-bye to Grandma and Grandpa Lewis before we go."

Abby laughed. "They're not buried over there, you know?"

"I know. But they would be upset with me if I didn't at least stop by one last time."

Abby knew the real truth. Jeff would never stop coming back to that little spot of earth. It had become a symbol to him, his connection to his forebears. So Jeff took William out to the garage and sprayed his pants and shoes with mosquito repellent, and then he did Abby's and his own. The three of them—or really four, as Abby was well aware—walked across the street. The last few days had been hot. Under the trees, the humidity was bad. She didn't mind the idea of saying good-bye to Jeff's grandparents, but she wasn't exactly thrilled to be walking into the woods. Still, she understood what it meant to Jeff.

This had been a good summer for Abby in most ways. She had gotten through her morning sickness a little more easily this time, and once she had quit work, she had tried her hardest to get Relief Society organized and prepared for a new president to take over. Sierra Farr was walking now, or at least learning to walk again. And Maggie Marshall was doing better emotionally. But what Abby knew now that she hadn't realized before was that virtually every family had struggles. It hadn't been her job to fix the troubles, but she had liked organizing the sisters so that they could all be part of helping one another. Abby had loved the role she had played in all that.

In the little clearing where they stopped, the canopy of tree limbs overhead was allowing columns of light to shine through.

Everything was peaceful, even beautiful, and Abby was surprised by her own emotion. She remembered the first time they had looked at this place and tried to imagine what sort of people old William and Elizabeth had been. She was glad that she and Jeff knew more about them now and had gained some sense of what life in Nauvoo might have been like. Abby had gradually come to feel a connection not only to Jeff's great-grandparents but to all the early Saints who had lived in Nauvoo.

Little William, on the other hand, was not really interested in breathing in the spirit of the place. He was twisting, trying to get down from Jeff's grasp, so he could run about. But Jeff told him, "Listen!" and William stopped struggling. "Can you hear all the birds?"

William looked up. He pointed toward the sounds in the trees. "Bird," he said.

Jeff took this chance to say out loud, "Grandma and Grandpa Lewis, I think you remember this other Will Lewis. As you can see, he's thriving now and growing fast." William was still looking about, not squirming, as though he caught the importance of what Jeff was saying. "We don't know what you know about us, or whether you get a chance to keep track of what we do, but I have a feeling you still care about Nauvoo, and maybe you like the idea that we're here. We're leaving in the morning, but you need to know, we plan to come back. We want to live here."

Abby had to smile to hear Jeff talk so naturally, as though he were talking to good friends.

"I think I understand better now what Zion meant to you," Jeff said. "And I know how hard you worked to make it happen. I just want you to know that we haven't given up on the idea. The Church is spread out now, and Zion's kind of everywhere, but it's not lost."

Abby had thought so much about that idea lately. In these last few months she had drawn much closer to the sisters in the ward. It had taken her time to comprehend what Relief Society was all about, but she had ended up learning a lot of things she had needed to know. She thought maybe the Lord had let her have the calling so she could comprehend what Jeff had learned in the elders quorum. What she had observed was that everyone, at one time or another, needed some kind of support. She had received help in Nauvoo, and now she had given some in return, and that was how she always wanted to live, surrounded by people who cared for one another.

"Grandpa," Jeff said, "I've read your life story. I know what you went through when you and Grandma were split up so many times, and I know how hard you worked all your life. But you need to know that your commitment isn't forgotten. It's been passed down through the family."

Abby surprised herself a little by saying out loud, "We promise to pass those things on to *our* children."

"Bird," William said again. The birds were singing lots of interlacing tunes and darting about in the trees. The light was becoming more muted and the cicadas were starting their noisy, rhythmic chorus. Fireflies would soon be flashing. It was like so many summer evenings in Nauvoo. Liz thought of William and Elizabeth Lewis living here on this little plot of land—the first land they had owned. She pictured them on an evening like this, their little boys playing nearby, and peace filling the air. It struck her that she finally understood what it had cost the early Saints to give up Nauvoo.

Jeff smiled at Abby and put his arm around her.

"You really are kind of weird, Jeff," Abby said. "You know that, don't you?"

"Why? Because I talk to my dead ancestors? Hey, you just talked to them yourself."

"I know. I'm getting as weird as you are."

"It's only weird if no one's listening to us. And I kind of think they can hear what we're saying."

Abby thought so too, and she thought she understood Jeff more fully than she once had. He questioned everything, and that had been difficult for her at times, but in the end, his heart was right. She loved that about him.

• • •

On the following morning Jeff and Abby got William up early, and they all got in the car. Jeff drove north on Warsaw Street—the old Rich Street mentioned in Grandpa's life history—but at Mulholland, he turned west, toward the river.

"Where are you going?" Abby asked.

"I just want to do this the way my grandparents did. You'll see what I'm doing." He drove past the temple, but he didn't make the turn with the highway; he continued straight down the hill and then turned left on Main and right on Parley Street. He drove to the river and stopped. "Grandma and Grandpa might have used one of the other landings, but let's just imagine they crossed here—drove their wagon and their animals out onto a flatboat and then crossed over to Montrose."

As Jeff spoke, he tried to imagine it all, tried to think what his great-great-great-grandparents might have felt that day. Grandpa must have been heartsick about leaving his home and his farm, but he hadn't said too much about that in his life history. He had talked about leaving Zion to go out into the wilderness, and about starting over in the West.

Jeff turned the car then and looped east past Joseph's store and his two homes, the Homestead and the Mansion House. But at the highway, he turned right.

"Now where are you going?" Abby asked.

"I want to pick up the trail where they landed, over in Montrose."

Abby was laughing at him again. "I can't believe how dramatic you're being. We're only moving ninety-five miles away. We're not crossing the plains."

"I know. I just like to imagine what William and Elizabeth—Will and Liz—were thinking that day when they left."

So Jeff drove to Keokuk and then north to Montrose, or actually a little north of the town. He had learned where the Saints had usually landed, and he drove to that spot. Starting from there, he drove on a gravel road to the bluffs that rose from the river plain about a mile beyond the river. Partway up the incline, he stopped the car. "We need to get out for a minute," he said.

"What about William? Where are we going?"

"We're not going anywhere. We just need to look at something."

Jeff got William out of his car seat. He wanted his boy to see this too, even if he wouldn't understand.

Jeff stood by the car and held Will in one arm and put his other arm around Abby. By then she had surely realized what they had come to look at. She was looking out across the mile-wide Mississippi and could see the temple in Nauvoo. "Oh, it looks so beautiful," she said.

"When the Saints had to leave their city," Jeff said, "they all had to make their way up these bluffs in their wagons, and then they headed from here out to a place called Sugar Creek. That was where a lot of people, especially babies, died in the snow and cold. But when the people got to this point where we're standing, just before they crossed over these bluffs, they knew this was their last chance to have a look at the temple. They knew they would never see it again."

"Just think how they must have felt," Abby said.

"The temple had cost them almost everything—their money, their time, their physical strength. They even kept building it when they knew they were going to leave it and never use it again. But they had promised to build it, so they felt they had to finish it. They kept working on it clear until spring—after quite a few people had left in the winter. They dedicated it, and then they left it."

Jeff let that sink in with Abby, and he tried to think himself what it must have felt like to stand here and say good-bye.

"When you read the journals from the people who left Nauvoo," Jeff said, "they usually say, 'We crossed the river,' and most of them don't explain much about that even though it was pretty frightening at times. But what almost all of them talk about is stopping to say good-bye to the temple."

Jeff hadn't been emotional until he looked over at Abby and saw tears on her cheeks. "Did your grandparents stop here?" she asked.

"Yup. Grandpa Lewis and Elizabeth—Liz—stood somewhere very close to this spot. It was cold, and there was snow on the ground. But he wanted that last look back at Nauvoo. He said he had given up everything in England, even his family, to come here, and he had finally been able to own his own land. Now he was giving that up. But he felt like his greatest work in Nauvoo had been in helping to build the temple. It just about broke his heart to leave it behind."

The two stood for a while longer. The temple was glowing white across the way—not the same temple that Jeff's grandparents had looked at, but one that was rebuilt to look almost exactly like the original.

After a time, Abby said, "Jeff, we're okay, aren't we? Everything's going to work out all right for us, isn't it?"

"Sure it is. We have to deal with some things people back then never could have imagined. But we're going to be okay. More than okay. With four of us, we'll feel like a real family."

"We just have to figure out everything as we go, I guess. I always want to know what's ahead and then avoid all the dangers. But it doesn't seem to work that way."

"It's the same for everyone, no matter when you live. You keep moving ahead. You do what you have to do."

"And I guess you have to trust."

"Yeah, that's right."

Jeff pointed out across the river. "Will, my boy, can you see the temple?" he asked.

But this Will Lewis didn't know where to look, didn't understand much about his world just yet. Still, it had been important to Jeff to visit this spot today, and he wanted to bring little Will back again when he could comprehend what a holy place it was. He wanted to bring all his children, even grandchildren, to these bluffs. He wanted them all to look out across the river, see the temple, and understand what it meant to them, what it had meant to the first of their family to live here.

Jeff liked to think of that bigger vision of things, to hold the concept before him that the events we call history are a piece of eternity, and each era is connected like links in a chain to all that have gone before, and to all that will come.

Jeff held William tight and pulled Abby close. His world was in his two arms. He wanted to do something worthwhile with his life, but more than anything, he wanted William and their expected baby—a girl, they now knew—to be linked to the chain of generations that had gone before. He and Abby had already made a decision. Their daughter would be named Elizabeth. They would call her Liz.

CHAPTER 29

Jesse's feet had swollen so badly that he could no longer get his boots on. Will had wrapped both feet and tied a layer of canvas around them, and he had fashioned a crutch from a tree limb. Jesse was able to make do that way, but he couldn't keep up with the main body of the marchers. His good foot was breaking down under the strain of carrying so much of his weight, so Will and Charley stayed on either side of him, and from time to time they got under his arms and supported him. That gave him a rest, but each day, as the afternoon wore on, Jesse was so tired that Charley and Will had begun to take turns carrying him on their backs.

The three had continued on that way and made it to Fort Hall, all of them exhausted. Will asked around at Fort Hall and found a trapper who had an old Indian pony he would sell for ten dollars. Will saw no other option. He would have to use a good deal of his remaining money to buy the horse. He knew they couldn't carry Jesse all the way to the Salt Lake Valley. But then Charley stepped forward. "Will, I'll pay for it," he said.

"No. I can't let you do that."

"I have more than enough. I want to do this for Jesse."

The trapper Will had bargained with was built like a bear and dressed in almost as much fur. He spat on the ground and laughed. "If I'd knowed you fellers had money to spare, I woulda held out for a higher price," he said.

Charley smiled and got his money out. "That's why I let Will do the bargaining," he said. He paid the mountain man the ten dollars and took the halter rope from his hand.

Will was amazed by what he was seeing. In the last couple of weeks he had watched Charley begin to be himself again, and he thought he understood how it had happened. When Charley had first helped Jesse, he had merely offered his physical strength, which turned out to be greater than Will had expected. But as days had gone by, Charley had begun to talk to Jesse, encourage him, tell him that his friends would never give up on him. And as he had begun to carry Jesse on his back, he seemed to get more determined each day, no matter how tired he was.

Will, himself, was giving out. The strain of packing Jesse was leaving him spent each night. The pain in his back and legs bothered him when he slept on the ground, and he had been waking up early, not sure that he could continue on the same way. He had known that he had to either buy some kind of animal to pack Jesse or leave him at Fort Hall and come back for him in the spring. It was Charley who kept saying, "No, Will. He needs to get to his family. I don't know what will happen to him if he has to winter up here by himself." What Will realized was that Charley understand loneliness and loss in a way that Will couldn't.

As they began their final trek south, the pony made a big difference. Will figured they had less than two hundred miles to go, but with the horse, they could manage much more easily, and it was October now; the summer heat was over.

What they hadn't considered was how swollen and painful Jesse's feet would become as he hung them down over the sides of the horse. Will had no doubt that bones in his feet had broken or that the bone and sinew had pulled apart. When the men helped Jesse down from the horse each day, it was all he could do to limp a few steps and sit down. Maybe some healing had begun, but the stiffness had become much worse. But they were getting lots of miles behind them. The company was pushing to reach the Saints before cold weather set in, and they were nearing their destination.

And then one morning they woke to find that the pony had gotten away from them. They had staked the little mare during the night, but she had pulled against her halter rope and jerked the stake out of the ground. Will wanted to let the company go ahead while he searched for the animal, but Charley said, "They say it's less than fifteen miles now. With a good day of walking, we'll be there tonight."

"But Jesse can't walk that far, Charley. You know that."

"I'll carry him. He hardly weighs anything anymore."

"Nor do you. You look like a scarecrow."

Charley laughed. "You haven't looked at yourself in a while, Will. You look like the ghost of yourself—all spirit, no flesh."

"Maybe I'm an angel."

"You might be, at that, but you're a dirty one, with a mangy beard."

Will glanced down at himself, saw how filthy and threadbare his uniform was. He had tied up his hair with a string in back, but he could only guess how ragged he would look to Liz. He wondered, too, whether his face looked as bony as his hands. "I'm afraid Liz won't recognize me," he said. But Will knew he had said the wrong thing. Charley had no wife to welcome him, even to be disappointed by his looks. "But I guess I shouldn't complain about that."

"It's all right, Will. I have a son to think of. Some men are saying that if their wives aren't at the Great Salt Lake, they're heading out to Council Bluffs. I've thought I might do the same—so I can see my little Andrew."

Will nodded. "After all this, you may want to winter here, then go in the spring."

"I know. I'll think about it. But I will go after him."

"And what about finding someone you can marry—so he'll have a mother?"

"I've tried to think of that, Will, but the idea of it feels wrong to me."

"That will change. You know it's what Rebecca would want you to do."

"Well . . . for now, let's just think about getting Jesse home to his wife."

"All right. But we'll carry him together. I'm thinking we can hoist him up between us, with his crutch under him, and it won't be quite so hard on either one of us." So he and Charley got Jesse to his feet and had him put his arms around their shoulders, and then they held the crutch under him so he could sit on it, and they lifted him up between them. They started the last leg of their trek.

The going was awkward and tiring, but they pushed ahead maybe a quarter mile at a time between rests. They put several miles behind themselves that way. By then, other men had offered to help. Almost all the men in the company took a turn or two, and all day they kept going. Jesse apologized over and over that he was causing such trouble, but Will felt good that everyone was working together to make sure Jesse made it to the end of the journey.

By afternoon, men were getting anxious to push forward and reach the Saints that night. Will told them to go on ahead. He and Charley would rest a little, then make the final push.

Jesse lay on the ground for a time, saying nothing, but Will could hear how rough his breathing was, and he knew the man was aching. "I think maybe we should camp right here," Will said, "and make our final push tomorrow."

"If you can keep going, I can," Jesse said. "I want to see Ellen tonight. I want to know this whole thing is behind us."

"What if Ellen and Liz aren't there yet?"

"At least we'll know."

But Will was afraid of knowing. He didn't think he could make it to Liz this fall if she was still in Winter Quarters, and he knew that Jesse couldn't go any farther. But he didn't want to be away from Liz another winter.

"The land doesn't look quite so bad as I expected," Jesse said. "It may be dry, but it's not all sand and cactus."

"I know," Will said. "I dug into the ground a little last night. It's not the loam we had in Nauvoo, but it should produce some decent crops."

"I don't mind the look of the place," Charley said. "I like the mountains, and I like the air. I don't think we'll get so sick out here."

Will looked up at the mountains, which stood stark in the light of the afternoon sun. The valley was beautiful, in its way, with granite mountains thrusting up against the sky and a wide, sloping plain stretching out toward the lake. But there were few trees, and nothing seemed truly green. The ground looked alkaline and the brush a shade of blue-gray. They had seen nice streams descending from the mountains, and Will planned to block one of those streams enough to run water onto a little piece of land somewhere. Still, it was hard to believe that he could ever do much more than survive. He remembered plowing the deep sod in Illinois and watching black earth fold off his plow. It was hard to think that *this* could be Zion when God had blessed the soil around Nauvoo a double portion and touched this land with little sign of love.

But he would make a go of it. He needed Liz now, and he needed his family. If he had his wife and children, he could do whatever he had to do. And if his children weren't so likely to be sick here, that had to be good.

After a time Will stood up. "Come on, Charley," he said. "Let's give Jesse one more ride."

So they set off, the same as they had before, but the thought that this was the last hard walk of the trip gave Will some strength. They still had to rest every few hundred yards, but they didn't stop long, and they covered what seemed a couple of miles that way. And then Charley said, "I think I see the camp. Aren't those wagon covers I'm looking at?" He pointed south.

"I believe so," Will said, and they started out again.

But the camp was farther off than Will had thought, and by the time he saw people, his legs were wobbling. What he could now see ahead was something that looked like a fort with an adobe wall built up around it. As they neared, Will could see several Battalion men crowded around an older man. Will heard the man say, "There's been companies comin' in these last few weeks. Some of the Battalion wives are with 'em. I heard that. But I can't tell you any names."

"Where would they be?" a man asked.

"The new companies are camped over on the east side of this fort. I think people pretty much stayed with their wagon trains. Some have started building sod houses, but I doubt the women without husbands would be doing that."

Will thought maybe Liz would. He knew what she had done the winter before. But he had heard enough. He nodded to Charley, and they picked Jesse back up and walked around to the east side of the fort. He saw a circle of wagons and asked a young man if he knew Liz Lewis or Ellen Matthews. The boy shook his head.

"Are there any Battalion wives with you?"

The boy only shrugged, but a woman came over to them and said, "We had a few of the wives with us, but not any with those names."

"Where can we look for them?"

"There are four more camps, all up that way." She pointed farther to the east. Will wasn't tired now, but he was scared. "Let's go," he said, and he and Charley lifted Jesse again.

But at the next camp, a man said they hadn't brought any Battalion wives, at least not that he knew of. And at the circle of wagons after that, no one knew of Liz and Ellen.

Will was beginning to feel sick. Not all the wives had come, it appeared. A kind of gloom began to set in as he thought of waiting out another winter. He decided he would get Jesse set up somehow, and then he would walk to Winter Quarters after all, and leave just as soon as he could.

Ahead, there were two more circles of wagons, so Will and Charley walked on to the first one. "Ma'am," Will said to a gaunt woman in a flimsy dress, "do you know Liz Lewis or Ellen Matthews?"

"Sure I do," the woman said. "That's their wagon, across the circle."

Will felt a jolt run through his body. For a moment, the idea wouldn't quite settle in as a reality.

"Put me down," Jesse said. "I'm going to walk over there."

Charley said, "Jesse, you can't do that."

But Will lowered the crutch and Jesse stepped down. His steps were more a shuffle than a walk, but the three men made their way across the compound, Will and Charley holding Jesse by the arms.

Two raggedly dressed little boys were running about, dodging through the sagebrush in the middle of the circle. As the men approached, Will saw something in the older boy. He was too tall to be Jacob, too thin, but his face was . . . and then he knew. "Jacob!" he called. The two boys stopped and turned to look at Will.

They both seemed startled, and Will suddenly remembered how haggard he looked. Still, he dropped to his knees. He had started to cry. "I'm your father," he said. "It's me. Do you know me?"

The boys stared at him, still seeming unsure.

"It's your dad. You're Jacob and Daniel. Don't you—"

And then Jacob ran to Will and jumped at him. Will caught him, and the boy wrapped his arms around his neck. Daniel walked closer too, but he was still holding back. Will reached out to him with one arm and pulled him close.

"Daniel, I'm your daddy, and I love you," Will said. "I've been gone a long time, but I won't leave you again." He tightened his embrace, but Daniel remained stiff. "Where's your mum?"

Jacob pulled away quickly. "This way," he said, and he took off running, Daniel with him. Will followed. There by the wagon was a woman, turned away from him. She was wearing a dress that was faded and torn, but he could see by the shape of her, by the way she held herself, it was Liz.

"Mummy, it's Daddy. It's Daddy. It's Daddy," Jacob was shouting.

Liz turned. Will saw the questioning look on her face. She had changed. She was browned by the sun, and her eyes looked tired. But she was beautiful. She looked at Will, took a second or two to be sure, then rushed to him as he continued to stride toward her.

He grabbed her up and held her, couldn't speak, couldn't imagine that all this was real. "Oh, Will, oh, Will," she kept saying. And everything felt as before, her lean body against his, the feel of her arms around him, the sound of her little sobs.

"I'm sorry I look this way," he said.

"No. No. It doesn't matter." And she continued to grip her arms around his neck.

Somewhere outside the little world that Will and Liz had suddenly formed, Will was vaguely aware that Ellen had appeared, that she had rushed past them and she and Jesse were surely holding one another too. But all that was distant. Will could only feel Liz against him, could only think that the ordeal was finally over. He had survived more than he could ever tell her, more than anyone would ever understand, but still, it was over, and he would never have to do anything like that again.

"We heard you might be coming, but we didn't know for certain," Liz told him. "I've been telling the boys to watch for you."

"They didn't recognize me."

She stepped back and looked at him. "I can see you under there, but I can see why they didn't know you."

"I'll clean up. I'll shave this beard."

"I know. But it really is you, Will. That's all that matters."

"It's not me, Liz. Not really. Not yet. I . . . ." But he didn't know how to tell her.

"I know. It's not me, either. But I'm stronger than I was. Maybe you are too."

He nodded. But he didn't want to talk. He wanted to hold her again. For all these months he had imagined himself embracing her, and now he could. "I love you," he said. "All this last year, it's all I could think, that I had to keep going so I could make it back to you." And then he realized something else. "Where's the baby? I want to see her, too."

So Liz took his hand and led him to the back of the wagon, but just as they got there, a young woman with a sling around her shoulder stepped down. She had a rag tied around her head and over one eye. He had the feeling he had seen her before, but he wasn't sure where or . . . and then he recognized Mary Ann, looking very different from how he remembered her. She had been fleshy before, and she was thin now and just as weathered as Liz, but she seemed prettier than he remembered her.

"It's Will," Liz said to Mary Ann.

"I really don't think so," she said. "The Will I remember wasn't all covered over in hair—and dirt."

"I know I'm filthy, and—"

"Don't apologize. It's how we all look." She finally gave him a hug with her one free arm. "It *is* good to see you—dirt and all."

"Are you all right?" he asked her. "What's happened to you?"

"Not anything too terrible. A wagon tipped over and threw me off." And then she broadened her vowels and said, "An English girl might have *busted* some bones. But us American girls, we don't break easy."

But Will saw more than a joke in that. She did seem changed.

Liz had Will by the arm again, pulling him closer to the wagon. She reached into the back for Mary Ellen, who had been asleep but was stirring now. "This is your little daughter," she said. She handed the baby to Will. But Mary Ellen set up a howl and reached back for her mother.

He understood her fear. She was half a year old now—more than that—and had never seen him. Will handed her back, and she tucked her head against her mother's shoulder. But after a moment she peeked back around, and Will saw that she had a lovely face, like her older sister she would never know in this life.

Will heard a voice behind him and turned to see that Charley—whom he had forgotten to introduce—was still there. He was talking to Mary Ann. He heard Mary Ann say, "Oh, Brother Buttars, I'm so sorry to hear that. It must have been terrible for you."

Charley said, "I think I died for a time. There was nothing left inside me. But Will and Jesse kept me going. And then I started to realize, I had to stay alive for Andrew, my son. He surely expects that of me."

"What a good man you are," Mary Ann said, and Will liked what he heard in her voice.

• • •

Liz felt as though she had finally caught her breath. It had taken her hours just to get the idea into her head that Will really was with her again. She wanted very much to be alone with him, but she wasn't sure when or how that would happen. He had insisted, not long after arriving, that he needed to wash himself, so he had walked to the nearby creek and had come back with his beard and hair wet, and his clothes soaked, too. "I took my clothes off and washed them as best I could," he said. "But I had nothing else to put back on. Is there any hope of getting anything better to wear?"

"Not that I know of," Liz said. "But we'll see what we can do."

She got out her scissors and cut his long hair, and then she heated water so he could shave. He looked much more himself when he finished, but he was thin, and something in his face had changed. His skin was not just darkened but seemingly thickened, and there were crow's feet by his eyes. She thought he looked ten years older. He was still very handsome, but under his happy smile, she could sense something more solemn in him than she had ever noticed before.

After a supper of beans and bacon and cornbread, which Will seemed to relish, Liz and he walked out a little—out among the sagebrush. It was mid-October, and the evening was cool. Will had no coat, but he said it didn't matter. He was used to being "too cold or too hot—or too something," all the time.

"There's one thing I haven't told you," Liz said. "We've been assigned a little plot of land where we can build a house. Brother Wade helped us women get started on it, but we haven't gotten very far. You can help us now."

"You mean, one house for all of us?"

"We didn't know when you would get here, Will. We knew we had to get the children inside before long."

"What kind of house is it?"

"They say it's sod, but the grass is sparse here. It's mostly just dirt."

"I've thought about that. I could make adobe bricks—that's better, and I've seen how it's done—but I don't want that for you. Inside the fort, the houses are built with logs. Someone must have cut timber in the mountains and hauled the logs down here."

"Yes, I think so."

"That's what I'll do, then. I'll cut logs. And we'll build a house for Jesse and Ellen and one for us."

"What about Mary Ann?"

"She can live with us for now, but when she finds herself a husband, I'll build a house for them, too."

"Can Jesse help you? What's happened to him?"

"Our boots wore out, Liz. We walked barefoot sometimes, or wrapped our feet with anything we could get our hands on. But Jesse's feet broke down. I think they'll heal when he stops walking every day, but he'll need help for now."

"Ellen told me that you and Charley carried him the last part of the way."

"Aye. But it's what we all did. There were times we had no water, and not enough food. We had to . . ." But he didn't want to tell her everything, maybe ever. He wanted to forget as much as he could. He only said, "Maybe the army did the best it could. I don't know. But nothing happened the way they promised us."

"We were short on food too, Will, and you never saw so many people sick. Lots of people died at Winter Quarters. *Hundreds.*"

Will looked down at the ground. "The Lord is refining us," he said. "But we'll be all right. I'll go to the mountains in the morning and start felling timber."

"You need to rest a few days first. You look so tired."

"That will be a rest to me, Liz. I won't have to walk twenty miles. I'll ride a wagon a few miles and cut down some trees." He laughed. "What could be easier than that?"

"But it scares me, Will."

"What's to be scared of now?"

"What this is doing to us—all this work. And never having time to rest."

"I don't know. Maybe it's using us up. But we have a city to build. It's not the right time to rest yet."

Liz hated to think that life would never be less demanding than it had been so far, but she did understand what Will was saying.

"But Liz, I want you to live better than we have so far. I'm still going build a fine house for you."

"I don't need one. And I wouldn't want it so long as others were still struggling to get by."

Will nodded. For so many years he had held himself to the promise he had made to Liz's father, but maybe, for the present, none of that mattered. Everyone would have to work together to build this place. Better homes surely would have to wait.

"I don't want to trouble the Lord for anything more than He's already given me," Liz said. "I have my husband again, and he loves me and cares about me—and loves the Lord. And my children are all strong and healthy. What more do I need?"

Will nodded. "I know. I have you, and it's you I've wanted all my life." He took her back into his arms one more time.

They walked back to camp then. After a time Mary Ann took the children and bedded down with them under the wagon, leaving the wagon empty for Liz and Will. So they went to bed early, and Liz only worried about Mary Ann being so close and probably still awake. But Liz didn't think about that very long, once she had Will in her arms.

CHAPTER 30

On the morning after Will reached his family in the Great Salt Lake Valley, he did some repair work to the wagon Liz had used to cross the plains, hitched up both teams of mules, and drove to a canyon in the nearby mountains. Will took Charley Buttars with him, and the two of them felled and cut to length a load of fir trees. The logs were full of sap and not thick enough to hew into squared logs, but Will thought they were better than sod or adobe. More than anything, he wanted his family to be safe and warm and as comfortable as possible this winter.

What Will soon realized was that he was more worn down than he had admitted to Liz. He remembered working much harder back in Nauvoo and not feeling the weariness he felt now. All the same, he and Charley loaded the wagon and returned to camp that afternoon, and then they went back a second day for another load. As they returned that second day, Charley told Will, "I've made up my mind not to leave for Winter Quarters quite yet. Some of the boys are leaving in a day or two, but I've pretty much decided to winter here."

"We can get a cabin built for you," Will told him. "Then, when you bring your son back—maybe next year—you'll have a place for him." Will smiled and gave Charley a little nudge with his elbow. "Say, I noticed you talking to Mary Ann again last night. She might offer you reason enough to stay for the winter."

Charley ducked his head. "She's a saucy girl, Will. She might be a little more than I know how to deal with." But when he looked up, there was more happiness in his eyes than Will had ever seen there before.

"She likes you, Charley. I can tell by watching her when you're around. She's lively, all right, but I think you two would get on well together."

"I'm not sure if we would or not. One thing I know, she's nothing at all like Rebecca."

"That might be a good thing."

Charley nodded. "Maybe that's right. But how would you feel about that—if I did court her a little, just to see how that might work out?"

"Nothing would make me happier," Will said, and he slapped Charley on the back. "We're brothers; we might as well be brothers-in-law."

They cut timber one more day after that, and then they began to notch the logs. Each evening, Charley ate at the Lewis camp, and sometimes he walked out in the evening light with Mary Ann.

Will and Charley built three cabins in the weeks that followed, with Jesse helping as much as he could. His feet were gradually improving, and that was a great relief to everyone. Each of the little houses had two rooms, which was more than most of the settlers had, but the floors, for now, were dirt. Instead of glass windows, the openings were covered with oiled paper that allowed some light to penetrate, and with shutters to close at night as days got colder. There were also no shingles to be had, and no proper timber to split

into shingles, so Will and Charley covered the tightly spaced roof-
ing poles with grass and weeds, spread twigs and branches over that,
and finally put on a layer of sod. They found stones in the streams
to build fireplaces, and they used mud and sticks and gravel to chink
the logs.

It was all quite crude compared to the houses in Nauvoo, but
after a year of living in tents and wagons—or in the badly chinked
cabin that the women had built in Winter Quarters—these houses
didn't seem too bad. Will and Charley also worked hard to get some
land plowed, and they put in winter wheat even though they feared
that they might be too late to see anything come of that in the spring.

The men each had a little money they had brought home, but
for now money was mostly useless to them in a place where no one
had anything to sell. The families had one cow to share—the one
that had trudged across the plains with Liz and Ellen—and a few
chickens had survived the trip, but otherwise, food was scarce. The
vanguard company had arrived in time to plant, and there had been
a small harvest, but the new settlers wondered how they would manage to survive this first year until better crops might be raised.

Life was all about work again, but Will found himself thinking
every day that he would never complain so long as he didn't have to
spend his days marching—or building a road—and wondering how
his family was faring, so far away.

• • •

By November the nights were getting very cold, and Liz wondered what winter would bring. America had required Liz to adjust
her thinking a great deal, but Nauvoo had at least been green and
wooded, and the place had looked, even at first, something like a
city. Gradually, there had been public buildings, and there had been
a society to be part of. But Liz felt the emptiness of this place, the

separation from everything civilized. It was true that cabins were going up, and on Sundays church services were held at the fort, but she wondered whether she would ever feel comfortable and secure here, whether the land would ever produce enough food to supply their family for winter, whether a true city could ever be established. On the Mississippi, cities had not been far away. Goods could always be purchased and brought in, and local businesses had begun to produce their own items for sale. But there was no city within a thousand miles of this valley, and it was hard to imagine that there ever would be.

Liz had little time to worry about such matters, though, and when she prayed at night, she always thanked the Lord that she had Will with her now, that she didn't have to build her own cabin this time, that he was plowing and figuring out what it would take to live in this remote place. She liked that he quit work at a reasonable hour now that the sun was going down early, and she liked that he took time to play with the boys and that he held little Mary Ellen and tried to make her laugh. Liz was also pleased that Mary Ann seemed so happy lately—and that she liked Charley.

• • •

One Sunday—a warmer day than some had been lately—Will and Liz walked with the children to the place that Brigham Young had designated as the spot for a temple. Will and his family had attended church services there under a bowery that had been built by the Battalion soldiers who had arrived first. It was a rough shelter, built of poles, with tree limbs spread across the top to keep the sun—or snow—off the congregation during meetings.

When Will and Liz stopped at the site, they stood where a stake had been driven to mark the corner of the lot, and they looked over the land. The boys ran off a little way and found some rocks to throw. Will stood next to Liz, holding Mary Ellen. Will was trying to imagine the temple that would stand there, wondered what it might look like out on this lonely piece of ground, where nothing but sagebrush grew. "I wonder how soon Brother Brigham will want to start building the temple," he said.

"Knowing him, it won't be long. But it almost seems too much to ask. Life is going to be hard here for many years to come."

Will did think things would be hard, but he didn't want Liz to feel his own concerns, so he told her, "Crops will grow well enough. If we get through this first winter, we should be all right."

"In Nauvoo, you used to say you didn't want to farm all your life. But there's nothing else to do here."

"Sure there is. There's money to be made hauling goods in from Independence or St. Louis."

She smiled at him.

"I know what you're thinking—that I'm just talking again, the way I did in Nauvoo."

"No. I'm not thinking that. But do you want to drive a wagon all the way to St. Louis while I'm here without you? I'd rather have dirt floors than have the money you could earn traveling back and forth across this whole continent—and gone from me again."

"I know. That's exactly what Jesse and I have been saying to each other. But if we made one or two trips and established ties with businesses back in the United States, after that we could hire men to drive the wagons, and we could sell the products out here."

"You mean, open a store?"

"Aye. Exactly."

"And then you'll give everything away to all the poor immigrants who'll be arriving here. I really doubt you ought to be a storekeeper."

"All right, then. I'll farm, and I'll hire someone to run my store. But I'm going to do some things. I know that."

Now Liz was laughing, and she looked so beautiful that Will couldn't resist reaching out to her with one arm and pulling her close to him. "We'll make a good life here, Liz. It doesn't seem possible right now, but this will be a city. This will be the Zion we thought we would have in Illinois. I honestly believe a day will come when this will be one of the great cities of the world. People will come to us to learn how a people ought to live. We'll also send missionaries out from here, and—"

"And you'll be gone from me doing that—preaching the gospel in some far corner of the world."

Will knew that could be true. He looked across this empty temple lot. He remembered when they had stopped to look back across the Mississippi at the temple they had had to leave behind. He felt tired when he thought of all the work that would have to go into building another one. All the rock was in the mountains, and that was a long haul. Will was sure he would be doing some of that. "We do have a lot of work ahead," he told Liz. "But our children will grow up in Zion, and if we raise them right, they'll preach the gospel to their children, and maybe a day will come when all that posterity will look back and appreciate the labor that went into getting this place started."

"I suppose. But people don't usually think much about those things. They don't look back; they look forward."

"I know. But we'll try to make sure our own children understand what it's all for."

"I only hope we'll have some nice years now, hard work or not, and our children and grandchildren will hold to the truth."

"We'll just have to pass our story down to them, Liz. One day I'll bounce my grandchildren on my knee and tell them about Nauvoo and everything that happened to us there. And I'll tell them that I married the most beautiful woman in all of England, and all my life I never stopped thanking the Lord that she agreed to marry me."

"I'll be ugly as a sod fence before long. So you better learn to love me how I am, pretty or not."

Will was laughing. "That's not my worry. I just hope that someday, late in life, you won't look back and wish you had never met up with me." But she was gripping him around the waist, and the truth was, he didn't really believe that would happen.

He looked up at the mountains and was reminded again that this valley was nothing like Wellington Heath, and nothing like Nauvoo, but he told himself it would be Zion in the tops of the mountains. He and Liz were still young and strong. They would help build this new city. Maybe Liz was right; maybe people wouldn't look back and appreciate the first settlers. But he hoped for a posterity that would at least continue the work he and Liz had helped to start. Zion wasn't a place. It was a way of living. He hoped his children, and their children, would always understand that.

AUTHOR'S NOTE

I have sometimes complained about all the hard work of researching and writing these long novels, but honestly, now that I've attached the final period to the final sentence, I'm a little nostalgic. For about six years I've steeped myself in the history of Nauvoo and the Saints' migration west. Now that I'm finished, I realize that I have only a beginner's grasp of the whole time period, and I won't have such a compelling impetus—a deadline for the next novel— to keep me poring over old journals. Still, I've gained some understanding of the people who established not only our Church but our culture—people who stood for things I want to stand for.

The more I delve into old records and personal accounts, the more I watch the stereotype of "the pioneers" disappear. They were simply not as noble and lofty in their motivations as we make them seem in our Twenty-Fourth of July celebrations. Many were astoundingly faithful and tenacious, deeply committed, but they were real people. They were not superhuman. They fought through the challenges of their time as best they could. For me, that's inspiring. I'm not as noble as I ought to be either, and I know how petty my motivations often are, but I vow to carry forward what the early Saints began, and to do my best in spite of my weaknesses.

When we speak of the Mormon Battalion, we almost always say something about the "longest march in military history." The problem is, that simply isn't true. But that, for me, is not the point. It wasn't the length of the march—over two thousand miles—that we should emphasize. People walk across the United States all the time—or make the trip on pogo sticks. It was the difficulty of the trip, out in the western desert, that we fail to understand. What I hope is that this book has shown what the soldiers—and, importantly, the four women—accomplished in holding out to the end. In many ways, the great test of life is to find out whether we can keep putting one foot ahead of the other in the same way that the Battalion marchers did. Working every day, raising children, preparing our Sunday School lessons, being true home teachers and visiting teachers—those are the markers of whether we carry on the traditions of our early members. If we can also grasp the big picture and keep track of the purpose of our mortality, we have a chance to rise above the mere level of drudgery, but we must start with the discipline to accept our callings and then work to fulfill them.

Some things about our lives are easier now, but other aspects of twenty-first-century life are more difficult. I wish we would stop talking about the perfection of the pioneers and model ourselves on the tenacity of those who stuck it out. Many failed back then, and many fail now, but I want to think of myself as one who keeps walking the walk. My third great-grandfather marched with the Mormon Battalion and then worked hard and raised a good family. I want to be like him. In one sense, we all have progenitors who walked that same trail. We're all connected to that heritage of strength, whether we had actual relatives there or not.

The strength of women in our history is something we should

never forget. Lydia Hunter and Melissa Coray were real people, and their stories are true. I made up their dialogue and put them in invented scenes, but the days without water, the pregnancies, and other details were all true. And Lydia really did die after the birth of her son in San Diego. Susan Davis and Phebe Brown also made the long march, but since I was using Company B for my story, I focused on Lydia and Melissa.

I always hope that readers will not see my fictional versions of history as the end to their study, but rather as an appetizer for further reading. In the previous volumes of this series, I've suggested books and resources for further study about the Church in England during the apostolic missions and about the Nauvoo period. Let me suggest now some good resources for the exodus from Nauvoo, the western migration, and the history of the Mormon Battalion. The best starting place, I think, is with Richard E. Bennett's two excellent books on the Iowa crossing and the winter settlements near the Missouri River: *We'll Find the Place: The Mormon Exodus, 1846–1848* (Deseret Book, 1997), and *Mormons at the Missouri: Winter Quarters, 1846–1852* (University of Oklahoma Press, 1987). Most of us know little about that period of our history, and yet it may have been the most daunting challenge our early members faced.

David R. Crockett covers the same period in an interesting way: he reports, on a day-to-day basis, what was happening not only on the pioneer trails but in Nauvoo or in other locations important to Mormon history. His two books are *Saints in Exile: A Day-By-Day Pioneer Experience, Nauvoo to Council Bluffs* (LDS-Gems Press, 1996), and *Saints in the Wilderness: A Day-By-Day Pioneer Experience* (LDS-Gems Press, 1997).

The biographies and reprinted journals I mentioned in the Author's Note in Volume 2, *Through Cloud and Sunshine,* continue to be useful, especially Leonard J. Arrington's *Brigham Young: American Moses* (University of Illinois Press, 1986).

On the crossing of Iowa and the continued migration to the West, there are many sources. *Journey to Zion: Voices from the Mormon Trail* (Deseret Book, 1997), by Carol Cornwall Madsen, contains a wonderful array of both women's and men's first-person accounts. Some additional published journals provide really fascinating personal accounts of life in a wagon train. I recommend especially volume one of the two-volume *On the Mormon Frontier, the Diary of Hosea Stout, 1844–1861,* edited by Juanita Brooks (University of Utah Press, 1964); *Mormon Midwife: The 1846–1888 Diaries of Patty Bartlett Sessions,* edited by Donna Toland Smart (Utah State University Press, 1997); and *The Pioneer Camp of the Saints: The 1846 and 1847 Mormon Trail Journals of Thomas Bullock,* edited by Will Bagley (Arthur H. Clark Company, 1997).

I know that some of these books are out of print and may not be available at your library, but here's the good news. The LDS Church History Library has made scores of transcribed journals available online. You don't even need a password. Go to lds.org and click on "Resources." From there, go to "Church History," and then click on "Overland Travel Database." You will find journals from 1847 to 1868, listed by the name of the journalist, by the name of the company leader, and by the year of travel. You can look up the name of your ancestor, the diaries I've listed above, or you can browse and read whatever looks interesting. I would recommend the journals of William Clayton, Levi Jackman, Erastus Snow, Heber C. Kimball, and about a dozen more who traveled with the vanguard company to the Great Basin with Brigham Young and then returned and made a second trek. But don't miss the many women's journals: Eliza R. Snow, Louisa Barnes Pratt, Sarah Pea Rich, and many others. Remember, too, the two volumes I recommended in my last book: *Women of Faith in the Latter Days,* vols. 1 and 2, by Richard E. Turley and Brittany A. Chapman (Deseret Book, 2011 and 2012).

One book I really enjoy, written by a "gentile" who lived among the Mormons and came to know us well, is *The Gathering of Zion: The Story of the Mormon Trail* (University of Nebraska Press, 1964). The author is Wallace Stegner, who is sometimes satirical, even condescending, about the quirks of the early Saints, but he's a true storyteller and he brings a wonderful writing style and fresh perspective to his account.

Many books have been written about the Mormon Battalion. An early book, written by one of the soldiers, is Daniel Tyler's *A Concise History of the Mormon Battalion in the Mexican War, 1846–1847,* first published in 1881, and reprinted by Kessinger Legacy Reprints. Colonel Philip St. George Cooke wrote his own version in 1878, called *The Conquest of Mexico and California, an Historical and Personal Narrative* (reprinted by the University of California Libraries). The most complete book on the subject is Norma Baldwin Ricketts's *The Mormon Battalion: U.S. Army of the West, 1846–1848* (Utah State University Press, 1996). Ricketts includes a daily log of the Battalion's progress. A useful illustrated portrayal of the Battalion's march is *The Remarkable Journey of the Mormon Battalion,* by Michael N. Landon and Brandon J. Metcalf (Covenant Books, 2012).

Sherman L. Fleek has added an excellent account: *History May Be Searched in Vain: A Military History of the Mormon Battalion* (Arthur H. Clark Company, 2008). Fleek, as a military historian, provides an important perspective. He argues that the Mormons in the Battalion had never been trained as soldiers and therefore misinterpreted many of the actions of their military leaders. Tyler's book and many of the journals, he believes, were unfair to Cooke, and especially to Dr. George Sanderson, because the men resented the rules and discipline that are basic to army procedures. Fleek has also written two historical novels that provide much more detail about the Battalion march than my book does: *Called to War: Dawn of the Mormon Battalion* (Digital Legend Press, 2010), and *War in the Far West: March of the Mormon Battalion* (Digital Legend Press, 2011).

An excellent collection of first-person accounts by those who marched with the Battalion is *The Army of Israel: Mormon Battalion Narratives,* edited by David L. Bigler and Will Bagley (Utah State University Press, 2000).

If you would like to read more about the Mexican War, two books that I read and found useful were: *A Glorious Defeat: Mexico and Its War with the United States,* by Timothy L. Henderson (Hill and Wang, 2007), and *So Far From God: The U.S. War with Mexico, 1846–1848,* by John S. D. Eisenhower (University of Oklahoma Press, 1989).

If you really want to grasp this history, travel the route. My wife, Kathy, and I, along with Kathy's sister Helen McKay) did just that as I was starting this book. We started in Nauvoo and drove the Mormon Trail across Iowa. We then used Norma Ricketts's daily account of the Mormon Battalion march, and we followed the Battalion's trail, at least as closely as highways allow, from Council Bluffs to Fort Leavenworth, from there across Kansas and New Mexico to Santa Fe, and then south and west across Arizona and California to San Diego. I took lots of photographs, got out and looked at the cacti and the other plant life, and we stopped in places where significant events took place. We took the wonderful tour at the LDS-sponsored San Diego Mormon Battalion Historic Site, and then we set out through central California to Sutter's Fort, crossed the Sierra-Nevadas and the Nevada desert, and continued back to our home in Utah. The round trip, starting and ending in Utah, was almost six thousand miles. We took about three weeks to make the entire trip (with a three-day stop in Nauvoo), but that was not actually quite long enough.

What we experienced, which we could have learned no other way, was a true sense of the distances (even though we were traveling at highway speeds), but more than that, we gained a feel for the vast deserts, the remoteness of the territory, and we saw up close all the "prickliness" of cacti and mesquite. We read the history as we traveled, and as we covered the miles, we thought of those long days when the soldiers—and Lydia and Melissa—marched without water and then found only muddy holes to drink from. Does a trip like that sound boring to you? Well, it surely isn't a Mediterranean cruise or a week on a beach in the south of France, but we had a good time, and I came home connected to my great-grandfather Robert Harris in a way that I could never match.

I wish to thank dear Emily Watts, my editor, who patiently slogged through this long trek with me. She caught my dumb mistakes and fixed my awkward sentences. After working together for many years, I think she still likes me—or at least she makes me feel that she does, and that matters during a long process like this.

Emily never sees a single draft of my book that hasn't been proofed and critiqued first. My wife, Kathy, patiently reads my manuscripts over and over. She marks the mistakes and turns down the corners of the pages so I can spot her corrections, and then she sits with me and lovingly tells me that I've done a really lousy job with some aspect of the plot or with some characterization. She watches out for my female characters and makes sure I'm sensitive to their needs. And in the end, she always likes what I've written (or at least she claims that she does). Love like that is hard to find. Saying "thank you" is clearly inadequate compensation for her efforts, but by the time this comes out, we will have gone on a grand cruise—as a way to rest a little. My guess, though—and my joy—is that she won't have any more fun doing the cruise than she did on our long drive across the desert. We sometimes annoy one another, but overall, after forty-seven years of marriage, we still like hanging out together.

I also want to thank the readers who let me know in various ways that they have enjoyed this series of books. Enthusiasm for historical fiction is not at the peak it was a few years back, but it's nice to know that some readers like something other than fantasy.

I'm not going to stop writing, but I am going to slow down a little. I have some projects of various kinds that I want to work on, and I think I'll step rather hesitantly into old age. I turned seventy last year, but I start out each day with as much enthusiasm as I've ever had. The trouble is, I end days more fatigued than I used to. All the same, writing is what I do, and I can't imagine life without it. So as long as my brain and my body can manage it, I do plan to keep telling stories.